NATASHA WALTER

A Quiet Life

THE BOROUGH PRESS

I

First published by HarperCollins*Publishers* 2016

A catalogue record for this book
is available from the British Library

ISBN: 978-0-00-811377-3

This novel is entirely a work of fiction.
The names, characters and incidents portrayed in it, while at times based on
historical events and figures, are the work of the author's imagination.

Set in Sabon by Palimpsest Book Production Limited,
Falkirk, Stirlingshire

Printed and bound in Great Britain by
Clays Ltd, St Ives plc

MIX
Paper from
responsible sources
FSC™ C007454
www.fsc.org

FSC™ is a non-profit international organisation established to promote
the responsible management of the world's forests. Products carrying the
FSC label are independently certified to assure consumers that they come
from forests that are managed to meet the social, economic and
ecological needs of present and future generations,
and other controlled sources.

Find out more about HarperCollins and the environment at
www.harpercollins.co.uk/green

For Mark, Clara and Arthur

Prologue

Geneva, 1953

How slowly the light dies on these interminable summer evenings. Laura is so keen for each day to finish that she pulls dinner earlier every night. She hurries Rosa through her bath. 'Rub a dub dub!' she sings with some impatience as she towels her daughter's hair. Rosa looks up, her flawless mouth half open, her dark eyes serene. 'Dub dub,' she repeats in a serious tone. Her hair is still damp, sticking up in spikes, as Laura settles her into her lap with a bottle of warm milk beside them.

The potatoes are already bubbling in their pan, the glass of cold vermouth is already poured and waiting at Laura's elbow, the way to Rosa's bedtime seems clear; but then the child suddenly pushes away the half-full bottle of milk and slides to the ground. 'Open, open,' she says, standing at the door that leads to the balcony. Laura fights her impatience as she lifts and encourages her – 'Come on, my sweetheart, for Mama' – to come back and finish her drink. 'Nearly supper!' she calls out to her own mother as Rosa finally drains it. Mother is reading some magazine on the sofa, still mapping the world of new autumn modes that will never be bought and new destinations that will never be seen.

Rosa is still saying 'More!' hopefully as Laura carries her

up the awkward ladder staircase to her attic room. For a two-year-old, every evening comes too suddenly to an end. She is never in a hurry for the day to close. Laura lays her down in her cot with a solitary white rabbit for company. 'More': that was Rosa's first word. My life is all run out, Laura thinks, stooping over the cot, but nothing is ever enough for you. Her daughter burrows into the mattress, face-down, a chubby starfish. Struck with unexpected guilt at wanting to hurry her into unconsciousness, Laura whispers, 'Lullaby?' But Rosa is gone suddenly into sleep, that enviable sleep that ebbs and flows over her with unpredictable tides.

Then Laura is back downstairs again, standing in the kitchen in front of the stove. As she downs half of her second glass of vermouth, she prods at the potatoes, cuts some tomatoes roughly, slides slices of ham onto two blue plates, and that's it. That's supper. Her mother's glance moves to the drink as she comes into the room. She doesn't say anything, but in almost unconscious reaction Laura lifts the glass and finishes it as her mother sits down and waits to be served.

'Potatoes, Mother?'

'Just two, thank you – now, what time is it that you want to leave this weekend?'

They have been over this a dozen times, and Laura pauses before she answers. 'It's this Friday, we can get a train just after three. It's quite an easy journey, really. Wine?'

'No, not for me, not tonight. And he has booked the hotel, has he, this – Archie?'

'That's right. He said it would be quiet at the end of the season, but still fun. He's got daughters himself, but doesn't see much of them – I think he misses that side of things, family life.'

Laura goes on talking, reassuring her mother that the weekend will be easy, that Rosa will enjoy it, that all three of them, grandmother, mother and daughter, might have a good time. Laura's voice is calm, yes, and measured too, until

2

her mother breaks in again. 'Have you remembered to tell the consulate where we're going?'

'Of course I have!' There is something too emphatic in the response, and her fork falls with a clatter to her plate. As the women's gazes meet, Laura tries to shift the tension in the room. 'If another trip feels too much,' she says, 'you know you could stay here without me. Or you could always go back to Boston.'

Mother pushes at some tomato on her plate with her fork. 'Would you like me to go?'

There is no answer to that. Yes, Laura thinks, I would like you to go; I would like not to have any need for you to be here. But her mother's presence is essential. The idea of being quite alone with Rosa in this fragmented world, wandering around Europe, uncertain of her welcome from friends and acquaintances, seems impossible to her now. As soon as her mother mentions leaving, the reasons why they are both here, joined together in their uncomfortable little *ménage à trois*, are present in the room again. Laura is back in the days immediately after Edward left, the telephone ringing and ringing in the hall, the black Austin car parked in the driveway, the cameras popping as she drew back the curtains. But when she speaks again, her voice is light.

'Why would I want you to go?' There is even the suggestion of a laugh in her words, as though her mother is being ridiculous. 'I think Talloires will be lovely this time of year. And you should see how much Rosa enjoys swimming now. Did I tell you what she said today? I was looking for a fresh towel and I took out the blue one that I used in Pesaro, and she said, 'Like on holiday, I all sandy . . .'

What, Laura thinks, would we talk about, day in, day out, if we didn't have Rosa, her life forcing itself up, like a tree cracking paving stones, between the hard, dulled edges of our misfortunes? As usual, the two women talk about Rosa's new words, Rosa's little habits, as they fork up their supper.

Eventually Laura picks up the plates and carries them to the sink. In theory the nanny, Aurore, is meant to tidy the kitchen in the morning, but in practice, Laura puts away the evening meal. She hates catching Aurore's disdainful look as she picks up the detritus from their pathetic suppers.

There is a slice of apple tart left over from lunch. Laura presses it on Mother, although her mouth waters as she looks at it. Boredom breeds greed. As soon as it is eaten, Laura refills her own wine glass and they go to sit in the little living room, on the uncomfortable slippery couch. They are talking now about whether they need to buy anything for the trip. Obviously, it is silly in their situation to waste money, but on the other hand, it is important to keep up appearances. Mother mentions that nylon is such a good material for packing, because it doesn't crease, and Laura agrees, and wonders whether it is worth getting Rosa a new dress now, since she is growing so fast that the two sundresses bought for her at the beginning of summer are already short. They sound ordinary and at ease, for a few minutes, just a mother and grandmother chatting, the last holiday of the summer approaching. When a silence falls that seems hard to break, Laura twiddles with the knob of the big grey radio. It comes on with a rush of static. A sudden cry rises from the top of the flat, as this noise or something internal – a dream? wind? – breaks Rosa's sleep. The tension flares in Laura's body as she wonders whether to go upstairs, but this time she is lucky. Silence falls again, only broken by the chattering voices of a couple walking in the street below.

'Well,' says Mother. 'Maybe it's time for me to get some sleep too. It's funny how tiring it is, doing nothing.'

'Isn't it?'

Mother pulls herself off the sofa. Her footfalls are so heavy, so flat. Laura recognises that she is being overly sensitive, that she is like a twitchy old husband, wincing almost deliberately at every example of his wife's bad taste and clumsiness. But she can't help herself. She is on edge as she listens to her mother in the bathroom, to the patter of her urine and the swoosh of the flush, and the endless coughs and rustles as she goes through her careful rituals of greasing her face and putting her hair under a net. At last her bedroom door clicks behind her. She turns in bed. She sighs. Laura walks into the kitchen and swings open the door of the icebox. Water is collecting under it, she notices for the twentieth time, and for the twentieth time she ignores it. She takes out the bottle of wine, still half full, and sloshes more into the glass.

I'm not, Laura tells herself, and never will be, one of those women who starts drinking in the morning and who looks ten years older than their age after six months of lonely self-comfort. But it surprises her how often she has to ask the wine-merchant in the rue des Alpes to deliver another crate, or a couple of bottles of whisky. A martini at lunchtime, a vermouth or two before supper, and then she finishes the evening, every evening, sitting out on the balcony, an empty bottle beside her, or a measure of whisky glowing in a tumbler.

Because the end of the day is the moment she longs for. When she can stop acting her part. When she can sit out on this iron balcony, looking out over the lake as it turns from the lucent blue of summer to the blank of complete darkness. In those empty moments she feels less alone than she does all day, because she has her past for company, and ghosts gather companionably around her in the dusk.

Until Edward left she rarely drank alone. He was the one to pour the first martini of the evening, the last whisky at night. 'Cheers, big ears,' he said sometimes, imitating that tedious couple who lived downstairs from them for a while in Washington. 'Bottoms up,' Laura would add, pretending to be the wife. She sits now, watching the darkness deepen, until she can no longer tell the mountains from the sky, until she can almost feel Edward's presence beside her and almost believe he could hear her if she spoke.

5

Every day, she looks for a sign. She catches her breath on so many occasions. When the telephone rings unexpectedly, or when she comes back to the flat to find an envelope sticking up over the top of the numbered mailbox in the hall. But also when people look at her too closely, and she wonders, are they about to tell me they have a message, are they about to say, someone was looking for you yesterday? Today it was the sharp-featured woman who came into the shop where she was buying a new summer dress.

When she saw the turquoise dress with its wide white belt in the window, she had pushed open the heavy door in the overpriced boutique in the rue du Port. It was almost as good as she'd hoped, the shade taking the sallowness out of her face, and the in-and-out shape giving back to her, generously, the lines of her younger body. Just as she said, yes, I'll take it, and turned to the changing room to put on her own clothes, another woman entered the shop. She didn't look at the clothes, she just stood there for a second and looked at Laura through her spectacles. 'Let me see,' she said in French, 'are you—?' Laura stood, caught in the woman's attention, hope rising as clear as a chime of music in the room. 'No, I'm so sorry,' she said. 'How absurd, I saw you through the window and thought that I knew you from the lycée in Montreux.'

Laura bought the dress and went out into the sunlight. She walked through the city, blinking behind her dark glasses. Soon she was by the lake. Among the swans a toy was floating, a child's boat with a stained silk sail, and to her surprise she picked up a piece of gravel from the sidewalk and threw it hard at the boat. She missed. Her hands curled into fists, she walked away, high heels clacking on the clean Swiss street, the shopping bag on her arm with the new dress all folded up in tissue paper, back to the sparse apartment where her mother and daughter were awaiting her return.

And when she comes in, it is the same as ever. Laura sinks as quickly as she can back into Rosa's world. She has a new doll that Mother has bought her, a rather fabulous creation that says 'Mama' when you punch its stomach. She punches and punches, and the curious thing says 'Mama Mama' in its low hiccupping tones, and every time Rosa smiles. 'Sad baby,' she says. 'Sad baby.' 'Maybe it's happy,' Laura says, taking it from her and cradling it, and singing one of the nonsense songs she has made up in the long evenings. 'Lullaby, lullaby, sleepyhead,' Laura sings, as her daughter watches her with sharp, bright eyes. And then Rosa takes it back and starts doing the same, crooning in her out-of-pitch singing voice, enunciating the words carefully.

Mother comes in at that moment. 'Look, Mother, how wonderfully she plays with it,' Laura says. She gets up, and immediately Rosa punches the doll again and then drops it and holds onto Laura's legs. 'Sing,' she commands, 'sing.' And so Laura spends the rest of the afternoon singing to her and her doll, and whenever her attention wanders, Rosa complains, vociferously. 'You give in to her too much,' says Mother, with the confidence of the woman whose child-rearing days are long over and whose criticism must be accepted. Laura wonders if she is right. She sees disciplined mothers every-where, mothers who can turn away easily from their children and pass them to the nannies or tell them to play on their own; but those mothers have lives of their own. What do I have, Laura thinks? Only these endless afternoons waiting to be filled.

Now, sitting on the balcony, in her mind she is explaining things to Edward, telling him how motherhood is so different from what they expected. For the two years of Rosa's life she has done this day by day, saying to him in her head, 'I cannot do this' and 'Look at this' and 'Help me' and 'How perfect'. She watches other fathers – disengaged, or authoritarian, or protective – and fits his character onto theirs, imagining herself telling him to let Rosa climb the slide – 'She can do it!' Laura says to him in her mind, 'She did it!' – or telling him that she is too young to learn table manners. And sometimes, when she hears Rosa in the night, and knows that she must swing her feet onto the cold floor and set off again to comfort her terrors or her thirst or her fever, Laura imagines that he will be there when she returns, to hold her as Laura is about to hold Rosa.

She is leaning against the iron balcony now, her cheek pressed against its cold hard edge. Down below, on the sidewalk, a young woman walks quickly. She is wearing a red dress and her shoulders are hunched, but as she passes under the street lamp her face jumps clearly into the light – she seems to be smiling. A memory of herself, a memory she cannot quite place, drifts through Laura's mind, but before she can catch it Rosa's cry rises again, and as she gets up she stumbles a little, and puts her hands to her temples, trying to press the drunkenness out of her mind. It doesn't do to go drunk to a crying child, it makes you clumsy and angry. Is this another reason why I want my mother with me now? Laura wonders. Can I be trusted, even with the daughter I love?

As soon as she is picked up, Rosa pushes her hot face into Laura's shoulder; if her sleep was disrupted by some dream, then her mother's huge, warm presence is immediately reassuring. But although she stops crying, she refuses to go back to sleep for a long time; every time she is put down, she sits up again and when Laura tries to leave the room she yells furiously. 'Sing, sing.' Laura sings a melange of songs without rhyme or reason. 'Saturday night is the loneliest night of the week,' she ends up singing, but she can't remember the rest of it, and goes on crooning vaguely, stroking Rosa's tense, warm back with her palm.

When at last Laura feels her daughter's muscles loosen and her breathing become stertorous, she gets up and realises how light her head feels and how heavy her limbs are. She is exhausted. She goes into her own room, drops her clothes to the floor and falls into bed. She hasn't slept properly for a while, but tonight sleep comes with smothering power, as though somebody is pulling a blanket over her face. And when she wakes the next day, she is sweating, twisted up in the covers.

It is a bad morning; everything seems wrong. Rosa has slept too long and her diaper has given out, her bed is soaked. That is for Aurore to do, but it puts her in a terrible mood. Aurore is a skinny Swiss girl with a fierce manner, but when Laura first interviewed her she could see that she genuinely liked Rosa. Even now, although she grumbles about everything else, she strokes the little girl's hair with a soft, light touch as she asks what to buy for lunch.

When Laura goes out onto the balcony, a cup of strong coffee in her hand, she sees the glass and empty bottle from the night before. She knows that Mother, who is sitting there, has seen them too. Mother is false and hearty, planning out loud what she is going to write in her weekly letter to Laura's sister in Boston. 'How do you spell Talloires?' she says, as though eager to tell Ellen about the trip that is weighing heavily on both of them, and Laura spells it out laboriously as she drinks her coffee.

Rosa cries when Laura goes back into the living room to pick up her hat and purse to go out, but Laura disengages her daughter firmly from her legs and clatters down the steps in the apartment building. There is no elevator here. It is the cheapest rental they could find that still looked elegant enough not to be embarrassing. The dark staircase smells of different people's cooking and the paint is peeling on the walls, but out on the streets Geneva's quiet order reasserts itself. In the café opposite the waiter is twitching paper covers straight on the metal tables and the only person drinking coffee there is a woman in an irreproachable blue toque. Laura walks her usual way to the kiosk on the corner for the *Herald Tribune*, and then back again to the garage where her car is kept. She has arranged to meet her cousin Winifred for lunch at a restaurant that she has found up in a mountain village, yet another clean Swiss restaurant with panoramic views of the hills. It is fair to say that she is not looking forward to the lunch; she knows that Winifred wants to talk to her about her future, and she has had to listen to her peremptory judgements too often recently.

The brilliant August sunshine is harsh, and her little straw hat is no use against it. She rummages in her purse, but she has forgotten her sunglasses. She can't face going back into the apartment to confront Rosa's anger and her mother's forced smiles again; whenever she leaves Rosa, she feels freed of some burden, and whenever she leaves her mother she is released from the part she is playing, even if only for the minutes before she meets someone else. She opens the door of the car and waits a few seconds for the hot air inside it to dissolve before she gets in and starts the engine. As she moves off into the road, she notices a small grey Citroën coming up behind her, which makes her self-conscious – she is naturally a careless driver, but even careless drivers pay more attention when there is someone close behind them.

The streets of Geneva and the lakeside road are crowded at this time, and the grey car drops back, but when she turns onto the road that ribbons up to St-Cergue there is no one driving but Laura, and she starts to go faster and faster, her mind running on something else altogether. She is thinking of the dress she bought yesterday and whether it will go with her prize acquisition for the summer, an electric blue cotton coat with a neat cut by Schiaparelli that Winifred had passed on to her as it was too small for her. Laura is wondering whether wearing it with something else blue will look so overdone it would be cheap, or, on the contrary, whether it would be just the right kind of over statement to be really chic, when suddenly a car behind her, another small grey motor – or is it the same one? Even in the moment she registers the parallel – overtakes her and then brakes, completely without warning, in front of her. Laura brakes too, so suddenly she stalls, and she realises how carelessly she must have been driving. She flings open the door without thinking, adrenaline propelling her out.

'What are you doing?' she yells. She realises she is in the wrong language. '*Qu'est-ce que vous faites? Vous conduisiez comme un fou!*'

'Mrs Last?'

The driver says her name through his open window, and Laura just says 'Yes' without thinking, and then he is opening his door too and they stand for a moment, and then she is back in her tirade, '*Vous allez nous tuer tous!*'

'Mrs Last, my friend has something to show you.'

There is another man in the car, whose face Laura cannot yet see. He pulls down his window and leans out; he is middle-aged, wearing a squashy grey hat and an overcoat which is too heavy for this sunny afternoon.

All of a sudden Laura is aware that there is no one else here. No cars are passing. There are two of them; their car is blocking hers. They could do anything, anyone could – her purse is on the front seat of her car, and the door is still open.

She takes two steps backwards, her hand reaching behind her for the handle of the door. The other man is holding something out of his window, and as she goes on retreating, the first man takes it and walks towards her. '*Je suis en retard,*' she says in her unsteady French, her tongue fumbling over the words. 'I am late for an appointment.' Then she sees what he is holding: a piece of card, half a picture – windows, roses, a pitched roof. 'This is yours, Mrs Last.'

She goes on opening the car door. She reaches for her purse and looks inside it. 'Please take a look,' he is saying, and she finds what she is looking for, folded within her black wallet. The matching half. She takes it out and holds it towards him, and he comes forward holding his half and they stand rather close as they put them clumsily join to join, a picture made whole again, a house in the sunshine.

'Your husband gave it to my friend,' he says.

'Yes.'

All the questions that Laura might ask run through her mind and are lost for the moment. She leans against the warm car, and feels her heart slowing from its panic, and over the woods below her she sees an eagle hovering in the warm winds, its huge wingspan in profile, so slow that it is still, suspended.

'I'm going away tomorrow,' she says to the first of the two men. 'I'll be gone for four days.'

'I see. Come up here on Tuesday. Just below here – you see, there, where there is a footpath into the forest – do you see?'

'Yes. At this time?'

The two men look at each other and nod. She gets back into the car and turns the key backwards and forwards. She presses the gas too hard and it roars and jolts. They move away, and then she does too, but quite slowly, so that soon the other car disappears ahead of her. When she gets to the restaurant on the outskirts of the village, she parks the car and just sits there for a while, tracing a pattern in her print skirt with her finger, and her mind is blank. This is the fork in the road, so long awaited; but now it is here she cannot see past it. It is as if there is only darkness ahead.

Water

To London, January 1939

Although Laura had said, time and again, that there was no need for Mother to come on board, in fact, when the moment came, she was glad that she was not embarking alone. They knew the steamer would be half empty, but half empty was quite crowded enough. Holding her smaller suitcase and pulling her muskrat coat around her, Laura had to push through a throng of middle-aged women just to get onto the pier on the Hudson River. She stumbled on an uneven step as they walked up to the tourist class entrance, and as she righted herself she realised how breathless she felt. Still, Mother being there made her determined not to show her uncertainty, or even at this last moment the whole plan might collapse, and she might be ordered home to wait out Ellen's recovery. So once on board she tried to walk with more confidence, as if she knew where they were going, up to the information desk where a steward rattled out the directions to her cabin so quickly that she had to ask him to repeat them.

'Take the elevator down one floor, along the corridor to the right, through the double doors . . .' As he was talking, Laura couldn't help noticing the sign above the desk: 'The company's regulations prohibit passengers from passing from one class to another. Passengers are therefore kindly

13

requested to refrain from applying for this privilege and to keep within the confines of the class in which booked.' The steward noticed the direction of her gaze. 'We do tours, you know,' he said.

'Tours?'

'Every day, you can visit the first-class deck. Or if you go to the movie, you'll go into their side.'

'Do they visit us?'

He laughed as if she had made some kind of joke, and then turned to the impatient elderly couple behind them.

The smell of old cigarette smoke hit her when she opened the door to her cabin and, putting her toilet case on the bed, Laura stood irresolutely beside it.

'Look, your trunk is already here,' Mother said, gesturing to the shiny brown box which they had given to a porter at the pier together with her cabin number. Mother always pointed out the obvious, was always fussily one step behind. But Laura was suddenly reluctant for her to leave. It would be so final, to be left here with these things that didn't look like her things at all. They were all brand new, that was why, bought in the splurge of shopping that had followed the sudden decision that the girls must go to London. Only Laura's name, written in her carefully neat lettering on the tag, told her the brown trunk was hers. The other bed – that would have been Ellen's – was a rebuke, but at least it looked as though no one else had booked it. Laura had quailed at the thought of sleeping with a stranger.

Mother was once again going through things that she had told her before, about how there would be a female steward who would look out for her, how she mustn't be afraid to let the steward know if anyone bothered her, and how Aunt Dee's maid would be at Waterloo to meet her. The thought of the maid brought Laura's anxiety up more sharply than ever. She was almost ready to interrupt the stream of admonitions about telegrams and underwear, food and gratitude, and say that she had changed her mind. Indeed, she had just turned to Mother, about to speak, when they heard the shout along the corridor, 'All ashore that's going ashore,' and Laura's face reverted to the still expression her mother hated. Contained, as Laura thought. Sulky, as her mother had described it only that morning. Laura opened the door to the corridor.

They walked together up to the point where the corridor split in two. All of a sudden Mother put her arms around her. They never embraced, and Laura stepped back without thinking. The abruptness of her move was tempered by the press of people converging at that very point; it was not a place to stand, not in the middle of the friends and family who were returning to the pier and the passengers making their way up to the deck. And so the two of them were carried forward in separate streams of movement. Laura thought to herself, I'll make it better, I'll wave. She saw herself in her mind's eye on deck, blowing kisses, borne backwards.

And she was leaning on the rail, looking for that grey fur hat in the crowd, when a woman beside her stepped right onto her foot. 'Sorry,' the woman said without turning, and Laura found herself looking at the curve of a cheek and curls of hatless hair rather than out to the pier. 'Why is leaving so—' the woman said, her last word lost in the scream of a whistle that rent the air. Her gesture was not lost, however. She seemed to sum up and then to dismiss the jagged Manhattan skyline as she brought her hands together and flung them apart. The view was full of sunshine and watery reflections, but Laura could not make out where Mother was standing, and she narrowed her eyes at the knots of people, pulling her coat tight around her neck. Then the wind was sharp in her face as the ship began to move, and she took a deep breath. The voyage had begun.

The woman next to her was wearing only a cloth coat, open over her dress, and a drab knitted scarf, yet she didn't seem cold. Laura turned to look at her again, but she couldn't have been more surprised when the woman turned too, and said in a matter-of-fact tone, 'How about getting a drink?'

Of course Laura had imagined meeting people on board; no young woman could step onto a ship that year and not think of Elinor and her doomed onboard romance in *Till My Heart Is Still*, which Laura had read in a creased paperback lent to her by a school friend, but she had not imagined such a quick advance into acquaintanceship with a woman who did not seem quite her kind. A part of Laura wanted to go on standing on deck, taking the measure of her solitude and the start of her journey, but the woman's nonchalance was appealing. So Laura found herself following her into a low-ceilinged, airless lounge on the floor below. As soon as she saw the people – mainly men – at the tables, she paused at the door, but the woman walked forward without hesitation, putting her purse and a book she was holding on a table and sitting down in one of the worn, tapestry-covered chairs.

When the waiter came up to them, the woman ordered a beer immediately. Laura was slower. She could not pretend that ordering alcohol would be natural for her, and she was thirsty and tired. 'A cup of coffee, please. And a glass of water.'

'Funnily enough, I was here yesterday – not on the boat, on the pier – welcoming those boys home—'

'You mean—'

'The boys they brought back from Spain. Heroes, one and all.'

'They were brave, weren't they?' Laura's comment was uncertain. She came from a home that was so lacking interest in politics that her father rarely even took a daily newspaper. He voted Republican, she was pretty sure, but she had never felt able to ask him about his views, or why, whenever he mentioned Roosevelt's name, he sounded so disparaging. As for her mother, an Englishwoman who was proud to under-

16

stand little about America, she often shook her head about what the world was coming to, or expressed grave misgivings about one leader or another, but she had never – in Laura's memory – stated any positive political view. Growing up in a home so insulated from the world had left Laura ignorant, but also curious, so she responded in a vague but friendly manner to the woman's statement about the heroism of the Abraham Lincoln Brigade. The woman continued to talk about one of the boys who had come home, and his experiences at the hands of the Fascists in Spain. 'No,' Laura said at the right moment, 'How – how terrible.' But she could tell that her responses were limp.

'There are lots of them still over there, you know – desperate to get home. I've been helping to raise the money. Shall I tell you something else? Such a strange coincidence, I've been thinking and thinking about it. The last person I know who sailed this way on this actual ship was a stowaway. This guy wanted to get to Spain, he didn't have a cent, so he crept in behind a wealthy family, just as if he were one of the entourage, and then kept walking once he was on board.'

'Really?' Again, Laura's expression was encouraging, although she was unsure of the right thing to say. 'Where did he sleep?'

'He said there was a steward involved – sympathetic to the cause, I guess, who slipped him food too.'

'It's hardly believable,' said Laura, whose imagination was suddenly stirred by the thought of a lonely man attempting invisibility on a crowded ship. She leant forward to ask more, but just then they were interrupted.

'It's true enough, though,' came another voice. Laura turned. At the table next to them was a young man sitting alone. Although he wasn't unattractive, with a mobile face and dark hair falling over his forehead, both women frowned as they realised that he had been listening to their conversation.

'How do you know?'

'I remember seeing a report about them. They were arrested

17

when they landed in Le Havre, though, poor boys. Didn't have the papers, didn't have any money.'

'The man I'm talking about, he wasn't arrested. He got to Spain and fought and was wounded and now he's in southern France somewhere. Can't get home, but he's written to his mother to tell her he's safe. That's how I know all about it.'

'That's a great story – do you know his name?'

'What's it to you?'

'Hey, don't be suspicious.' The man rose and stepped over to their table. 'Mind if I join you?'

'We're happy as we are.'

'Well, you won't mind if I perch here,' he said, sitting down anyway and tapping his cigarette in the empty ashtray. 'I'll be honest with you – I'm a journalist. Name's Joe Segal. I like stories like that. Wouldn't hurt the man to have the story told now.'

'What if the line came back at him for the stolen passage?'

'The French Line's got more on its hands than chasing a stowaway from years back.'

'Last year—'

'Tell me more about the story without the name. I can tell you're sympathetic. Wouldn't you like to inspire others to do what he did?'

'It's a bit late for that now, isn't it?' The woman shook her head. 'To be honest, I don't know a lot more. Just what I said: he stowed away, a steward helped him, brought him food – some of the best food he ever ate, you know, stuff that the people in the top suites hadn't bothered to touch – caviar, you name it. He had to hunker down in some equipment room most of the time, and then when he got to Le Havre the steward tipped him off to come out only when the staff were getting off, so everyone assumed he was from the engine room. He looked pretty grubby, you can imagine, by then. Apparently the staff here is so huge that he got away without anyone really knowing him. This steward just walked alongside him – and then someone met him at Perpignan station, and you know, there were loads of boys going over then. It's not impossible . . .'

The journalist smiled, and Laura saw how the story tickled him. 'The idea of a Red holed up in this ship – have you seen the first-class decks?'

'I've heard about them,' Laura said. Although in the rather down-at-heel tourist-class lounge it seemed unlikely, in fact the ship that they were travelling on was a byword for glamour. At this, the man seemed to notice Laura for the first time, turning his attention to her. He told her that he had seen someone he thought was Gloria Swanson getting onto the ship on the first-class side, and although Laura just raised her eyebrows at the thought, this, too, stirred her imagination. She thought of the lonely star, drinking martinis in her suite, perhaps, or taking a shower and feeling the warm water fall onto her ageing body, and the whole boat seemed to contain the extraordinary multiplicity of adult life and desire in a way that made her feel how right she was to have come, to have insisted to Mother that even now, even without her sister, a trip to London would be safe.

'If you walk through the engine room, you come out on the first-class deck and no one's going to stop you if you want to go have a look at those palatial surroundings . . .' the man was saying.

'Is that so? Will no one mind?'

'They say girls do it all the time – though the stewards might not be so pleased about the boys drifting over.'

Laura had finished her coffee by this time, and just then the boat dipped alarmingly in the swell. She felt, to her horror, a heat rise through her stomach. 'I'm going to lie down,' she said.

'You're not feeling ill already, are you?' The woman was looking at her with what seemed like real concern.

Laura shook her head. At not quite twenty, she still had

19

all the awkwardness of adolescence. Although she didn't want to be rude to these strangers with their interesting stories, equally she had no idea how to talk to them. She got up. To her surprise, the woman stood too, saying that she was going to go to her cabin.

'I'm Florence Bell,' she said, as they walked down the corridor. 'You?'

'Laura. Laura Leverett.'

'I didn't want to ask just then in front of him – seemed like he might be thinking of getting fresh – thought it would be better if he thought we knew each other.'

This statement, innocuous as it was, seemed to turn the woman suddenly from a stranger into an ally, so as Laura got to her cabin she turned to Florence. 'Will you knock for me when you go up for dinner?' The way the words came out, there was something needy about the request, and Laura braced herself for a dismissal, but Florence's assent was so matter-of-fact it reassured her.

Alone in her cabin, Laura still felt self-conscious, almost as though she were being watched. She even found herself, as she put her purse on the bed and took off her coat, composing the first few lines of a letter to Ellen. In her mind, she presented the cabin as having a certain charm – 'blue as the sea should be! With quite enough room to swing a cat!' – although in reality it was small and ugly. The fact that all the furniture was bolted down and the room carpeted in a springy felt only added to its claustrophobic feel, and here, she noticed, the reverberations of the engine seemed exaggerated, thrumming through the soles of her feet. Looking for the lavatory, she opened a door in the side of the room. It revealed a tiny toilet and shower stall, which smelt reassuringly of disinfectant. She stripped and got under the shower. For a while it puzzled her that her lavender soap would not lather, until she realised that the water was salt.

After her shower she dressed, but then lay down, and the

exhaustion engendered by all the strange new impressions pushed her into a half-sleep, so that when the rap on the door came and she heard the clear voice of her new acquaintance calling through it, she had to ask her to wait while she rebelted her dress. 'I fell asleep,' she said apologetically, opening the door, 'can you wait a second?'

She was looking for her lipstick, clipping on her earrings. 'Are you the only one in this cabin?' asked Florence, stepping inside. 'The boat isn't even half full, is it?'

'Actually we booked this whole room.' Laura explained how she and her sister had been intending to travel together, but how Ellen's sudden appendicitis had put paid to that plan. 'Mother was going to call the whole thing off, but I managed to convince her I'd behave myself for three days on a ship . . .' Laura paused, suddenly conscious that her mother's protectiveness might sound ridiculous to this independent woman. 'She still sees me as a child,' she said weakly.

But Florence, who was looking at the magazine Laura had left on the bed, hardly seemed to have heard her. It was a magazine about Hollywood stars, and Florence flicked through it for a few seconds while Laura lipsticked her mouth and slid her feet into her patent shoes, and then she dropped it on the floor. 'Come on, I'm hungry as a horse. Haven't eaten all day.'

They were early, so that only a few of the tables were taken, but rather than pausing for the waiter to show them where to sit, Florence walked directly to the table she wanted, in the middle of the room.

'Funny how your magazine puts that actress on the cover and doesn't say a word about her politics,' she said suddenly as they were sitting down and shaking out their napkins.

'Her politics?'

'She is committed, you know – signed a petition a few months ago for aid for Spain. I guess the studio doesn't want anyone seeing her as a Red, but even so, they could mention it.'

'Did you see her last film?' Laura asked. Here, she would be on familiar ground, since she had seen it and had decided views on it, but Florence shook her head and started telling Laura about some other actors who supported aid for Spain.

When the waiter came up with the menus, Florence took them from him with a quick nod, hardly interrupting their conversation, and even when she knocked a fork to the floor as she opened it, she seemed unflustered. Watching her read the menu, Laura realised that she was one of the first women she had ever met who appeared to have no physical uncertainty. Her dress was shabby, her hair unwaved and her eyebrows unplucked, but her gestures were expansive and her voice determined. Laura had been brought up into the certain knowledge that a woman's body and voice were always potential sources of shame, that only by intense scrutiny and control could one become acceptable. Hairy shins, stained skirt, smudged lipstick – anything could mark out one's failure. Laura thought she was doing all right this evening, in her wool crepe dress with the bow at the neck and the navy belt, with her pearl earclips and her unladdered stockings. These had all been bought for this voyage, and allowed Laura to take her seat in the restaurant feeling reasonably confident that she would fit in. Florence, however, seemed to be unaware of such concerns. Planting her elbows on the table, even though one sleeve was actually torn at the wrist, as the restaurant filled up and the waiter hovered to take their order, she went on talking to Laura as if they were alone and no one was watching them.

As she talked, Laura realised again that Florence was not the sort of girl she usually mixed with – not one of us, as Laura's mother would put it. She had been working since she was fourteen; first, she explained, in her uncle's glove-making business, and latterly in the offices of a large shipping company. But all the time her real work had been 'organising', as she called it. Organising. That could mean almost anything. But

22

in Florence's stories – she had told two or three stories by the time they had eaten their soup and their tough little chops – it was all about battles, of the powerless against the powerful. She told a story about how she had tried to insist on better conditions in her own uncle's factory, which had led to her banishment from that side of the family. 'But Father stuck by me. He is a Party member himself.' Laura said nothing at that, too incredulous to speak.

Indeed, at first Laura's role seemed to be only that of the listener. But after a while she began to ask questions, all of them positive, and at one point led Florence back to the story about the stowaway which had so flared in her imagination. After dinner both women felt too keyed up to go back to their rooms, and Laura agreed quickly when Florence suggested that they go up to the deck.

Out there, under the night sky, the wind came shockingly against the girls' faces. They struggled over to the railings, where they stood looking down into the foam-patterned ocean. 'You're going all the way to France, then?' Laura said, assuming that Florence would be trying to get as near to Spain as possible.

'No – just England.' There was a pause, and then she continued. 'I was really keen on my last job, it was just office work, but I was organising the girls, the typists, the kind of thing that a lot of boys in the Party don't really understand, but it's – important, frankly. To get them to understand. But I got into real trouble—' Then she stopped and looked at Laura. 'Hell, I don't know why I'm even thinking of telling you this.'

Laura was entranced. Was she going to be given a confidence already? Girls at school had rarely invited her into their circles of intimacy. Although she was trustworthy – as she saw it – there was something that put girls off giving her the linked arms and whispered secrets that they gave to others. Perhaps because she never shared confidences herself, being too scared that if she once let others scent the dismal smell of failure that hung around her own family, no one would like her, or perhaps because, as one girl once said to her, 'You're such a good girl, Laura, you wouldn't understand.' But here was this warmly energetic stranger, ready to entrust Laura with her inner life.

Laura had had an unaccustomed glass of wine over dinner, and it had made her movements more open than usual. She put out her hand and touched Florence's, where it lay on the rail. It was an untypically expansive gesture from her, but Florence was not to know that.

And so Florence launched into another story, about how she had been onto such a good thing with the girls in the shipping company, and how they had taken their demands for job security and paid holiday to their boss, and how he had pretended to give in, and then sacked Florence and some of the others and taken back his promise. She had been so humiliated, she said, after all the girls had put their faith in her, and one night, fired up by fury after visiting one of the girls who had been sacked and who hadn't eaten that day as she was so worried about how to pay her rent, she, Florence, had broken into the office and destroyed a whole lot of invoicing files. 'It felt good,' she said, obviously remembering with some pleasure and then catching herself up, 'but – ugh, it was the wrong thing to do.'

In Laura's mind, the action unfolded like a comic strip: the dastardly boss, the daring night raid. But Florence was now describing something much more real and complicated. 'He obviously suspected me, and the police came to question me. Luckily I was out when they called – I moved to a friend's apartment, but then I had to move again, and when I told someone in the Party, they called me in to discipline me. Very unhelpful for the revolution, they said. And when I went for other jobs the last few months I didn't get anything, I felt people knew about it – it was all horrible. Well, this girl I

24

met a couple of years ago, this English girl, has been writing me and encouraging me to come over to Europe. She was in Spain but she's back in London now, working in a printers. I just thought that it was time to make a fresh start. My uncle, the one who cut me off ages ago, gave Father the money for my ticket. I think everyone thought I'd gone too far in New York.' Her voice, which had been so strong and certain, seemed thin now, blown back in the wind.

'It sounds like you did the right thing.'

'No, no, the Party told me – I mustn't make things personal like that. We have to organise for collective action, not go off on our own.'

Despite the darkness that surrounded them, Laura was intensely aware of Florence's physical presence as she spoke, of her little sigh as she leaned backwards, her hands gripping the rail, and the scent of her – sweat, wine, laundry soap – which seemed so warm even in the chilly night air. She shivered.

'I'm cold too,' Florence said. 'Let's go down.'

'Are you tired?'

Laura was disappointed at the thought of the evening already coming to an end, but Florence said immediately, 'We can get a drink in that bar again.'

In her flat shoes, Florence was sure-footed on the iron stairs that led from the deck to the lower floor, but Laura clung tight to the rails. Florence said over her shoulder as they went down, 'So why are you going to London – family, did you say?'

'Yes, my mother's sister – my mother is English.'

'You sound English yourself.'

'Do I? That's only because of Mother.'

'You remind me of an English actress I once saw in a movie—'

'Who?' She was desperate to know how she might be seen by others. Was there someone she was like? How did she strike people? But to her disappointment they were already at the door of the bar and Florence did not reply. There were not many tables free in the lounge now, but Joe waved to them from a table to their left, where he was sitting with two women. It would have been too pointed to ignore him and so, after a quick look at Laura, Florence walked forwards and Joe pulled chairs up to the table.

Introductions were swift; the two new women were called Maisie and Lily, and Laura commented immediately on their English accents. These two women were clearly sisters, with tightly marcelled auburn hair and wide-apart eyes and small mouths, which gave them a look of almost doll-like innocence. That look was belied by their conversation. One of them was telling a tale about a casting manager for a big New York show where they had been working, who thought he was owed favours by every woman in the chorus.

'But he could never do the job,' Maisie said with a mocking tone. 'What he really liked was being told off for being a naughty boy . . .'

'Isn't that the English vice?'

'Oh, American men are quite as bad,' Lily said. Laura and Florence fell silent during the conversation, and quite soon Laura got up to say good night, and again to her pleasure Florence got up too and they went down the corridor together.

'Wait a minute,' Florence said at the door of her room, and Laura stood uncertainly as she went in and came out again. 'I thought you might like to read this – yesterday's now, but anyway.' It was a copy of the *Daily Worker*, which Florence obviously thought more suitable reading for Laura than the Hollywood magazine she had seen in her cabin. Laura thought she might feel criticised, but as she walked down the corridor to her room, she realised that what she actually felt was – what was it? – *noticed*, singled out, even if found wanting.

And that was why, after carefully wiping the make-up off her face with cold cream, the way that she had learned to do from magazines, Laura lay down in the hard, narrow bed and, despite the discomfort of the swell of the boat, she started reading the newspaper that Florence had given her. Most of the headlines, about delegates and conferences, policies and speeches, were too alien to hold her attention, but on an inside page she found a column about women's lives, by one Sally Barker, which mentioned the importance of men taking a role in domestic work if their wives were to take their place in the revolution. The writer talked about how too many women were trapped at home in America, while in Russia women were able to take their place next to their menfolk in the factories. 'There we see no selfish husbands who expect servants rather than companions, and no nagging wives who realise life has passed them by. We see women who proudly go out and put their shoulder to the wheel, and men who are not ashamed to rock the cradle.' Laura read it idly, but after she had put the newspaper down and turned out her light, its words kept drifting through her mind.

And as she slept, the words of the article seemed to thicken and take shape in her dreams, so that Sally Barker took on the form of one of her old teachers from school. She was sitting, in her dream, with Laura in her own living room at home and they were watching her mother sewing a skirt, but then gradually she realised that her mother was stitching the skirt onto Laura's own body, and she felt ashamed in case her teacher could see the little stains on the skirt where her blood was seeping. It was a surreal, nonsensical dream, she thought when she woke in the small hours, her heart pounding, but she could still feel her panic. As she woke properly, she realised that it was physical discomfort that had woken her, and she struggled out of the bed and staggered to the bathroom to retch over the toilet. As she lay back down again, the ship's swell seemed greater than ever, and the room horribly claustrophobic in the darkness, and she lay uneasily until she heard the sounds of people coming

27

and going in the corridor and thought it might be time for breakfast.

In the restaurant there was no sign of Florence or the journalist, and so she sat self-consciously on her own. When the waiter put the toast and coffee in front of her, to her horror she realised that she was feeling ill again, and she had to rush out of the restaurant to the nearest bathroom. As she washed her hands and mouth in the little basin, she saw how tired and pinched her face looked in the mirror, and rather than return to the restaurant she went out onto the deck.

'Feeling okay?' a voice said to her from a deckchair, and Laura turned to see Joe sitting there.

'Not my best,' she muttered.

'Sit here and eat this,' he said, offering her a bag of saltines with a casual gesture. Her instinct was to refuse, but then she realised she longed for one. 'You'll feel better soon. The weather's calming, it was a bit of a rough night, wasn't it? This ship has the worst vibrations of any I've ever known.'

'Have you done this journey before?'

'Just once. And once from Southampton to France, and down to Morocco and Egypt.'

Laura asked nothing about his travels, but someone as determined to talk as Joe was not to be put off by a lack of direct questions. He told Laura about the boat he'd taken to north Africa, about the film playing that afternoon in the ship's cinema, which he had seen the previous week in New York, and he called the steward over for hot coffee. In such loquacious company Laura could relax a little, knowing that nothing was expected of her.

At one point he stopped and looked at the newspaper which Laura had put down at her feet. 'You're not a Red too, are you?'

'Florence gave it to me—'

'Still, they're right about some things,' Joe said, taking the newspaper and looking at the front page. 'At least they get what's going on in Europe. They don't do the "if only, if only" – you know, "if only he was a nicer guy or he would accept this or that" – they can see that kind of stuff is all baloney, that there's got to be a showdown sooner or later.'

At this, Laura said nothing. She and her mother and sister had all convinced one another that war was a long way off, and even if they had done so simply because they wanted to believe that a trip to London was still possible, the conviction was now hard to throw off. Joe went on talking, about what he couldn't stand about communism, how they wanted everyone to toe the line. 'They want everyone to be the same,' he was saying.

To her own surprise, Laura found herself shaking her head. She had only that one article to go on, but she found herself saying something, which sounded inarticulate even to herself, about how it was everyone else who wanted women to be the same, and it was good if the communists thought that they could be free. Almost as soon as she had started to speak, she tailed off, and Joe laughed and started to tell her she was wrong, and that women wanted to be real women, not workers, but she was hardly listening. It was as though only on saying the word 'free' had she realised what she had been thinking all night – and not just that night, but forever, for as long as she could remember – about her home life, about her mother . . . yes, it was Mother who loomed in her mind, Mother's nagging, her carping, and even, from time to time, on dark nights full of awful yells and worse silences, her sobbing. She had always resented Mother, always blamed her, but that word 'free' had hurt her as soon as she had tried to say it, because it was the word that Mother had spoken once, on the one occasion she had tried to speak to Laura seriously, she had told her not to give up her freedom as she had done. Freedom. What had Mother given up? As the unbidden memories crackled through Laura's mind, she closed her eyes, the cracker she was eating an inedible lump in her mouth, and she heard Joe asking if she was going to be ill, and she made herself open her eyes and smile. That's what you do, you stay quiet, you open your eyes, you smile. Whatever you do, you never open the door to the place where the yells and the sobbing can be heard. 'I guess you're right,' she said quietly, as Joe told her that women didn't want to have to work in the same way men did, and that communists had no idea what women really wanted. 'Fashion, families, you know.'

'They have fashion in the paper,' Laura said, looking down at the newspaper that had caused the argument, and then knowing that she had been much too combative already, she smiled a dismissive little smile and asked Joe another question about what he was going to do when he got to Southampton – or Le Havre? He was happy to keep talking, and Laura found she didn't have to speak much more, while he was so eager to air his views and experiences.

As the swell did indeed die down, and the sun appeared weakly, one of the auburn-haired girls, Maisie, joined them. She complained of a headache, but she was still breezy company, one of those people who worked hard to match each anecdote in a conversation with one of her own, so that between the two of them Laura could sit more or less in silence, her fur coat buttoned up to her chin, beginning to feel better as the wind blew over them.

'Florence!' she called, seeing a tall figure, her hair whipping back, walking along the deck.

'Did I have a bad night . . .' Florence said, sitting down heavily beside them.

'Me too.'

'The woman in my cabin was being ill all night . . . ugh. Listening to sounds of someone else vomiting when you're trying to sleep . . . It stinks in there this morning, too.'

Laura commiserated with her, but Florence seemed less friendly than she had the day before, shrunk into herself. 'It's too cold to sit here, how can you stand it?' she asked and Laura could see her shivering in her cloth coat.

'We did the journey the other way in the summer – much better,' Maisie said. 'We went swimming – look at it now.'

They all looked down at the open tourist-class swimming pool, its water whipped into waves by the wind.

'Didn't you say that people go over to the first-class side to swim?' Laura asked, and Joe told them again that he had heard from other passengers that there was an easy way to the indoor swimming pool through the engine room. She found herself unexpectedly intrigued by the idea, and so, clearly, did Maisie.

'We could go,' she said, glancing at Laura. 'Not to swim, I suppose – just to look.'

'Are you coming, Florence?' Laura asked.

'You'll have to change – you can't go over in that dress, they'll see through you in an instant,' said Maisie, eyeing Florence's drab dress and worn shoes.

'I'm not going to dress up and pretend to be something – for what?' Florence said crossly. 'I've got a headache, anyway.'

'Why don't you lie down?' Laura said, regretting the words once they were said, for their fussy tone.

'Go back to that cabin? The smell of vomit?'

Laura was delighted by her next thought, which was to offer Florence her own room, since there was an unused bed in it. Florence accepted without any particular graciousness. All three women got up, and Laura walked back to her cabin with Florence while Maisie went to change, telling Laura to meet her by the engine room. Laura opened up her brown trunk to find a better dress than the one she was wearing.

'You have so many clothes.' There was a kind of rebuke in Florence's voice, and Laura looked awkwardly down at the folded piles of jersey and velvet and crepe, cerise and grey and peacock blue.

31

If she hadn't been with Maisie, there was no way that Laura would have crossed into first class. The roar in the engine room echoed in her stomach and almost seemed to lift her into the air. The couple of men at work on the engines did not seem to think it was their job to ask what they were doing, and when the two slipped through the huge double doors on the other side, it reminded Laura of being in a school play and coming suddenly out of the dusty, dark wings onto a brightly lit and confusing stage. Now the ceiling was twice as high above them, and the musty smell of cigarettes and old food was replaced by scents of lilies and polish. The wide, gilded corridors seemed to have been designed by a film director with delusions of grandeur, but you felt as though it had been flimsily realised, as if the marble might turn out to be painted and the inlaid wood just veneer. There were few people around, and they were moving slowly, a couple of elderly men walking with shaky steps down a staircase, a very overweight woman standing uncertainly in a doorway, as if each of them was overwhelmed by the decor. The pool room was the icing on this heavily sugared cake, a sweep of blue lined with multicoloured mosaics.

Once there, the girls perched on two of the white and gilt chairs by the side of the pool. Maisie got out her cigarettes and Laura found herself imitating the way that Maisie was sitting, with her legs crossed and her hand holding the cigarette out to one side, but it was a poor pretence of nonchalance. She asked Maisie questions about what she was going to do back in London, and learned how she had tried to start a career in the New York shows over the last few years, but things had not gone according to plan. After a while they lapsed into silence, and Laura found her gaze arrested by a woman who was swimming determined laps, up and down, up and down. Eventually she stopped and got out, a tall, straight figure in a belted white swimming costume, who removed her cap to show a bob of almost white blonde hair.

'Who's she?' said Maisie. 'I'm sure I've seen her before. Is she in the movies?' Laura didn't know. 'Or is she some society girl?'

It seemed more than likely. The woman walked to the side of the pool, her chin lifted, her shoulders back. 'Hughie,' she called to a tall man, who was reading a newspaper at the bar with a friend. 'I'm off to the hairdresser. See you for cocktails later.'

'At the bar upstairs?'

'Absolutely not. Come to my suite. The Landers will be along too.'

Ebslutly naut . . . Her voice was struck glass, ringing with a brittle tone, and as she walked past them again, her towel trailing slightly on the ground, her gaze hovered about a foot above their heads. Laura could swear she knew they were in the wrong place. She felt that it was time to go back, but Maisie started talking to her again, this time about London, and despite herself Laura started to ask her questions about the city they were steaming towards, which she had never seen.

'Is this yours?' It was one of the men to whom the blonde woman had spoken, a man with a young face but thinning hair, and Laura automatically shook her head and avoided his eyes. But Maisie was leaning forward, looking at the silver cigarette lighter he was holding.

'No, it's not mine,' she said, smiling up at him.

'I say, I haven't seen you around before.'

'Haven't you?'

Laura flushed. The man's voice had sounded mocking to her and it seemed clear that he knew they were not in the right class, but Maisie was oblivious as she introduced them.

'Are you having a good voyage, Miss May?' The man sat down next to them, unbidden, and Laura noticed him raise his eyebrows at his friend by the bar, who drained his drink and walked over to them. The conversation between Maisie and the first man seemed to be moving along quite easily. They were even laughing by the time the other man sat down. 'And we have drinks and you don't,' he was saying. 'Martinis?'

'I'll have a whisky sour,' Maisie said.

'I'm fine. I don't need a thing,' Laura said, in a voice that was too quiet perhaps to be heard, as the man seemed to take no notice and ordered them all drinks, which came quickly. In Laura's mouth, the spirits were bitterly strong, but she drank anyway, because it seemed to be expected of her.

'You're a quiet one, aren't you?' the other man said, leaning towards her, and Laura smiled, but it was a tight little smile.

Maisie and the first man, Hughie, were by now discussing various shows in New York, and he was talking about which of the actresses he had seen had the best shape, as he put it. He looked very obviously at Maisie's breasts as he spoke, and Maisie arched her back. 'I'll tell you who does better martinis than you'll get at the bar,' he said and his friend laughed. 'Mine are the best on the boat.'

Maisie immediately said something with a double entendre that Laura did not understand, but from the roar of the men, Laura could see it went down well. Before she quite realised it was happening, Maisie was getting up and the men were putting down their drinks, and they were all walking together from the pool room. Laura fell into step with Maisie and told her she was going to go back, and Maisie told her not to be a spoilsport. She turned away from her as she did so, and towards the men, and Laura felt hot with embarrassment and uncertainty. The suite turned out to be even more oppressively ostentatious than the public rooms – all gilt and glass and satin curtains, and even a baby grand piano at the edge of the room. Maisie sat down immediately on one of the blue velvet sofas, and crossed her legs so that her dress rode up to her knees.

Maisie asked them about the woman they had seen at the swimming pool. 'Amy?' Hughie said, as if they obviously knew who she was. 'She'll be at the hairdressers for the next couple of hours.' It was that statement, as though he had been let off by Amy for a little amusement, and his amusement was going to be these girls from tourist class, that made Laura flush up with embarrassment again. She replied monosyllabically to everything that was said to her, until the second man gave up on her and lay down on the floor, smoking a cigar.

Meanwhile, Hughie was talking to Maisie about shapes again and how he had once known a dancer with 'curves like watermelons'. 'Are you saying mine aren't?' Maisie said, and the man leant over and cupped his hands around her breasts and pretended to judge. 'That's just your brassiere, isn't it?' he said at last, and she laughed in a high, yelping voice.

At this, Laura got up. 'I must go,' she said, 'my friend's waiting for me,' but the man on the rug seemed to have fallen asleep, while Hughie was now engaged in a struggle with Maisie. Just as he managed to release Maisie's breasts from her dress, immediately putting his head down to lick one rosy nipple, Laura turned the handle of the door and went out into the corridor.

Out of the room, she realised that she was unsure where to go. She started walking to her left, but the corridor split in two. Seeing a steward coming towards her with a large tray, she stepped to the right, but after a while she realised she was walking down a passage she had not seen before. She saw an elderly gentleman walking towards her, and finally summoned the courage to ask where the pool room was. Once there she managed to retrace her steps back through the engine room and into tourist class again. The smell, the low ceiling and the dingy felt carpet in her cabin seemed more lowering than before. Florence was asleep in the spare bed, her face squashed into a flat pillow, and Laura sat down heavily. After a while, she watched Florence wake up, yawning.

Although she had thought that she was dying to tell Florence about the experience she had just had, and about the way Maisie had behaved, once she was awake Laura realised she didn't want to talk about it. She was no longer sure that she had behaved in the right way, leaving Maisie there. Part of her wondered if Maisie was all right, and the other part of her was full of hot anger. In her confusion, she said nothing about it.

'The other side of the boat . . . you wouldn't believe . . .' was all she said in a blank voice, 'more gilt than you can imagine.'

Florence sat up and stretched. 'Why aren't you travelling on that side anyway – your family must have quite a bit of dough?' Laura realised that she was looking again at the pile of dresses on the trunk.

'We're okay now. Not rich like those women in first class. But it was only last year we got our money. And we have been struggling.' Laura felt as though she were trying to excuse herself, to explain away the clothes, the earrings and the fur coat hanging on the back of the door. It was true, they had struggled. It wasn't the kind of poverty that Florence would be used to, of course – being hungry or cold – it was nice people's poverty. It meant that your clothes were last year's, faded and mended when the girls at your school came to class every term in clothes that were fresh and scented and glossy with newness. It meant that when there was a leak from the bathroom into the living room, there wasn't the money to make it better, and the ceiling and wallpaper stayed stained and a piece had to be cut out of the carpet, so that you didn't invite girls home. It was about saying no to invitations that you longed for – to the theatre, to parties – because you couldn't return them. It was about not going to college, but taking a secretarial course and then a little job at a real estate office, where you ate your lunch out of a paper bag every day. It was about your father being out of work and coming home smelling of drink late at night, every night. And it had

36

gone on, day after day, year after year, the little miseries of nice people's poverty.

Until suddenly, last year, with the death of her English grandfather whom she had never met, there was a lurch into a kind of wealth: shopping trips into Boston, the planned vacation in Europe, so many plans, so much chatter, which should have drowned out those years of humiliation. All that is behind you now, Laura reminded herself. Across miles of water now. This is where you are now, with this new friend.

At that thought, Laura smiled at Florence, and asked her if she wanted to stay in her cabin for the rest of the journey. Florence responded in a characteristically matter-of-fact way, and went to her old room to get her things – which turned out to be just a big old carpet bag, and when she came back in she said she was going to shower. Putting the bag down on the floor, she stripped carelessly. Laura and her sister had always observed a careful propriety with one another, and Florence's beautifully modelled back and buttocks and legs and, as she turned, the slopes of her breasts and stomach flashed into Laura's sight and stayed there even after Florence had gone into the shower room.

That evening they went up to the deck again after dinner and found a place behind a glass screen, where the wind was less bitter and they could sit for hours. Laura told Florence about the article that had made such an impression on her, and Florence immediately responded by agreeing that this was what things were like in Russia for men and women. 'A friend of mine made a trip there last year,' she said. 'She told me all about it.' The way Florence described her friend's experiences, everyone was able to participate in the happy-ever-after of equality. 'Everything that's so demeaning about relationships between men and women in America – gone.' Laura tried to grasp what this would mean, but Florence had already moved off onto other themes – dignity, fair wages, work.

37

Work. Florence asked Laura if she had ever worked. The memory of those months in the real estate office flooded back into Laura's mind. Of course she had been told many times how lucky she was to find a job, any job, that summer of 1937. It had been a humid, languid August to start with, and in Stairbridge almost everyone she had known from school was off on vacation, out on airy hills or beaches. Only Laura, it seemed to her, was condemned to this miserable office, where the summer days fell away pointlessly, unfulfilled, behind the windowpanes. She typed invoices and contracts line after line, page after page, rattle, rattle, rattle and bang, until she felt like a vase fretted all over with fine cracks, as though she would shatter at a touch. 'I hated it,' she said, a little shamefaced. 'I don't think I'm any good at working. It was so – repetitive.'

'That's the whole point.'

'What is?'

'There's so much . . .' and for a moment Florence seemed to hesitate, as if everything she wanted to tell Laura was too large to contemplate – and then she plunged in. She told Laura about the alienation of labour, and how capitalism reduced the worker to being an instrument rather than a person, and made work an endless sequence of repetitive actions. She told her that in a communist society every man and woman would be able to engage in meaningful work that really did spring from their personality. The alienation of labour. For some reason this abstract idea suddenly sprang into life for Laura, as she remembered those summer days and the sense, new to her and one she would never forget, that she was looking down at herself from far above, that she was not part of the life mapped out for her.

She made Florence talk more and more, as the swell rose and fell beneath them, and even when Joe stopped to speak to them, she shrugged him off. As Florence spoke, a gull momentarily landed on the railing like a white emissary from the future and the pared moon was suddenly naked as the clouds left it behind. Or was that just how Laura remembered the scene afterwards? Because she replayed the conversation in her mind for weeks and years to come, remembering over and over how she listened to Florence's words and how freighted with meaning they seemed. The promise of the new world that was mapped out for her that night seemed almost like a personal promise that Florence was making to her, that the petty humiliations of the life she had left behind would never return. More, that the bitter failures and pointless successes of ordinary middle-class life were unimportant, and there was a place ahead of them where women and men could find nobler and more vivid activities.

They went to their cabin late. But that night the sea was calmer, or maybe it was just that the girls were used to the motion. They slept deeply and woke more refreshed. There was an impatience in the air when they went up to the deck after breakfast, Laura thought, as if everyone was eager to get to the end of the voyage. But Laura did not want it to end. She watched Florence as she walked fast, as if with some purpose, around the deck. Bareheaded, her hair's natural curl tended, in the damp wind that blew constantly, to frizz around her temples and the nape of her neck. But the way black and brown and auburn seemed to mingle in the curls of her hair, the way the wind blowing at her eyes made them water and sparkle – something of the sea itself, some deliquescent light, ran over her and through her. In years to come, when events had irrevocably parted them, it would always be this Florence, this girl blown by the salty wind, who came back into Laura's mind.

Suddenly Laura saw Maisie and Lily talking to Joe, and felt a shyness rise up in her. But Joe called her over. They were all talking about what time the boat was likely to get into Southampton the following day, about how the bad weather at the start of the journey had held them back.

'You rushed off yesterday,' Maisie said in an aside to her. 'Well . . .'

'We had a wild time,' Maisie said confidently, and Joe said, 'So I heard.' Laura found Maisie's face hard to read. Was it all pleasure, or was there knowledge of how Laura had judged her? Laura could not be sure, but at least there was no anger there, and so Laura was able to stay talking. As they stood there together, Laura saw how intimate Joe seemed with Lily, touching her hand as he lit her cigarette and teasing her about how she seemed unable to throw off what she would call seasickness but he would call a plain old hangover. As she noticed how Lily shook her head at him in a mixture of laughter and annoyance, Laura wondered if there was something more than friendship now between the two of them.

But when Joe turned to Laura and started to ask her about whether she was going back into first class, his energy moved easily away from Lily and towards her, and she realised that there was no particular intimacy between him and Lily. He was just one of those people who wanted to create a flirtatious warmth with everyone he met. It was unusual in a man, Laura thought as she answered him, to see this constant attentiveness to every person. No wonder he had collected this little group around him in the few days on the boat.

And so she stood quite happily, chatting with the others, until she saw Florence again, now in conversation with a steward on the other side of the deck, and moved away to join her. The steward was, to Laura's mind, a rather unprepossessing man, a short dark boy with a bad squint. Florence and he had spoken briefly to one another before, Laura had noticed, and now with a transparent pretence of asking for coffee, Florence was talking to him again. As Laura walked up to them, she heard the words 'conditions', 'hours' and 'wages' and knew that Florence was becoming exercised about

40

some injustice that the boy was telling her about. She should have been pleased, she knew, that this was what Florence was doing, but instead she felt irritated that Florence's attention had shifted away from her, and was not sorry when the boy moved off as she approached.

In the evening a band was playing in the tourist-class restaurant, and after eating their steaks and apple tart Florence and Laura sat watching a few couples on the little dance floor. Florence was talking when Joe stopped at their table to ask her if she wanted to dance, and she shook her head. He raised his eyebrows at Laura, and she bit her lip. 'I can't dance like that,' she said, motioning to where Maisie and Lily were dancing with a couple of men. They were fast and slick, turning and turning on neat lines.

'Who cares?' Joe said, catching her hand, and on an impulse Laura stood up. He was not a great dancer either, and Laura felt that they were the clumsiest people moving in the room. There was something so exposed about dancing while people were dining, looking up from their plates to watch you turn and step. At one point she looked back at their table and saw that Florence was no longer there, and she loosed her hand from Joe's. 'I must just find Florence—' and then turned to smile at him politely, 'but thank you.'

She walked up the stairs to the deck, and sure enough there was Florence, her voice was clear in the night air. 'I think that you should be standing up to them,' she said. She was talking to the steward again. 'If they are really trying to bring down your wages because of that, well—'

'Florence!'

Florence waved to her, but turned back to the steward. Their voices were lowered as Laura walked towards them, but she heard Florence tell the man something about someone he needed to talk to in New York. As Laura came to stand next to them, she told them not to mind her, but the man looked at her with some embarrassment and then moved off.

'Was I interrupting?' She heard how her voice sounded, reedy and uncertain. Florence shrugged. They stood at the rails, but the urgency of their conversations over the last few days seemed to have left them. As they stood there, the music from the swing band downstairs was heard through an open door, spilling out onto the deck and the ocean. Laura felt its rhythms again, and remembered the touch of Joe's hand and his clumsy energy as they danced.

'There will be so much to do when we're in London,' Florence said, and Laura realised all of a sudden how near her aunt's house was. Her aunt, and the cousins, Winifred and Giles, who had sounded so formal in the letters they had written, were waiting for her in that grey city, ready to take her back into the embrace of family life. Florence, she knew, was thinking of a different London, a city that she thought was readying itself for war, a city where she thought she could be useful. They talked idly for a while about when the boat was likely to get to Southampton the next day, and then Florence said that she thought she would go back to the cabin and finish her book. 'Damn, I left my scarf in the restaurant,' she said.

'I left my handkerchief too,' Laura said, although she knew perfectly well that her handkerchief was in the pocket of her coat, back in their cabin, 'I'll go.' She left Florence on the dark windy deck and went back down. Through the doors to the restaurant, it was all warmth and light. A number of couples were dancing now, but in the centre of them were Maisie and Lily dancing together, moving even more sharply than when they'd danced with the men, the fastest rumba Laura could imagine. The music seemed to be shaking off their bodies as they tripped backwards and forwards.

'They're not bad,' said Joe, suddenly at her elbow. 'You rushed off . . .'

Laura apologised. 'I had to find Florence.' She saw Florence's scarf on the back of a chair, but rather than moving over to pick it up, she turned back to Joe. 'Dance again?' she said. This time they moved together with more ease, and as the number ended Laura could feel the sweat springing up under her arms. 'I must take Florence her scarf,' she said, but she said so looking at Joe, and this time they went together out of the restaurant. Upstairs, however, the deck was empty. Instead of moving back downstairs to look for Florence, Laura paused.

'Smoke?' Joe's voice was very near to her ear.

She took one although she hardly wanted it, the freshness of the salt air was so keen. As he lit it, Joe looked into her face, and Laura felt that their bodies were even closer than they had been when they were dancing.

'So, your comrade's preparing another lecture for you?'

'She doesn't lecture me.'

'I've heard her.' Joe flicked a match into the water. It spun, a tiny bead of light, in the darkness. Laura caught anger under his words, but before she could ask him about it, he turned back to her and smiled. 'Your eyes are shining in the moonlight. Has anyone ever told you what pretty eyes you have?'

Nobody ever had, but Laura laughed in what she hoped was a sophisticated way. She didn't know what to say, and felt shaken by the desire that rose up suddenly in her, a desire for his compliment to be not just an easy line but something that he had found hard to say, something that bore testament to his view of her. And then he did what she realised she was waiting for him to do, and put a hand behind her back and slid it down, over her dress, over her buttocks. Laura was unable to move as pleasure, so forceful it seemed to deny her a sense of consciousness, flooded through her, loosening her joints and heating her skin.

'What your friend wants,' he was whispering, 'I can see that . . . But what you want – what do you want?'

She hardly heard his words, she was so focused on his touch. He threw his cigarette away over the side, and put

43

his right hand up to Laura's face, stroking his thumb over her cheek and then putting it against her mouth. To Laura's own surprise, she did not move away from him, and her lips opened against his thumb, and tentatively her tongue touched it. 'So you do know what you want,' he whispered urgently into her ear. The hand that had been on her back was now between her thighs, and as it moved up to the skin above her stocking top her mouth opened suddenly wider, and a groan escaped her.

'Come on then,' he said, pushing his hand up to her underwear, which had become so wet that his fingers slid on the silk. Lost in the molten pleasure that his touch was giving her, Laura was unaware of anything but the pressure of his fingers, but then he stepped away and took her hand. 'Come on,' he said again. 'No need to provide the entertainment,' and to her shame she saw a steward walking past them and realised that Joe was smiling at her, as though she was amusing him. 'Let's get some privacy – my cabin mate is drinking in the restaurant, we can be alone for a bit. Long enough, anyway.' He raised his eyebrows at her, and suddenly his obvious amusement at what was happening made her feel ashamed.

'I must go and find Florence,' she said. Her words were clipped.

'Come on,' his hand held her wrist now, and it was too tight. Laura tried to pull away, but his grip tightened even more.

'Stop it,' she said, horribly aware that she could still feel the wetness between her thighs, that she wanted his hand back there, and that her voice sounded half-hearted.

'Don't go back to the lectures.'

'She doesn't—'

'What, does she give you any of this?' His left hand pushed up again, under her dress. 'Does she? Or is she just teaching you about how to be a good little worker, how to forget what you want for the good of the masses?' The hand still gripping her wrist was hurting her, and the other one was pushing her legs apart again, and though the sparks of pleasure were intense, so too was the anger, coming hard on the heels of the pleasure. He was smiling at her, and his teeth, which looked yellowy with nicotine stains in the daylight, were white.

Making a huge effort, she pulled away from him and smoothed down her dress. 'You have no idea—'

'No, Laura, *you* have no idea. You have no idea what she's talking about, all that claptrap that the Reds are trying to feed people while they knock down everything that's good in the world.'

'You're telling me about being good?' It was a quicker comeback than Laura knew she was capable of, and Joe laughed.

He went on talking, but he had lost her. She shook her head and told him she was going inside. As they walked to the stairs, Maisie and Lily came up laughing with another man, and Joe joined them. The four of them started dancing drunkenly on the deck, and Laura felt heavy and disappointed as she turned away from them to go down the metal staircase and back through the corridor to her cabin. She walked slowly, dragging one hand against the felted walls. There was something that had shocked her not just about the embrace and her overwhelming reaction to it, but in the lightness with which Joe had treated the sudden surge of desire. She felt confused, wrong-footed. How could he experience that energy, which had come across her with such an all-consuming force, as if it would fuse them together if they gave into it, as something so light and impersonal?

She opened the door to the cabin. Florence was sitting in her bed, her knees drawn up, reading. 'I've got your scarf,' Laura said.

'I thought you were still dancing.'

'No, I – I stopped.'

Florence said nothing, turning a page. Laura walked over to her and put the scarf down on her bed. 'Do you think—'

'What?' Florence's voice was not unfriendly, but it was rather clipped, as though whatever she was reading was more interesting to her than what Laura was thinking, and so Laura said nothing. She took off her clothes, facing the wall and pulling her nightdress over her body before taking off her underclothes. As she took off her garter belt, she remembered Joe's fingers, and she looked over her shoulder at Florence, but all her attention was on whatever she was reading, and Laura got into bed.

'Tell me if you want me to turn out the light,' Florence said in the same tight, reasonable voice. Laura told her not to worry and lay in the light with her eyes closed for a while.

But the rustling of Florence's pages and the shivery sense of her own body's warmth made sleep elusive, and she pulled herself up on an elbow and opened her eyes. 'Tell me about what you're reading,' she said to Florence sleepily, and as the girls' conversation began again and footsteps and laughter came and went in the corridors, the steamer pressed forward through the night ocean, and England came nearer in the dark.

When they went out on deck the next day, the coast of England was visible on the horizon. Clouds had come up in the night, and a drizzle obscured Laura's view as she stood watching the grey streak of land come into focus. About half of the passengers were disembarking, and in the crush to get down to the landing boats and the muddle of finding porters and a place in the queue for customs, Laura and Florence lost one another. After they had all gone through customs, she found Florence again, and Joe and Maisie and Lily, standing beside her, on the station platform. She saw that Joe looked terrible, as though he had been drinking all night. His face was dull and oily, and when he spoke a little line of spittle from his top lip to the bottom gleamed in the station lights. And yet there was a clench of desire in her stomach as she looked at him.

Suddenly the train came in with its great roar and shadow, and at the same time there was a press of urgent movement on the platform. It was the woman whose self-assurance had impressed Laura at the pool, walking swiftly, a maid and a porter behind her with stacks of luggage, a small red hat pulled down over her forehead. A pop of flashbulbs was going off in front of her. 'Amy!' 'Lady Reynolds!' came the shouts.

As the ripple of interest spread along the platform, the woman was being pressed on to the train with a man holding her arm, trying to push back the photographers. 'Do you remember her?' Maisie said to Laura. 'That Hughie told me all about her. She went away without her husband. The reporters will want to know if she's getting a divorce. They think she won't be Lady Reynolds much longer – but Hughie, he said her husband will forgive her anything. He said, she can do whatever she likes, and she does. Hey Joe,' she persisted as they found their seats together in one carriage. 'Call yourself a journalist? You missed the only story on board – these reporters have been waiting and waiting for Amy Parker.'

'I'm not here to do society gossip,' Joe said. 'I'm here because of the war.'

Maisie was scornful, sitting down and taking out her compact to check her face, as though the sight of Amy Parker had made her self-conscious. 'You'd think some people actually wanted a war.'

Joe started to tell Maisie that she couldn't bury her head in the sand forever, but there was a desultory feel to their talk. Laura was remembering Amy by the pool, and just now. 'She is lovely,' she said.

'She's got charisma, all right,' Joe allowed.

'Charisma – phooey!' Florence said, thumping her old carpet

47

bag onto the rack above them. 'She's got money. Money, money, money – and they all come running to sniff it.'

'It's not just money,' Maisie said. 'There were rich girls used to come to our show, lots of them nobody would look twice at, for all their minks and diamonds. Someone like Amy Parker, you'd look at her even if she was wearing your dress – though not so much, I give you.' They all looked at Florence's old purple smock dress, and even Florence laughed.

Laura said nothing, thinking both of them were right. There was the glistening, acidic aura of money around Amy, which gave her essential components of her glamour – the desirable brightness of her fashionable clothes, the scurrying maid, the piles of luggage. But there was also the strange character of the woman, the way she forged through that crowd, her tiny hat like a flag, daring the photographers to follow her rather than submitting to the shame she was meant to feel. In a way, Laura thought, that lack of self-consciousness was not entirely unlike Florence's, although in other ways they could hardly be more different. But both had a confidence born out of complete self-sufficiency, as though the approval of others meant nothing to them.

Once the train started, Florence closed her eyes and fell into a doze. But Laura looked out to the country that her mother had always spoken of as a kind of dreamland. There was the desolate flatness of the fields and the lowness of the sky which ran from grey to subtle turquoise, but seemed to be devoid of light, even though the fields themselves gleamed here and there with an almost unearthly sheen. By the time they reached London the shine had gone out of the air, and a heavy, freezing rain had begun to fall against the windows.

At Waterloo, people everywhere were hugging and saying their goodbyes. Laura put out one hand to Florence, but instead of embracing her, Florence smiled in her matter-of-fact way, picking up her big carpet bag and shaking her head at the porter who had moved towards her.

'You've got my aunt's telephone number,' Laura said. 'You will call?'

'Well, of course, there's so much to do – I'll let you know exactly what's going on.'

Laura nodded, unable to say more. As Joe wished her goodbye, she saw a questioning look in his eyes, but she turned away. She saw a dark, neat figure walking up the platform towards her with a porter, and as the woman approached her, calling her name, a current of knowledge of what was expected of her ran through her and she straightened her back and walked forwards.

Fire

London, 1939–1945

1

The first time Laura really spoke to her aunt was at break-fast the next morning. She was too tired when she got in to do much more than accept a cup of horribly strong tea and go early to bed. She woke with a jump, in a room heavily curtained against any light. Sitting up in bed and switching on the lamp beside her, she noted, as she had the previous evening, the solidity of her surroundings. Nothing here seemed new, or bright, or flimsy. Everything was covered in a patina of soft browns and greens, and as she pulled back the drapes the cloudy light falling through the window hardly seemed to illuminate the room.

Her watch had stopped in the night, and she found it hard to tell whether it was time to get up or not. After waiting a while she got dressed and made her way downstairs, and was relieved to find her aunt in the living room, reading a letter. Over breakfast they continued the conversation they had started the previous night, in which Aunt Dee seemed to be trying to build up a picture of their life in the States, and yet was hardly listening to Laura's replies. Laura felt throughout that she was rather a puzzle to her aunt and thought how much easier it would all be if Ellen were with her. 'I must send a telegram,' she said suddenly, remembering. 'I promised Mother that I would – to say I'd arrived safely.'

'I did that last night, dear, don't worry,' said Aunt Dee. 'I knew how Polly would worry. Sending you off on your own like this.' Laura caught a disapproving tone in her voice and was glad when she heard the quick step on the stairs that meant her cousin Winifred had got up. She came in with a citrus scent of cologne and a demand for more coffee. A tall, angular girl with fair hair and red lipstick, she seemed to jar against that room of sombre tones.

'Now,' she said as she drank her coffee. 'What to do this morning?'

Aunt Dee started to say that she hoped the girls would stay in quietly and do some reading, but Winifred shrugged her off, suggesting a walk and telling her with some impatience that of course they wouldn't be late back for lunch. 'Ten to one, we'll be back before Giles gets here. We're not going on an expedition, you know. Tomorrow, we can go into town, but now – I'll get my coat.'

Laura was glad that Winifred was so insistent they should go out; she had seen nothing of Highgate on arrival the previous day. But as they walked down the streets, Laura only thought how subdued the edge of this city was, how the brick houses with their many-paned windows, set back behind their hedges, drew away from your gaze, closing in on themselves. They soon came to a large park, almost monochrome in this dim January light, which Winifred called the Heath. It stretched uninvitingly into the distance. Laura suddenly realised that a question was hanging in the air. 'I'm sorry?'

'Just wondered if it was like that – the crossing?'

Laura had missed the comparison that Winifred had made, but did her best to describe the journey. She had not until that point decided to keep Florence and her conversations a secret, but something in her held back; the effect that Florence had had on her perhaps reached too deeply into experiences that she had never spoken about, feelings that she was nervous of exposing to Winifred's quick questions. And so she found herself mentioning Maisie instead, and the trip into first class, and Joe Segal, and how they had danced together on the last evening, and then she remembered the woman in the white swimming costume, the woman in the scarlet hat – what had her name been? 'I think she was called Lady Reynolds,' she remembered.

'Amy Parker?' Winifred said with interest. 'Giles knows her – or, well, doesn't know her exactly, obviously.'

Laura didn't understand how it would be obvious to know and yet not know her. It was only later that she came to see the way Amy sat at the centre of so many circles, how many and various her satellites were. But she was glad of Winifred's sudden spark of interest, and so she tried to recall everything that she had seen and heard of Amy. In return, Winifred told her about the speculation in the press about her marriage. While the girls' own lives were still dark to one another, Amy seemed to stand revealed and, in their comments on her, which moved from the admiring to the moralising, they hinted at their own desires.

After that the conversation led on to other things, but they felt more warmly now towards one another. Winifred mentioned how much she liked Laura's coat, and Laura expressed her interest in shopping with Winifred in London. 'I have an allowance now,' she said, almost wonderingly.

'Mother said that Grandfather's legacy would make a big difference to Aunt Polly – I'm sorry, that's an awfully crass thing to say,' said Winifred, but Laura was rather relieved that the subject had been broached and admitted to her, as if it were a mild joke rather than a humiliating shame, that it was odd for her to have money to spend.

By this time they had walked up a steep hill, and Laura felt she should say something about the view, which was confusingly vast, layer upon layer of buildings laid out under the hazy light, but still and quiet on this Sunday afternoon, and so, with an exclamation, she stopped. Winifred asked her about Boston, and Laura tried to explain that they lived far away from the city – 'Stairbridge is a small town, way west of Boston' – but she saw that Winifred, like Aunt Dee, was not really much interested.

The walk had taken a long time and the weather was turning drizzly as they came back into her aunt's street. Sodden, unswept leaves made the path slippery and Laura felt the shadow of the laurel bush, dark with soot, hanging over them as Winifred put her key into the door. 'Thank goodness, Gee's arrived already,' Winifred said, seeing the coat and hat on the hall table. Laura could hear the rumble of a male voice from the living room. 'He doesn't live here then?' she asked.

'No, only comes back on Sundays – the prodigal.'

Giles was a big presence, fair like his sister, his voice loud in the quiet, over-furnished room. Even with Winifred supplying repartee as quickly as she could, his performance was too fast and too expansive, Laura thought. The anecdotes he was telling were about work, and although they were difficult to follow in themselves, being about some developments in radio, the main thrust of them was easy enough to understand, about how Old Stevens was standing in his way, unable to get the funding released from air defence, and that the boy Pearson kept making a mess of the data, but how Giles himself was forging ahead.

The burble of his stories was continuing as they sat down to lunch – a meal of heavy roast meat and a sort of spongy pancake and indeterminate boiled vegetables – and Laura was just wondering if this family was always so easy, so reassuringly solid, or if this was a show put on for her. Then the telephone rang in the hall, and Mrs Venn, the maid who had met Laura at Waterloo the day before, put her head around the door. 'It's for Miss Laura.'

53

'Oh – do you mind?' Laura was getting up and going towards the door, only thinking that it must be Mother and hoping that Ellen's appendicitis hadn't entered some new complication. But down the line came the strong, clear voice from the ship, Florence's voice, dismissing Laura's questions about how she was and telling her about a march that was happening the following weekend. Laura felt a sudden sense of disjunction, a gap cracking open between the girl who was listening to Florence's voice, who would be expected to come to a demonstration in a few days, and the girl who would return to the dining room and pick up her spoon to eat the boiled pudding they had just been served.

'I don't think so,' she said to Florence, and then, as the directions continued, she fell silent. 'Yes – yes, all right, I'll see you then.' Once she had put the receiver back in its cradle, she stood for a while, wondering what to do, before going back into the dining room.

Entering the room, Laura stumbled over a lie that she had been speaking to a girl she had known from home who was visiting London with her parents. But she found that the others were not really paying attention to her. The conversation had shifted while she had been out of the room.

'You promised!' Winifred was saying, her voice rising, to Giles, who was spooning pudding into his mouth.

'Can't help it – away that week now.'

'Giles, dear, that is a bit rough – she has been looking forward to it.'

Aunt Dee turned to Laura and started to explain that Winifred had been expecting Giles to take her away to a country-house party next week, although Aunt Dee herself had thought it wasn't the right time for them to go away, given Laura's arrival.

Winifred pushed her bowl away. 'I even bought a new dress, you perfect—'

'Shall we have coffee in the living room?' Aunt Dee seemed

eager to turn the conversation. 'It's rather cold in here.' Indeed, the room felt damp and chilly, as the rain fell against the curtained windows.

'Freezing, yes. But Giles, why couldn't you—'

'Vennie's had a fire laid in the other room, as these radiators seem to have given up the ghost,' Aunt Dee said. Her voice held a fussy, conciliatory tone. 'And, Win, I got out a photograph album I wanted to show Laura. It's upstairs – could you get it?'

When Winifred was out of the room, Aunt Dee turned to Giles and began to persuade him to make it up to his sister.

'All right, all right,' he muttered eventually, promising that he would make sure she was invited to some other gathering soon. Laura thought it odd that they were relying on Giles, whose manner did not seem particularly engaging, to help Winifred with her social life.

In the living room, Aunt Dee began to show Laura the huge leather-bound book that Winifred had brought in. To her surprise, Laura found it intriguing. Her mother had almost nothing of the family, no photographs and no objects, and Laura had always dismissed her memories of a perfect childhood in a perfect world. So it was a shock to see these images of her mother's lost life: here was a sepia photograph of a timbered house in Oxfordshire, and here two solemnly starched little girls with their mother, whose face was long and lugubrious and who wore a tightly corseted dress. Here were the same two girls, adolescents in frilled blouses.

'Look,' said Aunt Dee, taking a breath as she held that one up to the light. 'We were just leaving for school in Lucerne, that's right – they sent us for a year, to finishing school . . .' In her voice was the memory of some richness, some freedom – but the page was quickly turned and here was Aunt Dee again in a posed studio photograph, alongside a man with a little moustache who seemed much older than she was. 'There isn't one of Polly and your father,' she said, and let out a breath. 'It was all such a rush. Father was so very sad when she went. He never quite forgave your father for living so far away – and . . .'

There was a pause, and Laura caught again the undertone of disapproval. Looking at Aunt Dee's engagement photograph, seeing the frank stare of the young woman with her hand resting on her fiancé's, Laura was struck by the thought of her mother at about the same age, and the force of desire that must have led her to follow the young man she fell in love with across the ocean at the end of the Great War. 'I think it must have been terribly romantic,' said Winifred, clearly also thinking of Polly's elopement.

Once again, images arose unbidden in Laura's mind. A window into the kitchen of her home opened in her mind, with her mother sitting there in her best blue dress, weeping. Her father had promised to take her out to dinner for her birthday, and had forgotten or got too drunk to come home. She heard Mother telling her never, never to marry beneath herself, and saw her red-knuckled hand grasping the glass of gin. Laura pushed the image away and looked back again at the photographs. Aunt Dee was pointing to one picture, and telling Laura that was her great-uncle Francis, her grandfather's brother, who had had a fine career in India, and Laura began to realise that there were all these stories that she did not know, about this English family she hardly knew.

When the fat album had been closed and coffee brought in, Winifred and Giles went on sparring, complaining to one another about old battles. As they spoke, Laura found herself watching Aunt Dee, trying to see how the confident outward look of the girl in the photograph could have developed into the watchful manner of the woman before her now. She was not unlike her own mother, Laura thought, seeing how her gestures seemed truncated and hesitant, how she seemed more eager than was necessary to smooth over the disagreements between her children.

When Giles moved to go, saying he was meeting a friend, Winifred said goodbye to him with bad grace. Laura could see that she had still not forgiven her brother for spoiling the planned weekend. Sure enough, as soon as they were upstairs alone, Winifred started complaining about him. Apparently he had some well-connected friends that he had met at university, and Winifred rather liked one of them, but there seemed to be some resistance on Giles's part to taking her about.

'I think he thinks I'm not worthy. It would be all right if I could do my own thing, but he doesn't seem to realise how little there is to do. I know, I've got my friends, but they are all such *nice girls*,' Winifred spoke the last two words with feeling. 'You are lucky, being allowed to travel so far – I'd love to do that.'

Laura almost asked whether she couldn't plan a trip somewhere; but when she thought of Winifred coming to visit her family in America, her stomach tightened with fear. The idea of Winifred's clear gaze falling on her undignified little home and miserable parents was a dreadful one. But Winifred started talking about other, more surprising, plans. Apparently she had a place at university, to study history. 'They accepted me last year, but Mother asked me to wait a year. She wasn't well in September. This year I won't put it off, whatever she says. She hates the whole idea of me going – I suppose Aunt Polly is exactly the same? You didn't go to university?'

Laura was too shy to tell Winifred quite how poor they had been, how it had been impossible, when she left school, for her to think about college, so she just shook her head and then asked Winifred more about her plans. Winifred became more and more honest about her frustrations with living at home. 'She still thinks we exist in the pages of that photograph album – she doesn't like me going around by myself.'

'You're not meant to go out alone?' This was more than Laura expected. She remembered the telephone conversation she had just had with Florence, and Florence's assumption that she would come to the demonstration the following weekend, and wondered hopelessly how on earth she would manage it. Winifred was explaining how her mother's protectiveness irked her. For instance, there was a rather nice man she had met recently at the cricket club dance, and he had asked her out for supper, but he was a divorcé, and Dee would not approve, so what could she do?

The two girls were sitting in Winifred's bedroom talking, their heads together, when Aunt Dee came in to tell them it was time to come down for tea. Winifred nodded, and once her mother had gone, she suddenly turned to Laura, her hands opening as if pulling apart a parcel, her eyes widening as if she could see a new vista. 'But now you're here – we could sort of chaperone each other, couldn't we?'

2

Although the march had begun to move off by the time Laura got to Hyde Park, there were still what looked like hundreds of people, dozens of banners, waiting in line. Laura thought she would never find Florence, and began to feel foolish for having made the complicated arrangements and spoken the shocking lies that had enabled her to be there. She had not even told Winifred what she was doing, simply that she wanted to have tea with someone she had met on the boat. That Winifred assumed it was a man, and that the assumption had made her eyes crinkle up knowingly, had embarrassed Laura but had not encouraged her to reveal the whole truth. So the two girls had told Aunt Dee that they were going shopping in town and then to tea with Cissie, an old school friend of Winifred's. Just as Laura was beginning to feel hopeless about the whole escapade, she saw the red lettering of the banner she was looking for, and then the familiar face she longed to see beside it.

Florence did not notice her immediately; she was talking to a tall, bareheaded woman who was holding one pole of the banner in her gloved hands. Laura had to push awkwardly past a couple of men and tap her on the shoulder, and then Florence only briefly acknowledged her before turning back to the tawny-haired woman. 'Elsa, this is Laura – I told you about her.'

But just to see Florence again sent a great chime of happiness through Laura's mind. This was where she wanted to be, even in this great crowd of people, so long as Florence was by her side.

Elsa nodded at her, heaving the pole, which seemed heavy in her hands, a little further upwards. 'Don't keep pulling it about, Else,' came a yell from a young man holding the other pole.

'Shall I take it for a bit?' asked Florence, but just then their part of the march began to move off.

After a few moments the first bars of 'The Red Flag' began to rise up from the crowd. Laura didn't know any of the words and couldn't join in the singing, but as she lengthened and slowed her steps to fall in with the rhythm, she felt that the crowd was fumbling for a sense of togetherness, and that the song, marvellously, seemed to give it to them. Even when the song faded, that sweet sense of being enfolded by a common purpose remained. Looking around her, she was rather reassured by the look of the people on the march; she had been nervous that the communists would be a raggle-taggle bunch, but in fact a drab propriety seemed to characterise them. Everyone was in shades of grey and navy, so that it was only the brilliance of their flags that brightened the streams of people. The walking and the singing seemed to go on and on, and Laura began to get nervous about time passing. 'When does this finish?' she asked Florence, who was now holding one of the banner poles.

Florence turned to her, and told her there would be speeches

59

in the square, but they would leave before that for the other protest. At Laura's puzzled look, Florence explained that a few of them were going to take the march to Halifax. Laura had never heard the name before. 'The Foreign Secretary, you know?' Elsa said. Her voice was low and brusque. 'We can't just do this, the marching, Trafalgar Square, just what they want us to do.' Laura could not see why this was not enough, the thousands of massed people as they got to the huge square lined with its grimy buildings. There were so many, she would have felt afraid of the crush, but there was a reticence about their movements, and one said 'Sorry, comrade,' in a gentle voice as he stepped on her foot. But as soon as their part of the march had filed into the square, Florence took Laura's arm and led her to what was obviously a prearranged meeting spot down a side road. Here, about two dozen women holding bags and rolled banners were waiting, and after a while they all moved off, down a broad avenue bordered by the chilly expanse of another London park.

'I have to go back soon,' Laura said, looking at her little silver watch. 'I told my aunt I was shopping with my cousin – we're going to meet at teatime.'

But Florence was not listening, and the pace of the women now was quicker and more urgent than the march had been. It was Elsa who was directing the group, with the help of a map, and at one point they had to retrace their steps to find their way into a wide square. Here, the sounds of traffic were muffled, the sidewalk unrolled smoothly under their feet, the trees opened huge branches under the quiet grey sky, the houses rose white and cold behind their sharp railings, a woman in a coat with a high fur collar was getting out of a car, holding a tiny dog, two policemen were standing indifferent in front of one of the blandly graceful houses – and that was the one the group was making for.

'Now, girls!' shouted Elsa, and suddenly all the banners were unfurled, some women were lying down, while yet others threw a pot of red paint at the shining black door of the house, shouting 'Halifax, murderer!' and 'Arms for Spain!' as they did so. Laura felt a spurt of fear run through her body, and stepped away from the group as the policemen moved towards them. A policeman bent over one woman who was lying down on the sidewalk and started to drag her along, so that her dress rucked up below her, showing the tops of her thick stockings, while another policeman started to blow his whistle in panicked bursts. The woman on the pavement in the fur-collared coat paused for a moment, and Laura caught her eye, expecting a secret sign of sympathy. 'War-mongers,' she spat. 'Stupid bitch.'

Laura started to walk away, almost into the path of a couple more policemen who were running along the pavement. As she hurried off, she could hear shouts behind her, and the noise of further struggle.

3

The memory of the march stayed sharp in Laura's mind. She had got to the tea room on Piccadilly only a little late, after asking directions from a woman once she had got away from the square. Winifred had been keen to tell her about the lunch she had had at the Criterion with the chap from the cricket club dance, and had hardly noticed Laura's distraction. All the way home and all the next day the voices of the singers, and the startling physical courage of the women in the square, had remained vivid. Part of her felt nervous about what she had witnessed, but the sense of urgency pulsed through her. What would change, now that the women had been so brave?

But she looked in Aunt Dee's *Times* newspaper, and saw no discussion about it at all; neither the next day, nor the following one. Reading the dense and impersonal reports of political speeches in the newspaper, she gradually came to understand that Halifax's policy of non-intervention in Spain had not shifted in the slightest. In fact, nobody but her seemed to have heard about the protest, and gradually she came to realise that it had not rippled the quiet life of the Highgate household, let alone the government.

As the days went on, it was hard to imagine what would create ripples in Highgate. There was a constant decorum to life here, which was both reassuring and claustrophobic. As Winifred said, Aunt Dee seemed to think that the best way for Winifred to behave was the way laid down during her own youth; it was a repetitive round of visits and walks and luncheons with girls who had much the same manner and appearance as Winifred herself, together with French conversation lessons and piano practice, and games of cards and reading aloud with Aunt Dee in the evenings, or the occasional concert or trip to the theatre. This round of activity quite easily accommodated Laura, and it was only her pact with Winifred, which meant that once a fortnight or so the girls said they were going shopping or to tea with a friend, while each went their separate way for two or three hours, that caused a secret rift in the tight tapestry of good behaviour.

It was a few weeks after her arrival, when Winifred was meeting up with her boyfriend again and they had told Aunt Dee that they were going to the cinema, that Laura went to see Florence at the local party headquarters in King's Cross. She had telephoned her that morning when Dee was busy with Mrs Venn, and Florence had told her where to come and explained they would go on to a meeting that Elsa was to speak at. But when Laura got to the little basement office, she found everything in confusion. Elsa was unwell, apparently, with a horrible sore throat, and Florence was talking to one Bill Ellis, the local party leader, about what to do. 'It's just a women's group,' Bill said.

'It's a branch of the Co-operative Women's Guild,' Florence said, 'Elsa was keen to bring them in – said that they should be receptive to the message about the struggle on two fronts.'

'Well, could you trot along and give them her apologies? If she really can't speak, there's nothing to be done about it.'

'She gave me her notes,' Florence said, and Laura noted the hopeful confidence that had so entranced her on the boat. 'I'll give the talk for her, it's fine. I did lots of talks to women's organisations in New York.'

'This isn't New York . . .' Bill seemed wary of giving Florence the go-ahead, but then someone called him to the telephone and before going he succumbed, only asking whether she really did have Elsa's notes and reminding her to stick to the line on the united front against fascism.

Florence reassured him, and turned to Laura, who was delighted at the thought of seeing her friend speak in public. It was the first time that they had seen each other alone since the protest, and as they walked to the house where the meeting was to take place, Laura tried to ask her about what had happened after the march. There was another one planned for Easter, and a fundraising pageant for Spain in a few weeks' time, Florence told her. Laura realised it was not just her ignorance that meant she had not caught the fallout of the protest. It was true that nothing had changed, but for Florence there seemed to be nothing surprising in that failure; all the planned activities would continue regardless.

The part of London they were walking through now was closely built, the houses rearing up above them and almost cutting out the sky. It was one of those evenings that Laura had realised were characteristic of the city, with a dampness in the air which was infinitely suspended, never falling as rain, studding Florence's hair and her old coat with tiny stars. But in the house where the meeting was to take place the light was cold from bulbs that hung bare from the ceiling, and everyone's skin looked sallow. There were only about a dozen women in the room, sitting planted on small chairs, their bags on the floor at their sides, a stillness surrounding them. As the first speaker went through various pieces of business and reminded the women in the room to pay their membership dues, Laura waited for Florence to stand up and break through the solid atmosphere.

But when Florence did stand up, she seemed physically ill at ease and her voice fell hesitantly into the room. She was not talking in her own voice, Laura realised after a while; she was reading from the notes she had in her hand, and the urgent rhythms of her own conversation were replaced by careful arguments that Laura kept following and losing. These were mainly about the logic of history and the correct understanding of the current situation in Europe, where Fascists in Germany and Spain must be defeated by a united front. The terms of the speech were all abstract, and Laura found her attention wandering. She began to watch the knitting being done by the woman beside her, fantastically quick and accurate, spooling off into a fine pattern of purple and green. When Florence stopped, Laura came back to herself and realised to her shame how much she had missed.

The woman who had spoken first now invited questions from the floor. There was a long silence, so long that Laura began to blush for Florence, but then the knitter beside her clicked the needles into her bag and asked her why she was advocating that they go off to fight fascism in Europe, with all the problems here at home. 'Two million unemployed,' she said, in a hoarse monotone, 'and that doesn't count all the ones like my old man, working short hours, not enough even to cover the rent since I was let go on account of falling orders. That leaves only my girl working, so she's sweating day and night now, and my boy can't get the medicine he needs for his pain – he's never been able to work, you know. Four mouths in the flat, damp running down the walls – that's not something another war will solve.'

Laura was horrified at the thought of the home that the woman had left to come here. She looked at her and thought, she's probably younger than Aunt Dee and yet she was stooped, her thin hair twisted at the back into a straggling bun. She would not know how to speak to her, but Florence was already talking again and Laura was glad to hear her voice return to the urgency Laura had first heard on the boat over the Atlantic. She was holding forth about how the workers had achieved so much in the past, and how this was no time to give up; and about what women could achieve too; and the rent strikes being led by women in the East End. As she recounted this concrete heroism, Laura felt flooded with light. But then Florence looked down at her notes again and stumbled, and started again, talking about the struggle on two fronts, about how it was important to link the struggle against capitalism at home with the struggle against fascism in Europe. Again she returned to abstraction, and when the talk finished and the women were invited by the chair to the tea table, where there was sweet, strong tea and cookies, Laura felt a kind of relief.

The woman next to her spoke to her as they stood up. 'You're a Red, too, are you?' she said, and Laura nodded diffidently. 'So you're all for war, then? It's an easy line. But you don't know. If you'd lived through the last one you'd know. We all said, never again.'

Laura was conscious of her own poor understanding as she began to repeat phrases from Florence's speech.

'That's what they said the last time,' the woman said before she had finished. 'A war to end wars. A war for a better world. They came home to higher unemployment, lower pay . . .'

'But that was an imperialist war – it was fought to defend the Empire . . .' Florence had come over to them. 'This will be a war against imperialism and fascism; it's quite different.'

The woman said something about how she sounded like the Conservatives, all this eager talk of war. Laura felt shamed by the criticism, but Florence hardly paused.

'If Churchill and Eden and Duff Cooper can see that Chamberlain is on the wrong path,' she said, and Laura wondered at her ease with these British personalities, 'that's welcome, whatever their motives. Of course that doesn't mean that they are right on anything else. In the long run we'll resist them just as we are resisting Adolf Hitler.'

Laura warmed to her certainty; how wonderful it must be to have such sure knowledge of what was happening and what was about to happen. But she felt, to her embarrassment, the other woman's gaze fall on Laura's fur coat and polished nails as she stretched out her hand for a cup. The conversation faltered, and the two young women stood in silence with their tea until it was time to go.

Outside, the air seemed to have cleared a little, and there was a frosty chill. When Laura asked Florence to show her the way back to the Underground station, Florence said she was going the same way. It was just along here, she said, that she lived with Elsa. A short silence fell, and then Florence asked if Laura wanted a quick cup of hot chocolate before going home.

So this was where Florence was living her independent life! The free life that Laura should be living if only she didn't have her family holding her back. As Laura followed Florence up the stairs, she felt a thick excitement rising in her. To be sure, the apartment seemed unprepossessing; there was a gap in one sash window that someone had tried to fill by stuffing it with newspaper, and stacks of dusty books and papers on the floor. But still, surely it was full of the hope of freedom.

It was only two rooms, Florence explained – so Florence slept in the living room, which was also Elsa's study, as Elsa's bedroom was so small. It was indeed very small, and when Florence opened the door to ask Elsa if she wanted anything, Laura could see Elsa in a bed which seemed to fill the room from side to side, with a large paisley eiderdown tucked over it. 'I think the fever's gone down,' Elsa croaked, and then asked Florence about the meeting. Laura heard Florence telling her that it had all gone well, that the speech had been delivered as Elsa would have done it, and that she was sure some of the women would come to the pageant. Laura sat on the edge of the hard blue couch as they talked, and then, when Florence came out to make some cocoa on the gas ring, she stood up and said she had only just realised what the time was, and that actually she should go. She asked if she could borrow a pamphlet which she had found on the floor, and Florence said she could, but hardly looked at her.

'We're out of sugar,' Florence called to Elsa.

'Open the condensed milk instead,' she heard Elsa order her from the bedroom, 'and help me up, for goodness' sake.'

4

'I get the feeling your boyfriend is not treating you well,' Winifred said to Laura the next day as the two girls walked up to Highgate High Street to do some errands. 'And I must say – my last dinner with Colin was dull as ditchwater. The wages of sin are boredom, don't you think?'

'Well,' said Laura, 'it's true – it's not . . .' But she tailed off. What could she say? After the last meeting with Florence, she had gone once or twice to other gatherings of the Party in King's Cross or Holborn. They had been full of speeches that constantly returned to abstraction, that never delved into the experiences that had brought her and, she assumed, others into the room. Even when she had sat with the other comrades over tea in the basement office, the conversations had been so far from the exquisite insights of Florence's discussions on the *Normandie* that she had almost cried with frustration. Instead, they had been mainly about procedure, with a great deal of discussion about who was on the right lines, and who was being bourgeois or deviationist or showing 'Trotskyist tendencies' in their approach. In all of this Laura sat in unbroken silence, and Florence herself said little, while Elsa was almost the only woman who raised her voice at all.

And the more she saw of Elsa, the less Laura could warm to her. There was the obvious scorn she showed towards those who did not come up to scratch, her grey serge dresses that smelled of sweat, the glasses she kept twitching up her nose. Laura knew she was wrong to judge Elsa in what Florence would tell her was a petty, individualist way, but she could not help herself, as she sat watching Elsa, and watched Florence watching Elsa, and saw Florence take on – without, Laura thought, knowing that she was doing so – some of the little mannerisms and turns of phrase that characterised Elsa's speech.

'Don't worry – you can keep him secret if you like.' Winifred broke in on her long silence.

Laura realised she had to say something, given how generous Winifred was being in helping her to meet her imaginary boyfriend, and so she began to tell a story in which the boyfriend took on the face and opinions of Joe Segal. At one point she mentioned something that he had said about communism, and Winifred laughed and told her she had been having a similar conversation with a friend of hers the other day.

'Cissie – can you believe, not a political bone in her body, really – had picked up some of that stuff. I told her to leave it well alone. Communism – can you imagine a more humourless, miserable way to live? I don't just mean no shopping. But the point is, some people really are special, that's the truth, and those are the ones who need to run the show. I don't know why it is that so many people at the moment seem to think it's the answer to bring everyone down to the lowest level.'

Laura was about to jump in, about to tell Winifred that communists didn't think that nobody was special, but luckily she caught herself in time. The last thing she wanted was for

Winifred to start arguing with her about communism even before she had it straight in her own head, and when she was feeling so . . . what was she feeling? Just then they came to the bookshop where Winifred was to find a particular novel for Aunt Dee, and Laura was able to go to the back of the shop where the poetry was kept, and under the pretence of browsing she went on with her train of thought.

Why was it that she had kept Florence and Elsa and the Party secret from Winifred all this time? Deep down, she realised this could not go on. Sometimes everything came straight. The pamphlet that Florence had lent her recently had laid things out for her in a beautiful order, showing that one did not have to accept the corruption and dishonesty and the stifling soullessness of the world as it was. While she was reading, she had said to herself, I'll join the Party properly, and tell Winifred, and move out and throw in my lot with Elsa and Florence. That's what I'll do. But once she had put the pamphlet away and gone out of her bedroom, she could not even form the words in her head that she would say to Winifred. The great impetus left her whenever she thought about living in the way that Florence and Elsa lived, rushing from tedious meeting to meeting, and returning to that cheerless apartment in the evenings. Just then, Winifred called to her and she put the book that she was pretending to look at back on the shelf.

After leaving the bookshop they walked up to the top of the hill where there was a dressmaker above a flower shop. Winifred bought most of her clothes ready-made, but wanted a dress altered for a dinner party that she was going to that weekend. They stood in the dusty light of the dressmaker's room while Miss Spark pinned up the hem of the dress.

'And I think I want these ruffled sleeves taken off,' Winifred said. 'What do you think, Laura? I could have it sleeveless.'

Laura had hardly been looking, but then she suddenly

69

saw Winifred turning to view herself in the mirror, her neck rising out of the stiff green silk like a straight narcissus breaking out of its leaves. Miss Spark was trying to convince her to put some trimming in place of the sleeves, taking out a length of white net that she thought would be right, and some small white silk roses, but Winifred looked at them and discarded them, turning around again in front of the mirror, lifting her arms. No, not a flower, Laura thought. A bird.

'I'm sorry you can't come to the dinner,' Winifred said as they walked down the stairs back to the street. 'Giles was reluctant enough to take me – not that he's taking me, of course, his friend Alistair is. One of the Initiates.'

Laura looked rather than asked the question, and Winifred explained how Giles and his very best friends had belonged to a society at university called the Initiates. 'All they mean, I think, is that they are initiated into adoration of one another; it's not that they are all that special, or all that gorgeous, or that successful, but you know what men are like – they need these secret societies, these movements and cliques, to feel comfortable. Wouldn't life be nicer if people didn't need all of that? *Clubs.*' Winifred's voice dropped into scorn on her last word.

Just at that moment the two girls had entered the park between the high street and Aunt Dee's house, and Laura stopped in surprise. On the way up, a morning fog had covered it, but now the air had cleared. For the first time she saw London revealed as a place of potential beauty, in this park full of its layers and layers of different greens, both deep and transparent, opening onto that now almost familiar view of a secretive city down below. She said how lovely it was, and Winifred casually agreed. As they walked on, Laura kept looking out at the city, its promise of energy, its distant song of movement, and she wished that she were able to go into it that afternoon rather than do what they were expected to do – go home and be idle in the over-upholstered living room, reading and playing cards. She knew that Florence and Elsa were preparing for a big concert for aid for Spain, and she longed to be with them. Even if in practice the preparation only meant the repetitive business of stuffing envelopes and typing out address labels, still it might hold purpose within it, and on this day full of the brimming hope of spring she longed for a sense of purpose.

As soon as they got into the house, Laura realised she was not the only one who was feeling out of step with the Highgate house. Winifred had seemed good-humoured while they were walking outside, but when her mother told her she had got her the wrong novel she slammed it down on the table and insisted that this had been the title they had discussed. Although Laura had seen Winifred irritated before, this was the first time that her voice had crackled into real anger. Perhaps, Laura thought as Winifred ran upstairs to her room, shouting about her mother's unreasonableness, the decorum of the household had been partly a response to her presence, as if everyone had been determined to put on a good show for the new onlooker. But now she was no longer new, nobody could be bothered to keep up the façade. The bitter atmosphere continued over supper, when Aunt Dee complained about the amount that Winifred was spending on dresses and Winifred countered by telling her that it wasn't her fault she wasn't allowed to earn any money.

The following Saturday, the day that Winifred was going to the big dinner party, Laura came down to breakfast to find the atmosphere between mother and daughter had curdled completely. 'I can't believe that you'd try to stop me again . . .' Winifred was saying.

'It isn't me, dear; it's the way that the world is. Laura, we should really talk about this too . . . Polly's last letter was definitely concerned, and I think she's right, that we should think about booking you a passage back quite soon. There's no hope of visiting the Continent while things are as they are, and I really think that—'

'Just because we can't go to France in the summer doesn't mean that I have to give up my place at university.'

'Do you mean you'd like me to go back?' Laura was, to her surprise, horrified at the thought. Suddenly she realised how she had got used to the pleasures of this life – on the one hand, the comfortable round of shopping and gossip, social engagements and visits, in which the expectations on her were easy and undemanding; and on the other hand, all the time there was the possibility of her next meeting with Florence, the sporadic crossings into a world where the future was being made and her growing familiarity with their discussions of the new world to come. But her horror was silent, confined inside her head, while Winifred was openly furious, the words tumbling out of her.

'I know, you say it's the war coming, and before it was because of your chest pains, but don't you see, Mother, it can't always be about other things – it has to be about me too. I can't stop living, I can't just sit here my whole life because you sat at home all of yours . . .'

Laura stood at the table, unable to sit down, riveted by Winifred's sudden honesty. How brave she seemed, in her green jersey, her hair pinned into curls in readiness for the evening's party, arguing with her mother while coffee cooled in their cups. Laura was not surprised, however, when Dee said nothing at all in response. It was as though Winifred had not spoken, as she turned to Laura and asked if she would like a boiled egg with her toast. Even when Winifred stood up and, throwing down her napkin, stamped out of the room, Dee simply folded her lips together and told Laura she was probably over-excited about the evening. To her shame, Laura colluded in pretending that Winifred did not know what she was saying. She sat down and ate her breakfast, and listened to Aunt Dee talking about whether the gardener had been right to plant the lilies right up against the house like that – how would they get enough sunshine? Aunt Dee wondered.

After breakfast Laura went to find Winifred, who was sitting in the garden in the thin sunshine, pretending to read a book. She listened to Winifred's complaints about her mother for a long while, and then reminded her that Dee had said it was time for Laura to go back. 'I don't want to,' Laura said. 'I really don't want to.'

She wanted Winifred to say, I don't want you to go either, but Winifred looked puzzled.

'Don't you? Is it about this man?'

'I don't know.' Laura wished she could tell Winifred about Florence and all she meant to her, but she still held back. It would seem ridiculous now to confess that she had not been meeting some dashing man from the boat, and also she was afraid that Winifred would find Florence and Elsa and their politics absurd and would never understand the importance of what Florence had offered her. 'Do you think I should go back?'

'God knows. Mother thinks – like your mother I suppose – that it's going to be 1914 and worse. Father was almost an old man, so he didn't have to go, but the men they had danced with . . . I don't have to explain, I'm sure you've heard enough stories from Aunt Polly.'

Laura could not tell her that her mother had never mentioned the war.

'No wonder they married where they could – sorry, I'm sure your father is . . . it's just Mother is such a snob, she thinks your mother only fell in with him because there wasn't anyone left in England.' Winifred turned to Laura, but she was unsmiling. 'And this time – you know what they're saying. Aerial bombs, all of that – but what are we supposed to do? We can't stop the world.'

Just then Mrs Venn came into the garden, saying Giles was

on the telephone for Winifred. 'God, if he's cancelling this evening, I tell you . . .' and she stalked off.

But he was telephoning to ask if Laura could come with Winifred. Apparently the girlfriend of one of his friends was unwell, and so there was a gap for another woman at the dinner, and at the dance afterwards as well. Winifred accepted without even consulting her, and immediately she came off the telephone she called to Laura to come upstairs and look over what she would wear.

'I suppose it is a bit of a winter dress, but it's the right one,' Winifred said eventually, after Laura had put on each of her two evening dresses and she had vetoed the grey one. 'You don't want to look like Jane Eyre,' she said, and although Laura wasn't sure of the reference, she could see that the dress she had thought of as silvery and subtle was in fact drab and drained her face of colour. Nobody could say that the red velvet dress was dull. Laura had bought it in Boston and had never worn it, but had been aware of it hanging up in the closet here in London, a brilliant rebuke to the dullness of most of her days. She wasn't sure that she wanted to wear it. Looking at herself in the mirror, she could only see the dress, not herself, but Winifred was so certain that she gave it to Mrs Venn to be pressed.

After lunch Aunt Dee suggested that the girls should rest in their rooms before the evening's outing. Winifred scorned the idea, and stayed reading in the living room, but Laura was thankful to be able to go upstairs. Lying on the big, high bed, she started re-reading old letters from her mother and Ellen. 'I think you should book a passage for April,' her mother had written. And now April was here. Laura laid the letters aside and wondered whether she was foolish to want to stay in London. It was true that nobody could ignore the sandbags on the streets and the trenches dug into the parks, not to mention the constant talk about what aerial warfare would be like and the Armageddon that would ensue. But despite

74

the fatalistic talk, despite the physical reality of the city's preparations, there was nothing concrete for Laura in the thought of war.

She looked into a drawer of the little desk where she had put the most recent pamphlet she had borrowed from Florence, *Will It Be War?*, which she had already started, but not finished. Its grand rhetoric, 'Never, never will we bow the knee to fascism', seemed too distant from her. Again she cast her mind back to the boat, and the moment when Florence painted for her a picture of what family and work might be like without false authority. That made sense to her; she felt it again, a taste of freedom, a world made in line with human desire. But the story of how they were all to fight as never before seemed dark to her, a summoning of something too large for her to comprehend. She found herself muttering some phrases from the pamphlet under her breath, as if she would commit them to memory to hold her to the right path.

Just then the handle of her door turned and Winifred came in, but to Laura's relief she did not seem to notice her confusion as she shoved the pamphlet under her pillow. She had just come to suggest that Laura might want to start getting ready for the evening and that the bathroom was free. Shortly afterwards, lying in the warm water and looking down at her body, her skin greenish in the water that was reflecting the tiles around the bath, Laura felt a huge reluctance weighing her down. The little she had heard about Giles's friends had not endeared her to the idea of meeting them.

Back in her room, she realised that the cherry-red velvet of the dress smelt of mothballs, as everything in this house did after a while. But it slithered with a cool touch over her breasts and legs as she pulled it on and zipped it tightly up the side. Lipsticking her mouth, looking for her pearl earrings, she was seeing herself only bit by bit in the mirror. Her lips – was the colour even? Her waist – did her garter belt show through the velvet? Her hair – should she push it behind her ears or fluff the curls forwards? But then, just as she was about to leave the room, she turned and saw her full reflection, as she had seen Winifred suddenly in the dressmaker's, and was startled. It was such a complete picture, it was so finished. It was only for a second that she saw herself like that, and as soon as she walked out and Aunt Dee commented on her dress and asked her if she had a wrap, she lost the image completely. She was fragmented again; she had no idea how others saw her.

Giles was waiting for them in the living room, and she and Winifred followed him to his motor car, which was waiting outside. Laura had never seen London from a car before, and the city surprised her, rolling past the windows with a kind of emphatic repleteness, as if it were being unfurled particularly for them. Giles and Winifred talked in their usual sparring way in the front seats, but she was hardly listening and was surprised when finally the car stopped outside a terrace of vast white houses rising sheer into the dimming sky.

Once inside, Winifred introduced Laura to the man who she understood was her partner for the evening, whose girlfriend had been taken unwell. Tall, thickset, with a ruddy face and even, for all he was only Giles's age, the suggestion of jowls.

'Good of you to come out at such short notice,' Quentin said to her. There was a note of condescension in his voice, clear enough for Laura to pick it out even in that room in which all the men seemed to speak with the same amused, arrogant tones. She was introduced to his father, who was a study in the fleshiness and loudness that Quentin himself was going to achieve, and to a Mrs Bertrand, a middle-aged woman with the most impressive black pearl necklace, who ignored Winifred and Laura and went on talking to the other two women who were already in the room.

Alongside Giles and Quentin was a young man who was

bending to put a record on the gramophone. He introduced himself as soon as the needle started to whirl, and Laura realised that this was Alistair, the man who was partnering Winifred. He was the most engaging of the men, with elastic, exaggerated hand movements and round blue eyes that seemed to take in everything about the two girls. There was a generosity in that; to him, they did register, even if their presence was a matter of indifference to the others in the room. Behind him was an untidy, good-looking man who did not even bother to come forward to be introduced, but put his arm around Giles and started telling him what was obviously a racy story, judging by the way he lowered his voice as he came to the end of it.

Despite the presence of Quentin's father and three other women, all the energy of the room came from the four young men, who seemed to be performing for one another, all talking at once, or almost, in quick, truncated sentences that would suddenly give way to protracted anecdotes, sustained as long as each could keep the floor. Laura had never been in such a relentlessly masculine atmosphere, she thought as they all moved to the dinner table. The women provided the colour between the black and white of the men's tuxedos, but that was all they seemed to be there for; these flashes – green, scarlet, blush and blue – between the black coats.

Sitting at the dinner table as the first course was brought in, she thought she should say something to Quentin. 'It's your sister's party we're going to later?'

'The redoubtable Sybil Last, indeed, her inevitable dance. Luckily, she has been persuaded away from providing entertainment for it in the style of last year . . . Do you remember, Alistair, the awfulness of the singers we were treated to then? The one good thing about the current situation is that no one thinks it's appropriate to ship one's entertainment over from France – too extravagant by far, not that that has ever put off dear Sybil . . . Do you remember, Giles . . .' and another anecdote, interminable, emphatic, began to roll. Laura was careful to laugh in the right places, and that was as much as she could do.

Although later on Laura came to see each of them – Quentin, Giles, Alistair and Nick – as individuals, at this first meeting she could only see the set of friends as one cawing mass. She could not imagine feeling at ease with them and picked up her spoon almost in gratitude to have something to do. At the first taste of the soup, however, she found herself grimacing. It was a creamy, pale green soup, pretty in gilt-edged bowls, but maybe it had spent too long sitting in a warm kitchen. Something – the cream, the stock, the potatoes – had begun to turn, and a rotten taste filled her mouth. She laid her spoon down, as did others, but Quentin went on eating as if he had noticed nothing. Her unease grew as she realised how physically uncomfortable she was. She had only ever tried this dress on standing up, and now, sitting down, she was becoming increasingly aware that it was too tight for her, that the cut was too rigid over her ribs and that she had to keep her back ramrod-straight if it wasn't to tear.

When the second course was brought in, she tried to speak for the second time, this time to Alistair, who was on her other side. 'You all knew one another at university?' she said, aware of what a lame gambit it was.

'Knew each other – loved each other,' he said with an exaggerated sigh. 'And here we still are, together as ever. Giles the scientist, Nick the joker, myself the writer and Quentin – Quentin the arranger of festivities.'

'What about Edward?' Quentin boomed across Laura. 'Just because he isn't here, don't forget Edward – what's Edward?'

'Edward, the philosopher – the absent philosopher.'

'Why isn't he here?' asked Giles.

'Have you only just thought to ask?' said Quentin. 'As a matter of fact, he'll be at Sybil's, but he said no to dinner . . . said he always has to work so late . . . said he couldn't bear

78

it . . . you know what Edward is like – the less . . .' he waved his hand vaguely around the table, 'the better.' Not knowing Edward, Laura could not tell whether he meant the less female company, the less dinner, or the less gossip, but that was all right, since very little of the conversation made any sense to her at all. It was all about mutual friends, shared history and absurd tales of other social engagements.

All in all, Laura was relieved when the dinner came to an end and they set off for the dance. They were offered cars, but apparently the other house was only a few minutes away, and everyone exclaimed that they would rather walk. The other women had fur wraps, but Laura was glad, stepping down to the sidewalk, to feel the air on her bare arms. The scene, as they turned into a neighbouring square, seemed familiar, and suddenly Laura was thrown back in her memory: shouts of struggle, the police, women with their pots of paint and slogans. This was the very place she had come to during her first week in London, on that extraordinary protest. There was Halifax's house. They passed it, and went on walking to another square, another row of white houses, and as they walked up the steps of one, the door was opened by a manservant. Beyond him was a wide hall painted turquoise, opening into rooms where lamps were reflected from mirror to mirror.

Here, Quentin's father and Mrs Bertrand moved on and into the party, but their group took up a place in the first room, and once they had been supplied with champagne, the chatter went on much as it had done over dinner, the women providing simply an audience for the gestures and conversation of the men. All except Winifred, who, Laura was rather impressed to note, seemed to be enjoying swapping stories with Alistair. Alistair was the only one of the men who appeared to imply, by his voice and reactions, that the presence of the women enhanced the evening for him, and he was egging Winifred on to talk about Giles as a boy. More and more little groups came into the room, full of expectant faces, but their group stayed together and few people came to greet them. Then Laura saw a tall, light-haired man walk in and scan the room.

'Edward! You made it,' It was Quentin's booming voice, calling the new arrival into the circle. 'Why haven't we seen you for so long? Has the Foreign Office been working you to the bone?' The men shifted to allow Edward to join them.

'Have you met our new friend?' Quentin said, as Edward shook hands with each of the group. 'Laura Leverett – Giles's cousin – American heiress from Washington.'

Edward nodded, his light gaze passing over her. 'Where is Sybil?'

The men looked around, and Alistair gestured to the other side of the room, where most of the guests seemed to be congregating.

'Don't rush off,' Quentin said. 'You haven't told us anything, and we do need the inside track – now more than ever. What did Halifax mean yesterday? Is he really trying to charm Germany again?'

The group seemed to hesitate as they waited for Edward's response. He paused to flick ash from his cigarette onto a silver ashtray on a mantelpiece, and then said, 'He's always wanted to avoid war . . .'

'But cosying up now . . .'

'Cosying?'

'You see him every day, how would you describe it?'

Quentin seemed irritated with his friend, leaning towards him and frowning, but Edward was unresponsive, his head tilted back.

Alistair burst in. 'If he was trying to negotiate a treaty, would the British public stand for it now?'

'The great British public would welcome anything that let them off a fight, wouldn't they?' Nick gestured at someone for more drinks. As the servant came forward, breaking up the group as glasses were filled, Laura turned to Edward.

'I'm not from Washington,' she said, 'and I'm not an heiress.'

'But your name is Laura?'

She nodded.

'Sybil,' Alistair said suddenly, stopping a blonde woman who was walking past them. She was tall, in a curiously cut, stiff turquoise dress. Laura would not say she was pretty. No, her profile was too dominated by the long nose and the high forehead, but one wanted to look again at that face, to understand the secret of its attractiveness. Quentin turned.

'I brought a new friend, Sybs – Nina was ill yet again.'

'Nina telephoned me. I think she is still coming – and this is . . . ?'

It was disconcerting to be addressed in the third person, Laura thought, as Quentin introduced her as carelessly as he had before. 'Laura, Giles's cousin,' he said. She realised again that she was only there as a stopgap, as everyone now began talking about the woman whose place she had taken.

'Nina takes to her bed for the attention,' Alistair was saying.

'Nonsense,' Sybil stated.

'Anyone less in need of extra attention . . .' Nick said.

'I think she is punishing me,' Quentin said, with a theatrically pitiful expression.

'Are you surprised? I did hear that you hadn't treated her with chivalry, exactly.'

The comments continued in that vein, crossing and recrossing, and after a while Sybil walked on, not having acknowledged Laura or Winifred at all. Winifred raised her eyebrows at Laura, but Laura was feeling too overwhelmed to respond. To her surprise, it was Edward who addressed her next, as the others went on talking about Nina.

'You're not with the embassy, are you? I know some of the chaps in Grosvenor Square.'

'No, I don't work, I'm not – I just drifted here to visit family, you know. Not the best timing.'

Edward said nothing, but Laura pressed on, feeling the weight of her embarrassment lessen as she spoke. 'My mother was keen for me to come – to see my cousins. But now she says I should go back. She's cottoned on to the fact that things may not be totally safe. It's taken her a while.' Edward nodded, again saying nothing. 'But it seems to be taking lots of people a while.'

'To see what's going on?' Edward said.

'Yes—' Laura was going to say more, when she found Winifred at her elbow. She turned to her cousin, but when Winifred asked her how she was finding the party, she wasn't sure what to say. There was glamour here, surely; the women's backless dresses, the men in their tuxedos. And yet there was a secret to the evening's energy that the others were responding to, as the colour grew higher in women's faces and men's voices became louder, which was eluding Laura. Instead, she was horribly aware of how uncomfortable she felt it was to be here as a replacement for a woman who – judging by the reactions to her illness – was clearly more of a character, more admired, than she would ever be. So she responded with some blank nothing to Winifred, and raised her glass to her lips, only realising as she did so that it was empty.

At that moment Edward took a silver cigarette case from his breast pocket. She took one when it was offered, just for something else to do with her hands. As Edward flicked the lighter, he spoke to her again.

'This American chap I've got to know at the embassy told me that he thought London was the saddest place he had ever been. Do you think so?'

Laura wondered. This question resonated. She stepped backwards from the group as she considered it, looking at Edward. 'Well, yes, – I wouldn't know. But you do feel that people would rather not be living in these times. There is that.'

'Rather Prince of Denmark.'

Whatever the exact meaning of his last remark, Laura took it to imply that he agreed with her. She waited for him to say more, but the pause that ensued seemed considering rather than empty. As they stood in silence, the conversations of the group continued beside them. This man's laconic manner might seem offhand, Laura thought, but surely it was just that his rhythms were so different from the starling chatter of the others. While they were striving for effect, their voices tumbling over one another, he was driving at something else.

'The time is out of joint,' he said as if in elaboration of his last point, and though Laura could not catch his exact meaning, she caught, or thought she did, the thought behind his words.

'Not for everyone, though,' she said, and a great rush of feeling ran through her as she thought of how Florence and her friends saw opportunity even in the danger, the possibility of remaking the world in these forces sweeping over Europe. 'Not if they see the struggle on two fronts, what it means for all of us.' The words seemed to have risen through her, and she was not aware until she had spoken them how odd they might sound in that dimly glittering room.

'The struggle on two fronts,' Edward repeated the words, but she could not read his expression as he did so. Clumsily, she reached for another subject, wishing that she had not said anything so political. She had spent too long with that pamphlet this afternoon.

'So, you were at university with Giles?' It was a false, bright tone that came out with the words, and her tongue felt thick in her mouth. She wondered if she had already drunk too much, and if it was obvious that she had done so.

83

'The struggle on two fronts: that isn't Giles's view,' Edward said, and again she could not read his expression.

Laura tried to explain that she didn't really know Giles that well, even though she was his cousin, and once Edward had made some polite response, she went on talking about staying with Winifred and how generous they had been to her. The ease she had felt between them had gone, though, and the small talk they were exchanging now was strained.

'But, Last, didn't Nina say to you not so long ago that if she was going to marry anyone it would be Quentin?' That was Nick's drawling voice breaking in over them.

'The emphasis was very much on the *if*, as I remember.' It was Giles who replied, smiling as he spoke, but there was sharpness there too.

'We have to dance, really.' This was Alistair. 'Sybil told me; she said, I'm not having you all turning up and just standing there like a party of gawkers.' Although he invoked Sybil, Laura could tell that in fact he was impatient to move away from his clique. Winifred and he moved off to the other room where a few couples were turning now to the music of a small band.

'He only did that to get away from this lot,' said Nick, motioning towards a couple of men who were coming towards the group, both of them in uniform. The two men who joined them seemed to be the target of some private joke in the circle, but they were perfectly friendly to Laura, and one of them was rather enthusiastic about the fact that she was American, telling her about a trip he had once taken to Boston and Maine. He was explaining to her at length the old cliché that Americans are so much more open and talkative than English people are, and then laughed with self-knowledge when he realised that she had said almost nothing as he spoke. When he asked her to dance, she was glad to move away from the little crowd around Quentin, who, she felt, had no interest in talking to her.

84

But after she had danced for a while she realised she had a stomach ache and, apologising to her partner, she moved away in search of a bathroom. The party was crowded now, knots of people standing everywhere in the two long rooms and in the entrance hall. A maid directed her upstairs to a bathroom, where she sat miserably for a while on the lavatory, feeling drunk and tired, before coming out and seeing herself reflected in the mirror. Just a fragment, again, just a flash; the lipstick worn off her mouth, a curl to tuck back.

Going down, she paused on the staircase, looking over at the gathering. 'We'll never see the like again,' someone said, going past her, and although the person's interlocutor quickly made clear – 'Oh no, I think they are breeding in Shipston' – that the comment was about horses, the words hung in the air as she looked down at the loud party.

Two women were just coming through the door from the street, one in a white satin coat, the other in grey. Laura recognised the one in white immediately. The face from the boat – unselfconscious, self-sufficient. She wore satin the same way she had worn a swimming costume, her shoulders well back and her movements quick as she shrugged her coat off into the hands of a waiting servant. Her companion was as pretty as she was, if not prettier, but it was Amy who held one's gaze. Laura saw Sybil making her way through the guests to greet the two new arrivals.

'Nina, you made it,' she said to Amy's friend. Next to her new guests Sybil looked dumpy, planted solidly on the carpet, but somehow it did not matter that she did not share their physical glamour, there was still some connection between them. The three women bent their heads together, whispering something, and then stepped back, laughing, looking at one another. They were the centre of the gathering, and as they moved through into the other room Laura saw many groups shuddering and re-forming, as people turned to greet them.

Walking down the stairs and entering the room behind them, Laura saw Quentin rushing forward to Nina, and bending almost double as he caught up her hand in an over-polite gesture. She stood irresolutely, watching them, and then walked on. She saw the RAF officer she had danced with earlier, now dancing with another woman, and she saw Nick and Giles in an entirely masculine group further on.

'Would you like to get an ice?' It was Winifred, taking pity on her, seeing her drifting through the party alone. Laura was glad of her company. She went with her and Alistair to eat a lemon sorbet from a silver dish and listen to them chatter. The evening dragged on like that until, very late, Winifred persuaded Giles to drive them back to Highgate. Winifred seemed to be riding high on the energy of the evening, talking over the gossip she had heard and pushing Giles for more stories about Alistair.

As she laid her cheek on the cold window of the motor car, watching the dark streets fall away as they drove, Laura felt rather ashamed of how awkward she had been all evening. What would it be like, she wondered, to feel that you belonged inside a party like that, inside the little group around Amy and Nina and Sybil, admired and envied, rather than uncom-fortably wandering through the crowds in a too tight, too bright dress? Then she thought of Florence, and how scornful she would be of such a desire. Florence – she must ask her what that conversation about Halifax meant. And then she found herself remembering the odd exchange she had had with Edward Last. The struggle, why had she mentioned the struggle, so pointlessly? She had seen him again, late in the party, but he was sitting with Sybil and Amy. He had looked up at her as she walked past but had not made any move towards her. Was it his arctic blondness that seemed to set him apart from others, or that quiet manner? As she remembered their conver-sation, she pressed a finger on her lip, as if she could stop herself blurting out words that had already been spoken.

Looking back on that summer, Laura sometimes let herself think that the inertia which gripped both her and Winifred was down to the fact that, along with the whole country, they were holding their breath for the great shift in September. But really, she knew it was not that. Despite their frustration with their lives, neither of them was ready to take flight from Highgate.

Winifred's life changed after the party. Lunch with Alistair and his publisher, tea with Alistair and his mother, theatre with Alistair and his friends; she would come in from each excursion with her energy high and the colour glowing in her face. As soon as she had spent some time with her mother, however, her energy would fade and she would recede into irritation and argument. If she wasn't set on taking up her university place in September, she told Laura, she would move out right away. But for now, she said, she would stay.

Laura's inertia was less explicable. She resisted all the attempts of her aunt and her mother to persuade her to book the passage home, and yet she could not take wing and leave her aunt's house. She saw Florence as infrequently as ever, and each time she saw her she felt it like a loss rather than a gain: Florence had been the only person who had ever recognised her, who had ever shown her anything about herself and her own desires. But since they had arrived in London, Laura felt that she was losing sight of Florence, watching her drift away down a road of new struggle and activity. She was always waiting for the moment when Florence would turn to her again, as she had on the boat, and paint for her the new world. But somehow each meeting always ended with the right words unsaid, with intimacy avoided.

And so the long, slow months faded away through the turgid heat of summer. Even though Laura had been told so often by Florence and Elsa that war was inevitable and desirable, when the announcement came through on the wireless on the third day of September, the concrete fact fell like an unexpected blow.

The scream of the air raid siren that rent the air sent them all, with Mrs Venn, out to the little shelter in the garden. Sitting there, Laura became aware that she was sweating: she could smell an acrid scent from under her arms. She had started her period the day before and in the enclosed space she was also sure that she smelt of blood. When you think of war, she thought, you think of action, but this is where it is beginning for us, stuck in this closed, bad-smelling space with four females.

Aunt Dee was talking to her about the need to book a passage back as soon as possible. She could not, she said, be responsible for Laura any longer. Laura put her head in her hands, feeling unwell. 'I was thinking of moving out . . .' she said in a small voice. Winifred pushed her hard in the ribs, and Laura realised that she was trying to silence her.

When the all-clear sounded and they could emerge, they realised that the telephone was ringing and ringing in the hall. Winifred ran ahead to answer it, while Aunt Dee stayed in the garden talking to Mrs Venn. Laura hung back, listening to their conversation. Mrs Venn wanted to go down to her sister's house, she was saying, as her own son, who lived with her sister, would now be evacuated and she needed to say goodbye.

Laura was startled. In all this time she had not imagined Mrs Venn's own life; she was guilty – as Florence said all the rich were guilty – of seeing servants purely as instruments. She had only seen Mrs Venn as an anonymous presence in the house, and now she looked at her properly for the first time. She was standing next to the straggling bush of late white roses, and as she spoke to Aunt Dee she reached out a hand and shook one of the flowers, which spattered its petals onto the lawn. It seemed to be an angry gesture, even though her voice was soft as she explained the urgency of her situation. She was a widow, Laura knew that, but she had never heard about the son who lived with her sister before. 'Well, I don't know, Vennie – must you go right now?' Aunt Dee was dithering. 'I suppose the girls can help get the lunch and there will be enough over for tomorrow.'

Winifred came back out of the house. 'It was Giles on the telephone,' she said in a high voice. 'He won't come to lunch today; they've been called into work. I might go and meet him later – will you come with me, Laura?'

'No rushing about today, Winifred.' In Aunt Dee's mind, it was clearly the first crisis of the war, the desire on the part of her housekeeper to take a few days off. As Mrs Venn stood waiting for her decision, Laura tried to persuade her aunt that they could easily manage without help for a few days. Mrs Venn did not express gratitude when Aunt Dee finally agreed that she could leave for a while. Instead, she frowned and then nodded at Laura in a way that Laura found puzzling.

Laura was soon in the kitchen, doing these now unfamiliar tasks that she had done so often at home: putting plates and glasses on a tray, making the gravy, draining the potatoes.

Winifred might have noticed and commented on her competence, but Winifred's mind was elsewhere. She was pouring herself a glass of water and drinking it down as if she had been running all morning. 'I haven't yet told Mother, but I'm not going to the university after all.'

'I thought . . .' Laura was disappointed by Winifred's declaration. Why would she give up her dream now? But as Winifred went on talking, Laura realised that another plan had taken shape in her mind. Although Winifred had never, as far as Laura remembered, talked to her about what she would do when the war started, it was clear that she had been thinking about it for a long time and was determined to be useful rather than following her dream of studying. What was even more surprising was her next statement. 'Cissie is looking for someone to share her flat. There would be room for you too – it would be easier to convince Mummy if we went together.'

Laura stood, startled, the gravy ladle dripping onto her apron. 'I didn't think—'

'I should have discussed it with you before – I know you don't want to go back to America, though I must admit I can't see why.'

It was both shocking and warming, that Winifred was being so friendly and opening this road for her. Not freedom, exactly, but a step towards independence . . . towards adulthood. Laura was not good – would never, all her life, be good – at expressing gratitude, but in hesitant sentences she gave Winifred to understand that she would like nothing more than to move out with her. Winifred explained that they needed to go and see Giles soon, to talk to him about jobs that he might be able to help them with. 'You worked for a time as a secretary, didn't you say?'

Laura was surprised that Winifred had even remembered that she had been a typist; she could hardly recall telling her about that. She wondered if she had been guilty of inflating her tedious, routine job into something more interesting than it had been. But she agreed that she had worked, and that she would like to try to do something useful. 'Will Aunt Dee ever agree?' she asked.

The tray was piled up, the beef cooling on its plate. Laura continued to pour the gravy into the gravy boat, while Winifred was looking straight into the future.

'How can she say no, really, if it's war work?'

As it happened, Winifred got a job through Giles easily, despite her lack of office experience. She looked the part, Laura had to admit, when she bustled off to interviews over the next few weeks in gloves and a grey hat and a glow of energy. Giles managed to put a word in here or there, in the bar at the Reform, he said, which got her onto a lowly rung in the newly formed Ministry of Food. Winifred did not mind much where she worked, she told Laura, but the offer of the job was simply the springboard that enabled her to tell Aunt Dee how difficult it would be to come back to Highgate every evening, and how much easier it would be if the girls moved into Cissie's flat in Regent's Park.

It was much harder to find Laura a 'berth', as Giles put it. In the end she took the job that Cissie herself had just left, part-time in a bookstore near Piccadilly. Cissie was herself moving on to war work of some kind, and was eager to leave her job behind. It was dull enough, she told Laura, and the owner was so crotchety she thought he would soon give up the store altogether. But this, thought Laura on the day that she and Winifred carried their boxes up the stairs to Cissie's little apartment, this is just the beginning. It would be pretty cramped here with the three of them, but luckily Winifred and Cissie had decided they wanted to share the big bedroom, so Laura had what they called the box room, looking over the trees. It was so different here, with the chintz cushion covers and the pot pourri in lustre bowls, from the atmosphere in Florence and Elsa's flat. Florence . . . she must go and see her, she could go right now, there was nothing to stop her, Laura thought as she pulled down the blackout blinds of the little room against the greenish light that was dying in the park.

'We're going out too,' Winifred said when Laura announced she was not staying in for the evening. 'Come with us, we're meeting Alistair and his friends.'

Winifred was drunk on the taste of freedom too, Laura could see. The two women looked at one another, complicit.

'Not tonight,' Laura said.

'We'll have to meet your secret man soon, you know.'

'There's no reason to keep him hidden now,' Cissie agreed, and Laura realised they had been talking about her strange assignations. How awkward it would be to come out and tell them the truth now. How much easier to look self-conscious and reply with the kind of giggle that they expected.

As Laura rode the Underground to meet Florence at King's Cross, she felt elated. The job in the bookstore was only two and a half days a week. The rest of the time she had free. Now, at last, she could become the girl that Florence wanted her to be, a faithful Party member who would stand by her side and contribute properly to the war against imperialism and fascism. To be sure, the day before, when Laura had telephoned Florence to tell her that she was moving out of her aunt's, Florence had hardly reacted to the news. But she had told her to come to the Party meeting which had been suddenly scheduled that evening for six thirty, and for once Laura could come on time, could come early in fact. And so here she was, looking for Florence where she often stood selling the *Worker* by King's Cross station.

Florence was there. But she was not, as she had been when Laura had seen her before, calling out '*Daily Worker*! Read the truth, not the capitalist lies!' and holding out copies of the paper. Instead, she was standing with her hands in her pockets and a scarf muffled around her neck, and the stack of newspapers was apparently ignored on an upturned crate beside her. When Laura came up to her, she hardly responded. After a while Laura offered to carry the unsold papers back to the office with her. 'We'll be late otherwise,' she said, but for once it was Florence who seemed to be half-hearted as she gathered them up, dropping a few on the sidewalk. Laura stooped to pick one up, and then she made out the headline. 'The communist aims for peace.'

That was nonsense. It was inconceivable. Only the communists understood the absolute necessity of war, how it would bring the great struggle between fascism and communism out into the open at last. It was like stepping through a mirror, seeing the headline there that night, and as Laura stood looking down at it, she realised why Florence was looking as if a spring had been wound down. What pushed them to the meeting? She could not remember how they walked, through indifferent streets full of people on pointless errands, their limbs weighted and words dying in their mouths before they spoke.

The room was already full, too full. But Elsa had saved Florence a seat near the front and Laura managed to squeeze in next to her. When Bill began to speak, a page of his notes slipped from his hands and he had to stop and retrieve it. It was heavily written and overwritten, Laura noticed, and as he was speaking he kept screwing up his eyes to read the next sentence. 'We must be clear . . .' The rolling timbre of his voice could always fill a room, but today there seemed to be resistance in the air and his words did not reverberate. 'This is not a just war, this is an out-and-out imperialist war to which no working-class member can give any support.'

Beside her, Florence was slumped down in her chair, not looking at Elsa or at Laura. Her legs were twisted around one another in a way, Laura thought, that must be uncomfortable. She wanted to put out a hand to those tense legs, to remind Florence that she was not alone. But they had never been physically close, had never been those girls you saw who walked with linked arms or who stroked one another's hair when they were ill, and Laura kept her hands in her lap, linking the fingers together, noticing how sweat slipped on her palms even though the room was chilly.

'The central committee has thoroughly endorsed the new line, and calls upon every member to endorse it too. There can be no room for wavering here: we must pay allegiance to this line not through mere lip service, but through conviction.'

As the meeting closed, Elsa and a couple of other women began the usual singing of 'The Red Flag' in their thin sopranos. Their dutiful octaves tried to enfold the crowd, but people remained separate, lost in individual thought. The girls did not usually go drinking after a meeting. There was not the money, after paying for rent and food, for Florence and Elsa to sit and drink beer in the evenings with the comrades; they were more likely to go back to their rooms for a cup of tea. But tonight it seemed necessary to remain with the group, to find places in the smoke-filled room, to sit down at a stained table, to shove along as more people joined them. They found themselves sitting next to Bill and two other middle-aged men. Drinks were being bought, cigarettes shared. A glass of what turned out to be beer mixed with lemonade was put down in front of Laura and, to her surprise, she rather liked the taste. Conversation stuttered around them.

'You'll accept the change of line publicly, but privately hold out against it?' Elsa's voice was already heard. 'That's ridiculous.' Her glance went to Bill's face for reassurance, and he nodded at her.

'A communist doesn't have a sanctum of privacy that they can hold out against the collective.' It was the way their conversations always fell, Laura thought, into phrases that seemed complicated, but in fact had always revealed themselves up to now to be straightforward in their certainties. Now nothing was certain, nothing was straightforward.

'But what is Pollitt's line on all this?' Florence asked. Laura remembered the pamphlet, *Will It Be War?*, with its grand rhetorical certainties, and one of the men beside her nodded, saying how well the pamphlet had been selling, how it cut through all the other nonsense.

'Comrade Pollitt has apologised,' Bill said, and put his hands down on the table in front of him, on either side of his pint of beer. 'He's confessed that he played into the hands of the class enemy by pressing the wrong position for so long. He's resigned as General Secretary.' Laura took another sip of her drink. Drops slopped onto her blue wool skirt. 'Comrade Dutt has started on a replacement pamphlet. We'll be getting it out as soon as possible. Explaining the need for the change of line. We cannot support an imperialist war. The International has made that quite clear. The directives arrived last week. We have been too slow at getting this out in public.'

Laura had been led here, to this London pub, by the light that Florence had shown her on the ocean crossing, when she had become convinced that a better world was possible. She was not giving up yet. But she felt suspended, unsure about what was happening now. This pact between the Soviet Union and Germany made too many things dark to her; and looking around her she saw she was not alone in her confusion. The table was breaking down now into separate conversations, and Elsa's rather hoarse voice suddenly fell into a silence as she told one man: 'Well, that's that. Either you accept the idea of a centralised world party, or you will find yourself in the camp of the enemy.'

The conversation that Florence had started with another man was different. They were talking about air raid precautions. It was a long-running concern in the Party, Laura knew – how the rich parts of London were well provided with shelters in basements and gardens, but in the poorer parts people were being left completely undefended, and the government was refusing to say that they would be able to use the Underground stations when the time came. Laura knew that; she had already been well briefed on that, on the fact that hundreds of poor people were going to die for every rich person. Florence was talking about the idea of direct action and how they could lead a protest to one of the big hotels where there were huge basement shelters that were apparently being fitted out comfortably for politicians and businessmen. Laura imagined such disruption in the Savoy, where she had been once for lunch for Winifred's birthday, and felt a ripple of – was it dismay, or excitement?

Meanwhile Elsa was now talking to a man on her left about the importance of showing workers how wages and conditions were being driven down by talk of patriotism. That made sense too. The man was saying that he had just come back from a tour of the Midlands where the factory workers had been up in arms about attempts to make them work longer hours for the 'war effort' rather than for extra money. 'You can't eat rhetoric,' he said.

There was nothing strange about any of these conversations. They were the conversations the comrades always had. But who would have thought that the massive disruption of the change of line would be so quickly laid aside? Laura felt too confused to join in the discussions and got up to go, and Elsa said something that Laura did not quite hear, about how Laura always had somewhere she had to be. To Laura's surprise, Florence got up too and walked with Laura to the entrance of the pub.

They stood there for a second, and then Florence asked her if she was all right going back in the blackout. Laura thought it an odd thing to say, since the moon was large in the sky. But Florence left the pub with her anyway, and walked along-side her back to the station. They were rarely alone, and some of the magic, for Laura, had gone out of those snatched moments when they were together like this. She had spent too long, she thought, waiting for Florence's sudden warmth to return, for her to look at Laura again, intently, energetic-ally, as she had done on the ship.

But to her surprise it was Florence who seemed to want her company tonight, and she asked Laura if she wanted to go to the café near the station before she went home. They sat for a long while over their hot chocolate, and it seemed to Laura that they talked about everything except what had been said at the meeting. They talked about Laura's new job, and about Florence's desire to find a new job; they talked about when America might join the war and whether they should go down to Richmond on Sunday for a special fund-raiser. If they were avoiding something, they did so with such energy that there were no spaces in their conversation, and it seemed that they were reaching for an intimacy which they had lost. At one point Laura even asked Florence about Elsa, and got her to talk about why it was that she was so in thrall to the older woman.

'It's always men who want to teach you,' Florence said. 'I don't want to be always taught by men. It's good when a girl feels she can speak too – not that the men in the Party like her speaking . . .'

Yes, Laura thought, she could see why Florence wanted to see her own potential strength reflected in that figure. She remembered the first time she had seen Elsa, carrying a banner at the march, and she had to admit that there had been power in that image. She couldn't tell Florence how much she disliked Elsa, of course, so instead she said in a rather pathetic way that she didn't think that Elsa liked her. Florence didn't deny it. 'It's not personal,' was all she would say at first, stirring her hot chocolate.

'She thinks I'm not good enough.'

'She doesn't understand . . . you're under pressure from your family. I know what that's like, I've had that. But you are a grown-up, Laura, you don't have to . . .'

For a moment it seemed that Florence was about to be honest with her, to express her own frustration with Laura's half-hearted commitment, and Laura felt her heart speed up as though she wanted the confrontation. But then Florence said something unexpected. 'She thinks – she thought – you were an informer. A government spy. Because you never commit, because you watch everyone . . .' Laura couldn't help a smile breaking on her lips, and Florence's face closed down. There is only so far you can go in criticising someone you love, and perhaps it was that evening Laura realised that Florence did love Elsa. 'It's not ridiculous, Laura. They've had to expel informers before. You shouldn't take that lightly. We are all under surveillance. We could all be being watched, any time.'

It was such a nonsensical thing to say, like a line out of the kind of movie that Florence didn't even go to, that Laura said nothing, spooning up the rest of her drink. 'It's late,' she said. They walked together to the station, and Florence seemed to want to smooth over the oddness of the evening, making Laura promise she would come to the next meeting. Laura wanted to put out her hands and touch Florence. There was the scent of smoke from the pub in her hair, the curve of her cheek white in the darkness; but she did not, could not, embrace her, and she went down into the Underground alone.

6

'I get along without you very well,' Cissie was singing to the gramophone, and holding up a new dress – or rather an old dress that a girl at work had given her – and dancing with it as if it were a person.

'Where do you get your energy from, Cis?' Winifred asked, lying on the sofa.

'Come on, we're going out tonight, aren't we?'

'We are, we are – and you're coming too, Laura.'

Laura said something about being too tired, from her place slumped in a green armchair. But Cissie and Winifred were having none of it. It was Cissie's birthday and Winifred felt it was incumbent on all of them to go out.

'You work fewer hours than we do,' Cissie reminded her.

Laura knew that was true, she didn't work nearly as hard as the other two, and she didn't have their social lives either, which took them out night after night with colleagues and boyfriends.

'Alistair said to meet him at the Ace of Clubs, if we were coming late – they're all going for dinner first, but frankly he'd only stand me a meal, not all three of us, so let's just go to the club.' Winifred and Cissie were feverishly energetic about having as much fun as they could on their budget, which was not limited in the way that Florence would have recognised as a limit, but which was still no match for some of Alistair's friends, as Laura understood from Winifred's constant gossip about their clothes, their dinners, their drinking, all unrestricted by the war.

As Laura was pulling on the blue dress with the wide neck that she thought would be suitable, she remembered that awkward night when she had first met Alistair and his friends. She looked at herself in the mirror. Her hair had been shorter then, falling forwards over her ears, but now it was longer and she wore it with a side parting, it was better to brush it back from her face. She picked up her brush and assessed her face, bit by bit. Plucking stray hairs from her eyebrows, finding the darker shade of lipstick: you had to concentrate on the details even if the whole was wrong, as she suspected it still was.

The women went through the streets holding their blackout torches; there was no threat in the darkness when they were all together like this, and they linked arms and chattered. As they walked, Laura felt buoyed up by the female friendship that she hardly deserved. Although she had never felt really intimate with Winifred, she had to recognise her generosity in giving her the independence that she had craved and including her in her own brisk, busy life. In response, she decided that for one evening she would try to be the cousin that she felt Winifred wanted. So she asked with apparent interest who would be at the club, and whether Giles would be there.

'Didn't I tell you? They've moved Giles's outfit out of London – too dangerous here, the risk of having it all blown up.' Laura realised she was still not quite clear about what Giles actually did. Winifred was vague. 'Aeroplanes, radios, you know. And Quentin won't be there tonight either, now he's joined up.' It was hard to square that development with the fleshy man who had held court over dinner. Winifred seemed to know what she was thinking. 'Anyone less likely to be the hero of the hour, I know, but apparently because he was in the Coldstream Guards for a year before university he can float back in now.' Laura asked if Alistair was planning to do the same. 'He can't bear the idea, really – but he isn't quite sure what to do. He'd like to be something really vital at the Ministry of Information, but he says they are just crammed with old Etonians . . . he's feeling awfully left out of everything . . .'

This was the way Winifred and Cissie tended to talk, as though the war were a kind of social gathering in which it was important to find the right clique. Through the big door in a road south of Oxford Street, through the blackout curtains beyond – going through these layers of darkness into light made the expectation rise in Laura's chest. But it was a rather drab nightclub, she was surprised to see, and the floor was tacky under her high-heeled shoes as she walked across it with Winifred and Cissie. It was crowded, and at first she thought it held nobody they knew, but then a waiter moved and there in the corner at a large table was the group: Alistair, Sybil and the man with the light hair whom she had not forgotten. He had already seen them and was rising to his feet in a way that made her wonder if he was leaving, but it was just his immediate politeness.

'Do you know Laura?' Winifred was saying to Edward as they sat down.

'We met,' he said briefly, but under cover of the chatter that accompanied their first order – champagne? Cocktails? Has everyone eaten? – he leant forwards, turning to her so that nobody else could hear his words, and said, 'The struggle on two fronts.'

Laura nodded, her consciousness of her mistake that evening rising through her, so that she said nothing and was glad when the martini was placed in front of her. It was Alistair who spoke to her next, asking her if she was terribly busy, as everyone was these days. When she described her little job in the bookstore, he tried to make it sound refreshing that she was not doing war work. How vital for the evening that he and Winifred and Cissie were people who generously spilled conversation constantly into the air, because otherwise the rather forbidding figures of Edward and Sybil would, Laura thought, have made the table impossibly reserved.

Now Alistair had moved on to a story about how he had joined his local Air Raid Precautions wardens, just to have something to do. 'Now the whole country is turning into an OTC camp – and you know I always was hopeless in OTC – I felt I absolutely had to . . . but the most exciting thing to happen so far was a false alarm when some poor old chap went to bed sozzled and set off a fire in his own bed with a cigarette . . . the flames leapt up just as a motor car backfired on Charing Cross Road, we thought we had a bomb at last . . . well, the relief when we realised . . .'

In return, Laura tried to overcome her awkwardness and present him with an amusing anecdote, but she had just started telling him about the night she thought she was talking to Winifred in the blackout when in fact she was talking to a complete stranger, when Edward took her by surprise by leaning over again. 'Dance?' he said. There were only a few couples on the floor, and it seemed strange of him to ask her, at odds with what she had seen of his character so far. When they started dancing, she was not prepared for the physical resonance of his touch, which left her unable to speak and even took away, briefly, any real awareness of the room around her.

Eventually he broke their silence. 'Things have changed so much since the spring,' he said.

She did not pause before replying. 'Everything seemed much clearer then.'

That was all she said, but the words seemed to satisfy him. They went on dancing for a while in silence, and then Laura began to find the silence was making her self-conscious; she should speak again. She made some vague enquiry about his work, and he gave her to understand there was not much he could say about it. Unlike Alistair, he had no easy conversation to offer her, and they soon fell back into silence. But when he dropped her hand at the end of the dance she felt it like a loss.

She felt Sybil's glance at her as they sat down, and without thinking she put her hand up to her hair, feeling how it had begun to frizz out of its careful wave in the damp atmosphere of the club. Sybil looked as impressive as she'd remembered her, her pale hair standing back from that aquiline face. Her dress was not fashionable, was not something that Laura would ever have picked out in a shop, but its silvery jacquard pattern and high neck gave her an almost queenly look. As Edward sat down, Sybil claimed him as her own, asking him for a cigarette, but Winifred was bolder.

'Do give us a dance, Edward. Alistair says he hurt his foot last week tumbling down some steps in the blackout, though I'm sure it was drink rather than darkness that was his undoing, but anyway now he can't stumble round the dance floor . . .'

Edward was all graciousness, and Cissie was deep in conversation now with Alistair about a mutual acquaintance of theirs who was in the same regiment as Quentin. Yet Laura felt unexpectedly loosed and confident, sprung into the dark air after dancing with Edward, and she turned to Sybil without thinking and asked her – it was the dullest opening in the world – if she had always lived in London.

She was surprised by how enthusiastically Sybil responded. She spoke of the park near to her house, and how her earliest memories included being taken there by her nanny, about how she always used to be sad when summer came and they moved to their house in the country, and how wonderfully lucky she had been that getting married had only meant moving around the corner from her childhood home. 'To think it could all be wiped out,' she said as her hand grasped her drink automatically and raised it to her lips.

As Sybil gulped her martini, Laura realised that she was living in a state of horror at the thought of aerial warfare and the possible destruction of a city that she clearly loved as much as anyone ever loved a place. Laura had never loved anywhere she had lived. Perhaps she had internalised her parents' own dissatisfaction with Stairbridge, the small town where she had grown up; at any rate, whenever she remembered it, a sense of looming claustrophobia attached to its tidy grey streets. And she had not fallen for London and its grim pride in its own ugliness. But it did not matter that she could not empathise with Sybil; something in her made her determined to seem sympathetic, and she went on asking Sybil about her childhood, murmuring appreciation at everything she said. 'Lots of people are moving out of London for the duration of the war,' she said, 'but you haven't—'

'I couldn't,' Sybil said, 'but I have sent some of our things to the country. It's very hard, though, to live without them, you know. There's a painting of Mummy by de László, Daddy gave it to me when she died, and I must say I want to cry whenever I see the gap on the wall.'

Laura felt the vibration of Sybil's sorrow and also her expectation – the expectation of the extremely privileged – that her sorrow could be paraded in public without mockery. But Laura did what was expected of her, telling Sybil how sensitive she was and how awful it must be for her to live without her lovely things. Laura had had a glimpse of the things that evening at the party, after all, and while at the time they had seemed no more meaningful than objects in a museum, the paintings and mirrors and carpets and tables in those rooms, now she realised what gorgeous evidence they must have been of Sybil's taste and wealth and family, and how hard it would be, if you were given that evidence every day, suddenly to lose it.

'You do understand,' said Sybil surprisingly, looking at Laura. Laura, who only understood that suddenly there was a vibrating chord of sympathy between them that she did not want to lose, nodded, and went on asking Sybil about her house.

When Edward and Winifred returned to the table, the conversation became general. They were talking about rationing for a while, and how grim life would be if it were imposed. Winifred, who was working for the Ministry of Food, had another view, the view that Laura had heard many times from Florence and Elsa, that rationing would be helpful for the working classes. 'You cannot imagine how poor their diet is,' she said incongruously in this room dedicated to hedonism. Unsurprisingly Alistair teased her immediately, asking her about the gospel of porridge, but Laura rather admired her courage for talking so inappropriately.

'You live in Highgate, don't you?' Edward's comment seemed not to follow anything, as he looked at Winifred and Laura. 'It's awfully far out – how do you manage in the blackout?' Winifred explained that they were now all living in Cissie's flat, although her mother had made them promise that they would move back if the aerial raids began. And they would go back for Christmas.

Christmas . . . was the year already so far advanced? The last letters that Laura had had from her mother had insisted that she must come home before Christmas, and now it was almost upon them.

'And will Giles be back in Highgate then too?' Edward asked.

'It's been so long! Quentin and Giles – how our circle is depleted,' Alistair said with a little moan. There had been another man in their circle when she had first met them, Laura remembered, an untidy, rude man who had not even spoken to her. But nobody seemed to be missing him as Winifred said that yes, she thought Giles would be back for Christmas.

'But you'll be at Sutton with us, won't you?' Sybil asked Edward.

'You all spend Christmas together?' Laura asked Sybil, trading on the intimacy that had sprung up between them when they had been talking about London, and she was not disappointed. Sybil turned to her and explained a new facet of these relationships, one which reoriented the people around her. Sybil's husband Toby was Edward's brother. And so every Christmas they went to Toby and Edward's childhood home in the country.

Toby . . . Laura had no sense of who he was; she had not remembered any man at Sybil's side at the party. 'He'll be here later,' Sybil said, 'or he said he would be. They are sitting late at the House, and this place isn't really his cup of tea. Too rackety.'

As if to underline her point, a woman in a rather bedraggled boa had just joined the small band and was singing in a voice that seemed flat on the high notes and sharp on the low ones. But under the music Laura was content to sit in silence, drinking the glass of champagne that was now in front of her, recognising that these people were no longer complete strangers to her.

Later in the evening Toby did arrive, and Laura looked at him, trying to pinpoint the similarity to Edward. Although he was fair, it was a sandy, freckly fairness, and rather than Edward's stillness there was something fidgety about him – he was constantly turning from one person to another, patting his face or straightening his tie, moving his glass or his napkin. But the group felt a little more balanced after he arrived, since he was happy enough to dance once or twice with Cissie and to bring Alistair new gossip from Parliament to refresh the conversation. It was late into the night when Sybil asked the waiter if taxis could be found. They were a long time coming, so all of them, except Edward, squashed into one – he would walk, he said, he liked walking in the blackout. The darkness was shockingly deep on that moonless night and he was quickly swallowed up into it.

7

'Go on, read it out – what does she say?'

Christmas Eve had drawn the two girls back to the quiet of Highgate. How strange, Laura thought, as she stepped into the brown hall that afternoon, it feels now like a return to a familiar place. She was in the living room with Winifred, reading through two letters from Mother that Aunt Dee had not yet forwarded.

'They must be pretty bad,' Winifred said, 'you haven't stopped sighing since you started reading.' Laura realised that was true. 'You can't blame her,' said Winifred. 'You could easily go back in January if you were sensible.'

'Ellen's got a new boyfriend,' Laura said.

'Change the subject, I don't mind. Tell me more.'

So Laura started to read out bits of Ellen's part of the letter about a boy she had met at the Bellinghams' dance. The Bellinghams! Before they had come into money the Bellinghams would have been unlikely to ask the Leveretts to anything at all. Ellen must have turned the change of fortune to real advantage if she was able to go to that big house by the river for a birthday celebration. And the boy was a cousin of theirs, from Boston. More to the point, Laura noted Ellen's rare humour coming out in what she said about him, and she wondered how much things had shifted for her sister over the last year.

That afternoon they walked through a freezing fog up to the church that dominated the village. Laura liked the smell of the church, a sourness from the old oak mixed with the sweet scent of mahonia flowers in the heaps of evergreen, but the cold was dense, unbroken by the small gas heaters at the sides, and she huddled into her fur coat, her voice following those around her in the carols she did not know. She thought about what Winifred had said, about whether she should go back home. Certainly it was hard now for her to pretend to herself that it was Florence who kept her here. Since the Soviet–German pact Laura had hardly been to the meetings in King's Cross or Holborn. Even though Florence and Elsa had been so keen to explain the new line to her, she found it opaque. The Party was clearly in disarray, and after her work at the bookshop was finished, she preferred to go back to Cissie's flat and read novels in bed, or sit in cinemas with other Londoners hungry for news and dreams. The long-awaited entry into an independent life seemed to have drifted into another kind of inertia.

Just then Winifred broke in on her thoughts, reminding her to put a coin into the collection. Laura did so obediently and hung back on the way out as Winifred and Aunt Dee greeted old friends and neighbours. Does one ever really take a decision, she was wondering as she pulled on her fur-lined gloves, or do outside forces – a chance infection, a chance encounter – conspire to place Ellen there and me here, one of us in this beleaguered city, the other at the Bellinghams' dance, without either of us actually deciding that this is where we want to be? But some people seem to be able to control their lives, she thought, remembering Winifred's decisiveness when she had planned their move into Cissie's flat. Is it my failing that I cannot do the same?

'Come on.' Winifred was leaving the church now, looking back for her cousin, and Laura stepped forwards into the shivering cold of the street where the clouds over London were already dyed lavender in anticipation of twilight. Christmas ran on well-known grooves for the Highgate house. Mrs Venn was back, so that warm mince pies were waiting for them when they reached the house. As Laura took one, she asked Mrs Venn awkwardly about her son and heard that he was doing well, thank you: a village in Dorset, a blacksmith's family.

'You must miss him.' It was the wrong thing to say, and Mrs Venn hardly responded. The mince pies had a strange dark taste that Laura could not like, and she left hers crumbled on her plate. Giles came back that evening from where he was working in Scotland. He was obviously exhausted; he said that he had hardly slept in days, and stayed in bed most of the time, only getting up for meals. The atmosphere among the family was much as Laura remembered it when she had first arrived – solid and easy, even if subdued, as if all the changes that had taken place beyond these walls had little effect on those within them.

When the telephone rang on the morning of Boxing Day, it was Laura who went into the hall to answer it, thinking that it was sure to be Mother – they hadn't spoken for so long and they should at least exchange Christmas wishes. At first she could not place the measured man's voice asking to speak to Giles, but when she asked who was calling the answer seemed unsurprising.

'Edward Last.'

She didn't lay aside the receiver and call for Giles; instead she remained still and told him it was Laura.

'I was ringing to see if we might all meet for luncheon,' he said.

Without thinking, Laura imitated his tone: bland and unsurprised. 'That would be lovely,' she said. He suggested the following Wednesday, and she accepted, and when he said they could meet at Manzi's, she agreed. She did not tell him that she did not know where the restaurant was or that she thought that Giles would be back in Scotland by then. His laconic manner, exaggerated on the telephone, allowed the space for her to behave in this uncharacteristic way. She thanked him, put the telephone down, and looked up to see Giles on the stairs.

'That was your friend, Edward,' she said.

'Last?'

'He wondered if we could all meet for lunch next Wednesday.'

'Lunch? Did he really? Odd of the old chap. I'll be back in Scotland. Got to get back to these tests, the pressure is on.'

'I'll just go with Winifred then – or I'll call him back and cancel.'

'Funny,' said Giles, looking down at her. 'I could have sworn it was Winifred on the telephone as I came down – you sounded so English.'

'Did I?'

'Yes. You don't usually.'

That made Laura self-conscious, so she went back into the living room where she had left Winifred playing Patience. Yet she did not mention the telephone call to her, nor did she ask Giles if he had Edward's number so that she could telephone to cancel.

The next Wednesday she was at work in the bookshop. Her supervisor was a middle-aged man who seemed to find her an irritant rather than a help when it came to most tasks. When she had asked if her colleague Ann could cover a long lunch break for her as she had to visit the dentist, he had agreed as if her absence would hardly be a loss to him. All morning she acted as if her mouth was bothering her, and at half past twelve she told Ann she was off. She went to the lavatory at the back of the shop and peered into the small mirror. Her pores seemed enlarged, her skin oily, and she took out her powder compact. Just then there was a knock on the door. 'Hold on,' she called. She still needed to urinate, and found when she pulled down her underwear that she had started to menstruate, earlier than expected. It was all right, she had only just begun, and she had a pad in her bag, but in her haste she pinned it crookedly, and all the way walking

109

up Piccadilly in the freezing wind she felt aware of her stained underwear and the pad rubbing against the top of her thigh.

She was just on time at Manzi's, but they showed her to an empty table. As the minutes passed, she began to worry that he was not coming. Should she go without eating, without paying? How gauche would that be? She shook her head at the waiter who came to find out what she wanted to drink, and then to her relief there he was, taller than she remembered, walking through the crowded room.

'Giles is back in Scotland, Winifred is working – it's only me . . .' She tried to sound casually amused, so that he wouldn't be able to laugh at her or be disappointed, but she wasn't sure she had succeeded. She was shaken by the effect of his physical presence and the blatant statement she had made by coming alone to lunch with him. She kept her gaze averted from his as she looked at the menu. 'I didn't have your number, you see, to cancel, so I . . .' Of course he would be too polite to make her feel uncomfortable deliberately. But as he said that he was glad to see her anyway, he seemed nonplussed, or was that just his usual uncommunicative manner? She could not read him, and she was suddenly sure she had done the wrong thing.

She did not like drinking in the middle of the day, and she knew it would make the afternoon at the bookstore harder than ever, but he had ordered a bottle of hock before she had time to say so, and recommended the sardines and the Dover sole to her. 'Yes, of course – that would be lovely,' she said, closing the menu and letting him order. That was the way they did it in London, she already knew; the men always recommended, always ordered, always decided everything.

When two people are very bad at small talk, Laura realised, and they have nothing in common, lunch together is not easy. A silence fell almost immediately. Simply trying to fill it, she asked about his work, and he answered politely. She asked after Sybil and Toby, and as he handled and dropped her questions, she felt more and more nervous. He was less luminous here in the restaurant than he had been at night, his blond apartness less obvious. He was a civil servant in a formal suit who was friends with her cousin; his world was dark to her. Their food came, and provided some distraction. The sardines were good; now she was living with Cissie she seemed to exist on boiled eggs and toast, so the strong, salty, oily flavour burst into her mouth. But they could not go on eating forever in silence. She asked about his Christmas, and he replied politely and asked how hers had been.

'It was my first Christmas away from home.'

'Did you miss it?'

She did not miss her family, but there was a physical memory nagging at her all the time that had become stronger over Christmas. She would not want to be back there, in the sadness and anger of home, but you cannot deny that the place you come from leaves a bodily imprint on you. She was becoming tired of London, she thought, its growing fear and darkness. Sometimes the brightness of the Christmas lights on Main Street recurred to her, or how the snow-covered hills west of Stairbridge reflected the winter sun. You never got that clarity of light and height of sky in London. She had fallen silent, she realised, and she had to say something. 'I miss the place a bit,' she said. 'It was pretty in winter. London is—'

'I know.'

'I mean, I don't miss the town much. But there were hills not far away; we used to go out there at the weekends sometimes when I was a child.' In fact, if she was honest with herself, there had only been a couple of brief vacations and they had been ruined by her parents' fighting. She was not sure why they had occurred to her now.

To her surprise, Edward responded, telling her about his childhood home, which apparently was somewhere in the hills in the west of England. Sutton Court. She remembered Sybil talking about it. Edward was saying that it was the most beautiful place in the world, and then quickly retracting, saying that it was just hills and trees, and pouring himself more wine.

'You should come out to Sutton one Friday. I know nobody is meant to be travelling about these days, but we get there when we can.' She felt that he had just said that to have something to say and she did not respond.

'Do you hear much from Quentin?' she asked.

'Yes. He's still in some godforsaken training camp on the coast. He's the only one of us doing the expected thing so far. Remind me, what are you doing? I know Sybil said you had a job.'

Laura grimaced, and explained her job in the bookstore, and how tedious it was. 'But it does sound self-indulgent to complain about being dull when we don't know what's going to happen next.'

Then Edward said something about how things that seem dull at the time are not always what seem dull later, when you look back, and Laura considered this idea. 'I suppose you never know what you are going to remember.'

'If you look back at your childhood, some things stand out, don't they, and you might wonder – why that, why that meal, or that teddy bear, or that moment of running through the wheat field? It's not always the moments of great happiness or great misery, is it?'

Laura thought again and agreed with him. 'But I don't have very clear memories of a lot of my childhood . . .'

'Neither do I.' There was a willed briskness to Edward's voice and Laura felt she knew that briskness, because it was something that crept into her own voice when she mentioned her home or her childhood. She would have liked to stop speaking and let herself wonder about it, but she knew that she had to go on talking.

'But I do feel that I will remember all of this,' she said. She meant this city, this year of her life that had been all change and newness – but the way it came out the words sounded

112

ambiguous, as if she meant that she would remember him and the lunch, and again she found herself averting her gaze, afraid that she had gone further than she intended.

He took up the conversation again, returning to how the war would be remembered. 'I'm sure one day some crass narrative will take over about the war, and we'll forget the way it really felt. There will be some story that everyone will tell about the way it was.'

Laura agreed with him without really thinking about it. 'Even though at the moment everyone experiences it quite differently,' she said.

'Exactly. Some people see it as a moral crusade . . .'

'And some as a tragic waste.'

'And some as a time to grin and bear it . . .'

'And some as an imperialist escapade.' It was Florence and Elsa she was thinking about, of course.

'You know people like that? Who see it that way?' His tone had crossed into more urgency than she had heard before. He was interested again in her, but she was silent. 'Do you?' he asked. A memory opened in her mind, like a frame from a film. It was Florence stirring her cocoa in a café, her brown eyes wide and her voice high as she told Laura that she should never forget that the Party was under surveillance, that they could all be being watched, at any time.

Immediately the memory nudged at her, she dismissed it. How ridiculous of her to imagine that Edward would be a government informer. But something had tripped in her mind at the thought that she should be careful about what she said, and she was self-conscious again as she nodded and then tried to turn the conversation with another query about his brother.

Edward looked at his watch and told her that he was sorry but he had to get back to the office for a meeting with some of the French chaps. Laura was smiling and nodding, reaching for her purse and standing up once he had paid the bill, and trying not to think about the fact that it had been a short

113

lunch. No doubt he was very busy. She had to reconcile herself to the fact that the lunch had meant nothing much. She was pulling on her coat, taking her hat from the waiter's outstretched hand, when he surprised her just before turning to the door. 'I'll ask Sybil, shall I, to talk to you about coming up to Sutton one Saturday?'

8

Spring had begun to touch the trees in the London streets with a tentative green as Laura walked up to Paddington station. At first there was the urgency about buying a ticket, finding the train, getting a seat, but then the journey slowed. The train came to a stop between stations and she gave up any hope of getting to the destination at the time she had been asked to arrive.

She had to change at a station where the spring wind blew cold down the platform, and the next train she stepped onto was packed with soldiers. She found a compartment of civilians, where a woman generously pulled her small boy onto her lap so that Laura could sit down. Then her knees were in reach of the boy's feet; he kept kicking her, but Laura felt it would be rude to complain. She tried to read her book, but it was a volume of essays that Florence had lent to her months before, and its abstract discussions of working-class history could not hold her attention. All of a sudden, turning her gaze to the window, she saw the landscape open up in a way she had never seen in England before. Here, on the western side of the land, she saw the earth lift, pulling away from the flat dull plains and low bulges that she had seen as England's inescapable physical aspect, pulling up into real hills with strong curved lines and tumbling back into valleys.

When Laura got out of the train her legs felt heavy from sitting so long. There was no one there to meet her, but she was not surprised; she was hours late, and she asked the station master if she could use the telephone to ring the number that Sybil had given her. It was a servant who answered and asked her to wait at the front of the station. Eventually, an old-fashioned Daimler pulled up and the very elderly driver came out to pick up her case.

Laura thanked him in a bright voice, but he said nothing and remained in total silence throughout the drive. Although she never usually smoked alone, Laura fumbled in her purse for an old pack of cigarettes and lit one. The lane they were driving along wound between high hedgerows, so that one couldn't see much from side to side, and curved sharply over and over again, so that one couldn't see far forwards. As they drove, a burst of rain came pattering on the hedgerows. But as she stepped out of the car on to the drive, light broke through the clouds and lit the raindrops to sparkles on the gravel and on the camellias that were blooming in sombre white and crimson by the russet walls of the house.

The elderly driver opened the car door and took Laura's case, and she followed him up to the house. She was cold and stiff after the long journey, as well as thirsty and desperate for a lavatory. But as the door opened and she was ushered on through an oak-panelled hall whose ceiling was two or three storeys high, she realised that she would be immediately on show. From the hall she was led into a huge drawing room, with six large French windows that looked out onto a formal garden and the hills beyond. It was the view that dominated the room; your gaze was pulled on and on to the gauzy verdancy of the garden and the shadowy green heights beyond. It was like a dream or idea of a view. But there was no time to contemplate it, as there was Sybil on the sofa in the room and beside her was Mrs Last, Edward's mother.

As Laura took them in, she noticed immediately, crowding out all other impressions, that the clothes she had thought would be just right for this weekend with Sybil were quite wrong. She had remembered Sybil's queenly look, and so that morning Laura had chosen a rather formal cobalt blue skirt and silk blouse, with patent black shoes. In her mirror in the bedroom the outfit had said confidence, but now she realised she looked like a shop girl next to Edward's sister-in-law and mother. Both Sybil and Mrs Last were wearing tweed skirts and jerseys in muted, heathery colours, and polished brogues. Around Sybil's throat was a necklace of large cabochon amethysts, which meant that she still had that regal look, while Mrs Last wore a double row of perfectly matched pearls. In contrast, Laura felt that she looked both overdone and underdone; there was nothing of value in what she wore, and yet she had obviously tried too hard. Miserably, she sat down when asked, and told Mrs Last what a beautiful house it was and thanked her and Sybil for inviting her.

'You can't see the house the way it was, I'm afraid,' Mrs Last said. 'It's looking so ragged now we don't have the staff any more. And we are just using one wing – I'm afraid you'll be in a tiny room tonight.'

Laura, still unused to the English way of constant apology, muttered something about how she was sure that it was fine. Mrs Last immediately passed her another conversational ball, asking her whether she had seen much of England, and Laura tried to respond with some sprightliness, telling her how fine the hills had looked from the train, but she was afraid that she came over as naïve, and American in the worst sense. They went on talking in this way, but there was a brittleness to their conversation that made Laura feel the oxygen was being sucked out of the air, and Sybil hardly spoke at all. That chord of sympathy she had felt with her in the London club had gone, and she felt that Sybil was already regretting having asked her down for the weekend.

All in all, she was relieved when Mrs Last said that no doubt Laura would like to go to her room. 'We won't dress for dinner,' she said. 'We haven't, since the war started.' It seemed a curious sacrifice to make to the patriotic cause. As they walked, Mrs Last asked Laura about her family. Laura had learned something now she had been in England for more than a year, and she gave very little away. To say her father was an architect, to say they lived in Massachusetts – this could mean so much or so little, and she knew that English people had no way of placing her. 'Your cousin is Giles Frentham?' Mrs Last said at last, and this placed her, she knew, and obviously not in a good way in Mrs Last's eyes, judging by the suspicion in her voice. 'He used to come here sometimes in the long vacation. My son is fond of him. I hear he is doing very well – in air defence, isn't he?'

Left in the room she had been told was tiny, Laura crossed immediately to the big window under which was a deep window seat. The cushions were worn, the chintz all faded to a dim turquoise, but if you sat there you could see the view that had opened from the drawing room, miles and miles of wild slopes and open sky. Turning back to the bedroom, Laura saw there was a generosity to its structure – the high ceiling, the detailed cornices and the large white fireplace. But everything was fading, dust clinging to the little cracks in the hearth tiles and the old paintwork, even if the mahogany wardrobe was polished to a high shine.

Her nightgown was already folded on the pillow, and when she opened the wardrobe she saw the clothes she had brought already hanging up. She regarded them now with despair. What did Mrs Last mean by saying that they would not dress for dinner? Did that mean she had to stay in her inappropriate skirt and blouse? And where was the bathroom?

She opened the door of the bedroom, and there was a young girl on the other side. 'Sorry—' they both said automatically. 'Mrs Last asked me to come and help you,' said the girl, and Laura realised that this must be the maid. She was either absurdly young or tiny for her age, so that her dress looked too big for her. She showed Laura to the bathroom and when

Laura came back, there she was, standing by the fireplace, looking as lost as Laura felt.

Laura asked the girl, Edna, what she should wear that evening and together they looked at her clothes. 'I'd wear that,' the maid said at last, pointing at a rayon jersey dress in deep crimson. 'Do you really think it's all right?' Laura asked, but Edna could not bring herself to say yes. 'I think it's the best one of these,' she said. Young and untried as she was, even Edna could obviously see Laura was not really part of this milieu. Her presence made Laura feel even more ill at ease, and she was glad when the girl went away to run her a bath.

The low spirits persisted as she went back downstairs to join Sybil and Mrs Last. They had been joined by another couple, whose names Laura did not catch in her confusion. 'The boys have just come in, they'll be down soon,' she heard Mrs Last say to the others, and just as she said that the door opened and Laura was caught by the gaze that she now saw when she was falling asleep at night, every night.

Over dinner Laura was separated from Edward, sitting between Toby and the other man, and the conversation of the table was dominated by local gossip. There was a great deal of discussion about what would happen to the house for the duration of the war. Apparently this was part of a conversation that had been going on for months: whether Mrs Last would have to take in evacuees, whether the house would be requisitioned for a hospital or training camp, and what effect this would have on Sutton Court itself. Laura was struck by the tone of the conversation, which disguised bitter complaint under a pretence of being game for anything. It was a tone she had already heard a great deal of in London. 'Of course we are prepared to do anything . . .' Mrs Last kept saying, 'but it does seem a pity if . . .' And everyone kept agreeing with her, telling her that it was an awful shame that Sutton might be spoilt, and how sad it was that the garden was already being ploughed up, and how the evacuees in the village didn't appreciate anything at all that was done for them.

The dinner was served by the elderly man who had driven Laura to the house, and Edna, the very young girl who had helped her in her bedroom. Their presence threw the complaints of the diners into sharper relief, Laura thought – though she was aware that it might only be her consciousness of what Florence would say if she were there that made her think that. Laura knew about the custom of the women leaving the dining table before the men, but after dinner everyone moved back into the drawing room together, and Mrs Last clicked on the wireless, as everyone always did nowadays, evening after evening after evening.

There was little to add to the previous day's news of the capitulation of Finland, and as the light died in the garden and the little maid drew the curtains across the French windows, the wireless was turned off. For a moment Laura saw them as a huddled, scared group, gathered on the faded sofas, intent on one another as the world collapsed outside, but then her vision cleared and she saw the youth and beauty of Sybil and Toby and Edward, the confidence of the older people and the solidity of the room's gracious lines. The double vision that was induced by news of the war often took her like that, bringing on a transitory clouding of her mind.

'You'll play?' A game had been suggested, the kind of thing that Laura was not very familiar with but had played a couple of times with Winifred and Aunt Dee. Everyone had to think of a character to be, real or fictional, and then others would ask them questions that could only be answered with yes or no. Laura was at a great disadvantage in such games, not sharing any of the literature and lore that the others took for granted. But when Alice's cat, Peter Pan, Antigone, Demosthenes and Pitt the Younger had been unmasked, there was only Laura and Edward left in the game. 'He's a he, a real person, dead, foreign, not a king or queen, has written books, not a book that is in this house, books that we are unlikely to have read, books we are certain to have heard of,' said Toby, counting off on his fingers the answers to the questions that had been asked of Edward.

'Are you Karl Marx?' Laura asked, surprising no one as much as herself, and Edward nodded.

'Jolly well done, Laura,' Toby said in a hearty voice, obviously trying to encourage her. 'Now your turn, come on, what do we know about you? A woman, fictional, not in a book, not played by a famous movie star, never seen on stage.'

'We give up,' Sybil said, and Laura felt a kind of rebuke that she had not chosen something more knowable.

'Betty Boop,' she said, and was not surprised to see a look of bemusement cross Mrs Last's face. After that, Mrs Last said she didn't feel like more games and the conversation became stilted, until Sybil stood up, yawning, and said she would go to bed. She was wearing a strangely cut dress in green and yellow, with long sleeves and a wide skirt; not quite an evening dress, but nothing Laura could imagine wearing during the day either. The other couple stood up too, saying something about seeing everyone at church tomorrow, and the good nights were all general. Laura felt the cue too, and stood, but she noticed that Toby and Edward were not leaving the room. Rooted, holding their drinks, it was as though they felt called to an audience with their mother, who was still sitting on one of the sofas, her knees and ankles pressed together, one finger moving up and down her pearl necklace as she said good night to everyone.

This time Laura gained her bedroom with a sense of achievement. She had got through the evening, and there was only one day to go. There was a chill in the bedroom as the fire had been allowed to go out. Laura felt keyed up and a little drunk as she sat there with her coat on over her nightgown, filing her nails, remembering how Edward had looked when he walked into the room, reliving one moment when Toby had laughed at something she had said, replaying the evening as if she was trying to make sure she would not forget anything, when there was a tap on the door.

She opened it. For a moment Edward said nothing, and then he whispered, 'Should I go?' There was an uncertainty in his expression that she could never have imagined. She stood to one side, and he walked in. For a few moments the space between them was unpassable, and then it was passed. He bent his face to hers and there was elation, so great it overpowered her, the ecstasy of knowing that the physical hunger that she thought would never be assuaged was matched by his, that they fitted, that they could make everything right. She could hear half-sobs in the room, but they were rising from his throat as well as hers as they fumbled their way not onto the bed, for some reason, but onto the carpet in front of the cold fireplace. By the time they had made one another come to orgasm – not through intercourse, but sweating and pushing against one another, humping and fumbling – both their faces were wet with tears of relief. It wasn't the graceful embrace that Laura had imagined to herself at night, but under the fumbling was a confident, certain rhythm of joy, a music that sang through the clumsy movements.

Afterwards they lay for a while without speaking, Edward's hand moved down over her back and thighs over and over again, until Laura felt she lost the sense of where she ended and his hand began. Then they undressed fully, and got into the high, narrow bed, and lay holding one another. For a few moments Laura felt she would never sleep, all her nerves seemed so alert, her pulse fast, but then suddenly sleep over-took her, and at some point in the night he got up and left her, so that she woke alone.

As she emerged from sleep, she was aware of every inch of her body and how it was lying in the heavy bed linen. She felt the edge of the pillow pressing into her cheek. She felt the sheets, warm under her legs, and cold where she stretched out her arms. She sat up, and then got out of bed, naked, and walked over to the window. She pulled back the heavy curtain, feeling the raised pattern of the damask under her fingers. Everything she touched touched her back. She felt the smoothness of the floorboards under her bare feet. She saw the slopes of the hills to the sky, running like live things into the morning light.

After dressing she walked with confidence down the oak staircase, aware of each step with its slight depression where generations had walked up and down, aware of the way the banister had been rubbed to its high sheen by innumerable hands. Edward was not there when she entered the breakfast room. It was a dark room, hung with uncleaned oil paintings and papered in grey-toned greens, but even this seemed just right, a kind of harmonic counterpoint to the lightness of the drawing room. She drank her coffee and ate her toast and bacon, feeling rinsed and new for the world. When Edward came in, perhaps no one else would have seen anything different about his uncommunicative demeanour as he poured himself a cup of coffee and started on a plate of toast and bacon, but Laura felt the pause in his breath as he looked at her and felt his gaze rest on her.

Conversation between herself, Sybil and Toby was going on reasonably well as Edward read a newspaper, and then Mrs Last came in, telling them that everyone would be late for church if they didn't hurry up. Laura got up with the others, but Edward remained at the table. 'You don't have to go, you know,' he said to her.

His mother heard him. 'You are such a heathen these days,' she said, but it seemed like something she had said before and Edward did not react. For a moment his mother stood there, as if she would like to say more, but then she went into the hall with the others.

Laura and Sybil were putting on their hats and pulling on their gloves when Edward came out of the dining room. 'I'll go down with you,' he said, addressing himself to Sybil, but Laura felt he was speaking to her.

The walk was long, first along a path bordered by two straight lines of lime trees, where the light was sifted by their still-bare branches, and then down a lane to the village. It was not sunny, but there was a warmth in the misty air. Sybil and Mrs Last strode ahead together, while the boys and Laura went more slowly, and soon there was a distance between them. Laura was still in her over-sensitive mood, and the turn in the lane that revealed the spire of the little church by the green seemed to her like a revelation of a particularly English picturesque, the possibility of cliché ironed out by the poignancy of seeing such peacefulness during these days of war. 'Come on in,' Toby said to Edward. 'It would mean a lot to Mother.'

'Hollander is such a ham. How can you stand it?'

'Would you believe it?' Toby said to Laura. 'He was the most devout of us when he was a boy.'

She smiled.

'Was he? Were you?'

Edward admitted that he had been, and Toby reminisced about how he'd used to harangue the family about correct Christian values, and how he would read the Bible and even correct the vicar over Sunday lunch. 'You discovered Jesus as some kind of socialist – Mother didn't think it very funny. It lasted until you went to university, as I remember. Then you seemed to forget the kingdom of heaven.'

Laura felt Edward's sudden discomfort. He reached out a hand and broke off a thin branch from a bush of white flowers next to them. 'I'll see you at lunch,' he said, turning away. In the church Laura sat in rainbow lozenges of light that fell from the stained-glass window above, and all of a sudden, in the middle of a hymn, she imagined Edward as a little boy in the pew, turning his face to the windows and feeling faith rise in him.

Sunday lunch was another long, tasteless meal, this time

with other neighbours to join them. Afterwards a kind of languor descended on everyone. Edward sat down at the piano and began to play something with only the slightest melody; repetitive chains of notes that rose and fell on disciplined lines, but the music seemed to irritate rather than calm the room. Sybil suggested cards and a game of bridge began. Laura, who did not play, got up and wandered around the room, looking at the photographs in tarnished silver frames that sat on the small tables. One she thought was Edward, that arctic blondness and indifferent expression, but when she lifted it up to look, she realised it was not him but a slighter man, older, without the broad shoulders and with a more delicate cast to his mouth and chin.

'He's terribly like Edward, isn't he?'

It was Toby, standing near to Laura, the game of cards having finished.

'Yes – exactly like, who is—?'

'My father.'

'He was a politician like you, wasn't he?'

'Not at all like me. He was one of the inner circle. Mother—'

And then Mrs Last spoke. 'I don't know why we are all stuffing in here – the sun's shining at last. Sybil, why don't you take our American visitor and show her the gardens?'

Sybil rose and opened the French windows, and she and Laura stepped out onto the wide terrace. It was not particularly warm, but feeling that they should go on, they walked down a path towards the pond. Soon it became too muddy. 'The rose garden was wonderful last year,' Sybil said, but of course they were just stumps right now, frilled with the beginnings of their new leaves. Laura could see how even this part of the garden was already ragged – the grass unkempt, the borders beginning to spurt with spring weeds – and beyond this formal part were now beds of vegetables. The two of them stood for a while by a large stone fountain, dry now and green with lichen, looking up at the hills. All this weekend

Sybil had been absolutely reserved, only polite, and nothing more. Why had she invited Laura if she had not even wanted to talk to her?

'It was sweet of you to invite me to join you this weekend,' Laura said, hoping to break through the reserve.

'Toby remembered how you hadn't been out of London at all. I think the boys felt sorry for you – they believe country life lifts the spirits. These Sundays in the country . . .' It did not sound as if she agreed with the boys' opinion of a weekend at Sutton. 'You mustn't mind if Mrs Last isn't very friendly. She bullied me rather, when I first visited.'

Laura was unnerved by this criticism of Edward's mother. Was it allowed, then, to speak about how cold she was, and how her sons seemed to be unable to relax in her presence? That would go against all Laura's instincts, which were to act as though such an uncomfortable family life was merely normal. And so she said something formal about how it must have been hard for Mrs Last since her husband died.

Sybil said nothing for a few moments. 'Yes, it must have been hard,' she said finally.

'And for the boys,' Laura said.

'Yes, Toby took it hard. It was quite unexpected, quite recent, you know.' She said nothing about Edward. 'Your parents are both alive, aren't they? They must miss you so much.'

'I'm not really sure that they do,' Laura said. For some reason, her words came out in a kind of imitation of Sybil's, and the rather regal judgement that had dominated Sybil's tone when she spoke about Mrs Last crept into Laura's own voice. It surprised her. She had never spoken like that about her parents, however resentful she had felt about them. But she felt it was the right thing to do in that moment.

'I know,' Sybil agreed with her. 'I haven't seen my father since the war began and, frankly, I don't think he cares.' The two women stood there, looking up at the grandeur of the Malvern

125

Hills, and Laura realised that her pale imitation of Sybil had brought them back into sympathy with one another.

'But the boys love it here, don't they?' Laura said, wanting Sybil to go on talking about Edward.

'They do. It's the bond, isn't it? Hard to break.'

Not long after, they all left, squashed into the Daimler to the station. Laura had been told by Winifred that she should tip the servants, but when it came to it she could not meet the eye of the little girl who closed her case or the old man who took it to the car, and she preferred to pretend she did not know about this convention. The train was crowded again and they could not sit together. In the end Sybil and Laura took seats in a carriage with a large family who were prepared to squash up, and Edward and Toby stood in the corridor, smoking and talking. Laura didn't mind sitting apart from him. She felt that she was moving tentatively, but with growing confidence, through a new medium, like a child who has just learnt to swim, buoyed up by the memory of sensual pleasure.

9

It was a few days before she heard from Edward again. Should this have worried her? For a time she could not imagine worrying ever again. At night, on waking, or at odd moments stepping off a bus or wrapping a book for a customer, the wealth of pleasure she had been given suddenly recurred to her and she felt her senses sway and her stomach clench. She relived that night so often that she hardly noticed the hours and days passing. But even so it was a relief when she came back to the flat one evening and saw that Cissie had written Edward's name and a telephone number on the pad that they used for messages. When she rang him they arranged to meet that Sunday, at a public house he knew. She knew it too, as it happened to be in Highgate, near to her aunt's house; she had seen it once on a walk with Winifred.

That it was another fine spring day was an unnecessary boon. The pub was dark, and they sat in an alcove, eating something that Laura hardly noticed. Edward drank beer, and then brandy, and this time Laura enjoyed the feeling of drinking at lunchtime, the shuddery warmth engendered by the glasses of wine that Edward ordered for her. After lunch they walked out onto the Heath, where they sat on a bench looking out over a small hill and artificial lake below them. The crocuses scattered all over the green lawn, and the child suddenly running by with a red kite, his mother calling after him – images danced past Laura's eyes. Greatly daring, she touched the side of her hand to Edward's, and he took her hand, crushing it in his, and lifted it to his lips, inhaling the scent of her skin, closing his eyes. She closed her eyes for a moment too, and when she opened them he was looking at her, still holding her hand.

'Here we are,' she said. Or did he say it? They were both smiling.

'At last,' he said. 'Now I might find out who Laura is, this mystery.'

It was extraordinary to her, that he saw her as a mystery, that he wanted to know about her.

'Come on, it's time.' He turned properly to her, hitching one knee up on the bench and hooking that foot under the other leg, putting his right arm along the bench and touching her shoulder with his hand. It was a gesture both open and controlling. 'Tell me. Here you are, with your decidedly revolutionary political views, but looking like a debutante at a tea party . . .'

She was shocked. He had noticed, had been thinking about everything she had said to him that she thought had gone unnoticed or been misunderstood. She was so used to being the dullest person in the room that this caused a strange shift in her sense of herself. He was still talking.

'There wasn't anyone else at Sybil's party that night that could have told me about the struggle on two fronts – not that you did tell me. You clammed up right away, which said more than anything. What did you feel about the struggle on two fronts, then? Why were things less clear in November? Do you think the war is an imperialist escapade, or aren't you sure?'

Laura felt as though the breath was being squeezed out of her. What was behind this forensic questioning? And then she realised that in fact it was a relief. She didn't have to hide or pretend any more. For the first time, she could tell someone, and so she did. She told him about Florence, about the protest she had seen when she first came to London, the pamphlets she had read, the speeches she had heard. He listened and then asked her how open she had been about what she was doing. 'I didn't tell my aunt and Winifred,' she confessed. 'It seems silly, doesn't it – but I thought they would never understand.'

Edward nodded, as though this made absolute sense to him. 'And you – are you a Party member? Do they know you, does the Party know you?' His pressure on this point seemed strange. Again she remembered Florence, intent on warning her, her high, energetic voice telling her that she might always be under surveillance. So she was under surveillance, was she? This irreproachable civil servant was a government informer, spying on radical elements?

'You tell me first,' she said. She said the words without any particular forethought, but when he reacted so quickly, pulling back from her with such shock in his eyes, she pushed on in a way that was more intuitive than rational. 'Tell me – go on – your secret is safe with me.'

'My secret.'

She had not expected him to react like this, turning away from her and leaning forwards, putting his hands on his knees. She spoke again, thinking from his reaction that her guess must be right, he must be trawling for information. However terrible that truth was, she wanted to clear the air between them. 'You can tell me—'

But she broke off from what she was about to say, as he suddenly stood up. Pulling her hand, he was dragging her down the gravel path and towards the artificial lake, down to where the trees grew thick and there were no walkers, further on, off the path. He was pulling her still, too quickly, between the trees, she was stumbling as she walked, the brambles snagging at her stockings. Then he stopped, and held her by the shoulders. 'To tell you – my God, it would be . . .' And then he did tell her.

Of course she had had no idea. How could she? Nobody could ever have guessed. It was only a misunderstanding that had made him think that she had an inkling of the way he lived. The secret was so much larger than anyone would have imagined. It was almost beyond Laura's comprehension, even when he spelled it out. At first she was unable to judge it. She judged him, however, as he finished telling her. He looked exhausted and stood there lighting a cigarette, smoothing back the blond hair that was always falling across his forehead. As he put the cigarette to his mouth, Laura saw his lips tremble. She reached out her hand, took the cigarette away and kissed his trembling mouth.

As they held one another, Laura heard a blackbird singing from a nearby tree. She felt as though she had lost all her boundaries. The song ran through her, through her mouth and thighs. Edward's hand was hooked inside the top of her stockings, pushing her thighs apart almost too roughly. She straddled as wide as she could in her narrow skirt, rocking back on her heels. She would have fallen if it hadn't been for his other hand, around her back, pressing her chest into his. She grasped his thighs with hers, moving her body up his so that his erection was in the right place, in what she experienced just then as the entirely open, entirely wet centre of her

129

body, even though their bodies were touching through layers of clothes. The blackbird's call, liquid, honeyed, sprang through them before falling into the green spaces of the park. Laura felt the song running through her, she felt Edward's closeness, she groaned, his mouth was so hard on hers that it hurt, and tears came into her eyes.

10

Even in the blackout, dawn made itself known: the birds calling the city to wakefulness, the bluish glow at the edge of the blinds. Laura was already awake, alone in her narrow bed, pictures and words from the previous day tumbling through her head. After the revelation, they had gone on walking around the muddy lake, and although their conversation had stopped and started, at times there had been a rush of surprising clarity. She had begun to understand what he must have been like eight years ago, at the time when he entered this secret life: an undergraduate at university, a young man who seemed to outsiders to be a perfect fit in a world that was moulded for him, yet who felt all the time that everything was out of kilter. 'But I don't have to explain that to you,' he said to her, and this assumption of their mutual understanding startled her.

He had been an open socialist then, he said, having moved away from his youthful Christianity and into a greater understanding of how one might create a better world here on earth rather than waiting for the kingdom of heaven. One evening in a friend's room, he mentioned his desire to go to the Soviet Union after university, and then another undergraduate had followed him out into the night at the end of the discussion and asked him to reconsider, to make a deeper and more secret commitment.

'And so I told everyone that I had lost interest in

communism. My parents were so delighted when I started to talk about the Foreign Office.'

He had told her with a kind of sad pride that nobody had ever suspected him. She considered that. She had seen enough of him with his friends to see that he was entirely accepted in his social circle – more, he seemed to take for granted a sort of deference. She thought about how he spoke, how he moved; the pauses in his conversation, the stillness of his bearing, the way he encouraged revelation from others rather than opening up himself. Now that she knew what lay beneath this aura of controlled authority, she could see how brittle his manner was. But she knew how she had seen him at first: invulnerable, bright with the armour of his social status.

At the same time that she now saw his vulnerability, she also saw his heroism. She had been convinced by Florence that there was an answer to the failures of the world around her, that there was a better future ahead. Yet despite their apparent certainty, Florence and Elsa had not shown her a straightforward path to the promised world; she had seen how their lives were overwhelmed by all those meetings and marches that seemed to achieve so little. But Edward had found a way through all of that impotent activity. Lying there, as the clock ticked on the hours she should be sleeping, it was not doubt or fear that kept Laura awake: it was happy anticipation.

She would see Edward again that evening; they had arranged to meet in a restaurant near to Shaftesbury Avenue. She would not quiz him, she thought, she would not ask any of the obvious questions, about how he got away with passing secrets and how he could bear to spend so much time with people who understood nothing about him. She would ask him nothing, she decided as she lay there, but she would show him . . . The memory of their kiss, and that moment when he mentioned a connection between them which meant he did not have to explain himself, flooded her with pleasure so intense that she turned over and buried her face in the pillow, smiling. She would show him that she understood.

As she got out of bed and pulled off her nightdress, walking over to her closet to find clothes for the day, she found that every action felt imbued with a sense of purpose she had never known before. As she ate toast and drank strong tea with Winifred, who was yawning after going to bed too late the night before, she felt her secret trembling inside her – not wanting to get out, no, but there like an extra dimension to a scene that would otherwise be too flat to be real. And as she opened the door to the street, the very city around her seemed changed, because out in it was somebody who might also be thinking of her.

As she had decided, she didn't quiz him, and so that evening started off with more inconsequential conversation. He asked her about her day and she replied with unaccustomed talkativeness, telling him about a woman who had come into the shop asking for a novel whose title she could not remember, by someone whose name she could not remember, but she said that there was a very nice dog in it. 'Can you believe,' Laura marvelled, 'that she thought we might know what the book was?'

He responded in kind, telling her a story about a man he worked with who had picked up the book Edward was reading, which happened to be *Madame Bovary*, and said, 'Any good?' Laura did not quite understand the humour in this story, but it did not matter, she still appreciated the spirit in which it was told. As they talked, their gazes were constantly drawn to one another, and a small smile kept coming and going on Edward's face.

Because she was so determined not to question him, but to show that she fully accepted him as he was, and was satisfied with whatever he wanted to tell her, Laura only gradually came to understand how Edward's double life was organised. Details came slowly, dropping now and again into their conversation and always after a hesitation, as though he was eyeing a gate that looked closed and only gradually realising that it could swing open. That evening, for instance, he reminisced about his interview with the Foreign Office when he had first applied to them. 'They asked me about my interest in communism . . .'

'How did they know?'

'I hadn't kept it a secret at university, not at the beginning. So obviously they had to ask. I said that I had been interested, but I had come less and less to admire it. I was ready to go on, you know, if I'd been asked, but the odd thing was, I don't think they were even listening to my answer. The chap who interviewed me, he'd been at the same college as my father, and he'd seen my father the night before the interview, in the bar at Pratt's. So it wasn't as though they wondered about me, it wasn't as though . . . I was never outside . . .'

Never outside – was that what he said? Laura hadn't quite heard the end of the sentence in the noise of the restaurant where they were sitting, and was about to ask more, when he asked her something instead, about the last time she had been to a Party meeting.

In fact, strangely enough, he seemed more interested in the details of her world than she allowed herself to be in his. He kept asking her about the Party members she had met, about the meetings, about what they had talked about, what was in the *Worker* that day, what people said about this or that writer or event. Laura sometimes struggled to answer, and often she felt that her anecdotes fell short of his expectations. If she tried to express to him her sense of the impotence of the British communist movement, he seemed not to understand her. She came to realise that he thought she was lucky to be openly part of that world.

One evening they talked about the change of line on the war. They were walking arm in arm back to Cissie's flat after going to see an American film. He listened to her confusion, her account of how the Party members had tried to adjust themselves to the new line, but how uneasy it had all felt, and then he told her that it wasn't Stalin's job to pull the imperialists' chestnuts out of the fire for them. 'It won't be long, though,' he said. 'Really, Britain drove the Russians into Hitler's arms. If we'd only been able to create a united front . . . but when the Soviet Union has built up its strength and can confront fascism and imperialism – it won't be long.'

'I know,' Laura said, warmed by hearing from him the same arguments that she had heard from Florence and realising that he would have heard them from some inner Party source.

They did not talk about world events all that much, however, even in those first few weeks. Politics might be the key in which their love song was placed, but it wasn't the melody itself. That lay in the rhythm of their bodies. They were intensely aware of one another from moment to moment, their blood beating up at any touch – knee to knee as they sat in the cinema, or hand to arm as he steered her out of a restaurant, or during the brief luxury of an embrace as they said goodbye in a blacked-out street. Somehow those fleeting touches were enough, during those first weeks. More than enough, at least for Laura. For her they added up to an unexpected excess of happiness.

In May it was her birthday, and when Edward discovered the date he made a point of asking her to meet him at a more expensive restaurant. He had also mentioned to her, in a tone whose carelessness seemed studied, that his flatmate was away for a few days.

Laura arrived early. Sitting alone in the crowded restaurant took her back to the very first time that they had met for a meal, for that stilted lunch in Manzi's. How changed everything was. She shook out her napkin and ordered herself a martini. She felt so connected to the noise and colour around her that the clatter of cutlery and the burble of other people's conversations seemed to be a rhythmic accompaniment to her own thoughts. She could not think directly of the night ahead of her, but there it was, sharpening every sensation. As Edward entered the restaurant, she saw him greet two men who were sitting near the door. He had not yet seen her, so she could luxuriate in watching him walk through the restaurant, and take pleasure in seeing how women at other tables noticed him too.

It was to be a celebration, and so they ate more extravagantly than usual, although the food was nothing special: tough little lamb cutlets, creamed spinach that had been too heavily salted. At one point, as he poured her wine, she put a finger on the inside of his wrist, where his skin was silk. But it didn't take long before she noticed that something was off, that he was distracted. He was doing an odd thing that she had never seen him do – before he spoke, and sometimes in the middle of sentences, he would move his glass or his fork half an inch to the left or right, as if lining them up. She had never before seen him betray any kind of fidgetiness. She had said something about emotions that last, and suddenly he said, 'If only one could know when things would last.' At first she went on speaking, and then she realised that he had given the words a strange weight, and she stopped and asked what he meant.

It took him a while to explain. The salt cellar was moved to line up with the pepper pot, and the wine glass with the water glass, at every pause. Gradually she began to understand. They had told him that the situation could not continue. She was too openly a communist, visiting Party meetings and spending time with known Party members. Even if her cousin and her aunt had never noticed what she was doing, the taint of her being associated with that world was too obviously a danger for him.

'You mean . . . ?'

'They want me to stop seeing you – it's too dangerous. An ultimatum.'

The shock of it stopped her talking or eating for a while, but then she realised he had not stopped talking. He was saying something about how he couldn't ask her to give up her freedom. He was talking about how it would be too much to tell her that she had to live the way he lived, with everything kept dark from everyone. She tried to cut through what he was saying. 'So it isn't an ultimatum,' she said. 'I just have to break off with Florence.'

'She's your only friend,' he said, shaking his head. He believed that it would cost her too much, not to see Florence again and to stop going to Party meetings. He was saying that she wouldn't, if the situation were reversed, expect him to give up his friends. This was true, but the situation was not equivalent. At that point, as they were struggling to understand one another, the waiter stopped by their table, asking if they would like anything else. There had been Queen of Puddings on the menu, and Laura ordered it although she had no idea what it was. 'I can't walk into your life and destroy it,' Edward said after the waiter left. Again, the wine glass was brought into line with the water glass. She realised she had not made herself clear, and quickly she told him that of course she would give up Florence and the visits to Party meetings.

'But I can't say to you, just give up everything that matters to you. You know the penalty if I'm found out. I can't do that to you.'

Something had shifted. Although he was saying that he couldn't say it to her, he was saying it. He had stopped playing with the cutlery. He was looking at her. The clouds cleared. He was asking her to throw in her lot with him. Nothing else mattered.

'I don't want anything else.'

He went on speaking about why that was impossible, but his tone said otherwise. He told her that the penalties were too harsh, the strictures too difficult, what she would be giving

136

up was too great. 'If you do this – it's pretty odd, the way I have to live. Pretty lonely.'

Pretty odd. Pretty lonely. At the time, she could not see through his English understatement, and she brushed it aside. 'We won't be lonely. We'll have each other.' Just then the Queen of Puddings and the brandies were set down on the table, and so Edward's reaction to her statement was gone in a nod to the waiter. There seemed nothing more to say for the moment. The die had been thrown. She picked up the spoon. 'How nasty,' she said, grimacing. 'It tastes like soap, sweet soap.'

'Let me order you something else.'

'There's no need.' He called back the waiter and ordered her an apple pie instead, and pushed a brandy towards her. As he did so, his foot touched hers under the table. She pulled her chair closer into the table, hoping to press her knee against his, but just then the friends he had greeted on his way into the restaurant were at their table. They were going on to the Ace of Clubs for a drink, they were saying. Nick would be there, back from Washington, and Amy was in town. Edward was polite, and said they might see them later.

When they had gone, he looked back at Laura. 'Do you want to go to the club?'

'No.' Her mind was running on how she must break with Florence. 'I should tell her immediately – I'll think of a reason. Immediately, don't you think?'

'I'm on ice until I either break off with you or you come in.' He pulled his knuckles across his lips, and she realised how hard it was for him to speak clearly about his work after so many years of silence. He told her that they had told him that he might be no further good, having broken the primary and absolute rule of secrecy, and that he had had to spend time trying to convince them she might be trustworthy. 'The first bad judgement I've ever made, that's the way they see it.'

137

She was puzzled by the tension in his face as he said that. It was as though he feared the people he was talking about, and yet he must surely be their treasure, their darling, with his extraordinary fidelity to their cause despite the fact that it worked so entirely against his own self-interest.

After that brandy they had another. She was beginning to get used to the constant drinking, and to ending the evenings dazed with alcohol. Eventually, very late, they left the restaurant. Blackness, warm and dense, surrounded them; wrapped in its cloak they walked up the Strand, through Covent Garden and into Bloomsbury. They walked with the whole sides of their bodies touching, Edward's arm around Laura's waist, her blood flushing up at the touch of his body. Time seemed to slow, they spoke little, finishing each other's sentences, as they walked through the hidden city.

When they entered his flat, they did not turn on any lights, they did not speak to one another. But they reached out for one another with a silent confidence. That night, she began to learn the softness and hardness of his body, and she felt those qualities mirrored what she was learning of the harshness and vulnerability of his character. She felt as though she touched his spirit as well as his body, as though his spirit was made flesh. At one point she pushed him away, holding him by his shoulders. 'It's too risky,' was all she said, and he said, 'I'll make it safe,' getting up and looking in a drawer. She disliked the interruption of the rhythm of their embraces, but his response to her fear was completely reassuring to her.

From listening to Winifred and Cissie and their friends, Laura had found that other women spoke of their first experiences of intercourse with a kind of resigned cynicism, but her reality, the knowledge she gained for herself in the dark room, in the cries of the night, was different. The consummation of their desire seemed to Laura a cataclysmic ending and beginning. It was as if she lost any sense of herself as an individual, and then regained it with redoubled force. After they were

138

exhausted, she lay awake for a long time, listening to his breathing, and for the first time in her life that she could remember she felt lulled by the precious sense that she was no longer alone, that she could be entirely at rest in another's presence. A phrase she half remembered from the reading in that Worcestershire church a few weeks earlier floated through her head. She grasped it and turned it over in her mind. Yes, she fell asleep thinking, this is the peace that passes all understanding.

11

Monday saw Laura back at work. Out of the bubble that had enclosed Edward and herself for the weekend, everything in the bookshop seemed far away and hard to understand. But nobody else seemed to notice anything different about her. At the end of the day she walked over to a left-wing bookstore that she remembered seeing near the British Museum, and looked among the shelves. A few weeks earlier she had heard Florence arguing with someone about some essays by a writer who was trying to convince the Left that the communists were a busted flush. 'He sees communism simply as an instrument of Russian foreign policy,' Florence had said, 'as if this was just about one country, not the international struggle.' The writer's name had become hazy to Laura, and she was too shy to ask the assistant for help, but eventually she found the – thankfully slim – volume she thought would be useful.

There was a café in a side street nearby, and she ordered a cup of tea and some toast, and began to read. She had no faith in her own ability to build an argument with Florence about why she would be breaking all contact with the Party, so here, in this orange-covered book, it was a relief to find an argument laid out for her. The writer believed that communists in Britain were simply being led by the nose by the Soviet government. 'Every communist is in fact liable at any moment to have to alter his most fundamental convictions, or leave the Party,' was how he put it.

Laura put down her teacup. How strange that the writer, who was clearly respected in many circles, was so all at sea; did he not understand that one's own most fundamental conviction could be faith with the Party, with something greater than oneself? It need not be a struggle, but an immersion. She went on reading, but found the essay hard-going, since so much of it assumed familiarity with literature she had not read, and since it was written from a point of view that she found so alienating. Her attention kept flickering from the page to the conversation that was going on at the table next to her, where a woman was describing in detail a recent operation her mother had had.

When she pushed her attention back to the essay, she got stuck on a single sentence. 'We live in a shrinking world,' it ran, 'the democratic vistas have ended in barbed wire.' Laura felt a shudder pass through her when she imagined what it would be like to believe that. To believe that all idealism ended up in the battlefields and concentration camps of totalitarianism. She did not want to read this essay and to understand how somebody could come to such a view of the world. She wanted to stay in the sunlit place where Edward and Florence were, where everything was going to get better and clearer as time went on.

But she made herself re-read some of his sentences over and over again, trying to understand them well enough to use them. Then she finished the tea, which had gone cold, and the toast with its thin coating of margarine. Already, food was turning out to be a constant disappointment in London.

She had told Florence she would try to get over to her flat that evening, after Florence came back from selling the *Worker*. She found both Florence and Elsa there, and Florence started talking to her about the actions on air raid precautions. A first

140

demonstration at Underground stations was planned for that weekend, but Florence was still keen on the idea of protesting in one of the big hotels.

Laura listened for a while in silence, and then spoke. 'It's a good plan,' she said, 'it's so necessary. I can't see it convincing more people to join the Party, though. That would mean persuading them to support Soviet foreign policy, and it's a waste of time trying to convince English people of that now.' Laura dropped her voice a little, and added an almost plaintive tone to her next words. 'And you can see why.'

The last words seemed to resonate in the room. But then Elsa moved the conversation back to the demonstration, talking about what the banners should say. Laura stirred, as if she was feeling physically uncomfortable, and spoke again. 'Sorry,' she said, and then stopped. Florence looked at her. 'Especially when the bombs begin to fall, how can the Party go on with the line that we can't support this war? The working class is never going to buy that – it's like conniving in one's own defeat.'

To Laura's surprise, Elsa looked sympathetic as she turned to her. 'It is hard. We all know that. We've got to try and show how the ruling class is using this war as a tool to enforce more inequality. You know wages are going down in the factories while hours are going up . . .' Laura was impressed by the way that Elsa had engaged so quickly with her apparent shakiness of faith. She was intelligent, no doubt about that. Laura wondered how differently she might have seen her, if she had not been so jealous of Florence's affections. But Florence burst in on Elsa's reasonable response, and there was something unreasonable about her reaction.

'Don't tell me you've gone in for that patriotic mush,' she said, almost spitting out the consonants. 'Next moment you'll be telling us that this is a war to defend democracy, when you know perfectly well by now that it's about defending the British Empire, not defeating fascism.'

'I'm not saying that it isn't! But I'm saying—'

'If you can't see that all this defending democracy stuff is a lot of baloney, given what this country is really fighting to defend, you must have blinkers on. It's all about the empire. There are millions of Indians and Africans that the British can't even see as human. Good God, even Hitler can't make the workers work for a penny an hour, do you know that's what Indian coolies are expected to work for . . .?'

'But Flo, doesn't Laura have a point when she says it's going to be hard to convince the workers—'

'Laura's so worried about the workers, is she? Or is she a bit more worried about how her posh friends see it? Laura, you are like a flannel, just soaking up the slogans.'

Laura was shocked. She had not expected Florence to explode so quickly and it seemed to her that the reaction was fuelled by something other than ideological dissent. Florence must have felt that Laura had failed her. Was the failure her inability to commit to the Party up to that point? Was it her involvement with Winifred and her friends, her glossy clothes and make-up, the nights she spent drinking and dancing rather than coming to Party meetings? Or had Florence recognised the withdrawal of her affections, did she feel the awakening of Laura's energies in another direction?

In the moment, there was no time to pursue those thoughts. Laura went on talking to them both, trying to defend the point of view she had found in that book of essays, that the Communist International was now being seen as all about the interests of one power, rather than the interests of the international working class. The strange thing was that by taking on the words of someone else, she felt swept along by them. She had more confidence arguing a view that was not hers than she had ever had in trying to express her own ideas. Eventually she decided to leave, but as she stood up she found she could not walk away immediately. She walked over to Florence and put a hand on her shoulder.

She could not have expected the roughness with which Florence pulled away, nor the distaste in Florence's face. Funnily, she felt no sympathy with Florence's anger, or any desire to win her back. If she had cared about me, she wouldn't have minded my arguing with the Party line, she found herself thinking as she clattered down the stairs. She knew that emotion made no sense, given that their whole relationship had been founded on Laura's adherence to Florence's politics, and yet she could not help feeling resentful and betrayed. It was anger, not regret, that stayed with her that evening, an anger that was slow to fade.

The next day Laura was surprised by a telephone call early in the morning, before she left for work. It was Edward. 'Can you meet me at the Lyons' on the Strand, at one?'

She didn't have time to ask for a more convenient meeting place before he rang off, and because she was only allowed to take her lunch break from one, she arrived breathless, late and sweating. The roads were so congested it had seemed easier to walk. She wondered whether Edward realised how conspicuous he looked, so tall and formal, in the tea room crowded with shop workers.

She sat down. He only had a coffee in front of him, and he said nothing about her being late. She wanted to touch him – just the sight of his hand reaching for his cup reminded her of how and where his hands had touched her the previous weekend – but he was already speaking in a low voice, about instructions he had been given for her. They were for the next day, Saturday afternoon, two o'clock. 'The tobacco shop, Alfred's, by Clerkenwell Green. Go in and say to the man at the desk, "Do you have Quintero cigars?" He will say no, and you'll say, "Do you think you will be able to get any in?" and then, if the shop is busy, he'll ask you to wait while he finds out, and if it isn't, well, you'll see.' He asked her if she had heard all of that, and she nodded, and he asked her to repeat it back to him. She was word-perfect, because she was so alert to him.

'I can't stay for lunch, I'm afraid, do you want anything?' He was gesturing to a waitress.

Laura asked for a cheese sandwich, feeling winded by the thought that he was going so quickly. 'I'll see you soon,' he said, 'I'll telephone.' It was a cursory meeting, but before he got up, he put his hand across the table and put it over hers, parting her fingers and stroking the skin between them. His touch stayed with her, despite his haste.

When Saturday came, Laura arrived at Clerkenwell a little early and looked in the windows of the jewellery shops in Hatton Garden for a while – rows of diamond rings, winking at absent shoppers. At two o'clock she went into the shop. It was small, with that sweet scent of expensive cigars, but the only customer was an elderly man buying cheap cigarettes. She hung back for a second, so that he could leave before she spoke, but strangely she felt no hesitation about asking the question that Edward had given her. It felt more natural than she thought it would, to speak words that were not her own.

The man behind the counter, a middle-aged man who she thought looked Greek or Italian, showed no surprise at her question. He waited just for a few seconds, looking at the door behind her, before lifting the top of the counter and gesturing her through to the back. Behind him was a small room where boxes of cigars were stacked high on shelves and the scent of tobacco seemed even headier. Laura waited there a long time on a faded green armchair. The novelty of her situation was impossible to grasp, and instead the passivity of the moment bore down on her and she began to wish she had brought a book or newspaper with her.

When the door finally opened again, Laura was surprised that it was a woman who entered. She sat down on the other chair and pulled a pack of cigarettes from her bag, but did not offer Laura one. 'I'm Ada,' she said. 'That's the name you'll know me by.' She went on talking, and though Laura was listening carefully to her words, she was also puzzled by her tone. What was it? Irritation? Belligerence? She was explaining that she needed to find out about Laura, to understand the nature of her commitment. She mentioned Edward, and how Laura had threatened his work. The way she put it, it was as though Laura was all at fault. She was older than Laura, severely dressed in a belted grey coat which she did not take off, her hair bobbed. She would have been good-looking, if it hadn't been for a squint which seemed to set her whole face at an odd angle.

She spoke in a clipped tone, but Laura realised from her voice that she was American, or had spent a great deal of time in America. Laura remained under her interrogation, or so it felt, for some hours. She had to explain exactly what had drawn her to communism, who Florence was, why she had not become a Party member, who her associates in the Party had been and her precise understanding of current Soviet foreign policy. None of her answers seemed to make Ada happy. She would correct Laura from time to time, or make little notes in a book she was holding, in a manner that showed she was not impressed. Once Laura had told her all she could, Ada began to lecture her.

The lecture was all about the nature of secrecy. It was a secrecy, Laura was given to understand, that far surpassed anything Laura could have imagined. It must now encompass every aspect of her life, even in her relationship with Edward. She was told that they should not discuss anything about his work, in case he let slip something that would endanger him if she was questioned. 'The less you know, the better. Everything you know makes him more vulnerable.' Laura began to understand the tension Edward had expressed that night in the Savoy. This woman was clearly deeply disappointed in Edward for breaking the rule of secrecy, and deeply suspicious of Laura. She was being seen as a threat, not an asset. Laura began to feel rather sick and tired, as the hours drew on in that stuffy room and Ada went on lecturing her.

145

At last Ada seemed to be bringing the conversation to a close. She had been chain-smoking through most of their conversation, but finally she ground a cigarette down in the ashtray and did not light another. 'I will report on this meeting. We will find out the response in time. Until we do find out the response, you are not to see Edward.'

Laura said nothing, but nodded.

Ada found her passive response unsatisfactory, and was stirred again to lecture her. 'Do you understand what you have taken on? Do you understand what would happen if Edward's work was discovered?' Edward had also spoken of the penalty, and Laura said she supposed she did know, but Ada felt the need to spell it out. 'Life or death,' she said. Laura did not know how to respond to show that she understood. She simply widened her eyes, saying 'I know,' and suddenly she realised how hopelessly naïve she must seem to this woman, who had passed through God knows what struggles to land up in London handling this precious traitor, and here came this little ignoramus, this stupid girlfriend, threatening everything.

The shock of seeing herself through Ada's eyes made Laura want to stand up and tell her she wasn't like that at all, she was faithful and sure. But she knew it would be no good. She pursed her lips and looked at the carpet, and wished the interrogation would come to an end.

Ada was speaking now about how Laura would know whether the report of the meeting had been received in Moscow and what the response was. She must return to the shop, using the same code words, in a fortnight. If she was told the cigars would be in soon, she must return the following fortnight, and so on, for the next two months. Laura, desperate to go, repeated the instructions back to her, and only then did Ada nod her out of the room. The shop was closed. The Italian man unlocked the door for her without speaking, and she went out into the street whose normality seemed exaggerated after the strangeness of the scene she had just passed through.

The days dragged slowly over the next fortnight. Laura could not quite believe that she and Edward had been forbidden from seeing one another, but she was so keen to prove that she could be trusted that she would not have thought of trying to get in touch with him. Cut off from Florence as well, she spent a lot of time in the flat, bored and restless. She threw away all the political books and pamphlets that Florence had lent her, and went back to reading magazines and the paperback novels that Winifred left around.

As it happened, Laura had to return only once to the tobacco shop. This time she had to wait for a while before it was clear, pretending to look along the rows of pipes and cigar boxes. And when she was ushered through to the back-room, there was somebody already waiting, but it was not Ada. It was a short man with receding dark hair, wearing a worn grey suit, who introduced himself as Stefan.

Perhaps the words he spoke were no more friendly than Ada's had been. But somehow, Laura thought, there was not the same hostility. He went through again the need for extreme secrecy, and asked a couple of other questions about her feelings about the Soviet line on the war, but that was all. She did not mention her sense of confusion, but repeated Edward's phrases, and found as she did so she longed for the certainties she had found in the old communist pamphlets before the war. He told her that she would not now have to come back at any time unless she received a telephone call from a John Adams, in which case she should return the first Saturday after the call, using the same words as before. 'But we should have no need to meet,' he finished shortly. 'That is just a back-up.'

Laura felt dismissed, but relieved by the dismissal. 'And I can see Edward again?'

He laughed. 'Why would I stop you and Edward meeting? I am not some ogre.'

Laura felt puzzled as she realised that Ada might have been overly zealous in keeping them, even temporarily, apart. Walking into the street, she looked for the reassuring red box of a public telephone and went in and dialled Edward's office number, as she knew he worked Saturdays now. That evening they met in a cheap little restaurant in Bloomsbury, and although they didn't discuss anything that either of them had been told by these emissaries from the other world, the knowledge of what Laura had passed through was there. A barrier had been lifted, and they had been allowed through.

And once that had happened, other things began to shift. One evening Edward asked her to go with him to a party the following week to celebrate the publication of Alistair's first book. Quentin, apparently, would be expected too, as he had a few days' leave coming up. 'It's a pity that Giles can't make it,' Edward said, 'but he says that there is no way he can get to London mid-week, his work is so busy now.'

Laura understood that this invitation constituted a kind of presentation of their relationship to his circle, and she felt that she should at least match his frankness, so that evening when she got in, she told Winifred that she would be going to Alistair's party with Edward. Winifred was immediately fascinated.

'You are the secretive one,' she said, with an almost admiring tone. 'What happened to your other boyfriend?'

Laura screwed up her mouth in a dismissive expression, hoping Winifred would not probe further.

'Last – I wouldn't have thought he was your type . . .'

Laura was, as ever, keen to know what others thought of her and pressed Winifred to say more, but Winifred shook her head and seemed uncharacteristically reticent.

On the day of the party, Laura met Edward beforehand in a hotel bar in Bloomsbury, and they walked to the party

148

together. Now, she thought, stepping into the crowded room next to him, for the first time she was part of the group, she was at its heart.

That sensation did not last long. Edward was quickly claimed by his male friends – by Alistair, who was eager to hear what he thought of the book, and by Nick, that untidy-looking man she had not seen since that first party at Sybil's, who started whispering some gossip in Edward's ear and roaring with laughter, in a way she felt was almost calculated to exclude her.

Laura soon found herself moving away from them and around the edges of the room. It wasn't much of a party, really; it was just a crowd of people and a lot of cheap, warm wine in a room at the top of Alistair's publishers' office. The book they were celebrating was a short biography of a nine-teenth-century writer, which Alistair had attacked in a style, Laura understood from Edward, that some critics found shocking and others found refreshing. There were shabby elderly writers and shabby younger writers at the party, and also a number of the confident, loud people – not necessarily more elegant, but if they were shabby it felt like an affecta-tion rather than a necessity – of the sort she remembered from Sybil's dance. Among them Laura saw nobody she knew until, to her relief, she found Winifred sitting in a window seat next to a man who was rolling a cigarette, and went and sat on her other side.

Winifred made room for Laura with alacrity, and started asking her whom she had been speaking to. 'Was Alistair a bit offish with you? I think these men are always funny with each other's girlfriends – it's all a bit Darcy and Bingley.' Laura did not really know what she was talking about, but they both looked across the room to where Alistair and Edward and Nick were standing close to one another. 'Although do you think they really love each other as much as they say they do? The things they sometimes say about each other . . .

149

about Giles, of course, there is no question. I can't believe how much Alistair misses him.'

Thinking back, Laura realised that Edward, too, had spoken more about Giles to her than about any of his other friends. 'Yes, Alistair loves him so much,' Winifred went on, 'sometimes I think he is only with me because I remind him of Giles.'

'This is interesting,' said the man on the other side of Winifred, his heavy accent – was it German? – making his words sound particularly emphatic. 'This transference from brother to sister, I have a case just like this right now. With my patient, I think it may have something to do with the pattern of intimacy laid down early at these boarding schools. These English boys are never allowed the natural Oedipal development, being thrown out of the family so young.'

'I love the way you always have an explanation for everything,' Winifred said to him, and Laura noted her amiable, almost flirtatious tone. It made her feel rather on the outside of this conversation too, and as she looked back into the party she saw Quentin and his girlfriend Nina entering and steering towards Edward, Alistair and Nick. As they did so, Edward looked across the room, and Laura saw, or thought she saw, a summons in his gaze. She stood up.

As she came back to that group of men who were at the centre of the crowd, Laura felt shy. Who was she to think that she could break into this conversation, in which Nick now had his arm draped across Alistair's shoulders, and Quentin was lighting Edward's cigarette? All the energy of the men seemed directed towards one another.

Edward made room for her in the space, stepping to one side so that she could join the ring, although nobody spoke to her. She tried to join in the conversations, greeting Quentin and Nina, asking Quentin how things were going in the forces, and complimenting him on his newly slender physique. She was struck by the joking tone with which Quentin replied, telling some absurd story about his deluded major whose false memories of the Great War were a source of great mirth in the regiment. But before he had finished his story, Nina broke in, asking where on earth the drinks were. Alistair called to a young man in a loud voice, and soon wine was being sloshed into glasses, and Quentin was free to resume. The burble of men's voices continued and Laura was content to sip her drink. But Nina remained sullen, watching Quentin with her cold blue stare.

'Come on,' she said suddenly in an aside to him that everyone could hear, 'the others are at the Café Royal.'

Quentin seemed embarrassed as he turned to her, and she laid a hand on his arm. Laura expected them to leave, but instead he went with her to the side of the room, where they seemed to be having an argument. Laura caught a little of it, when Quentin's placatory tone seemed to break and he said loudly that he only had two days in London. Nina left alone, and Quentin rejoined the group.

'Here you are, my duck,' Nick was saying, putting his arm around Quentin. 'I must tell you I heard something about that major of yours – but this definitely is not for the ladies . . .' He looked at Laura and Winifred, who had now joined them, and Laura stepped backwards, feeling dismissed, but Winifred looked at him and lifted her chin.

'You don't think we'd be shocked, do you?' There was something quick and confident about the way she spoke. Laura was impressed. Nick said something about how she was probably less shockable than Edward, and Laura caught a nasty undertone in his voice. Although Winifred came back with another retort, Laura drifted away again to the window seat where the German man was still sitting. He offered her a cigarette.

'You're a doctor?' she said to him idly, remembering what he had said about a patient. He explained to her that he was a psychoanalyst, and she started talking to him about what that involved, but without really listening to his answers. She had learned from Florence that psychoanalysis was an incorrect interpretation of the world which personalised problems that could only be cured by class revolution. Her sense that there was something decadent about his work was not dispelled as he started to tell her a story about a man he knew who had only come to accept his homosexuality after a dream involving a cricket match which turned into an orgy. Laura thought the story rather shocking, but realised after a while that he seemed to be telling it simply to put her at her ease. The end of the story involved a stupid pun and Laura found herself giggling at it.

Just then, Winifred rejoined them. She was bitter about the way that Alistair and Nick were apparently now talking about going on to a club where women were not allowed. 'I don't know why we bothered to come,' she said. 'Much easier if they just put "women not wanted" on the invitations.'

Laura shook her head and told Winifred that it wasn't really important; that of course the men would want to spend an evening together while Quentin and Nick were in town. That didn't mean that Alistair and Edward didn't really put Winifred and Laura first.

Winifred looked at her sceptically. 'You *are* in the first fine flush,' she said.

Laura could not say what she thought, which was that this kind of social activity didn't really have much to do with their real selves, with their intimate selves, with the Edward she loved. Laura looked over at him, to where the men were roaring with laughter at some story that Quentin had just told. But Winifred was right to some extent – there wasn't much point in staying. The psychoanalyst was inviting Winifred to go on with him to another party, but when they asked Laura to join them, she shook her head.

She went over to Edward and touched his arm. He turned immediately. When she said she would be leaving, he went out with her into the corridor and said he would take her back to Cissie's flat. She demurred. She didn't want to be a Nina, trying to break up the group, but he insisted, and as he walked her down the stairs to the street he suddenly ran his hand up her back and into her hair, pulling her hair a little so that her head lifted. Unusually for those evenings, they found a taxi quickly.

'It'll be empty?' he asked about the flat, and when she nodded, he came in with her. She unlocked the door and led him into her small bedroom, suddenly shy when she realised that she had left a tangle of stockings, underwear and a dress she had tried on and discarded that morning on the floor. She kicked them under the bed. He did not kiss her face or mouth, the way he usually did, but immediately pushed her onto the bed, restraining her arms above her head with one hand and putting the other hand over her mouth. She found the restraint overwhelmingly sensual, and the explosion of her orgasm arrived almost as soon as he entered her.

They lay for a while afterwards, holding one another. Laura told him about the psychoanalyst she had met, and what he had said about boarding schools. Edward seemed to be considering, and then said something about the friendships you make when you are young and how they form you. Laura had never made a close friend at school, but she said she understood, because she could see it, in the moment, through his eyes. 'It's not as though family life is always so benign,' said Edward, and Laura agreed. She loved it when they talked like this: they said so little, but they communicated so easily; there seemed to be no distance between them. Still, she was not surprised when he soon rose from the bed.

'Are you going out with the others?' she asked.

'Do you mind?'

Why should she mind? she thought to herself, sitting up and stretching. She had the best of him.

12

'This is John Adams, can I speak to Laura?'

'Speaking.'

Laura heard the buzz as the receiver clicked into place. It was a Friday morning and the telephone had woken her; she did not work on Fridays and she had been sleeping late. Apprehension filled her as she made herself a cup of coffee. She had never expected such a call to come. In fact, Edward's double life had simply not impinged on her recently. Since the fall of Paris the previous week there had been little time off work for him, and although they managed to see one another a couple of times a week, they were brief meetings. Surely, Laura thought about the call, it must have been a mistake. She was about to telephone Edward and ask him about it, but she remembered Ada's bitter lessons about secrecy. She must show she understood, she thought; maybe this was just a test. She would not even mention this meeting to Edward.

There was no one in the tobacco shop other than the owner. Wartime deprivation had already taken its toll on the shelves, with boxes of cheap American cigarettes rather than fine cigars dominating the shop. Laura felt a new nervousness when she found Stefan waiting for her in the backroom.

He was standing up and shook his head when he saw her. 'I didn't think there would be a need for this,' he said, and without asking her to sit down, he explained the situation. Edward had begun to experience some problem with passing papers to them; the arrangement they had had before had fallen apart, and he was working such long hours that he could not get to different meeting places. They needed someone who could assist in photographing and passing documents. Laura listened to the explanation without, at first, understanding that she was being asked to play a role herself in the work. She was nodding along to Stefan's words, and then, once she had recognised what was being asked of her, it felt as though she had already said yes. Stefan told her she was a good girl and that they would start teaching her the ropes the following day. He gave her a time and place for Sunday and dismissed her, telling her to leave this time by the back way. She had not been aware of this way out: it led through a yard into an alley that stank of a bad drain, and then into the street. Laura walked back to Cissie's flat in a hurry, as if by walking fast she did not have to think of what lay behind or ahead of her.

When Laura got to the basement flat that was their meeting place the following Sunday, she found the key to it as instructed, next to the bins, and let herself in. Stefan arrived only a minute or so later, in a bad mood. He told her that he had followed her there and she had done everything wrong. She listened to his instructions about how she must learn to move around London with more awareness of what was around her, and she felt a weight settle in her stomach as he spoke. She had no idea how she could live up to these expectations.

Then he put a camera into her hands; the smallest camera she had ever seen, a slender rectangle only a little longer than her palm. She had never really used a camera before, and he spent the next hour instructing her how to use the little Minox: how to position papers to catch every letter written on them, how to ensure that there was enough light for everything to be seen. He had papers with him that she had to photograph herself, and when the lesson was over he flipped the film out of the camera and said that when it was processed he would tell her how she had done. Laura was sitting at the table, a headache beginning to grind in her forehead. All this time he had not even offered her a glass of water. 'You can go now,' he said. 'Same time, same place, next week.'

The rules that Laura learned over those months she never forgot. Was it Stefan's intensity that made them so memorable?

Or was it just that once you begin to believe that someone might always be watching you, that you might at any point walk into danger, it awakens a paranoia that is latent in everyone? Laura learned how to take unlikely routes through the city, how to choose streets with only one sidewalk, to find shops with more than one entrance, to hang back until the last second when boarding a bus or a train, to use a dead-letter drop, to remember emergency signals from the coded telephone call to the chalk circle next to the Underground sign. She had no natural talent for this behaviour, but slowly she began to change from someone who drifted through streets and shops and restaurants with little visual awareness of her surroundings, intent on her own mood, to someone who found herself looking at entrances and exits, noticing men whose faces were obscured and women who looked at her too sharply.

The worst day of all the weeks of teaching was when Stefan drove her in his own little grey car deep into the Bedfordshire countryside. They parked up on the side of a road and then walked up a track into a wood. 'Private: No Entry' it said, but Stefan showed her a place where the wire fence was cut and told her the owner was expecting them on his land that day, so they would not be interrupted. They walked further and further into the beech wood. In other circumstances one would have noticed the beauty: the layers of overlaid green above them and the ground made soft by a carpet of years and years of leaf-fall. Finally they stopped, and Stefan came to the point.

He took a pistol from an inside pocket and told Laura it was time she learnt to protect herself. If she had ever thought she might say no, and put a stop to his strange games, this might have been the moment, but it all seemed so unreal: he in his homburg, she in the yellow summer dress that she had chosen because she was hoping to meet Edward later; the two of them standing there as if they were meeting for a picnic. But there was the dissonant element in the picture: the gun, with the shifting sunlight glancing off it. He showed her how the safety catch was lifted, how the trigger was pulled, handed it to her and asked her to aim for a certain tree.

It was cold, heavier than it looked, and the report was louder than she expected. After she had fired it, she stood with her hands by her side. If she had ever disappointed him, this was the time. Over and over again she tried to hit the target, but failed every time. With each failure the awkwardness grew, and she realised it looked as if she were being deliberately clumsy. Finally he took the pistol away from her and put it back in his pocket. He lit a cigarette and offered her one. They stood there, smoking, listening to the alarm calls of the birds throughout the wood. 'I hope you never have to shoot your way out of trouble,' he said.

Was she wrong, or was there a note of humour in his voice? She looked at him. Up to now she had been nervous and formal with him, but she tried a small smile. 'Stefan,' she said, 'I'm never going to be a heroine.' She meant a heroine in the kind of film where girls aim pistols and make quick getaways.

He gave her a little bow. 'To the Soviet Union, all who risk their lives for revolution are heroes.' It was a rhetorical answer, and yet it seemed to put them both at ease. They were both nothing, he seemed to imply, and yet they were both everything, in a bigger picture. They walked back to the car more companionably. 'I have to drop you at the St Pancras station,' Stefan said. He often spoke like that – I have to, you must, it is necessary that – without any explanation.

'Don't let me forget the film,' Laura said, taking it out of her bag as the car started up.

'You have some more? They say your photographs are good, very clear. Make sure you don't cut off the left margin, sometimes you angle a bit to the right.'

Laura considered that. She had not expected this praise, but she had already found, almost to her own surprise, that she liked using the little camera; of all the jobs and instructions she had been given, it was the only one that made sense to her. After Stefan had dropped her off at St Pancras, she walked down to Tottenham Court Road to a camera shop she had seen. She had decided she wanted to buy a proper camera, for herself. The tiny Minox was fine for the work she had to do, but it was no good for ordinary photography, and she fancied that it would be useful cover for her – if anyone found the Minox on her – if she could present herself as a real amateur photographer. She spent some time talking to the man in the shop. He was patronising towards her, but she didn't mind, and in the end she spent a lot more than she could really afford on a Leica. He told her it was a beautiful machine, and she could believe it, as she put it back in its glossy leather case and handed over the money for it.

After that, as the dusk began to fall, she walked over to Edward's apartment. His flatmate had recently moved out, and Edward had made no move to find someone else to share with. He was already there when she arrived, and passed her a packet of papers. As he fixed drinks for them, she pulled down the blackout blinds, moved the 100-watt lamp she had bought previously into position, and started to photograph them, one by one – sometimes taking more than one picture of a document if she wasn't sure that she was getting everything in, and being careful to leave more of a margin on the left.

As soon as she had finished and started to put the papers back in the packet, she felt Edward's hands around her waist. With a sense of luxuriant surrender, she turned to him.

Afterwards, as she was washing and dressing, he was standing there going through his post. 'Look, a postcard from Giles.' He was smiling. 'Says they've moved his outfit – he can't say where, but he says it's not far from my childhood home. Tell you what, I'm owed a few days off, we should go down to Sutton, and I'll get him to come down too. I think Toby and Sybil will be there as well, as the House will be on recess. But there's masses of room.' It felt like a reward he was offering her, an escape from the drudgery and secrecy of London.

13

This time they left London together for Worcestershire, settling down in the train carriage beside one another, Laura holding a copy of *Vogue* and Edward a book of French poetry. At one moment he leant over her to pull up the window. She felt so flooded by the scent of his skin that it was all she could do not to press her lips to his throat above his shirt collar, but the presence of two elderly women in the carriage prevented that. Once they were in the back seat of the Daimler, they succumbed to a brief, open-mouthed kiss, but Laura quickly pulled away, conscious of Mrs Last's servant in front, the back of his head in a grey cap and his gloved hands on the wheel.

The house had still not been requisitioned in any way by the military, and as the car pulled to a stop in front of it, Laura saw it with a shock of recognition, as if its restrained beauty had entered deeply into her after that one previous visit. It seemed only enhanced by the growing wildness of the garden, the ivy breaking over its walls, the gravel blurred with blown leaves. Edward's mother was not waiting for them in the drawing room, but Sybil, who had already been up there for a few days, was there. She had obviously been playing Patience, and shuffled the cards together when they walked in, yawning.

'Your mother is busy with her war work,' she said to Edward. She told them that she had hardly seen Mrs Last the last few days as she had taken some kind of job with the evacuees and was out of the house a lot. 'And Toby is busy with his writing . . .' There was something almost dismissive in the way Sybil talked about the work of others. 'I asked for a cold luncheon – do you mind?'

They walked through to that dim, high-ceilinged dining room, where even without Mrs Last their behaviour became rather formal. The sunlight did not penetrate the room, but after they had eaten they went to get their bathing costumes and the warmth of the day came back with a shock as soon as they stepped onto the bright terrace. Sybil walked beside Laura through what had been the formal garden; the box hedges were ragged now but the elegant gestures of their lines were still apparent, holding the blown borders in a hopeful frame. Beyond a final hedge the ground suddenly dipped and gave way to a meadow with cows grazing at the further edge, which in turn gave way, under willows and long grasses, to the brown, slow-moving water of a river. Sybil threw a couple of blankets onto the grass and the three of them lay there, Sybil and Laura talking and Edward reading, the sun dappling through the willow leaves, spots shimmering in their eyes and then flicking away. They had been there for some hours when someone hallooed from the top of the meadow.

'Giles! Thought you wouldn't be here until tomorrow.' Edward put down his book and sat up.

'There was nothing doing at work today, the aeroplane we were meant to be running the new tests with got smashed up over the Channel last night. Pretty poor show.' Giles sat down, unbuttoning his shirt. 'Old Bales didn't know where you'd got to, but I thought you'd be down here.' He pulled off his undershirt and started unlacing his shoes. 'I feel like I could sleep for a week and never look at a cathode ray again. You can't imagine the way we have to work out there – in a bloody field, really. Hardly any time to develop the new stuff either, they're trying to get us to fit as many planes as we can with what we've got. Sybil, you look like Titania in this sunshine.'

Laura couldn't help noticing that other than a nod towards her, Giles didn't greet her. She knew that Edward must have told him that she would be there, but he was behaving as though she was no more interesting to him than the manservant, Bales. Edward told him that they didn't know what he was talking about, since he was always so secretive about what he was doing, but he said it in an affectionate way, looking at Giles with pleasure.

'And even if I explained you would be too stupid to understand. It's not Pindar, my dear Edward, it's what our American friends call radar. I must swim – is the water freezing?'

'Absolutely. I'll go in with you.'

The water was not really deep enough, but both men managed to swim a bit. Laura found it odd seeing her cousin here, so comfortable in Edward's territory. She remembered how Mrs Last had spoken of how Giles used to come here in the school vacations. She imagined them as boys, slipping down from the big house to their spot by the river, tasting the freedom from the grown-ups. It was as if even now, as adults, they felt the return of childish freedoms as they entered the river. Sybil splashed into the water too. She was built on a larger, firmer scale than Laura, her white body in its blue costume statuesque as she sat on a boulder, shaking back her hair. Laura looked at her tall, deep-breasted figure admiringly.

Afterwards they all lay again on the grass, lighting cigarettes to drive away the midges that were now rising from the water. Edward's gaze rested as often on Giles as it did on Laura.

'You're getting quite a paunch there. Food good in – where did you say you were?'

Giles groaned. 'Malvern – it's not the food, it's the lack of exercise. I'm just sitting on a bench all day, tabulating the bloody results. Sometimes I get into one of the aircraft and do the same in the air. You're right, I'm turning into a pudding. I'll be as fat as Quentin soon. Though I hear he has slimmed down – all that square-bashing.'

Laura told him he looked fine. 'Let me take a photograph,' she said. 'A record of the perfect day,' Giles said in a voice that seemed to be mocking her with its light, girlish tone. Laura had brought her camera with her, and she picked it up and set the shutter speed low for the light that was now falling more obliquely over the meadow. Even though she had only used the Leica a few times, she had beginner's luck that day. The photographs stayed with her through all the roaming years. From time to time, in Washington, in Patsfield, in Geneva, she would come across them: there was Sybil, her upright posture, her blonde hair almost white; there were the boys lounging beside her on the grass, the willow tree a blurred frame in the background. Edward's looks did not transfer as well as Laura had expected onto celluloid, but there he was, pale hair falling across his forehead, showing off the legacy that school sports had bequeathed him in his broad shoulders and muscular arms. The shutter fell, their glances froze.

That night Toby and Mrs Last were there for supper, and the table seemed to fall naturally into two halves: at one end Laura, Edward and Giles; at the other Toby, his mother and Sybil. Giles and Toby were easy talkers, and their burbling conversation needed little stimulus. It was about food, and then it was about Churchill's character, and then it was about the weather, and then it was about Toby's chances of promotion: topics ranged from the large to the small, but always continued with ease. Mrs Last joined in too, handing down her judgements, but the other women and Edward said little.

Laura was quite content to concentrate on what she was eating. She liked the solid, English food: boiled gammon, peas and potatoes in buttter, followed by berry crumble and thick cream. Out here, there was no sign of the privations that affected wartime London, and Mrs Last was pleased to discuss at length with Toby how well the home farm was doing that summer. Once the dinner was finished and they went through to the drawing room, Laura made an effort to join the conversation, but at one point she said something about how bright

162

the stars were tonight – the curtains were open and they could see the studded sky over the hills – and Giles said, again in that breathy tone, that they made him feel so small. She realised she was being mocked again, although she wasn't sure why, and after that she lapsed into silence.

When the evening finally broke up, she felt tiredness washing over her as she opened the door to the guest bedroom, but she stayed awake, anticipation skidding through her body, until she heard Edward opening the door and all the desire that had been building since the warm train journey, since the golden hours by the river, since the long dinner, could finally find its release.

The next day, the others went down to the tennis court, and Laura, who had never learned to play, sat and watched them, an abandoned magazine beside her. Giles and Toby went on talking between strokes, sometimes arguing about politics, which they seemed to see solely in terms of clashes of ego, and sometimes discussing their friends in that way that was becoming familiar to Laura, in which harsh judgements were masked by humour. At one moment Giles asked Edward if Quentin was still as wrapped up with Nina as ever.

'Yes – it is rather a bore.'

'She is rather a bore, you mean.'

'I suppose she thinks with those looks she can behave rather badly.'

Laura remembered the first time she had seen Nina, coming into Sybil's party with Amy. She started to speak about that moment, thinking she would tell the story of how she had only been invited to Sybil's party as a replacement for Nina and how small that had made her feel. But as soon as she started to talk, she realised that she didn't have the confidence to go on and expose her own vulnerability to Giles and Sybil. So she turned the story around quickly, stuttering a bit as she did so, and simply said how gorgeous Nina and Amy had looked, and how she remembered seeing Amy disembarking

163

from the *Normandie* a few months earlier, surrounded by photographers. 'I suppose Amy is quite – well known?'

'That kind of fame . . .' Sybil's tone showed what she thought of it. 'Lately, she's been lucky – I mean, one can't call it luck, it's the war – but the papers haven't been free to take her on. Not so much interest in gossip now. And Anderson, her new husband – he'd be absolute bait to them in peacetime, but now of course he's joined up so there isn't much they can say.'

Sybil returned to the subject of Amy that afternoon, when the five of them – Mrs Last being absent again – were eating tea at a table set out on the terrace. She was talking about how Amy had gone up to Scotland as her new husband was in a training camp in the Highlands and wondering how on earth she was coping there. Giles agreed with her that it was absurd to think of Amy in Edinburgh.

'The scattering – I hate it,' Sybil said. 'You in Malvern, Quentin God knows where now. It's so lucky that Toby and Edward have to stay in London.'

'Yes, we must keep the clan together as long as we can,' Toby said rather lugubriously, drinking his tea.

Laura spread cream and jam on her scones as she listened to them. She wanted to believe that she was happy, here in the sunlight with Edward and the people he was closest to. But she was finding Sybil and Toby and Giles more rather than less forbidding as she got to know them. They had been a group for so long, so homogenous and so inward-looking, that every sentence they spoke was loaded with assumptions that they had never thought to question. How could Edward bear to live within this tight circle every day? Laura wondered, looking at them as they talked and ate and nodded and judged.

Giles had just started saying that one of the dour Scottish men he was working with had got into a terrible argument with their boss about his refusal to do any work at all on a Sunday. 'Old Penrose's riposte was that he should see work against the invasion as a kind of prayer. I could see that wasn't going to cut the mustard in convincing the deluded chap. It's funny how there is never any point arguing about really heartfelt beliefs, is there – you can't be rational, and if you try to beat them at their own game, like Penrose did, you just end up sounding mad yourself.'

In response, Toby began to tease Edward again about his adolescent devotion to Christianity. Giles broke in with interest, and for the first time that weekend the conversation drifted onto ideas. Giles was remembering how Edward had been a passionate Christian when they had first met at school. 'There is a Christ – not the Christ that we're served up in school services or this war, that one has to love, that's what you used to say.'

'Not the Christ of the church, no,' Edward said, putting down his teacup.

'How can there be a Christ not of the church?' Toby said, his voice quickening with irritation.

'You were always trying to get me to read Tolstoy on that,' Giles continued, talking to Edward. 'He's dead set against what the church made out of Christ's actual teaching, isn't he? Thinks it's a joke that it's used to justify the state and that the church colludes in that.'

'And why are we listening to a Russian nihilist's view of our religion?' Toby said in that tense voice again.

'For goodness' sake,' said Giles to Toby, 'you don't have to sound quite such an MP.'

Toby clearly wanted to shut down the conversation, but now Edward and Giles were talking further about Tolstoy and whether he would have stuck to his views if he were alive now.

'What, if he'd seen the storming of the Winter Palace? Or Dunkirk? You think he would have seen how pure force is sometimes the only answer?'

'Unless you want to sleepwalk towards the wreckage of our civilisation.'

'But whether he would see it as a civilisation worth saving . . .' said Edward, and there was energy in his words.

Laura was startled when she heard Mrs Last's voice and realised that she had come onto the terrace without them noticing. 'Are you enjoying the strawberries? Rather fine this year, I think.'

'Very fine – enjoying them hugely, Mother, if only Edward and Giles wouldn't depress us with talk of the wreckage of civilisation,' said Toby.

'Surely we don't have to talk about France today?'

'It wasn't the news, Mother. You know Edward, the usual vision of a universe falling into hell if we don't change our ways.'

'Can I pour you some tea?' Sybil said. 'Actually the pot is rather cold, I'll just go and catch Edna and have some more hot brought out.'

'Yes, why not? Looks like we could do with some more scones too, I'm sure they baked enough to keep us going.'

'We've tucked in already, but let me see if there are some more for you.'

The conversation, which had momentarily taken that turn into passion and politics, seemed to have returned safely to its old groove, and as Sybil poured Mrs Last some fresh tea Toby started to opine about whether they could stop inviting their neighbours to dinner; apparently they had done something quite unforgivable with their boundary fence.

'I might just go and have a last bathe,' said Edward.

He stood up and left the terrace. Laura waited for a moment, as the conversation eddied on, and then murmuring something vague she got up too. She walked down, through the box hedges, over the ha-ha and into the meadow. For a moment she thought he wasn't there, and then she saw him, flung down on his back in the grass, his arms over his eyes. When she touched his hand, he uncovered his face and sat up. Laura sat next to him as he lit a cigarette.

'I used to love this field so much,' he said. 'When things used to go wrong for me at school, whenever I felt miserable, I used to go down, in my mind, into this meadow – you know, the bees, the smells, the feel and the sound of it, the noise of the river.'

'It is the most beautiful place.' Did Laura really love it, or did she love the little boy who had come longingly to the light on the river, through the meadow studded with speed-well and buttercups?

'Yes, but I thought it was paradise. It was only later I realised. It was horrible, really, to realise that everything I thought was good was rotten.'

'It's still a beautiful place.'

'But you know,' he took her hand, 'you can't – you know you can't – rely on this kind of beauty. Not when everything it relies on . . .' It was as if he could not trust himself to go on, and he fell silent. Finally he muttered, 'It's all rotten.'

Laura felt she knew what had caused his sudden sense of despair. She had felt it too, the rift between the passion that was within him and the cold gossip of the others. 'Did you mean what you said, about how force will carry the day?' she asked, wanting to relive the conversation in order to understand what he thought lay ahead, but his body stiffened as she asked the question. Rather than answer, he picked up her hand and put it over his mouth. His lips moved over her palm. He inhaled her skin. There was something yearning in the gesture. Laura ran her fingers through his hair. His beauty was, to her, the gathering up of the afternoon, his hair a distillation of the golden sunlight, the warmth of his skin a giving back of its heat. She wanted to give herself up to him, to be taken up into his physical strength, into his sunlit warmth. As they kissed, she felt him relax. 'We should go back,' she said. He drew back from their kiss, and smiled. 'We could stay here.' By saying it, he had freed them from the group. They sat for a moment longer, holding one another, but there was a lightness now in their mood, and after a minute they were happy to get up and to walk back to the house.

Sutton Court was sinking back into the late afternoon light. Was its beauty rotten? She contemplated it through the eyes of Edward, the eyes of Florence, its stones built on the wealth of a cruel empire, the garden laid out by the hands of the oppressed. Its cool, ordered beauty rose up nonetheless, its perfection so studied as to have become entirely nonchalant. The others were still sitting out on the terrace with his mother.

'Cocktail?' Toby asked as they approached. Giles was sitting back in his chair, an unreadable expression on his face.

'Dinner won't be long,' demurred Mrs Last. She was looking at them as they stood there, but Laura did not take her hand out of Edward's, and then his mother turned and walked into the house.

14

'Post for you – goodness, you look well. Your hair needs cutting, though.'

Winifred was sitting in the kitchen when Laura got into the flat on Monday evening. It had felt strange to leave Edward at Paddington station; being in his presence for four days had reoriented her to such an extent that she felt unbalanced now without him. She was glad that Winifred was there, smoking and drinking tea and listening to the radio and reading a magazine – Winifred never seemed to be able to do just one thing – or else, she thought, she would have felt rather maudlin. As it was, she was able to take a cigarette from Winifred's packet and rip open the letters from home without having to think too much. But the letter she opened caught her attention.

'Trouble at home?' Winifred said.

'It's from Ellen, she's wondering about whether to marry this – Tom.'

Winifred was immediately interested, and started to fire off questions about him. Laura had to admit she didn't know much; neither she nor Ellen had been great correspondents these eighteen months. But one thing she did remember, from Mother's previous letter, was that Mother approved. She remembered thinking how lucky she was that she did not have to think about what her parents thought of Edward – or, so much worse, what he would think of them. When she told Winifred that Polly thought it was a good match, Winifred stubbed out her cigarette with a look of distaste.

'So long as she doesn't marry to please Aunt Polly. You should hear Mummy on the subject of Alistair. She's so delighted with him, I can't face telling her that our affair is breaking up.'

Laura had not known that things were going wrong with Winifred and Alistair. She sat down and touched the side of the teapot to see if it was still hot as she began to commiserate with her. Winifred reached for a clean cup, brushing off Laura's sympathy. 'It isn't killing me. I'm so busy at work anyway. Promoted – not bad less than a year in.'

Laura congratulated her, but maybe she looked unconvinced. 'No, really,' Winifred said, 'I'm not weeping over him.' She explained that she didn't really think that Alistair cared for her, and then said she wondered whether those men cared for anyone, and whether it was something about their early lives that prevented them from ever caring. Laura caught an echo in what she was saying of the words spoken by the man they had met at Alistair's party.

'That psychologist or therapist – what was he? – wasn't that what he said?'

'Yes, Lvov – I was talking to him about it. He's very interesting on the effect of boarding schools. But you know all

169

about it. Last is just the same, isn't he? Does he ever talk about what he is really feeling?'

Laura said she didn't feel he held back so much, but then changed the subject. She didn't want to expose her feelings about Edward to Winifred; she knew that deep down Winifred was unimpressed by what she saw as Laura's naïvety when she talked about him. Winifred was not to know, thought Laura, that their understanding was so beyond anything her cousin had experienced with Alistair. What was the point of trying to explain? It was much easier to turn back to Ellen's letter and to read bits out to Winifred and speculate about what Tom was like.

The next day Laura only worked half a day, so in the afternoon she went to have her hair cut and then walked over to Bloomsbury. She had her own key to Edward's flat now; he had given it to her on their way back to London, and she had told him she would be there just before he was due back from work. There was a precious intimacy about the act of putting her key into his front door, and when she was inside she automatically went over to the sideboard and poured herself a small gin and tonic, realising only after she had done so that it was what he would have done for her, that she was imitating his actions even though he wasn't there.

Holding the drink, she went into his bedroom and pulled up the blinds. His apartment always seemed quite spartan. The landlady cleaned it, but Laura felt that even if she hadn't he would have kept it like this: tidy and functional. Some shirts, just back from the laundry, sat folded on top of a rosewood chest of drawers. They smelt of starch and soap. There were no photographs on the mantelpiece, just a couple of old invitations and address cards pushed behind a Lalique lamp; on the desk were a few papers and a new book, a translation of Virgil's *Georgics* by an English poet.

Without thinking, Laura opened one of the drawers, noting the letters folded back into envelopes, personal letters and

170

letters from his bank stacked together. There were a few small notebooks, and she took one out. Its cover was soft thin leather that yielded under her fingers. At first the pages were uninteresting: mainly notes of people's telephone numbers, details of train times and totting up of small accounts. Across a couple of pages, however, a poem was written, with many crossings out and then a neat copy on the next page. 'My house', he had written across the top in another pen.

> A windowed room, a spacious lawn
> A view from hill to hill
> This is the breadth that gave me breath
> The space that let me grow.
>
> The slope to the sky was once alive
> The curlew called with hope.
> But now I see the view is framed
> I feel the walls are close.
>
> Where is the air to catch a breath?
> Why is the world locked out?
> The footfalls pass from room to room.
> No house, but prison this.

Even Laura could see that it was not much of a poem, but it drew her back again to Edward's anger that afternoon at the weekend when his family had broken through his conversation with Giles with silly chatter about tea and scones. Again she remembered how he had seemed to find peace with her; and again she felt a sweet confidence as she considered how they understood one another without the need for explanation. She replaced the notebook with the others, with no sense of guilt, and turned back to the room.

The wardrobe door was half open and she went to close it. Before she did so she stood looking inside, revelling in the memory of his presence that his clothes held: the dark suits he wore every day in town, tweed jackets for the weekend, pale flannels for the summer, and two tuxedos – she put her face to the sleeve of one, was it the one he had been wearing when they first met? As she did so, a tie slipped from where it had been hanging inside the door, and she bent down to pick it up. She saw something – was it another tie? – a flash of something pale, under one of his shoes. She moved the shoe. It was a slip, pink, crumpled as if it had been pushed suddenly into the closet. Laura herself had never worn such a thing – it was cheap, untrimmed. She found herself holding it, and then she dropped it and walked out of the bedroom.

Her gin and tonic was still sitting there on the coffee table. She drank it and found herself pulling at her own fingers, twisting them. That, she realised, is what they mean by wringing your hands. Had she assumed he'd been a virgin too? No, of course not, not if she had stopped to think, but she had not stopped to think, and how long had the slip been there, and how many, and when, and . . . Laura had been living in the present for months. It had seemed to be a comfortable place, but suddenly the past and the future had opened up on either side of her and she realised that the present was a narrow spit of land, and she felt dizzy.

She thought of leaving. She reached for her purse and stood up, but as she went towards the door, it opened and there he was. For all these weeks, it had been such a revelation to her that this man's attention was on her; she had experienced it as a complete loss of boundaries. Now, as he came in, she felt their separation again, and a distance that she had not felt since their first kiss seemed to arise between them. He moved towards her, but she moved back, into the living room. They exchanged some stilted sentences; she didn't know how to bring up what she had seen, but then as he poured himself a drink and sat down on the sofa, pulling at his tie to loosen

172

it, she was overcome with desire and sorrow. She put her head in her hands.

He did not ask her what the matter was. 'Cheer up,' he said and turned her face to his. She let him kiss her for a few seconds, the desire rising up in her as ever, and then she suddenly jerked away from him.

'I was talking to some chaps at the office last week,' he said, 'and it would be possible to get you home on a convoy now that things are getting so hot.' He thought she was scared by the start of the air war. He thought she was missing home. Or did he just want her to move on?

'Do you want me to go?'

'Do I want you to go?' He almost laughed, and told her it was the last thing he wanted.

'Is it? Is it really?' She could not dissemble any more, and so she told him what she had seen. It would have been hard for her if he had been dismissive, but he immediately seemed to recognise her anguish and to want to reassure her. He spoke quickly and confidently; it had been some time ago, before the first evening she had come here, yes, definitely – and who had it been? Well, hadn't she known? He thought she had known. Ada.

With a rush, Laura's world was rearranged. She remembered Ada's hostility that day in the back of the cigar shop as she had questioned her.

'Do you still see her?'

They never talked about meetings that they had with Ada or Stefan; the need for secrecy was being drilled into Laura week by week. 'Everything you don't know makes you safer,' Stefan would tell her over and over again in his flat East European accent. 'Everything you know is a danger to yourself and those you care about.' The direct question was a challenge to that new habit of secrecy, and Edward paused.

'No,' he said finally. 'I don't. It's someone else now. I don't know what's happened to her.'

He seemed lost in thought for a moment, and then when Laura picked up his drink and drained it, he spoke again, telling her that there was no need for her to be jealous. 'She meant a lot to me at one time. I suppose, like Florence for you. All the questions I had, she seemed to have the answers. I think I relied on her. When she was photographing . . .'

Laura's fingers slipped on the glass. So Ada had been the one who had photographed his papers before Laura showed up, and then Ada had been moved on – or maybe she had asked to be moved – and Stefan had had to find some other solution. There were so many questions Laura wanted to ask – about how long they had been together, and why on earth the slip was here when she knew that it would threaten all the protocols of his secret world for Edward to have brought Ada to his own flat.

But as knowledge flashed through her, she saw how Edward was looking out over her shoulder towards a past she could not share. A rift had opened between them. It was a rift that she wanted to close, and it seemed that Edward felt the same. They reached for one another gently at first, and then as the passion took over they made love with a curious, almost angry abandon, Laura's nails scoring down his back as he pushed inside her.

Maybe Laura's uncertainty would have stayed with her, but later that evening when they were lying naked in bed, Edward said something she did not expect. He was smoking, the window was open, and the noises of London were magnified to Laura in the aftermath of love-making; she could hear the rush of buses down Gower Street, a swing band on the radio from a room below, a rattling clang as someone pulled down the shutter on a shop. They should get married, Edward said. He thought they should get married soon. If he wanted to bring her back into the present, she was ready to be there with him. She luxuriated in the moment. Above the sounds of the streets she could hear the soft screaming of the swifts as they chased each other in the still-peaceful London skies. She ran a finger down the line of Edward's throat, where the sandpapery shaved neck gave way to the silk of his collarbone. Yes, she said, breathing in the scent of his skin and relishing the fact that doubt had disappeared.

15

Laura stood on the steps of the registry office, her husband beside her.

'Stop!' Winifred said. They stopped and Laura smiled into the sun. Across the road a woman pushing a pram looked at her with a weary face. A few scraps of confetti were thrown.

Laura had lent Winifred the Leica to take a photograph for Mother, but she had had to talk her through how to use it, and in the end none of the pictures came out well. All in all, it was lucky for Laura that a wedding day had never been at the centre of her dreams. Because if it had, the rushed ceremony, the paucity of guests and the rigid demeanour of Edward's mother, who even refused a glass of champagne at the dull lunch in the Savoy, would have disappointed her. There was Alistair, of course, and Toby and Sybil, but Nick had gone to Washington and neither Giles nor Quentin had been able to get leave. Winifred had organised the day, and had tried her best to give it a festive air, but Laura could not help picking up the low mood of the others.

Laura had thought Aunt Dee would have been most pleased of anyone. Everything about Edward – his family, his position, his Englishness – should have delighted her. But strangely, when Laura went over to tell her, the week after Edward had proposed, Dee seemed puzzled and anxious. She kept saying that she wished Polly were here to meet Edward, and that maybe they had better wait. It was Winifred, who had gone with her, who told her how happy Laura was and how delighted Polly would be. Laura was grateful to Winifred for stepping in, even if she knew that her cousin was not entirely convinced herself. And it was Winifred who persuaded everyone that as it was wartime, a small wedding at a registry office in London, followed by lunch at the Savoy, would be the right thing rather than carting everyone off to a church in Highgate or, worse, Sutton.

But in Laura's eyes the lack of celebration was not as important as it seemed to be for Winifred and Sybil, who looked rather glum as they embraced her at the end of the lunch. To Laura, this union had been sanctified long before. For her, their walk up the aisle had taken place through the blacked-out city in May; their honeymoon had been enjoyed in the sunshine of Sutton Court. The absolute nature of their union could not, to her, be enhanced by a public ceremony, let alone this rather ordinary day in which she was irritated by the adenoidal voice of the registrar and the way the humid weather made her hair curl out of its set. When the women asked to see the little ring that Edward had bought her, when Mrs Last presented her with an old velvet case which turned out to contain a double-strand pearl necklace and matching earrings, and particularly when Toby stood up at the end of the lunch to speak rotund phrases about how glad he was that his brother had found happiness, she felt that their conventional actions and reactions really had nothing to do with her connection to Edward.

At the end of the long afternoon, Alistair, who was unbelievably drunk on wedding champagne, came back to Edward's apartment with them, unable to find his keys to his own, and fell asleep on the sofa in the living room. Laura found it an almost unbearable intrusion, but there was nothing she could say; it was still Edward's flat and she felt it would be unwelcome if she questioned the ways of the group. She walked into the bedroom and asked Edward to unzip her dress. It wasn't white; Winifred had told her that for a registry office

176

wedding she didn't need to wear a real wedding dress; it was pale grey. It fell off her arms, and she looked at herself in the mirror in her white slip, Edward behind her. Now she looked like a bride, alone with him.

Maybe it was because Alistair was in the living room that they felt constrained as they made love that night. Edward put one hand over Laura's mouth, to tell her without words not to cry out. She was never aware in the moment that she did cry out when they made love, but sometimes afterwards her moans replayed in her head, to her own embarrassment. But tonight she remained just outside herself enough to control her voice, even as her body shuddered.

The next day Laura woke late, the aftermath of the champagne throbbing in her head. Neither of the men was awake, and she went and made coffee in her housecoat and took it back to bed with her. Someone was practising the piano across the square; she had heard them before on these summer days when the sash windows were pushed up. They had still not got the hang of those scales, but the waltz was going better now, and it dripped smoothly into the Sunday morning air.

Perhaps it was the contrast with the beginning of the bombardment that meant Laura remembered the sounds of that summer in the city so clearly; the whistling screams of the swifts in the evenings, the broken melodies of the piano in the mornings – how poignant they seemed in retrospect.

The first night of the raids, Edward was at the Foreign Office, working late. Ivy, the landlady of the house, called up the stairs to Laura when the siren rang out and asked her to come with her to the public shelter in the nearby square. Laura wished that Edward had been with her – for sure, he would be safer in one of the Whitehall shelters, but she missed his certainty about the right thing to do. She went with Ivy, holding a pillow, a torch and a paperback book, but the thin-walled shelter seemed more fragile than the house she had left. It was not just the doom in the sky that made her so restless; she was desperate for the lavatory, but could not contemplate using the chemical toilet, which was hardly screened from the rest of the room by a cotton curtain.

That evening she told Edward she thought they should just brave out the raids in their flat, but he refused to contemplate it. And her irrational sense of invulnerability was challenged when they emerged from the shelter a few days later to see the end of the street sheared off, water spurting from broken mains and turning the rubble into a swamp. She and Edward stood looking at it, feeling a new recognition of what might be in store for them running through their bodies.

'Why don't you go to Sutton too?' he said to her. Sybil had telephoned them the previous evening to say that she was going there now the bombing had started – not to the house, since it had finally been requisitioned as a nursing home, but to the lodge, with Mrs Last.

Laura turned to Edward, almost laughing. 'You know I couldn't,' she said.

As they walked back to the flat in that grey dawn, Edward went on talking. 'Toby suggested I should go and live with him in Chester Square – otherwise they will give it up, you know. Another chap from the Home Office has moved in, but still, it's ridiculous to keep anywhere so big going now.'

Laura knew that Toby had created a shelter in the deep basement kitchen of the big house. When they went to see it later that day, she found it claustrophobic, despite its size. Toby had had the ceiling reinforced with railway sleepers and the windows were all thickly covered with sticky tape; while he had also included a Morrison shelter, like a kind of table under which they could all sleep on mattresses when the raids started. 'As safe as St Peter's, I should think,' Toby said, referring to the church nearby where many of his neighbours went at night.

She did not want to move into this house. Walking through it with Toby and Edward felt intrusive; it was all wrong being in Sybil's house without Sybil. True, it had changed so much since the first time she had entered it. With that tape over the windows and its railings gone, even the face it presented to the outside world was a downcast one, and inside it was almost empty, most of the rooms closed and shrouded in dust sheets, dark patches on the walls and light patches on the floors where the pictures and rugs were missing. Still, she felt out of place in its cold, grand spaces. But it would be graceless of her to tell Edward that she did not want to live there, especially as it would be so much easier for him to be nearer to Whitehall. So they took possession of one of the bedrooms that overlooked the square and, for the fourth time since she had arrived in England, Laura unpacked her trunk and laid her clothes into different patterns in different drawers.

The first few times that Laura came back into the house in the afternoons, opening the front door with her own key and walking into the hall whose parquet floor, bare of rugs, now showed scuffs from the many heels that walked up and down it, she could not help remembering the fear and expectation she had felt the first time she had entered it, and she averted her glance from the reflection in the hall mirror almost nervously. Sybil wrote occasional letters to Laura about local affairs in Sutton, and whenever Laura received them she felt a surge of guilt, as if Sybil were observing her and noting how poorly Laura was looking after her home.

Laura had not realised that Toby would assume that she, Laura, would take responsibility for running the house once she moved in. There was only one general maid now in the house, unlike the large staff they had had before the war, although another woman came in daily to do the heavy work, the scrubbing and the washing. The live-in maid, Ann, spent her days working slowly from top to bottom of the three floors they were using, and Laura came to realise, hearing her brush and pan on the stairs before breakfast and the plates clattering in the kitchen after supper, that her hours were excessive and that the work was beyond her ability and that of the daily. But rather than trying to give her any direction, or take on other staff, Laura instead allowed old standards to be left behind. Dust collected in the unused rooms, and the formal meals gave way to one course, left on the table by Ann for them to help themselves.

If the very absence of Sybil – the fear of what she might think if she could see Laura's failures – made her uneasy, so did the presence of Toby. Like the rest of the group, he was apparently loquacious, even humorous, but it was always a humour that seemed to exclude, dedicated to highlighting anything that marked out somebody's difference or failure. So, although he seemed to laugh at the scratch dinners that appeared, beneath his comments about the eternal mutton hash, Laura knew he was scornful of her failure to run the household more effectively. And although there was the constant appearance of politeness between the brothers, she was aware that in Toby's presence, Edward's defences were always up, and that the constraint of living in this way seemed to make it harder for Edward to slip into intimacy with her, even when they were alone.

What's more, on the nights of bombardment, even the solitude of their bedroom was out of bounds. Instead, they had to seek the unquiet haven of the basement shelter, where it was not only Toby and Ann who shared the space with them. Between them, Toby and Edward seemed to know dozens of people who had not left London, or who had to visit London, but had been bombed out of their homes or whose houses had been shut up and let out for the war. Many nights, before the sirens sounded, there was someone extra drinking whisky in the ground-floor living room and, after the alarms went off, bedding down on a spare mattress in the basement.

Even Winifred came, one or two nights when she was working late at the Ministry of Food, while for a time Alistair was quite a regular visitor. He had joined a searchlight battery in west London, but most of his energy was still taken up by writing for various periodicals and a novel that didn't seem to be going very well. Once Laura read one of his articles in a weekly magazine, in which he had described the work of the air wardens over a few nights, and was surprised by his ability to turn the horrors of the blighted city into a narrative that ran like a surreally comic film. In the spring, Giles started coming down to London for meetings at the Air Ministry, and he too tended to stay in Chester Square on those nights.

One evening around nine o'clock, Laura had gone upstairs, about to change for bed before the sirens' expected call.

'Giles is here.' It was Edward, calling up the stairs, and on the last word the familiar wail began. Laura came down in her pyjamas and bathrobe and greeted Giles – unembarrassed, since they had seen one another *en déshabillé* pretty frequently on these broken nights.

'Nothing coming over yet,' said Edward. 'Shall we have a drink?'

'I think I'll go down,' said Laura. It wasn't so much that she was tired, but conversations with Giles never seemed to go well for her. Giles made as if to do the same, but Edward was reluctant.

'It's further east, still – it usually is,' he said. 'Come on, have a whisky before we turn in.'

Laura went down into the basement. Edward had left the door to the living room ajar – it opened into the ground-floor hall, so that his and Giles's voices travelled quite clearly down the basement stairs. She could hear them as if they had been in the kitchen with her. At first their conversation drifted. They were talking about Aldous Huxley's new novel, which Giles liked and Edward thought was tosh, and about the levelling effect that the war seemed to be having on accents in London, which Edward thought was rather a good thing and Giles thought a pity. Laura realised again as she heard

181

them talk that it was a while since she and Edward had had a serious conversation of any kind. She thought of getting up and closing the door, but there was an odd pleasure in lying there, hearing them talk when they thought nobody was listening.

'I'll be back again in two weeks, if that's all right,' Giles was saying. 'We're getting everything ready . . .' He paused, and then, oddly, told Edward not to talk about what he was saying to Alistair. 'If he writes about it or mentions it in the wrong place there will be hell to pay.'

'Is that fair to Alistair? Is he untrustworthy?'

'It's still all about himself, and how he wants to be in the know. Don't you remember when he blabbed to Rogers Minor about us smoking by the Lower Pond? Just because he wanted to show off. But that's how it all got back to the Head.'

Laura could hear Edward's half-laugh, as he told Giles that it was absurd to hold that fifteen-year-old schoolboy contretemps against Alistair now.

'I don't know that he's grown up as much as all that. Whereas you – you are a changed character, aren't you? I used to think you were on a mission to change the world. Well, maybe you're right – maybe we all have to turn our idealism into pragmatism. I never thought I'd be working all hours trying to find someone to manufacture these new magnetrons. Things should move faster than this in wartime. You know what it's like working with bureaucrats. But the Foreign Office's still keeping you happy?'

Footsteps, as Edward presumably crossed to the sideboard to refill their drinks. 'Laura keeps me happy.'

'Well, that must be love . . . an American girl with nothing in her head except movie plots and fashion tips . . . sorry, Edward, I know she's my cousin.'

'Come on, Giles, that was beneath you.'

'I've said I'm sorry.' A pause. 'Forget it, can't you?'

'I'll try.'

'Anyway, I'll be back in a fortnight.'

'Anything in particular?'

'It's pretty exciting.' Giles's tone was conciliatory now. He began to tell Edward about his work, explaining that he was going to America to join the mission that was taking the latest research findings 'right to the top. Even this magnetron. If the Americans can throw their research energy into this new stuff we've got going, we could start driving ahead. I'm not going alone, of course, but it's pretty good – I'm putting together the package, even if old Penrose will take over a lot of the talking once we're there.'

'Good God, is it safe to cross?'

Giles said that if they got attacked, they would dump the black box at sea. Laura, who was lying with her eyes shut, saw a sudden image, like a scene in a movie, of a boat plunging on a foam-patterned ocean, Giles heaving a great box overboard, a hero of science. Was that how he saw himself? Giles was still talking about how that was one of the big fears, Germany getting at their new work through captured equipment. 'Every time we lose a plane, we wonder if they are going to have the wits to work it out. But we have to go – if there's even half a chance it will help. It's the dream, cracking the night-fighting – the new stuff gives us a hope of being able to do that. But I don't think we can do it alone.'

Edward then said something rather muffled, about whether the Americans would give anything in return. Giles's clearer voice resumed, saying that they could only hope, that they had to try to break the stalemate or the war could go on for years. 'Doing some more research with us won't put them in danger. Even those cowardly sods should be up to that. It's sickening isn't it, them and the Russians, sitting it out while we get the brunt.'

Laura turned in her bed. She was used to the scorn that everyone in London expressed about America. 'Cowardly sods' was one of the milder phrases they used. She knew that it should mean nothing to her; Toby had once told her, meaning to be kind, that she could consider herself English now she was married, while Edward had once commented that it was good their secret commitment to an international cause meant they had left the pettiness of nationalism behind. Yet the criticism of America still seemed to have a personal thrust, and made her quail a little before she gathered herself to reject it. There was a longer pause, and then Edward said he might turn in. There seemed to be no bombs falling, however, and Giles asked him if he fancied a game of chess first. Quiet fell, punctuated only by their comments on the moves.

The next morning, everyone woke before dawn with the all-clear, bleary after a short night's sleep. Laura was planning to go back to bed for a while, but once they were in their room, Edward suddenly said that he had some papers he had forgotten about and wondered if she could photograph them immediately, as they had to be back in their place that day. Laura agreed without thinking. She knew that her work was necessary now; Edward was working such long hours that he could never have managed to cross this chaotic city to meet Stefan frequently enough to deliver papers. So she used the thin dawn light to photograph as Edward fell back to sleep for one more hour. Click, click: she heard Toby come into the house after his night with the Home Guard, and she put down the camera as he came up the stairs so that he wouldn't hear her and wonder why someone was taking pictures at dawn.

Usually when Laura met Stefan the focus was simply on handing over the films. They had evolved a process that had become almost nonchalant: both holding a copy of *The Times*, they would exchange newspapers by leaving them apparently casually on a café table or a park bench between them; the films were taped inside her newspaper, and there was no need, very often, for them to speak at all. But that day the meeting place had been fixed in a square near to City Road. It was

184

entirely empty at that morning hour, and they were unseen, so for once Stefan didn't get up from the bench once the newspapers had been laid between them. He said he had been asked to pass on thanks for her hard work. Was she happy?

Laura did not answer at once. She had no problems doing the work, but the first few months of aerial bombardment had affected her in a more visceral way than she had expected. Sometimes in the middle of the night one felt that there was no end in sight, that the pounding and the fear would go on forever, and then when morning came it was only the breath between one night and another. She remembered the great certainties of the pamphlets she had read before the war, their airy summoning of war and victory, but it all felt so different now, in the muddle and mess of a city under attack, in a conflict in which the Soviet Union was not even involved. But she did not feel she could speak of her fear and uncertainty to Stefan, so in an effort to lay those thoughts aside she remembered what Giles had said the previous night, and she started telling Stefan about how perhaps the war might enter a new phase soon, how a friend of Edward's was taking new research over to the States, in the hope that together the Americans and British could crack the night-fighting.

Laura caught the importance of what she had just said at the same time that Stefan did, and she was not surprised when Stefan began to grill her on everything she knew about Giles and his work. She had little enough to pass on, but when she mentioned the improved magnetron that Giles said was their precious new development, she saw how Stefan's hands gripped *The Times* that he had picked up. He spoke to her for a while about what might be possible, what was needed. 'If Edward . . .' he said, but she responded quickly. No, it was not Edward who should be asked to do this to his friend. She was the one who had brought the secret to Stefan, she would see what was possible. As soon as she had spoken, she felt unsure that this was right, but then it was too late to go back,

185

Stefan was already getting up and walking away down the grey London street.

It was a dark winter morning a couple of weeks later that Edward mentioned as he was shaving that Giles would be coming over that evening, passing through London on his journey to America.

'Shall we meet him at a restaurant?' Laura asked, standing at the bathroom door and brushing her hair, trying to ignore the apprehension in her stomach at his words. 'Or will he eat at the Ministry?'

'I'm sure they'll feed him. If not, we can go over to the restaurant by the station after he gets here.' Was Edward avoiding her gaze? No, he was always like that now in the mornings, a little tired and anxious. He rinsed his face and went back into the bedroom to dress, saying nothing more. Laura got dressed more slowly once he had left. Even though the conversation with Stefan had been beating in her head for the last fortnight, she still had no idea how she was to fulfil her allotted task, and all day at the bookshop the evening loomed in front of her.

For once Edward was home at a normal time, and the three of them were drinking in the living room when the doorbell rang. The cab driver brought in Giles's suitcase, while Giles laid down a large black box with an almost tender gesture, and then took off his overcoat.

'Have you eaten?'

'They fed us after a fashion at the Ministry, but I could do with something more. Do you have a sandwich?'

'I'll go and ask Ann,' Laura said, going downstairs. When she came back up, the black box was still in the hall. She ran her hand over it. It was large, heavy, locked. As she heard the rise and fall of voices in the living room, she quickly slid a hand into one pocket and then another of Giles's overcoat, standing so that if someone came out of the living room they

186

would see only her back. Her fingers touched some scrumpled paper in one pocket, a box of matches in another, but no keys. But she already knew that would be the case. Of course the key would be in the breast pocket of his jacket – where else would you keep something so precious? Footsteps behind her made her turn, but it was only Toby, who showed no surprise at seeing her in the hall apparently rehanging the coats.

She followed him back into the living room, and Edward poured her a whisky and soda. Toby had a Scottish friend who was able to keep the brothers supplied with the whisky they loved, and which Laura was becoming used to. Giles was talking about whether there was likely to be a raid that evening.

'God, I hope not,' said Toby. 'If I don't get some sleep soon I'll be good for nothing. It's not the bombs that make that impossible so much as the guns in the park.'

'Are you a light sleeper?' Laura said to Giles. She gave her voice the bland tone that he had mocked in the past. He replied with the characteristic garrulousness that she found so irritating.

'I'd say I was. But in fact once I'm asleep I'm all right. It's more that I find it hard to fall asleep. My friend Grey – his work's all in neurology – came up with an interesting finding. Most people, when they close their eyes, their brain waves immediately slow into a more regular pattern – alpha waves, they are called. For most people that's automatic: you close your eyes, your brain waves calm down, you open your eyes, they go back to being spiky and jumpy again. But a significant minority of people, if you ask them to close their eyes, their brain waves don't change. They remain just as spiky and jumpy, they are just as engaged as with their eyes open. And I'm one of that small minority—'

'Is that such a breakthrough?' Edward broke in, asking whether it wasn't just a physical observation of something one already knew by experience, that sometimes it was hard to switch off. Giles began to argue immediately, telling Edward that it showed that people aren't as in control of their minds as they think they are.

'But does it show that? It doesn't show that you couldn't change it if circumstances were different – we're not just machines, made to work one way only . . .'

'Come on, if it's in the patterns of your brain waves, then that's it, you can't just change those.'

Edward and Giles went on arguing about whether such experiments proved that one didn't really have free choice. They seemed to believe that they could change each other's minds if they argued passionately, that Giles could convince Edward that his brain's patterns were already laid down for him by biology; that Edward could convince Giles that people could be changed by force of will, while Laura remained silent, smoking and looking into the fire. For once, the hated sirens and the descent into the basement came as a kind of relief.

For a long while they lay there, Toby snoring, Giles reading by the light of a small torch, until the raid began and they started to hear distant thumps and explosions and the answering clatter of the guns. As always, Laura felt excessively aware of the fragility of the walls and the ceiling. After an hour or so she crept out of the kitchen. She hoped that the others would assume she was simply on her way to the lavatory, but instead, step by soft step, she made her way upstairs. On the second floor, she shone her torch into the guestroom. Giles's clothes from the day were folded over a chair – like Edward, he had the boarding schoolboy's spartan neatness in his blood. She ran her hands over the pockets of his jacket, but there was nothing there apart from a folded piece of paper. Then she saw on the desk a wallet next to a small heap of change, a couple of paperclips, an envelope, and some keys. Clearly, he had emptied his pockets before taking off his jacket. There was a set of keys on a plain brass keyring, and one steel key lying separately. With her handkerchief over her fingers to avoid prints she scooped it up and put it into her pyjama pocket, where it lay heavy against her thigh.

She did not know whether this was the right key, but now she had taken the first step, she went on without considering the alternative. She went back downstairs and stepped into the hall. Yes, the key turned easily enough, and she lifted the lid of the box. If someone came up from the basement now, it was all over, but ever since she had spoken to Stefan about the magnetron she had seemed to be walking down a road with no way to step off. Luckily no one seemed to be stirring. What she saw inside the box made her heart sink. There were stacks of papers in folders, and a long wooden box. She grabbed her handbag from the hall table, and put three folders of papers into it. Immediately, she put the lid down and relocked it, and went upstairs again. She shut the door to her and Edward's bedroom and pushed a chair against it. Checking the blackout blinds were firmly fastened, she turned on the top light and moved a side lamp onto the table too. Hoping that was enough light, she rested the camera on a makeshift tripod of a stack of books, and one by one she laid out each diagram, each set of equations, and clicked the shutter.

Time slowed. She was moving as fast as she could through each of the three folders she had brought up. She was wearing gloves now, according to the instructions that Stefan had dinned into her, so that there would be no fingerprints, and although they were thin cotton gloves she had bought just for this purpose, her palms were wet with sweat and her forehead beaded. There was no sound in the room but her short breaths and the shutter falling, but the pounding of the guns in Green Park meant she could not hear what was happening in the house. What if Toby was wondering about her absence? What if Ann was coming up to see whether she was all right? What if Giles thought of checking on his box?

Yet when the guns suddenly fell silent it was worse, as the sound she was dreading, the sustained note of the all-clear, wailed out.

At least she had finished the folders she had managed to bring up with her. She moved the chair away from the door. But then she heard footsteps on the stairs. Giles, going back to his room. A physical shudder of nausea ran through her at the thought of him noticing the lost key, but carefully she tucked the papers into the waist of her pyjamas and tied a cashmere bathrobe around her. She must look bulky and odd, but as she was going to claim a stomach ache it might be all right to hold her arms around her belly. She went downstairs as insouciantly as she could. But there, on the hall floor, was a gap where she expected to see the box. She was standing in the hall when Edward came up the basement stairs and she looked past him into the kitchen. There was the box, in the basement. Giles must have moved it down there for safe-keeping. Had he tried to open it? She felt sweat start on her back under her bathrobe. She went into the kitchen, where there was only Ann now, putting a kettle on the hob.

'Mrs Laura, are you all right?' she said.

'I'm really not well, Ann – could you do me a favour? I think there are some powders in Toby's bathroom. Could you get them for me?'

Ann nodded and went out, and to Laura's relief she was alone with the box again. Again, there was no time to think; however risky the moment was, she knelt and opened it, and slid the papers inside. Ann returned just as she was straightening up.

'Goodness, I'm still not feeling well. I think I'll go up again.'

She took the powders from Ann and went upstairs, as quickly as she could, into the bedroom, where Edward was lying in the bed, apparently asleep.

Presumably Giles was getting a last couple of hours' sleep too before his journey; but she could not rest. The key was still in her pyjama pocket. She sat on the edge of the bed, wondering what on earth to do, when she finally heard movement, followed by the taps running in the bathroom. Going quickly across the hall and into Giles's room, she put the key on the floor, half hidden by the leg of the chair, as though it had slipped from the table. And then she went back into the bedroom. Her knees seemed almost to give way as she sat down on the bed.

'Darling,' she said, leaning over Edward. 'I think Giles is leaving soon.'

'Is he?' Edward groaned. 'Must get up to say goodbye.' But he did not move, just lay there, his eyes closed. Laura touched her lips to his smooth shoulder and his hand rose and pulled her to him. With an odd urgency their mouths suddenly found one another; an intense current of need seemed to pin them against one another, so fierce and hard, there was no time for her orgasm to mount and yet she still experienced an intense relief, a melting rush, as his energy was spent.

Dressing quickly, they both went downstairs to say goodbye to Giles. When Laura saw herself in the hall mirror, she felt her exhaustion was written too clearly on her face, the dark shadows under her eyes and the rather clammy pallor of her skin showing that she had not slept. But as she met Giles's eyes, there was no knowledge or question in his cursory glance.

'Are you off, Giles?'

'Just waiting for the chap from the Ministry – they are sending an escort or two with me – absurd really, you know, but it's in case any spies get on the train. They rather wanted somebody with me overnight – they are paranoid. Makes sense after a fashion, I suppose. Have to do these things the right way.'

Eventually a knock on the door announced the arrival of his escort, a bowler-hatted man who lifted the box into the car.

'I'll see you when I get back, then,' said Giles, shrugging on his overcoat. Laura watched his back, unconcerned, jaunty, as he went down the steps, and felt both sickened and superior. Edward had already turned back into the house.

'I may be late tonight, endless meetings planned,' he said, straightening his tie in the hall mirror. Laura wondered at his tone. Was there knowledge in it? She realised that if he did not know, she did not want to tell him, in case he might judge her. But immediately she thought that, she told herself she was being absurd. Who had brought her into this work? Had he not already betrayed his friends over and over? Did he not sit with Giles and Quentin and Alistair day after day, year after year, pretending to be on their side, in their world, and yet selling out everything they believed? Only she, only Stefan, were really in his world. And yet still Laura felt an inchoate fear that her action had gone too far, that by breaking open his friend's work under his brother's roof, she had broken bonds that were stronger than she knew, that had been forged over long years of friendship. She would not think of that now. She still had work ahead of her.

Before she left for the bookstore, she transferred the film from the camera to a tiny canister which she pushed into a pocket in her purse created between the lining and the outer leather. She was due to meet Stefan that afternoon, at four o'clock, in a café near to Charing Cross Road. She spent the day stocktaking in a haze of tiredness, always aware of the bag which she had left in a backroom. At last, at half past three, she reminded her boss that it was her early afternoon, and she went half running along the Strand. When she got to Charing Cross, however, she found the street was closed. 'Time bomb,' said a man at the barrier. 'Don't know where I'll spend the night if they can't get the thing.'

'Don't know why it took them so long to get started on this one,' said a woman beside him.

'There've been so many unexploded from last night, streets closed all round the West End today.'

'They won't think themselves so clever when our lot go over there. They'll get a taste of their own medicine then.'

These eddies of bitterness were the same every day. Laura was tired of the impotent chorus, but she stood weakly at the barrier, not knowing what to do next.

'Nothing to see – pass along now,' said one of the demolition squad to no one in particular. Laura began to walk away, taking an aimless course as she thought through her options. She had a series of instructions about what to do if a meeting was stalled for any reason. There was the dead-letter drop in Camden Town, and there was the Clerkenwell tobacco shop where she could speak in code to the owner ('Can you let me know when you will get more Quintero cigars?') and leave them a number. Then, in theory, she would be contacted. She decided she had to try the drop first. She was desperate to get rid of the film. Although it carried no weight, it felt like a burden. But when she got to Camden Town she wondered why she had wasted her time. It wasn't that the wall had been destroyed, but there was so much rubble and broken glass, the area had obviously been a target more than once. It seemed absurd that Stefan thought she could risk leaving something precious in the fragile fabric of this breakable city.

Laura turned and began to make her way south again. But she had never walked in this part of London before, and as the road stretched on its dusty way she began to be unsure whether she was taking the most direct route. She asked a young woman, who told her to take a bus. Laura waited at the stop for a long time before someone else told her the buses were being diverted due to another time bomb on the previous street. Laura's once shiny patent shoes had lost the rubber to one heel at some point during her walk, so she went along with an uncomfortable limp. Finally she came to the road in Clerkenwell. The shop now stood in a row of boarded-up frontages. A scrawled notice in the window said, 'Closed due to bomb damage'.

She began to limp back along the street, and just as she thought to wonder what the time was, 'Here it comes,' came the shout from across the road and the sirens began to wail. Laura knew no shelters in that part of town, and she meant to go on walking, but as she crossed towards Farringdon, a warden shouted, 'Are you deaf?' and she realised she could hear the thrumming of planes, already coming near. With other people, she started running towards Farringdon station. The noise was suddenly all around, and they crushed together as they entered the station. 'Careful there, no need to push,' voices said as they struggled into the ticket hall, stumbling over people who had already spread mattresses on the floor. A great rustling and sighing filled the air around where Laura was standing in the station entrance, as the bombers began to release their first loads.

'Incendiaries,' said a voice behind her, as the chandelier flares began their crazy descent. 'Incandescent incendiaries.'

'Incredible incendiaries,' said another voice.

'Inglorious, insidious, Indescribable, intensifying incendiaries,' said the first voice again.

'Alistair,' Laura said, recognising the voice, but her words were covered by the rising force of the anti-aircraft guns, and she had to shout, 'Alistair!' before he turned and saw her, his face lit by the green-white flares of the incendiaries bursting on the road outside.

'They've got St John's,' someone shouted, and she saw the light further away change to yellow and then blue where a gas main had been hit.

Alistair said something about this being an absurd place to meet as he struggled and failed to move closer to her. Laura replied, saying the bombardment had come early, but then she saw the station clock and realised she must have been wandering the city for hours. Her mouth was dry, her bladder burning, and someone's bag was jabbing into her side.

She asked a ticket inspector who was trying to gather up

mattresses from the people who had got there early, to encourage them to stand up to make more room, if there was more space further in. He told her that the escalators had been turned off, but people had already filled every step. 'They're getting it bad in Holborn,' he said. 'Watch yourself, what are you doing?' The press of people was making Laura feel claustrophobic, and she had stepped into the road.

'Wait, Laura,' Alistair called to her. 'Wait till this lot have dropped and I'll come out with you.'

She stepped back in, and they waited for a few minutes that extended like elastic around the whooshing of falling bombs, the rumble of falling masonry, the dirge-like voices of the commentary of the people around them.

'Come,' he said, as the skies quietened. 'Or do you want to wait it out after all?'

'I can't stand it, I'd rather walk.'

Alistair asked the friend he had been standing with if he was coming with them, but the young man shook his head, and Alistair and Laura went out into the exposed road, where other desperate people were beginning to emerge. As they were walking up Farringdon Road, they heard the low roar of aeroplanes again. 'We'll never get you back to Chester Square tonight; you should have stayed in the station.'

'What about you?'

'Can't bear these nights. Tell you what, how about the Ace of Clubs, have you tried it? It's reopened, safe as anywhere else, I would have thought, in that basement.'

Laura agreed, hardly knowing what she was agreeing to. She was limping again. She slid her feet out of her shoes and started to walk in stockinged feet.

Alistair shook his head, saying she was crazy to walk like that, in these streets. They were littered with shrapnel and glass, but she managed to pick her way in the glare of search-lights to the west. Somehow the madness of the situation made them elated, and they found themselves half laughing as more incendiaries fell to the west of them, until one bigger bomb sucked up the air as it fell too near and they were pressed against the side of a wall. But they went on like that through Holborn, with other scurrying ants who had come out of hiding. As they turned the corner into Red Lion Square, they saw two or three ambulances and muffled figures with stretchers. 'Look where you're going,' said the person holding the end of one. It was a woman, whose gaze sought Laura's, and Laura looked down at her burden.

'Come on, Laura, we're nearly there.'

They went on, but the sight of the bleeding body had taken away their ebullience. Could it have been a child? Eventually they made it to the club, and Laura walked down the stairs, clinging to the banisters. The room was stuffed with people, and a small band was desultorily playing songs from before the war. 'Let me buy you a drink,' Alistair said. 'You look terrible.'

Laura asked for a telephone, and Alistair pointed to it at the bar. She dialled the number of Toby's house, but the line was dead. She put out her hand to the brandy that Alistair had bought her, downed it, and then went to find the lavatory. A flagrantly exhausted face, streaks of dust on her cheeks, looked at her from the mirror. Alongside another woman Laura washed her face and hands and lipsticked her mouth. The woman beside her said something about how the noise would get you down if nothing else would, and Laura smiled the usual response.

'They say it's coming down hard over the East End again,' Alistair said.

'Any news of Belgravia?'

'Not that I've heard. Another drink?'

Laura hadn't eaten since lunchtime, but he was right, they had to keep drinking and trying not to think of what might be happening elsewhere in London. At one point the room seemed to sway, as if a high explosive had landed too near for comfort, but although the woman beside her clutched her arm, nobody left, nobody screamed. Eventually they heard, as if from far away, the all-clear.

'I have to get back, Alistair.'

'I'll go with you.'

Soon after they started walking, they saw a bus coming through the lightening gloom, and Laura ran to the bus stop.

'To Marble Arch, that will do – no need to come with me now. Thanks so much.'

'Any time you want another drunken night . . .' Alistair seemed untouched by anxiety, speaking as if they had been drinking in a city dedicated to pleasure rather than bludgeoned by war. It was the pose that many of Edward's friends took these days, Laura knew, but no one did it with such panache as Alistair, smiling at her, overly smug, she thought, about their own courage in drinking and socialising despite the horror around them.

As the bus swung down Oxford Street, she saw the gaping holes of department stores, but that was old damage. Once she got off she started running, in stockinged feet again, longing to see the white row of houses, their ample doors, their blind windows. But when she rounded the corner she saw the worst: an ambulance at the head of the street, a fire engine, women in tin hats, dust in the air. She was running past them, forcing her way through a knot of people, calling out to ask what was gone.

There he was, walking towards her through the dust, blood running down his cheek – but it was only a cut, it was only a splinter of glass, he was unharmed. 'Where have you been?' It would have taken too long to explain, so Laura just shook her head and held him, revelling in the warmth of their bodies. 'Dying to sleep,' she said, and she went in, her feet bleeding and filthy on the once fine parquet floors. Their house only had more windows blown out, but a few doors down a house had taken a hit, and all morning, as Laura slept fitfully, she heard the sounds of digging, shovels scraping through foundations, through the London clay, into the dark.

It was weeks before a meeting came together. Finally she left a note in the dead-letter drop. A few days later a strange man stopped her on the way to the bookshop and asked her about the Quintero tobacco she wanted, and told her to come and meet him at the Lyons' Corner House in the Strand the following day. She had never seen him before, and when she slid into the seat opposite him, he frowned at her.

'You missed your last meeting.'

'I couldn't help it – where is Stefan?'

She said it before she remembered the prohibition on direct questions. Unsurprisingly, he didn't respond.

'I have something to deliver,' she muttered. 'What should I do?'

'Small?'

'Very small.'

'Use the drop.'

'Too precious. I can't risk it. Can I pass it now?'

'Not at this meeting, I can't be sure you weren't followed. Next time. Come in three days.'

Laura tried to tell him that it was urgent, but he was already getting up. She was left there, with everything unsaid and the film still in her bag, powerless to stop him.

The next time, they passed the film in the way that Stefan had taught her, placing it in the newspaper that she left between them. Laura tried to mutter an explanation. This is it, she said in broken whispers, the drawings, the night-fighting, but who knows what chaos in the east had drawn Stefan away from London, and this man seemed ill at ease, as if Laura might present some danger to him. He stayed silent for a while, and when there was nobody around them he spoke two sentences only. 'You must go on ice for a while. There have been too many breaches of security, too many missed meetings.'

'So long as you give that to them.' The man showed no interest in the film, but it was now in his hands and Laura walked back through the scarred city free from it. As she waited at a traffic light at Marble Arch, she realised gas was seeping from a mains somewhere and she covered her nose and mouth against the smell.

16

As the months of bombardment went on, Laura became more and more conscious of the silences that fell between her and Edward when they were alone. She wanted, so much, to talk to him about the political situation. When would the promised conflict between capitalism and communism become clear, or would this grim struggle between fascism and imperialism, both sliding more and more deeply into darkness, go on interminably? Sometimes she tried to bring their conversations towards the political, in her desire for elucidation, but always a barrier seemed to close between them when she did so.

Still, there was no physical barrier between them, and Laura found Edward's constant desire for her as sweet as ever. One night he came into the bedroom as she was getting undressed and wordlessly pushed her onto the bed, face-down, so that she could not even see him. She felt her desire rise to meet his, as always, but something in her stood outside them, and she saw how oddly aggressive their coupling must seem. Afterwards, in the melting sensation that followed, they lay holding one another. 'It's as Lawrence had it,' he said, 'two single equal stars, in balance.'

Laura was silent for a while, thinking of what he had just said. 'Stars?'

'This balance – it goes beyond love.'

She asked him why it had to go beyond love, and felt his unease begin, as he struggled away from her a little, reaching for his cigarettes. As so often, she recognised how much he disliked questions, and told herself that she must stop pressing him. Hadn't she promised herself from the start that she could show him that she could understand him without interrogating him? If he believed that they were two equal stars, that was surely wonderful enough for her. She turned the conversation.

'Will you take me out again?' she asked him. 'It's my birthday next week – can we go out for dinner?'

Laura knew that despite the bombs, behind closed doors the clubs and grand hotels of London went on with their chattering, swaying life. She stood irresolutely in front of her closet on that Friday evening, and in the end took out the cherry-red dress she had been wearing two years ago on the night they first met. The zip moved more easily than she remembered; perhaps rationing meant that she had slimmed down a little. First she pulled her hair back, but she felt that looked much too severe, so she curled it and rolled it in front in a way that she had seen in a fashion magazine that Winifred had left behind the last time she had come over. They walked to the Dorchester in the darkening city. 'Do you like this dress?' she said in a flirtatious tone, and in a vague voice he asked if it was new and said how pretty it was. When she reminded him it was what she had been wearing when they first met, he stopped and looked at her, and smiled, and said that of course he would never forget, he had just been distracted by something that had happened that day at work. But when she asked what it was, he said it was a long story and fell silent.

The ballroom was crowded, but it did not take long for Laura to notice, across the room, two women picked out by the way that the gazes of others turned to them – Amy and Nina. Both of them were in black. Nina was wearing heavy amethyst earrings and a silver scarf around her shoulders, but Amy seemed to have no accessories, and her white-blonde hair was brushed back severely. Immediately Laura was conscious of her too-bright dress with its pre-war style and the absurd way she had dressed her hair, and she was not eager to go and say hello to them. When Edward saw them, however, he rose without hesitating and steered her across to their table. She was not surprised that they hardly acknowledged her. Presumably the man next to Amy was the husband that Sybil had once spoken about, the one that the newspapers would have mocked if he had not acquitted himself in some distinguished way in a theatre of war. He hardly looked the part, while Nina's partner was an overweight man who had not even bothered to wear evening clothes.

'This is Michel Blanchard,' Nina said, and the man merely nodded at them before saying something to her in an undertone. They did not ask Laura and Edward to sit with them, and Laura was relieved when they went back to their own table. She tried not to let their chilly manner bother her; neither of them had a partner to match her husband, she thought as they sat down. And in the noise and energy of the room it did not matter if there was still a pool of silence around her and Edward as they drank and danced. It was well into the small hours when they paid their extortionate bill and went into the lobby, where Edward stopped short.

'Good evening,' he said, as an elderly man with a hollow-cheeked face stopped in front of them and greeted him in a polite way, asking what brought him there. 'Celebrating my wife's birthday – Laura, have you met Lord Halifax?'

The protest that she had once seen at his door danced through Laura's mind as she took Halifax's hand. She remembered what they had called him in the Party: the old appeaser, the old snake; she had expected someone with an air of devilish certainty. But he seemed to hold his power in the distracted, accidental way of all the men in Edward's class, there in his evening clothes in the lobby of the hotel, shaking her hand in a distant manner and muttering that the pleasure was all

201

his. As they walked on, she noticed that Edward was tense with irritation, and she asked him what the matter was.

'Of all the people to meet . . .'

'But he lives here, doesn't he? Hard to avoid him.'

It seemed strange, stepping out of the hotel and into the city's blind blackness, to think that he lived in that gilded interior, but she remembered hearing that from Toby or Winifred.

'I see enough of him at work – you'd think we could go for a drink without bumping into him. No doubt he'll have something to say about me dancing all night if I don't go in at dawn tomorrow.'

At first Laura was surprised that he felt so rebuked by being seen by his boss. But as they walked on and he put his arm around her, she realised that his reaction wasn't rational, that there was something about always being surrounded by his work that was eating into him. So as they walked she tried to steer the conversation elsewhere, and for a few moments it worked; they talked about after the war and how they might one day have a small house where they could be together – in the hills, Laura said, or by the sea; or in the forest, Edward said. They left open which country their idyll might be in – maybe the hills of Worcestershire or Massachusetts came into their minds, or some unidentified snowy valleys or birch woods in a country they had not yet seen. But they would be free there of the bitter secrecy which made Edward so miserable, Laura thought as they opened the door in Chester Square. The evening had been quiet so far, but as soon as they began walking upstairs the sirens sounded.

Downstairs, under the table, Laura and Edward both found sleep eluding them as the morning came near and the guns began to rattle. Ann got up and made tea, and they all sat, sleepless, drinking it. For some reason they began to talk about how they didn't really know anyone who had died in the raids: some distant acquaintances, yes, the wife of one of

Edward's colleagues at work, who had been unluckily caught in a public shelter that had taken a direct hit, and a whole family in the East End whom Ann knew a little – but no close friends or family. But as they went on with the conversation, both Ann and Laura suddenly felt superstitious, and they stopped. It might be tempting fate, Ann said, to sit down under the bombardment and say that they didn't know the dead, and Laura agreed with her.

Nobody could have remembered that conversation except Laura on the evening in early June when she and Ann were sitting in the kitchen, drinking tea after supper, and Toby came in late and tired from the House. 'Edward in?' he said, pausing at the door. When Laura told him that she didn't expect him to be home until later, Toby asked if she could tell him the news, as he couldn't get him on the telephone and he had Home Guard duty to go to. 'Don't want it to wait until the morning.'

For some reason Laura thought first of Mrs Last and Sybil, though it was ridiculous given that they were safe in the countryside. The actual news made much more sense. Quentin was dead, not missing in action or taken prisoner, but dead of bullet wounds in Crete on a beach, seen by his men. Sounded quite horrific, Toby said – no need to tell anyone that, though. He had heard it from one of Quentin's fellow officers, so the news would only be getting to his father today. Toby was gabbling rather, and Laura felt she should make him sit down and give him a drink, but he was already making his way upstairs to change into his Home Guard uniform, his feet stamping as if he were pressing down on whatever he was feeling.

When he had gone out, Laura and Ann sat in silence for a while. Then Ann tried to tell Laura she was sorry, but Laura told her there was no need for condolences, that she had hardly known Quentin. It was a shock, of course it was, to think of all that confident, unquestioning energy gone, but the shock had little resonance for her. How easy it would be to romanticise the part he had played in taking her to Edward, but he had always been dismissive of her and she had hardly seen him as an individual. To her, he had just been part of the group. The worst thing was that Toby had given her the job of telling Edward, and as she waited there with Ann she thought that she must have a drink first, and she went to the cupboard to where the whisky was kept. She offered some to Ann without thinking, and Ann accepted with a look of surprise.

'You must have seen him in the house often,' she said to Ann, and Ann agreed. 'Before the war I was usually in the kitchen, but still I saw him. It's very sad for Mrs Last,' she said. Laura knew she meant Sybil. 'And for their father, he'll be so cut up, his only son. They've got a beautiful house up in Derbyshire, was going to be his.' Laura thought about this, and asked Ann why Sybil hadn't gone there on the outbreak of the war rather than to Toby and Edward's mother. Ann started to tell her that Sybil had never got on very well with her own father, and then they stopped, knowing that it wasn't the done thing for the two of them to gossip about Sybil as though Laura was a maid too, or as though Ann was a friend of Laura's. Laura felt the weight of embarrassment at the same time that Ann did, and the possibility of Toby's disapproval if he were there. How ridiculous, she told herself, you know you don't believe in these barriers. Still, the self-consciousness persisted, and Laura said she would go upstairs until Edward got in; as she went up the hall stairs she heard his key in the door.

Did he take it badly? He hardly seemed to react at all. Laura said they should have a drink and they went into the living room. He seemed almost confused, sitting there with his hands in his lap, then saying he would read a bit before going to bed, and standing in front of the bookshelves with an indecisive air. After sitting with him for a while, Laura realised her eyes were closing, and she said she would go up.

She said again how sorry she was, how awful it was, but he was not looking at her, he seemed deep inside his book.

She went to bed in their own room, as the skies were unexpectedly quiet. When Edward came finally to join her, near to morning, she woke and rolled over to hold him. She wanted to wake up properly and talk to him, but he soon started to descend into sleep, snoring loudly in a way he had never done before. His breath did not hold that hint of apple which was one of his most striking physical characteristics. It was sour with the smell of whisky. He must have been sitting there drinking for hours. A good wife would have been sitting with him, she thought, but she knew that whatever it was that he and Quentin had shared, whatever memories of first steps into university or London life, this was not something that Edward had ever told her about. This grief was not something she could share.

The next day, after checking with Edward that she was doing the right thing, Laura wrote a formal letter of condolence to Sybil, and soon received a brief acknowledgement in return. She had gone to her father's house, she said, and for a long time after that Laura heard nothing from her. Edward and Toby never mentioned Quentin again, and after a while Laura came to believe that in fact he had not meant so much to them, as they had forgotten him so quickly.

As the weeks of war continued and rationing began to bite, Laura spent more and more of her days in queues. Since that house with four people living in it created much more work than Ann could manage on her own, if Laura had not helped with the shopping they would not have had enough food in the house. One Friday in July, having missed the meat queue in their usual butcher's after getting there just an hour or so late, Laura bought sausage rolls in a shop she had never frequented before, and they had all come down with the runs. Edward got up, grey-faced, on Saturday and went to work as usual. He didn't come back that evening; it was no longer

205

unusual for him to work such long hours, but Laura had to resist the temptation to telephone him at work and ask how he was feeling.

Eventually she went to bed alone, feeling rather weak and maudlin in the aftermath of the illness. Winifred had lent her a novel about a teacher in an English private school, but its humour was that of the group, and although she could now pick up some of the tones of irony, most of it baffled her. Though the sirens sounded in the night, she stayed in her own bed, a heavy inertia pinning her down, and lay there for a long time even once light pulsed through the edges of the blackout blinds, the covers pushed off because the air was already so close. At last she got up, splashed her face with cold water, and went down to breakfast feeling light-headed. Toby was there, head bent, munching through toast and margarine. 'News,' he said thickly, gesturing to the radio.

Laura caught the tail end of the bulletin: 'Hitler now has new fields of slaughter, pillage and destruction.' That gravelly voice had become familiar to everyone, but it seemed just for a second to be speaking directly to her. 'I see the Russian soldiers standing on the threshold of their native land, the ten thousand villages of Russia where there are still primordial human joys, where maidens laugh and children play. We shall give whatever help we can to Russia and to the Russian people.'

'There we are,' said Toby, 'not alone any more.'

Laura was nodding at a meaning he could not guess beyond his words, as she asked Ann if there was any more toast and coffee. They sat talking idly, and not long afterwards they heard the front door bang and Edward came down the basement stairs. The expression on his face was one Laura had not seen for so long. Without thinking of the others, she stood up and went into his arms, and he held her for a moment, smiling. 'I am sorry,' he said, 'so much going on, I couldn't get back last night. It's a lovely day. Shall we walk up to the park?'

Laura went upstairs and put on a dress that she had not taken out of the wardrobe yet that summer. Sleeveless and low-necked, it seemed almost too bare for the city. There were no deckchairs free, so they sat on the dusty grass under a sycamore tree. At one point Edward picked a daisy and tucked it into her hair. It fell out and down the front of her dress and, without thinking of the people around them, he bent and kissed the hollow where it had fallen. They lunched at the cafeteria by the Albert Memorial and the sparrows came to their hands to be fed. It seemed easy to talk now – about everything, about politics, yes, if they had wanted to, now that the world had fallen into place, now that good and evil were ranged on opposite sides of the great conflict, but also about why the leaves of chestnut trees looked glossy and the leaves of plane trees looked dull, or whether they should go to hear this pianist that Alistair had been raving about last week. At one point Laura misheard Chopin as shopping, and Edward laughed so much that his coffee went up his nose, and when they watched some park warden sweeping the gravel path he quoted some nonsense rhyme about how many maids it would take to get a beach clean, and she made him repeat it until she'd learned it too. They felt drunk with their sense of relief.

17

One grey Thursday Laura saw the Red Flag fluttering over Selfridges; the only splash of colour she had seen for a long while in that grimy, shattered city. Later in the day, with hindsight, it seemed like a precursor of the telephone message that Ann shouted up to her. 'It's for you, Mrs Laura,' she called up the stairs, and when Laura came down Ann handed her the receiver. 'Someone called John Adams, he says your sister gave him your number.'

207

It had been months – no, years – since Laura had heard from any contact, and it was as hard as ever to slot herself back into that frame of mind. She had not missed her role in that secret work. The world around her had fallen into place more coherently since the chaos of the first years of the war. Now that Londoners spoke of Russians as the bravest of all, she felt more in step with the dogged hope that was the only acceptable attitude in the city. Tired and shabby, as all Londoners were after years of war, she went on day by day shopping for rationed food and doing shifts in that half-empty bookshop, but just putting one foot in front of another felt like enough of a journey. Perhaps she should have felt proud to be called back to the bigger struggle, but going into the dim café in Balham and seeing Stefan's familiar ugly face at a back table, she was as nervous as ever. Once she had sat down at the next table, where he could hear her speak, she hoped for some words of reassurance or explanation. But there were only two muttered passwords, and then silence.

He seemed to have aged much more than a couple of years, she thought, looking sideways at him. His hair had turned greyer and he had put on weight; when he put out his hand to his cup of coffee she thought she saw it shake. She had brought *The Times* newspaper with her, although she had nothing to give him that day, and she saw he had one too. She assumed it held fresh film for the Minox, and she put her hand on it in a would-be casual manner as she got up, and put it into her bag as she left the café. She had been there half an hour at most.

Rattling back on the Underground, she decided to get out at Trafalgar Square and walk along Piccadilly to see if she could find a shop Winifred had mentioned that had been selling new nylon stockings. As she came out into the pale light, she heard voices raised in a song that she recognised. It was a communist rally; red flags and the plangent tones of the 'Internationale'. A couple of passers-by had stopped beside her to watch and she heard something about the bravery of the Red Army and how they could teach other armies a thing or two. Everyone loved Uncle Joe now.

As she stood there, years disappeared for her, and she had a flash of how she'd felt when she had just arrived in London, freshly in love with the idea of freedom. She scanned the rows of people for a familiar face. Was that the back of Elsa's head, there, by the banner? The woman Laura was watching began to turn. It was not Elsa, but then for a moment Laura thought she saw Florence's dark hair a few rows in front of that; no, the woman she was looking at was not tall enough. She saw the banner they used to march with far across the square, but just as her body was about to push forward, going towards the familiar sight, her mind caught up. It was dangerous to stand here, waiting to be recognised. Long ago she had promised to turn her back on all of this. She walked quickly away, skirting the square and taking a long route to Piccadilly. One day soon, she said to herself, secrecy will be at an end.

Once the meetings with Stefan had been regularised again, they gradually began to induce less anxiety in her. In fact, they became routine, and gave a kind of structure to the weeks; they took place on Wednesdays and Saturdays, on her half-days from the bookstore. And gradually Stefan began to change their tone. In the past he had cut short every rendezvous, leaving immediately after the newspapers had been exchanged, his whole body exuding fear of discovery. But now, he sometimes chose spots where they could sit and talk, in the corners of Hampstead Heath or unprepossessing cafés in Balham or Elephant and Castle. He asked her about all sorts of subjects: who was staying in Toby's house and what they were saying about the Soviet Union; what her friends felt about rationing and what Winifred's role was in the Ministry of Food. . . . If she had stopped to think about it, of course Laura would have recognised that she was simply being pumped to provide useful information, but his

209

attention felt flattering to her, as if he was interested in everything about her. Sometimes she found herself wondering about him, and what his life was like, and how his cover worked, but she knew it would not do to ask him anything. And in fact the one-way nature of their conversations was oddly seductive: Laura felt released from the feminine necessity of encouraging her male interlocutor to open up; she luxuriated in being the one who was listened to. All week she found herself saving up observations and nuggets of information for him.

One cold autumn afternoon they met on Hampstead Heath. Laura passed the film as usual under a newspaper on the bench between them. 'If only everyone was as reliable as you, Pigeon,' he said. Theoretically, she knew it was a breach of protocol for him to use her codename, or Edward's, but they seemed to have become terms of endearment for him.

'But Edward is—'

'Yes, Virgil is impeccable,' Stefan said. 'How does he get his hands on all this stuff? Sometimes my bosses don't believe you both are for real. Fools.'

Laura found it shocking, that suddenly bitter note of criticism. But he didn't seem to notice that he had said anything out of the ordinary. She asked if he was having problems with other agents. She did not expect any kind of direct answer – if she had been honest with herself, she would have realised that she was just fishing for compliments. But he surprised her again, by answering with detailed irritation, opening up to her for the first time, telling her that one of his other sources had just come under suspicion.

'For years he has brought us information not just from his country, but also from Germany. Now some of it has been checked from another source, and it is false – he is tricking us. I have to know who he is really working for now. After all, if Blanchard . . .'

Blanchard – Laura remembered the name, and the man,

210

sitting there at the edge of the dance floor in his office clothes, and she repeated the name as if to remind herself.

'You know him?'

She shook her head. She couldn't say she knew him, but if it was the same – a tall, middle-aged man . . .

'With a limp.' Laura had to admit that she hadn't seen that, but after all he had been sitting down. Stefan was irritated with her for not being more certain. He was clearly eager, even desperate for Laura to be acquainted with him. 'I need to keep an eye on him,' he said. Laura was trying to backtrack, explaining that even if it was the same man, she didn't know him, in fact was only acquainted with his girlfriend, and even then hardly at all. But Stefan had already moved on, explaining that it was essential that she build on this acquaintance. 'We used to have a good supporter in the hotel itself, one of the waiters, who would do little things for us, but he has now been called up. I need to know what Blanchard is doing and who he is talking to. He is the press attaché at the Swiss embassy, so he has many, many contacts. We can see what he does when he is not in the hotel or the embassy and we can look at his letters, but what is he doing in there, and who does he see?'

Again Laura tried to explain that she had only seen him in passing, and Stefan started to get impatient with her.

'You must make an effort.'

Laura felt rebuked. She had been Stefan's good girl all these months, and now he seemed ready to be angry with her. As she left the meeting place, she felt curiously shaky. She wanted his approval, she realised; she wanted to be told how well she was doing. Over supper that evening she asked Edward if they could go to the Dorchester again soon. She was hardly surprised by his reluctance, but pressed him, and perhaps it was because it was so unlike her to do so, he agreed.

When she and Edward walked through the doors of the ballroom, she realised that the atmosphere reminded her of nothing so much as the first-class quarters of the ship in which she had crossed the Atlantic, oppressive in its ostentation and gaudiness. But now, in this shattered city, it could not seem more out of place. There was a tackiness about it; even the glass in which she was given her cocktail was sticky, and there was no ice in it. But there was energy here too: London's nightlife had received an injection of new blood, and there were a number of American uniforms among the dancers. In fact, it was so full that there were no tables free immediately, so they sat at the mirrored bar drinking their sweet cocktails. It wasn't long before Edward saw someone he knew.

'There's Percy,' he said. 'Let's pretend we haven't seen him – he wrote a vicious review of Alistair's first book.' And then, with an expression of distaste, he continued. 'There are all those Polish chaps I was in a meeting with just yesterday. I suppose they'll come and say something.' But instead of talking to any of these acquaintances, Edward ordered more and more to drink.

It was after midnight when they saw Nina come in, together with the overweight Swiss man Laura remembered. They were not with Amy, but with another couple, a thin dark man wearing suede shoes and a very young girl, as well as a tall man who looked too young for his shock of striking white hair. Unlike with Laura and Edward, the waiters were quick to find the group a table, and Laura and Edward went over to say hello. Nina introduced them to her friends. The girl, who looked about sixteen, didn't open her mouth, but the dark man stood up and bowed politely to Laura. When Edward heard this man's name, however, his smile became fixed. He nodded to the table and walked Laura back to the bar.

Laura tugged on his sleeve as they went. 'I told you, I want to talk to Nina.'

'That man is a notorious Polish arms dealer,' Edward said, draining his cocktail, 'who made his money selling weapons to Franco.' And as soon as the drinks were finished, he insisted they left.

When Laura imagined telling Stefan that she had seen, but completely failed to talk to Blanchard, she felt angry and embarrassed. So the next morning after Edward had gone to work she telephoned Alistair. At first she chatted a little about his novel, which he said he had nearly finished, and then she moved the conversation to the point, telling him that she had been dancing at the Dorchester with Edward the previous night and had had such a good time, but that Edward was too busy to go very often, and she wondered whether they couldn't go together, just for fun. She remembered Alistair's easy-going attitude on the night that she had been caught by the bombardment, and sure enough he only sounded a little surprised and agreed to come and pick her up on Wednesday evening.

Alistair was just the right company for that environment. He was all interested observation and quick conversation; he was happy to steer her around the dance floor and to look around for acquaintances; there was the editor of a magazine he wanted to write for; there was an American officer he knew slightly, who asked Laura to dance. And then, when Nina came in again very late, he naturally went with Laura to greet her. This time Laura stood solidly by Nina's table until she had to ask if they wanted to sit down, and Laura made sure she sat next to Nina.

Laura tried to give Nina the kind of sympathetic flattery that usually resonated with other women. She asked where on earth she had got that beautiful dress. She asked if she had heard recently from Sybil – how lonely Sybil must be in the countryside without her friends. She asked what she was doing now that women had been called up, what a bore it was that they were all expected to work. But to all the questions, Nina said very little. 'Aren't you dancing?' Laura said at one point. 'This band must be better than any I've heard since I left the States.' This was simply a pretence at sophistication, and she was afraid that Nina could see right through it.

'Well,' Nina said in a tone of indifference, 'Chéri doesn't, you know.'

Laura was surprised to hear her inappropriate endearment for Blanchard, but she turned to Alistair, sensing an opening. 'You'd love to dance with Nina, I know you would.'

Once they had got up, the space between Laura and Blanchard was empty, but Laura could not believe how hard it was to flirt with a man who did not seem interested in her. There was no energy there between them, and so Laura found herself acting in an absurdly exaggerated way to try to make him notice her, batting her eyelashes as he lit her cigarette, brushing his fingers as he passed her glass, and even touching his leg with hers lightly under the table. She felt like a wind-up doll, turning on a music box, while Blanchard watched her sleepily, with the manner of someone who was used to being amused rather than exerting himself to amuse.

At first Laura was relieved when the other couple she had seen them with before – the Polish man and the young girl – came over to the table, but then she realised that meant the men would talk to one another rather than to her, and when she spoke to the young girl she did nothing but smile.

'Don't worry about Ingrid,' said Victor. 'She doesn't talk much.'

'You like quiet women,' observed Blanchard.

'She makes some noise in bed,' Victor said.

'That's where I like a woman to be quiet,' Blanchard said. Laura tried to break into the men's conversation with a funny story about life in Toby's shelter, but she felt her voice falling shrilly over the table and she was aware that she was much too callow to amuse these dissolute, secretive men. When Alistair came back to the table, she was trying to draw Ingrid out, but either because Ingrid was scared of her or had poor English, she only answered in monosyllables.

214

That Saturday afternoon she went to meet Stefan with a sense of a job badly done. In the café in Balham with steamed-up windows, she told him that it was pointless trying to stalk Blanchard at the Dorchester, that Edward refused to go and she could not ask Alistair to take her again, he could not afford it. Stefan cut the meeting short with an air of disappointed resignation, and Laura was surprised how she replayed and replayed his manner, how much it hurt her. At the next meeting he told her briefly that she had to try again, and before she had time to reply he was gone. This time in *The Times* newspaper was a brown envelope, and in the envelope was a stack of five-pound notes. Clearly, Stefan had decided to assume that the only barrier was the one she had mentioned, that she could not ask Alistair to treat her.

When she telephoned Alistair, he seemed puzzled by her desire to go back to the Dorchester. She understood why; it had been an uneasy evening at best. Laura looked at herself in the hall mirror as she talked to him, and saw herself raising her eyebrows and laughing as she told him how lovely it was going out dancing when everything else was so grim. 'My treat, this time,' she said, and wondered how foolish she sounded.

Each time she and Alistair went back to the Dorchester over the next few weeks, she had to put on that persona; she had to become that woman who was a bit of a butterfly and couldn't see when others weren't quite in the mood to join her. Every time it became a greater strain. She knew that really she was too dull for Nina and her friends; she had to learn to drink much more than she was comfortable with, and stay out until the small hours, laughing at their jokes.

'I hate it, Stefan, and I'm not learning anything about anyone. They just flirt and drink. It's horrible.'

Stefan nodded. Now that this had been going on for a couple of months, he too had realised that Laura was learning nothing except the way that Blanchard liked to get drunk with his girlfriend on his nights off. But if Laura expected to be released, she was disappointed by his next words.

'If you can get into his room alone just once, I want you to put a bug into it. Then we can hear him. Then we will know. He must be making contact with the other side somehow. We need to know what he is telling them.'

Laura did not even know what he meant by a bug.

'A listening device – like a radio receiver.' Stefan's voice was impatient. It was too cold for them to meet outside, and they were in that little café again. Laura suspected that the owner was a Party member and that was why Stefan felt at home there, but she had felt safer in the old days when they used to meet in open spaces. Their conversations were always so rushed here, and she felt that she had not even really heard what Stefan was saying before she had agreed.

The next day they met in a prearranged spot in Tooting, and he drove them south out of London in his little grey car. They pulled into a lay-by and he showed her the device that she was to fix in Blanchard's room. The instructions he gave her were detailed, and she nodded as he talked, but back in her bedroom that evening, alone, she got the bug out of its box and looked at it disconsolately. It was bigger than she had expected, a long antenna connected to a silver-plated can in which, Stefan had told her, were the wires and plates that would act as a microphone when radio waves were transmitted to it, which another agent could do from a different hotel room once this bug was fixed in Blanchard's room. He had talked to her about the best way she could fix it: it need only be temporary, so she could put it in the furnishings of the room, on the underside of the desk or the back of a bedside table, for instance. There was no need to drill a hole into the skirting board, he said, as though that was reassuring. He had given her a little tube of glue, a tiny tin of epoxy resin and some small tools, but Laura felt incompetent as she looked at the kit, and could not imagine how she could carry out her task without discovery.

That evening, getting ready to go out with Alistair, she decided to leave it behind; she packed it into an old hatbox at the top of her wardrobe. While she was making up her face, Edward came in unexpectedly early, and she asked if he felt like coming out with her and Alistair, but he shook his head, saying the Dorchester wasn't really his thing.

'I know,' was all she said. She assumed he knew why it was that she was going there; not in detail, of course – they both knew not to discuss their work – but he must know that she would not be going if she did not have some kind of mission there. He paused behind her, looking at her in the mirror. For a moment she was about to tell him what lay ahead of her and how she felt sick with apprehension at the task Stefan had given her. 'Do you ever—' she started, about to ask him whether he ever found that Stefan gave him things to do that he balked at, but the words were slow in her mouth and at almost the same time he was telling her not to stay out too late.

'I know it's fun,' he was saying, 'but they are such an odd crowd there.' She thought she heard in his voice an anxiety about her, about what she had to do, and she stood up and put her arms around him.

'Bother,' she said, 'I've put lipstick on your collar.'

'It's going into the laundry anyway,' he said, disengaging himself and picking up a book that was lying by their bed.

By now Nina and Blanchard seemed to have accepted that Alistair and Laura would come over to their table at some point during the evening. Alistair had done most of the work of making them accept their company; he was happy to dance and flirt with Nina, while Laura still felt she faced an uphill struggle to get Blanchard to notice her. But Nina seemed languid that evening, and almost as taciturn as Ingrid, and Alistair went wandering off to the other side of the room to gossip with a journalist he knew. Nina had said the previous week that she would soon be going to visit Sybil in Derbyshire, Laura remembered, but when Laura asked her about the visit, Nina looked vague.

Blanchard, too, seemed distracted, and Laura thought suddenly, as she was drinking her second cocktail, that she was going to give up after that evening and give Stefan back that bug. What was the point of trying to make headway with Nina or Blanchard, or to pretend that she was this girl who wanted to get drunk and dance with people who didn't even like her much? Just then she noticed that Nina was looking at her with an oddly glassy stare, and she asked if she was all right. Nina nodded, but Laura saw how her gaze wavered even when her head stilled. Nina got up, saying she was going to powder her nose, and Laura got up too. Blanchard asked why girls always went to pee together, and Victor laughed and made some smutty innuendo. As they walked through the room, Laura felt Nina's hand suddenly on her elbow, a tight pressure. 'Feeling a bit tired,' was all Nina said when Laura turned to look at her. They went into the ladies' powder room; it was large, with little peach-coloured armchairs and a maid whose job it was to lay out the linen towels by the peach basins. It smelt of shit and tuberose perfume. Laura, feeling nauseous, sat down by a basin as Nina went into one of the lavatories. The door was locked. There was silence. Laura was pleating the silk of her dress in her fingers. The silence lengthened. Another woman, middle-aged and respectable in green crepe, came, urinated and left.

'Nina, my sweet,' Laura called out, 'are you all right?' There was no answer, so she knocked at the lavatory door. Again, no answer. Laura turned around and saw the maid still folding linen towels. 'My friend is in there – I'm not sure she is all right.' Why did she have to spell it out? Surely it was obvious that something was wrong. The maid tried the door and knocked too, and then shook her head and left the room.

Laura was still knocking and calling when she came back with a key that opened the door from their side. The maid had not said a word. Laura pushed open the door, but something was keeping it closed, and the something was Nina's foot. Nina had slipped off the lavatory and was on the floor, unconscious. There was vomit on her grey velvet dress. Her underpants were around her calves, her dress rucked up. The maid was pulling up Nina's underpants and straightening her dress, and Laura was wetting a handkerchief and putting it to Nina's face, calling her name. 'I'll get the doctor,' said the maid. Nina opened her eyes and gazed at Laura with the same glassy stare as before.

'Not their doctor,' she said clearly, 'my doctor.'

'I'll get you to a room,' Laura said. 'Blanchard's room?'

'Yes, let's go to Chéri's room, and he can call my doctor. Ugh,' and Nina shuddered, turned and vomited again into the lavatory. Laura asked her if she could stand, and then supported her into the corridor and to the elevator, where Nina leant heavily against Laura, so that Laura could smell her tainted breath. She felt repulsed by her. Nina had a key to Blanchard's room in her purse, but her hands were so shaky that Laura had to open the door and then usher her in. Clearly, the room had been used just before Nina and Blanchard had come down to the ballroom – it was a mess. The bedding was a swirl of linen, there was discarded underwear on the floor, and a bottle of brandy and other things – pill bottles, medicine bottles – on the table by the bed. Nina picked up one of the bottles and shook it, but it was empty. She fell clumsily onto the bed and Laura attempted to straighten it around her.

'Are you going to throw up again?' Laura asked, when Nina sat up restlessly.

'I need Chéri – I need my doctor.'

Laura told Nina to lie down and put the wet handkerchief in her hand so that she could wipe her face. Nina asked her to unzip her dress, and Laura did so. She was not wearing any undergarments except the blue silk underpants, and Laura saw bruises on her skin: a yellowing one on her breast, a fresh purple one on her thigh. Laura straightened up and left the room, telling Nina she was going to get Blanchard.

Walking through the ballroom was like moving across a stage, through the colour and chatter of the crowd, with lines that seemed laid down for her. When she reached Blanchard, she bent down and whispered in his ear that Nina was ill and that she wanted her own doctor. Blanchard got up and Laura went with him, back up to Room 248. He seemed to take in Nina's condition at a glance, and went to the telephone to call someone. As he did so, Laura went to Nina and wiped her forehead again with the handkerchief, asking, with exaggerated concern, whether she was feeling any better.

'I'll go now,' she said to Nina, with honey in her voice. 'You ring me if you need me. I'll leave my number here,' and she scribbled her telephone number on the pad next to the telephone, noting Blanchard watching her.

He followed her out into the corridor, then asked her exactly what she expected him to ask her, which was to say nothing to anyone.

'What would I say?' Laura said with false matter-of-factness, as though every day she saw a drugged girlfriend collapse in the ladies' room of the Dorchester and left her in the care of her violent boyfriend. There was a total lack of surprise or concern in her voice; she was acting, in fact, as she thought Nina herself would act in a similar situation. Blanchard looked at her assessingly, and Laura looked back at him. 'Maybe Nina needs a rest,' she said in her blank voice. 'She was talking about going to visit our friend Sybil in the countryside. It might be a good idea.' Blanchard nodded. 'I mean,' Laura said, 'I'll miss her, obviously.' And then she did something that was so out of character for her it made her feel momentarily dazed, as though she had lost her own sense of reality. As she said 'I'll miss her', she stepped right up to Blanchard, so close

220

her breasts almost touched his chest, and looked directly into his eyes. Then she withdrew and turned and walked down the corridor. She wasn't quite sure what she had done, but somehow she knew she had made him an offer as directly as it was possible to make one, and had told him that Nina was too much trouble for him.

At the next meeting with Stefan, Laura said little about how things were going, only that she was trying her best. But less than a week later the telephone rang one Wednesday afternoon and Blanchard was speaking to her. 'Little Nina is gone to the countryside,' he told her, 'and I wondered if you would like to have dinner with me?' Laura agreed to meet him at the Dorchester at eight. As soon as he put down the telephone, Laura put on her coat, calling to Ann that she had to go out to buy some more cigarettes. She went out of the house to a telephone box, where she rang the cigar shop and left a coded message for Stefan. It was beginning to snow, and she felt foolish as well as freezing as she stood in the phone box in her old muskrat coat.

After ten minutes of tense waiting, Stefan called back and Laura told him briefly that she might be able to do it if he could detain Blanchard somewhere at eight.

Her voice was confident as she spoke to him, but as she came back into the house she wished she could pretend to be sick and go to bed and forget about the whole thing. She felt like trash, so she was careful to dress in a way that made her look as sleek as possible. She had bought a fox wrap second-hand a few weeks ago, and she wore it over a plain black dress that Cissie had given her, and a pair of perfect nylons Ellen had sent her. She had to carry a large bag in order to fit in the bugging device, rather than the little purse the outfit demanded. She put tissue paper around it and an American cake of soap in its box on the top. Then, if anyone looked inside, she hoped it might just look as though she had been shopping that day. When she got to the hotel, she leaned over the desk. 'Mr Blanchard asked me to go up to his room.'

'He is not there.'

'He wanted me to wait for him there – Room 248.'

The man knew Laura, of course, how could he not? In the weeks she had been chasing Blanchard, she had been careful to smile at all the staff she met and to tip them lavishly with Stefan's money. He passed Laura the key as if it was nothing, and she went to the elevator. At Room 248 she knocked first, in case Stefan had not been able to get to Blanchard, and then put the key in the door.

She remembered the disorder of the room when she had accompanied Nina, and in an odd way she was expecting it still to be in the same state, but of course that was all gone: it was hotel clean. There was a large desk under the window, with an onyx lamp on it and a green leather blotting pad. At first she thought of fixing the bug under that, but the telephone was next to the bed, and surely it would be more useful for Stefan to be able to hear Blanchard's telephone conversations. She sat on the bed, putting her hand behind it, but it was too close to the wall for her to consider gluing the bug behind the headboard. The bedside table was flush against the wall too, so she opened the top drawer to see if there was space to fix it inside somehow. Lying there in the drawer was a pistol, among papers and coins. Laura closed the drawer and stood up. With the sight of the gun, her feeling of suspended animation had shifted. It had only ever been false courage driving her on, she realised; a sense of unreality. But this was real. Fear overwhelmed her.

Just as she put her hand on the door handle to leave, it was rattled from the other side. Blanchard was there, standing bulkily in the door, although it was only quarter past eight.

'Why are you here?' he said without preamble.

'You told me to meet you here.'

'I didn't tell you to sneak into my room.'

Laura tried to look innocent and stupid, as she muttered that she was sorry, that she had misunderstood.

'You should be sorry. Give me my room key.' He came into the room and shut the door with a slam, before gripping Laura's wrist with his hand and taking the key out of her fingers. The fear was hot now, filling her stomach.

'Shall we go down for dinner, then?' she said, with an awkward attempt at insouciance.

'A drink first,' he said. Somehow she had to change the temper of the evening and withdraw the invitation she had made when she had offered her body to him silently a couple of weeks ago. But here she was, in his room, and here he was. Her thoughts dashed and dashed, but she saw no way out.

He was mixing martinis of a kind, pouring cheap gin into glasses and splashing vermouth on top. Laura sat down on the sofa and he gave her a drink, at the same time putting a hand on her knee, pushing her legs open. Instinctively she moved away, stifling a desire to slap him.

'I'm so sorry, it's so embarrassing, I'm not feeling very well. I ate oysters at lunchtime – I'm not sure . . . may I use the . . .'

'It's over there.'

In the bathroom, Laura washed her hands in cold water, wishing she did not have to come out again. She would have to pretend she had been taken ill, she thought. She came out to find him waiting for her by the bed.

'I'm so sorry, I'm really not well. It's such a pity; I had been looking forward so much—'

It was as though he had not heard her. He grasped her arm with his hand, bending his face down to hers. Automatically Laura pushed at his chest to get away.

'I think I'm really unwell.'

'I think you are playing a game. And girls who play games with me get punished.'

With no more warning, Blanchard threw her face first onto the bed. She felt his hand force her legs apart, ripping the silk

223

of her underwear, and then his fingers were thrusting inside her. Laura screamed, but his other hand was on her mouth, pulling her head back so hard that she could hardly breathe. His fingers were pushing into her so roughly, as though they wanted to rip her softness apart. She found herself limp under him, unable suddenly to resist.

'You like it like this,' he grunted. It was terror that prevented her from moving. He moved his hands away from her genitals to undo his flies, positioning himself just above her. Laura moved very slowly under him, turning over and putting her hands up to stroke his shoulders, as if she had succumbed entirely to him, allowing a little moan as if of pleasure to escape her. Somehow, she did not know how, agency had come back to her. She was able to dissemble, she was able to act as if she desired him. He allowed her to move under him, he put his mouth to her breasts and she felt him biting her right nipple through her dress. Then, just as he finished unfastening his trousers, she suddenly flung herself sideways and grasped open the drawer in the bedside table. Before he realised what she was doing, she had the pistol in her hand, pointing it at him. He started back, his exposed penis slowly becoming flaccid.

'It's not loaded.'

Without speaking, Laura called his bluff, lowering it a little. He tried to grab for it but she held on, pulling back from him.

'How did you know it was there?'

'You left the drawer open.'

He must have known she was lying. But maybe he began to compute each of the potential scenarios ahead of them, as she did. Denunciation and counter-denunciation, and possible exposure. If he began to wonder who Laura was working for, whether she was a Fascist spy come to demand more information, or whether she had come to him from the Soviets to demand he come back to them, or whether, more likely, she was from the Americans – whatever conclusion he came to, the realisation must also have followed that no knowledge was good knowledge. It was better if they remained ignorant, if they stopped here.

He sat up and rebuttoned his trousers.

'All right, Mrs Last. Put that down. Look, I will open the door to the corridor and we will talk quietly. Let's have a real drink rather than these filthy cocktails.'

Laura still had the pistol in her hand while he poured two glasses of cognac. She didn't want this drink any more than she had wanted the first, but strangely she still felt a kind of social pressure to remain here in the room in a dignified way for a few minutes, trying to recapture a semblance of normal behaviour. When they were both holding their glasses, he raised his. 'To . . . ?'

'To our leaders?'

'To our leaders, Mrs Last.' Neither of them mentioned who those leaders might be as they drank. He said nothing as she got up, smoothed down her hair and left the room.

As Laura let herself into the house that evening, she realised, as though looking down on herself from above, that her hand was shaking as she turned the key in the door. She paused by the telephone in the hall, wondering why, all of a sudden, she thought of picking it up and speaking to someone – but there was nobody. Winifred was probably working, or out drinking somewhere; she could not place a long-distance call to Ellen or Mother out of the blue, and Florence . . . why did Florence's strong voice recur to her now? Florence was long gone, her marches and speeches blown back into the past.

Surely it was Edward she needed. Yes, she thought as she went upstairs, dragging her hand on the banister, if only she could come to rest in his arms. She needed his understanding of the necessity of their work, a necessity that could outrun shame and failure. He was not in the bedroom. She pulled off her now hated black dress, threw out her torn underwear, and put on a grey utility dress which was the only spring

225

garment she had been able to get with her ration book. She went downstairs, into the living room, put on the gramophone and poured herself a drink. Why didn't he come home?

At last, she heard Edward's key in the door. 'Drinking alone?' he said in a quizzical voice as he came into the room. She poured him a drink and sat down next to him on the sofa. She was waiting for him to notice her shakiness and ask her what was wrong, but he seemed distant and distracted himself. Still, the simple fact of his presence was reassuring to her in that moment. She felt her pulse slow, as they sat for a while in silence. How clean and strong he looked. She could not imagine how to start the story of her evening, but she was about to begin, when he spoke.

'Do you ever miss home?' he asked.

It was an unexpected question, but at that moment she was glad to be asked something personal that did not lead her back into the shock of the evening. 'I suppose I do,' she said.

And it was true; something like homesickness had become stronger in her lately. She had recently had a letter from Mother that had startled her into a kind of guilt about staying away so long. Father was sick, it was clear from the letter, although what kind of illness and how serious it was had been left vague. Ellen had got married two years ago, had moved to Boston and now had a daughter. Laura could tell from her letters how for Ellen the breathlessness of being courted had already moved into the slower pace of family life.

But perhaps, if she was honest, it wasn't her sister or her parents she missed so much as the lost rhythms of speech of her home country. Sometimes, when she talked to Americans in London, she felt a shock of what she realised was nostalgia. She was about to tell Edward this, but stopped. He would find it odd, she thought, if she talked about how American she sometimes felt. She knew what the group thought of

226

Americans: so crass, so uncultured – and 'so frightened all the time', as Alistair used to say about the American officers in the Dorchester. And as new battle lines were being drawn, surely in Edward's eyes any loyalty to her country would become more and more absurd.

Her thoughts had made her fall silent again. She tried to say something honest about how she did miss home, and her mother and sister, even though she knew how little she really got on with them. Edward listened for a while, and then got up to pour another whisky. Over the glug and gurgle of the new bottle being poured, he told her the news. They were to leave London. They were to go to Washington. In May. A shock to him as well as to her. Though obviously they had always known he would not be in London forever. Working for the Foreign Office meant a certain amount of moving around. And this was a good, an enviable posting.

'It's quite a promotion, actually.'

'And I'll see Mother, and Ellen . . .' Laura's voice sounded uncertain even to herself.

'You were just saying how much you missed them.'

Laura was not sure what to say to that, and asked more about the job. Edward told her that it was Halifax's doing. Laura knew that the elderly man who was forever tainted by his attempts to prevent war was now in Washington, dispatched there to try to charm the Americans. And he had called on Edward to be by his side. She felt Edward's uncertainty. As they went on speaking, he tried to frame his hesitation as the thought of leaving London at this time, at the end of the long war. She told him it was a good time to leave, and they brushed over, with silent understanding, the real meaning of the new job. There, he would be perfectly placed for all the secrets Stefan could ever want; as the trusted subaltern of the British ambassador, he would go like an arrow into the heart of the new empire – targeted, precise. But they did not talk about that.

'My father would have been pleased,' Edward said at one point. 'He talked about Washington when I first went into the Foreign Office.' He spoke, Laura thought, as if he were fulfilling his father's dreams rather than blowing them to dust. But Laura too, in the moment, talked about it as if it were a straightforward promotion and suggested opening one of the old bottles of champagne that were being stored for the end of the war.

As he went to get it, Laura felt that now was not the time to tell him about her evening. Here was enough strangeness. When he came back with the champagne and gave her a glass, he put out his hand and stroked back her hair with that familiar gentle gesture. 'Yes, we'll get away,' he said. For a moment she believed he knew, and understood, why she wanted to leave London, why they needed to reach a new world. And so she chose to let the horror of the evening recede, and drank her champagne while they talked about planning for the journey.

A few weeks before they left for America, Sybil returned to her house. Laura worked with Ann to try to make it look its best, but it was so dilapidated now, scuffed and scarred, paint peeling, half the windows boarded up and the doors no longer fitting properly into their jambs. The mice on the top floors scurried and scratched all night, and there was a suspicious smell to the hot water in the faucets, Laura had noticed, as though something had fallen into the tank and died. As Sybil came up the stairs to the front door, both Laura and Ann stood in the hall, and Laura felt almost as though she too were a kind of maid or caretaker, a failed one.

Sybil walked slowly with her up to the first floor, running her hand over the dented banisters. 'It's good to be back,' was all she said at last, and then asked Ann to bring tea to the drawing room, as if it were a pre-war spring Sunday in Belgravia. Laura and Sybil sat together on the one sofa in the room. At first conversation was difficult, and then Laura said

228

how very sorry she had been to hear about Quentin. As soon as the words left her mouth, she was unsure that she had said the right thing, but Sybil turned to her.

'Nobody talks about him. Father never talks about him. Toby never talks about him. It was such an awful waste, you know, they were all retreating . . .' She got up, as though it hurt her to keep still. 'He was the only person I could ever talk to.'

Laura was surprised. She had only observed a rather cold, almost needling relationship between Sybil and her brother in the couple of times she had seen them together. She wondered if Sybil was not guilty of putting on the rose-tinted glasses of the bereaved, but she did not judge her for that. And then she wondered what it meant for Sybil's marriage, if she could not talk to Toby. She simply said, however, how sorry she was.

'At first I just couldn't face seeing anyone,' Sybil said. 'It was a relief, burying myself in the countryside and helping with the evacuees. But I have to face reality now. Toby says there will be a general election quite soon, and he wants me around.' People were coming back to London now that the end was in sight, she said, adding that it was such a pity that Laura and Edward would be leaving soon. Laura could not quite tell, in the formality of her tone, whether she was really sorry or not. Surely she would be glad to have her house back to herself, and indeed, over the days before their departure, Sybil seemed to be trying to do what she could to remind herself of its former splendour. She brought some of the rugs out of storage and had them laid through the big drawing room, but against their glossy warmth the dirty walls looked more depressing than ever, Laura thought.

And a couple of weeks after she returned to London, Sybil asked some of their friends round for drinks. It was still not the time to bring people together, Laura felt; the city was too chaotic, the mood too uncertain, with war not yet over, even if the endgame had begun. But there seemed to be a kind of imperative, for Sybil, in pretending that they could recapture the social ease of the past, and Laura tried to match her alacrity, sitting with her and Toby and Edward in the living room, a glass of Scotch and soda in her hand, as though she was looking forward to the evening.

Laura had met Stefan, she assumed for the last time, that afternoon. He had told her to meet him in a cinema – a new and unexpected instruction. It had been full and she had had difficulty finding him in the fourth row as instructed. Under the cover of the blaring newsreel he had told her the passwords that other contacts might use in America, and thanked her for trying with Blanchard, although even in the dark she felt his disappointment that the bug had not been fitted. Then his attention had turned back to the screen. She had never mentioned to Stefan what had happened to her that evening because of his failure to detain Blanchard; her mind was closing over the experience, burying it deep. And as the newsreel rolled in front of them that afternoon, she was reminded how trivial her own little actions would always be. There above them, in irrefutable black and white, the horrors of fascism, so much greater than anything she could ever had imagined, were being uncovered at last. A cold silence fell through the cinema as they watched the walking corpses. The heroism of the Soviet Army could now never be forgotten. Perhaps this was why Stefan had asked her to meet him here, so that together they could be swept back into certainty.

When Alistair came into the room that evening, complimenting Sybil on her dress, complimenting Edward on his new job, all smiles and dapper gestures, the memory of the night in the Dorchester stirred, and Laura felt the fear again in her stomach, but she kept her composure. She noted how Alistair spoke to her, as if they shared some complicity after those nights of drinking. When Toby said something about the election and the serious mood of the public, Alistair responded in an undertone to her that if the Germans couldn't close the Dorchester, the Labour Party never would. That was the price she had to pay for making him take her about; his assumption that she was the social butterfly she had pretended to be.

But for some reason she still felt at ease with him; he was full of smiling confidence that evening. His novel had finally been published and the reviews had been prominent, even admiring. She had not liked the book; set in a dystopian future, it had shocked her in its obvious belief that the world was set on a path into misery. That seemed a strange view to take now that the world was in fact emerging from the fog of war. While she was reading it she had wondered, did he see everyone like that, like the people in his book – easily controlled, easily cowed? But now he was charming, exuding warmth and teasing her about the life she and Edward would have in Washington, imitating some American officer from the Dorchester and his belief that America was leader of the free world.

Just as she was laughing at what he said, Winifred came in and Laura got up. She wanted to find out what Winifred thought of her imminent departure, and the two of them stepped out onto the balcony that looked out over the huge square. It was not yet time for the blackout. They could stand there, facing away from the room, into the fading light, and Laura could tell Winifred how grateful she was, how she remembered the first time her cousin had brought her here.

But Winifred cut her off, as though Laura was being too sentimental, and asked her instead if she had read Alistair's novel. Laura confessed she hadn't liked it.

'You see, it's what I've always said – he doesn't really believe in people's full humanity. That's how he sees us, like the regimented idiots in his book – the only person Alistair believes in is himself.'

Laura thought Winifred was being too harsh, but rather than argue with her she asked after Giles, and whether he would be coming by that evening. He was still working too

231

hard, Winifred said, it was impossible for him to get away. 'He always thinks he is on the verge of some great discovery. I don't think he will recognise us unless we are plotted on some graph.'

'No . . . Does he have a girlfriend?' Laura realised she had never heard about any relationship of his.

Winifred looked at her in an almost pitying way. 'You are an innocent. You must have noticed that girls aren't his thing at all.' It was Winifred's prickliness in conversations like these, Laura thought, that did not always make her a relaxing person to talk to at parties, and in a way she was not sorry when they had to step back into the room, as the blinds were rolled down. 'It won't be long now,' someone was saying. 'Soon the lights will be going back on.'

'And how boring will that be,' came a reply. 'How will we hide our vices when the cloak of darkness is snatched off us? Our nakedness, darling, all exposed again.' It was Nick, who seemed drunk, even though it was so early.

'You're dragging Edward back to America, I hear?' he said, his attention coming to rest on Laura for the first time that she could remember.

She answered in a serious way, explaining that they were going because Edward had been promoted, turning to him for corroboration, but he was at the other side of the room, sitting on the arm of the sofa, talking to Toby.

'Yes, yes, I know,' Nick said as Laura went on talking, 'he'll be covering for old Halifax in the land of the free. They'll work him hard. He'll miss us, he'll miss all of this so much.' They all seemed to be looking at Edward suddenly, but he was oblivious, deep in conversation, his legs crossed, looking so elegant and assured, Laura thought, the old happiness stirring as she revelled in the knowledge he was hers.

Alistair also said something about how Edward would miss London, and then how lucky it was that Edward had lost his

232

Red sympathies after university. Nick grunted a laugh. 'Bloody lucky he kept his boss sweet, more to the point, even when Halifax was trying to suck up to Hitler before the balloon went up. Edward knows how to keep older men happy, doesn't he? I remember how old Carruthers could hardly operate in 1941 unless Edward was taking the minutes.'

Then both Alistair and Winifred started talking at once, Alistair asking Nick whether he was likely to go back to the BBC after the war, and Winifred telling Laura she must be sure to send her some American stockings once she was settled in Washington. Laura was not sorry when Nick turned away from them and crossed the room towards Edward. As she watched, Nick walked up to him and trailed his fingers across the nape of Edward's neck to get his attention. As Edward looked up, he bent towards him, whispering in his ear.

Laura's attention was now being claimed by Sybil, who wanted her to ask Ann to bring up more glasses, but soon she had had enough of the evening. As soon as she could, she left the room and went up the wide carpetless staircase, into the bedroom with its boarded-up windows where they had lived out the long years of the war. She sat on the edge of the bed, listening to the sound of voices coming up through the floor. She knew she wouldn't miss the group, this drunken and solipsistic circle, who seemed uncowed by the devastations of the last few years. For a while she felt, lying back on the bed, that she might miss this dark city, this scarred house, the first frame of her love. But there will be more rooms that hold happiness, she thought; wherever Edward is posted will simply be a new frame. We will carry our happiness with us. She held onto that sense of promise as she fell asleep.

Earth
Washington, 1945–1950

1

'What a pity that Edward couldn't come this weekend.'
The words were bland, but Laura felt their hard
undertone. She had come alone to where Ellen was spending
the summer on Cape Ann, because Edward was too busy, in
his first months in Washington, to get away. For the week
she had been there, she had felt her solitude as a failure. So
often she had rehearsed her re-entry to her family, and in
her mind she had been an object of admiration, with her
husband by her side, her tales of living through the bombardment and her European experience putting distance between
herself and them.

But as soon as she had arrived she felt a different reality
surround her. She had not moved on from the way she had
always been seen by Ellen. She was still the little sister who
needed to be corrected and pitied; the same little sister whose
dress always seemed to be dirty and crumpled after a day at
school, while Ellen's remained pristine; whose breasts remained
flat while Ellen blossomed into curves; who stood alone for
hours at the first evening party Ellen had taken her to when
she was just fifteen, until Ellen had got some unwilling boy

234

to dance with her. Laura did not speak about such memories with Ellen, but they were there, and sometimes an echo would become almost painful.

That afternoon she had tried to amuse Ellen's daughter while Ellen and her maid prepared the house for Mother's arrival. It was the first time she had looked after such a young child, and when Janet began romping around the living room, pulling cushions off the sofa, Laura sat happily in the middle, glad to see her laugh. There was a wildness about her that came unexpectedly from her small frame. Then Ellen burst in and was irritated by the mess and the noise, and she remembered how Ellen had always been so angry when Laura played with her things when they were children. That doll that Laura had been so jealous of, the one with the long hair made of yellow wool – once Laura had tried to comb the hair and pieces of it had fallen out in chunks. The memory stuck like a barb as Laura asked in a meek voice if there was anything else she could do, paying tribute to Ellen's competence.

Ellen asked her to put a couple of lanterns out on the porch while she gave Janet her bath. It was at that moment that she said what a pity it was that Edward could not be with them, and Laura found herself apologising again for his absence. Surely Ellen understood, Laura thought to herself, that the needs of the embassy in the endgame of the war might overtake the need to come and introduce himself to his sister-in-law.

After tying the lanterns onto the wooden frame of the porch, Laura stayed out in the garden, sucking her finger where a splinter had lodged under the nail. It was too early to light the lanterns, the day was not yet fading. It was as though the ocean were giving up a last luminosity to the sky, and everything was bathed in a salty light. This house that Ellen and Tom were renting for the summer, a worn family home filled with braided rugs and old bric-a-brac, was in a fine setting. Its yard ran all the way down to where grass gave way to pebbles at the edge of the shore. But all she had heard from Ellen during the week she had been there were complaints: the living room was too small, the bathrooms too few, the kitchen too inconvenient down that narrow corridor, and their hired maid too lazy.

Laura recalled how, when they were at school, the most envied girl of all, Mary-Lou Bellingham, had always taken her summer vacation along this part of the coast. She had come back every autumn bearing the physical marks of her privilege – the tan on her long legs, the bleached streaks in her fair hair – and with tales of parties on the beach, flirtations with cousins, sailing and tennis. It had seemed, then, a world away, but now Ellen was a part of it. Laura sat on the porch, looking into the garden, and considered how their lives had moved on and yet between herself and Ellen there was still the same weight of frustration and anger, even if unacknowledged.

Ellen was upstairs settling Janet, and Laura heard Tom's car returning from the station in a crush of gravel, yet she remained outside, listening to Ellen come downstairs to greet Mother. She heard the chatter in the hall, she heard Mother saying, 'So how is she?' and she heard Ellen say, 'Oh, you know Laura,' with a bitterness in her voice. She stayed still, eager to hear what they did know, but then they all came out onto the porch and saw her standing there, and their conversation was overtaken in the embrace that Laura and Mother had failed to complete more than six years ago.

'Well,' said Tom as they broke away from one another, 'you can't miss the family resemblance here.'

Laura was not flattered. As they sat down, she looked at Mother's over-made-up face, in which a determined girlishness kept warring with the lines that age and sadness had drawn on it – was that really what she looked like? Or was that her future face? Mother was thinner – she had always wanted to stay slim, disapproving of women who got fat – but there

236

was a slackness now about her slenderness, as though by losing flesh she had lost energy. Tom offered them drinks, and Laura asked for a highball, which was what she knew Tom usually drank, though Mother and Ellen stuck to lemonade.

As she sucked down the first cold gulps, Laura asked about Father; she knew already from Ellen that his chest was worse and he was very sick now. Laura remembered his cough from the past. It had been deep and rasping, though his voice was light for a man's, and he would try to suppress it over breakfast as he lit his first cigarette.

'I don't know why you didn't insist he come,' Ellen was saying to Mother, 'the sea air would have done him good, and Laura hasn't seen him for so long.' That was characteristic of Ellen; she was always the one whose self-righteous certainty made others doubt themselves. Mother said little, and Laura found herself unexpectedly in sympathy with her; she seemed almost to quail under Ellen's critical voice. Laura looked at Tom as she thought about Ellen's character; how rigid she always was, unable to see anyone else's point of view. How would it be to fall in love with someone like that?

But from their first meeting Tom had been opaque to Laura. She had learned something from Ellen's letters during the war about his background, his connection to those envied Bellinghams, and about how he had been excused military service due to a heart murmur. Those facts had led Laura to invest him with some aura of glamour or delicacy; his actual presence, red-faced and inarticulate, was puzzling, as was his attitude to Ellen. He seemed not to notice her complaints, but treated her with a kind of casual dismissiveness.

After a while they stood up to go into dinner and Laura felt the drink weighing down her movements, but when she sat down she asked Tom if she could have a beer along with him. She said it in a light tone, as though she simply wanted to try what he was drinking, but in fact she felt thirsty for the cold bubbles. She did not see how she could get through evening after evening here, already she could feel a needling pain rising up through her shoulders, which were hunched up to her neck as if to protect herself. She looked at Ellen, and saw that her mouth was folded together as if she too was struggling for composure. But then Laura felt rebuked when Ellen caught her eye and smiled, and said something about how wonderful it was that they were all back together again.

'All except Father,' said Laura.

'Yes, things aren't really very good with him,' Mother said, but then she was distracted, or chose to be distracted, by the plate that the maid, Ora, was passing her. 'Not so much for me, and no sauce – my stomach can't take such rich food, Ellen.'

'You don't have to watch your figure, Mother,' Laura said. Her mother shook her head.

'You know it isn't that, Laura, but . . .'

But yes, God forbid that you should ever relax, Laura thought, drinking the beer Tom had brought her and taking the rejected plate for herself. Already, Ellen was into her usual complaints about how much work this summer was creating for her. Tom's brother was to arrive that evening; he had been wounded – a shattered wrist – in the Pacific, Tom was explaining, although both Laura and Mother already knew the story. His month's convalescence leave had just started, and the hope was that he would not have to return to service, that demobilisation would overtake the end of his stay. Ellen was wondering if he would mind that dark room at the end of the corridor, and Laura was saying in a small voice that maybe it would be easier if she went into a hotel. Tom talked over them, enthusiastic about the possibility of more people in the house. He wanted to get the tennis courts rolled. It was a pity the garden here had become such a mess; he remembered it from years back, it had been a great place then.

Laura remembered the garden at Sutton Court, and started to tell them about it – the long formal hedges and the rose garden all turned over to vegetables for the war, the meadow given to grazing. She realised almost as soon as she started speaking that it was as though she was telling a fairy tale, something childish, about a distant and uninteresting land. She had noticed this reaction time and again whenever she started to say something about England and the war. It was natural, she told herself – why would her family want to hear about the wartime deprivations she had known; as if America had not made its sacrifices, was not still making its sacrifices? She stayed almost silent for the rest of the meal, and as they went into the living room she realised that her back was damp with sweat, even in her cotton dress.

In the living room the windows had been left open, and moths were blundering around the lamps. Ellen exclaimed in irritation, pulling the blinds down over the windows and flapping a magazine at the insects. Laura had quite forgotten about Tom's brother, and when they heard a taxi drawing up, for a moment she thought it could be Edward after all, and she went out to the door with Tom. There was a tangle of roses by the door, and as she brushed past them their scent seemed almost wet, it was so refreshing in the night air.

'God, this is a nice spot, Tom – just like the old days.' Kit was at first glance rather like Tom, the same fairish, freckly colouring. But there was grace in his manner as he threw the butt of the cigarette he was smoking onto the gravel and advanced into the house with what was almost a dancer's posture, his feet turned out.

Once in the living room and furnished with a cold beer and another cigarette, Kit was the centre of attention, as Ellen and Tom began to quiz him about his health and his plans after demobilisation. His wrist, he said, was completely recovered. It was his left hand anyway, and as good as new now. As he talked in a rather diffident way about how he was thinking of going into journalism, Laura realised that the attention bothered him. She sympathised with his obvious shyness and wondered what he had been living through; it

239

was much harder to imagine him in active service than it was to imagine Tom there – particularly dressed as he was tonight, in a pale lavender shirt and cream pants. Now he was talking about a friend of his who was also eager for demobilisation, a man called Joe, who had been a newspaper man until he had enlisted, who was planning to go back into it, probably in Washington; it sounded like a good life – Kit was thinking of something like that.

Laura found her mind travelling back to the Joe she had known, with his anecdotes about reporting and travelling, and without thinking she said, 'I met a journalist called Joe,' and although Ellen obviously thought she was interrupting the conversation, Kit turned to her and they started discussing the journalists they knew until they realised it was the same man, one Joe Segal, and that the strange vagaries of fate had led them to know him at different times, on different boats, six years apart from one another. Laura thought little of it in the moment, simply smiling and nodding, exclaiming about the coincidence.

But as she gained her room that night, she realised how the discovery had destabilised her. Joe, smiling at her in the smoky bar, his hand warm on her leg on the dark deck. There was no escape from memories; the memories of her childhood that Mother and Ellen brought with them, and now the memory of those days when she thought she was escaping. She felt the web of the past restricting her, pulling her back when she thought she could move forwards.

She woke blearily to breakfast the next day, and found that the influx of new people into the house had energised Tom. He was insisting that they should all go sailing, and had borrowed a boat from a neighbour he had known from childhood. Ellen demurred, saying that she had to stay back with Janet, and Mother said that she didn't see how, with her knees, she could clamber in and out of a boat. Part of Laura also longed to stay back in the shade of the garden; the air would be damp and cool under the old elm tree. But that was where Mother would be lying all day in a deckchair. It was better to get out, then, onto the sea.

When she went down to the beach, Tom and Kit were reminiscing about making exactly this same trip in the past; they were talking about their parents, about old neighbours, about the time when their boat had sunk and they had been stranded in a distant bay for a whole day and half a night. She felt out of step with them; she was just a passenger, and while they were soon busy with ropes and sails and anchors, she was clumsy and tentative in the boat which seemed so unpredictable, and she sat gingerly on the wooden benches.

The short trip in the small boat felt exposed, out on the naked water under the cloudless sky, but when they got round to the cove that Tom was aiming for, Laura could see its charm; it was enclosed, hard to scramble down to from the road. There was just one other family there already, an image of what Tom and Kit's must have been years ago: a silver-haired father with tall adolescent boys. Laura stumbled getting out of the boat – the rocks were slippery under her sandshoes – and Kit reached out a hand to help her, but his fingers seemed inert on hers.

'We must swim,' Tom ordered, and obediently they shed their outer layers. Tom and Kit swam far out, as if racing one another, but there was a breeze coming off the sea now and Laura stayed standing in the shallows, goose pimples coming up on her arms. 'Don't you swim?' Kit said to her as he came back in, and Laura told him not to worry about her. They wanted to recreate something from their past, and although they were polite to her, she felt that she was a drag on their enjoyment. Soon after a picnic lunch they decided to return; Laura wondered whether they would have stayed longer without her.

When the boat was moored, it was a long walk back up the shore to the house. Laura excused herself and went in, going upstairs without talking to Mother and Ellen, whom she could see on the lawn. This week, she had gotten into the lazy habit of sleeping for a while in the afternoon, and she pulled off her slacks and her bathing costume and slid into bed, realising as her sandy legs rubbed against the linen that she would have to shake the sheets out later. She had already fallen asleep when she heard a hard rap on the door – 'Laura?' For a moment she wasn't sure where she was, coming too quickly out of unconsciousness into this high, hard bed and the sunlit room, but then she saw Edward standing by the bed.

'I wasn't expecting—'

'I know – I managed to get away, things had quietened down for the weekend, but I have to get back Monday morning. I called from the station – your brother-in-law picked me up. Is there room for me there?'

Laura rolled to one side and opened her arms. 'I'm all sticky and sandy,' she said, with happy expectation, as Edward pulled off his tie and his shoes, but as soon as he got into bed he simply said, 'I'm so tired,' and, putting one hand on her shoulder, he closed his eyes. Laura watched his face as he fell asleep. She could relax now. Nothing in the past could touch her, not now she had her present and future beside her.

She was full of easy anticipation when they went down to dinner that evening. How patrician Edward looked, pausing at the foot of the stairs to wait for her to come down, his light hair luminous in the shadows, his green gaze resting on her. Now that they could see the quality, the beauty, the intelligence of the man who loved her, she would take on a different value in her family's eyes. She felt released, finally, from the burden of being the old Laura as they went into the living room.

It was odd, though, to see how pale and tired Edward looked next to the other men; Kit must have picked up his bronzed sheen on the ship and Tom from the beach. What's more, the other two were in soft-coloured shirts, without ties or blazers, and when Kit crossed his legs you could see the flash of a bare ankle above his loafers, but Edward had dressed as he always did at weekends, in a flannel jacket and white shirt and tie. In England, Laura realised, Edward had always worn precisely what all the other men of his class did, right down to the design of his shoes and the colour of his tie. There, he knew line by line whatever unspoken codes governed men's clothes, but here he seemed to be working in another language, and its formality made him look absent-minded, as if he had not expected to find himself here, in the heat of summer and the languor of a vacation.

Tom and Kit were quick to include him in their conversation, asking him about work and telling him about people they knew in Washington. As Laura listened to them talk, she remembered how struck she had been when she first met him by the glacial pace of Edward's conversation, and how the chatter of his friends slowed down to meet his rhythms. But what had seemed part of his unquestionable authority in London now seemed less sure-footed. Kit soon overtook his slow responses with a quick anecdote he had heard about the editor of a Washington newspaper, and when they moved to the dining room to eat, Ellen and Mother seemed to be struggling to get anything out of Edward. 'And your ambassador?' Kit suddenly asked, throwing a conversational ball down to Edward's end of the table, to Laura's relief, continuing something that Tom had said about the effect of the war. 'What does he think of the future of the empire?'

Laura knew that Edward would shine, as he always did, with his inside knowledge of the powerful players in British government. But he simply forked up another piece of duck, and said in a rather toneless voice, 'There's an inevitability about the way things are moving.'

Kit said something about Halifax's point of view being moulded by his own career, and when Tom asked him what he meant, he explained that Halifax had once run India.

'I heard someone say that the Indians are the biggest problem that Britain will face after the war,' Tom said.

'I don't know about that,' Edward said in his slow manner. 'You don't have any problem with *your* Indians, of course. You killed them all.'

For a moment Laura did not pick up the extraordinary rudeness of his statement, as it was delivered with such diffidence, but when she did she turned to Mother and said, 'It was so lovely going out sailing today. You should try it before you go. It's a pity we never learned to sail.'

'There are so many things we didn't learn,' said Ellen. 'I can't even play tennis.'

'I always wish I'd learned to play the piano,' said Laura, but she was only talking for the sake of it, trying to move the conversation away from her husband.

The next morning the light seemed to have shifted up to a different wattage. Was it just her hangover that made it so ferociously bright, Laura wondered as she drew back the curtains? Over breakfast Tom insisted that everyone should come out to swim that day. The preparations seemed to take so much time and so much discussion about what was needed, from Janet's hat to bottles of lemonade. It was a little way, just far enough to feel tiresome to walk, to the beach that was good for swimming, and each of them felt as though they were carrying too heavy a load.

This time Laura went into the sea, walking into the great greenish waves until they reached her shoulders, and swam until the cold clamped her chest too fiercely. Even in the sunlight, the ocean water was freezing at depth. She swam back in and walked up the sand, shuddering.

'Your mouth is blue,' said Ellen, who was beached in a deckchair. Laura flung herself down on a towel, and looked back into the rinsing sea, and saw Edward swimming further out than all the others, right into the horizon that was too

244

bright to look at. He came out last, when everyone else was already lying on towels and deckchairs under the three big beach umbrellas pushed into the sand. As he came towards them, he seemed transfigured by his swim. There were droplets running all over his shoulders and his hair was slicked back; he was framed in light.

For the first time since leaving London, Laura felt the cloud of war lift from her. Was it going to be all right, would peace inflect their lives again, in a country ready to re-dedicate itself to comfort? The sky was high and silent, and all along the shore they could see families playing in places they had known from childhood.

'Would you like to build a sandcastle?' Edward asked little Janet. She was too shy to reply at first, and it surprised Laura, who had never seen him with a child before, when Edward took her spade and started to mark out and dig a moat. Then Janet responded with pleasure, toddling up and down to the water with her bucket. 'It won't stay in the moat, wait till the tide comes up,' Ellen admonished her. Laura began to sort the stones beneath her fingers, picking out white ones for the castle walls. Smooth, rough, small, big, the pebbles fell through her fingers in their uncountable diversity.

The sun began to strike fiercely at their faces, and Laura rummaged in her bag for a hat. It was a big straw hat that she had borrowed from Ellen, having nothing suitable herself, and unexpectedly Edward bent under it and touched her nose. 'I believe you're getting freckles,' he said. As they walked up the beach back to the house for lunch, Janet put her hand into Laura's: a sudden shock of sweetness, this touch of small fingers.

After lunch, Tom insisted on tennis, and Laura remembered Edward and Giles playing at Sutton, and recognised echoes of the upper class from England to America – serious about their games, honing what they thought was character with boats and bats and rackets. As she sat with Ellen and Mother and Janet, she heard the men laughing as they reached for the balls and argued over points. She walked over to watch them and saw that now Edward seemed to have lost some of the weight he was carrying, he and the others were as full of their physicality as children. But it was not childish, she knew; there was status at stake as they drove the balls to one another, and she was disproportionately glad that her husband was prepared to join in these games that were only superficially trivial.

After the game Edward looked at her, his eyes crinkling around the edges. They went hurriedly upstairs, and before dressing for dinner made hungry love. What did it remind her of, the absolute surrender to his sun-warmed body? Lying there in the aftermath, she remembered. 'It's like that summer at Sutton in the phoney war,' she said.

'It's always the phoney war,' Edward said, and his words were enigmatic to her.

'Why were you so awful last night?'

Edward looked puzzled. He had got out of bed and was standing naked by the closet, looking for a clean shirt. 'Was I?'

'Don't wear a tie tonight—'

'You have to wear a tie with a shirt like this.'

'Please. You sounded so distracted last night.'

'Was I? I'm sorry if I wasn't much fun. I'll be more on top of things tonight. Washington tires you out. It's the heat, I think, and—'

'I know, I've been so tired too. I think it is coming away from the war.'

'That reminds me,' Edward said, 'I've got a message for you. It's not Stefan, it's—'

'I don't want to hear it tonight,' Laura said. 'Tell me tomorrow.' It wasn't that she had given up on the work, but something in her wanted to hold onto the mood of their lovemaking, the rinsed, voluptuous summer mood, for a few more hours.

But it was pointless for her to wish for pleasure, because the telephone that was now ringing in the hall was ringing

246

for Mother, with news of Father's death. The summer's promise was already withdrawn.

What a horrible fraud Laura felt, sitting with Ellen and Mother through the long night in the first rush of their grief. The beat of guilt rather than sadness drummed through her. Why had she not gone straight to Stairbridge when they arrived, rather than following Edward to Washington and then coming out to the coast to see Ellen? Why had she not realised that it was not Father's laziness that prevented him from coming to join Mother here? Why had she not come home years ago, to see if she could salvage some kind of relationship from the years of disappointment and misunderstanding? What kind of daughter had she been? She could say little of all this to the others, of course, because when she began to speak of her guilt, she could see in their eyes that they agreed she had done wrong.

The next day they began to prepare for the journey back to Stairbridge. Tom was all busyness, arranging to come with them, and telling Kit to close up the house, as they would not be back that summer. Laura went upstairs to pack her few things, the couple of new cotton dresses, the white sandals, the paperbacks she had bought for the summer. Edward was sitting on the bed as she packed, and she came over to him, letting him hold her, but she could not relax into his arms. 'It's all right,' she said. 'You go back to Washington. I know you can't get time off work. I'll let you know when the funeral will be and you can come for the day.'

'Is that all right?' he asked, but there was relief in his voice.

2

The church was not empty. Custom and expectation cover up a man's worst failures, and although Laura had little awareness of her father's friends or the sporadic work he had done here and there, designing renovations for houses on the cheap, he had left enough of a trail through ordinary society for a number of people to be sitting with them the following Wednesday for his funeral.

Edward was not beside her; he had been called back to London, absurdly, for a huge conference of European leaders. He was skimming the skies with Halifax on an aeroplane while she was grounded in Stairbridge, trying to recognise familiar faces in the small group of people who came back to their childhood home for drinks after the funeral. Hands clutched hers, voices asked her about her husband. She found herself standing with two elderly men who, she thought, had once done building work to her father's designs. Their conversation stuttered to a stop, and then she found that the two men were talking, instead, about the bombs. They could not find it in their hearts to be sorry about the deaths in Japan; one had a son who had been standing by to go across. Oh, it was kill or die, the other said, and then they realised how inappropriate their conversation might sound to Laura, and stopped. She smiled at them, and walked on.

The house itself was looking so much better than she remembered. Grandfather's legacy had been put to good use here. Laura did not like Mother's taste, but at least the veneer cabinets with their spindly legs and the yellow sofas were shiny and new, and there was clean decking at the back door and lilies in green vases on the mantelpieces. But even now there was a smell she remembered – what was it? Maybe the scent of the brewery blowing from the west of the town or rotting food from the trash outside the kitchen door, something bitter that the perfume of the lilies could not cover.

There was a photograph album out on the tables. Laura did not want to look at it, but at one point Ellen passed it to her, and she saw herself standing next to Father on the front steps in a forgotten green dress. Before Grandfather's legacy had transformed her life, it had been her only party dress, and even that had been passed down from Ellen. 'Look at you, so young,' Mother said. She said it in a longing voice, as if they were looking at a picture of happiness. But the picture . . . the picture. Laura put it down.

She had forgotten that evening – no, you never forget, but you bury it deep – the night of her high school dance, how she had longed not to be the symbol of social failure. At least a boy was taking her to it, even if it was only Walt Eaves. She could not stand his flat-footed walk and the way he talked down to Cristel, their coloured maid, but at least he had asked her, it was a chance. The evening had been horrible enough – when he kissed her it was like being choked, and she had pushed him away and said, let's go in, Father will be waiting. And he was, but as soon as they came in she saw it, she smelt it, the drink, the stumbling, and Father came too close to her, and asked what she had been up to – it was as if she had to be shamed. She would not follow the memory, down the path where Walt had looked at her with pity in his stupid eyes. Her shame – she would not allow it. How could they grieve, she thought, looking at Ellen and Mother mouthing their platitudes? The perfect façade of drinking their tea and telling half-hearted stories about Father's favourite books would keep all the memories hidden in the dark. But the stain was spreading now in Laura's mind, and she felt her hand shake as she picked up her cup of tea: she could not swallow it and had to put it down.

After the guests had left, they sat in the living room facing one another on the new long sofas. 'You must come to us in Boston,' Ellen was saying to Mother, returning to a theme that she had already opened up the previous day. 'There's lots of room for you. Janet will love to have you with us.'

'It seems an awful lot for you – and for Tom.' With Mother's words, a gap opened in the conversation for Laura to make some offer. But she said nothing.

'You should come back with us tomorrow,' Ellen said again, pressing.

'But there's so much to do here . . .' Mother gestured to the rooms around her.

'You can come back and sort out Father's things when you've had a break. You can't do it all when you're still in such shock. Laura or I will come back with you next month.'

Laura was still sitting in her puddle of silence. She saw a glance pass between Ellen and Mother. She got up and picked up the teacups and took them into the kitchen. She stood at the window, looking down the street where the trees seemed dusty now at the end of summer. How often had she looked down at that view! Yet she remembered it being larger than this, the houses more looming. She realised she had dreamt about this street since she had left, and in her dreams it had had such an aura of menace that now the reality seemed oddly quotidian. She would not stay, now that her path away was clear. She went back to the living room. 'Is there any brandy?' she said. 'Couldn't we all do with some?'

On her way back to Washington, the inertia she had felt throughout the funeral stayed with her. Perhaps over the last six years she had become too used to the small scale of the English countryside, its low skies and patterned fields, because as she looked out of the train window on the way back to the city, she felt she could hardly comprehend the scale: everything looked too big and the train seemed to be tiny, scuttling through the hills and forests. And the entry into Washington itself overwhelmed her – the humid, dirty air as she left the station, the pulse and roar of the traffic. She had hardly taken in the city in their first weeks there; just the wholeness of the streets and all the brash colour in the store windows had been strange enough without noticing any details. But in the taxi back to their apartment in Connecticut Avenue she felt she was passing through streets built on too massive a scale, oppressive in their inhuman size. Except for the apartment itself, which was miniature, a little box with a clattering tiled floor. They were lucky to have it, she knew. The city was crowded. Everyone was flocking here, to the heart of the new empire.

Laura looked into the icebox, where there was nothing but some sliced cheese and a half-drunk bottle of gin, and ate and drank some of both. The air in the apartment was thick and even when she opened the windows she felt as though she could hardly breathe. It was one of those heavy days she had already come to know in Washington, when the heat beat back off the pavements all day and into the night. Away to the south, dark clouds hung in the sky and the light seemed brassy, but even when the storm broke she knew that the pressure would hardly lift. The tastes of the gin and the cheese went badly together, and she felt nauseous, sitting on the sofa and listening to the radio with a magazine on her lap when Edward's key turned in the door late that evening. He bent to hold her, but she was unmoving in his embrace, feeling the sweat spring between their arms where they touched. 'I am so sorry I didn't get to the funeral,' he said.

Laura told him it didn't matter, and asked him for news of London. She would much rather hear about their friends there than talk about her childhood home. Edward started telling some story about how hard Toby was finding life without his parliamentary seat, but Laura was slow to respond. 'Your mother, how is she taking it?' Edward asked.

'No different from what one might expect. Have you eaten?'

'I've been eating round the corner. Let's go.'

They had gone to this restaurant on their first night in Washington, but now the steaks seemed quite a normal size rather than some absurd mistake, larger than a week's ration. At least here the air conditioning blew hard and cooled the sweat on their cheeks. Because it was so noisy it did not matter that Laura found it hard to talk, and Edward had other stories of their friends in London, as well as plans for the next few weeks. 'I've got an invitation for you to the embassy luncheon this Saturday,' he remembered at one point. 'I was going to reply for you and say no, but then I thought maybe you'd like to have something to do – I mean, something different, new people to meet. Remind me to give the note to you.'

As they walked back, the thunder sounded and rain began to steam on the sidewalks. Neither of them had brought an umbrella, and when Laura caught sight of them in the lobby mirror as they went into the apartment block she was struck by how bedraggled they looked, her damp hair sticking to her face and her mascara smudged. Before they went to bed, Edward gave the note to her, a few impersonal lines from Lady Halifax. Laura looked at it and wondered if it would be a formal affair, but Edward said not, and that he would go over there early as Halifax liked a game of doubles before lunch. Laura turned that over in her mind: that pale, thin man playing tennis with his subalterns in the embassy garden. Strangely, she dreamt about it that night, but in her dreams Edward and the other men were playing with snowballs – 'Don't worry, your lordship!' he was saying as they melted in the sun. 'Your point, I think!' She walked onto the court in the dream, and a snowball landed on her arm, but as it melted it left a red stain.

The next morning as Edward was about to go out of the door, he suddenly stopped. 'Do you have the reply for Lady Halifax?'

'I thought you'd tell them I'd be coming—'

'If she writes, you have to write.'

He waited while Laura found a piece of paper to scrawl her acceptance on; the ink smudged, but she folded it anyway and pushed it into an envelope.

That Saturday, after Edward had left for his game of tennis, Laura found herself going through her closet without relish. The couple of summer dresses she had bought to take to Ellen's house in Portstone seemed out of the question – they were too obviously vacation clothes – but her entire wartime wardrobe was also impossible with its shabby, skimpy lines. So she took out the only possible things she had: the clothes she had bought in Stairbridge for the funeral, a pleated black silk skirt and tight black jacket with elbow-length sleeves.

She walked the short distance over to Massachusetts Avenue, past well-kept houses with liriope and pansies blossoming by their front steps, smoking a cigarette, barely noticing the river flashing among the richly coloured trees. In the aftermath of the storm the weather had cooled a little, but in the embassy garden the air was unstirring around the English women on the garden terrace, all of them dressed in similar printed dresses, whether they were in their twenties or their sixties.

'Mr Last is just finishing a game with my husband. He's rather pleased that they have players for doubles now,' Lady Halifax told Laura when they were introduced, folding her mouth down at the end of each sentence.

'Yes, Edward likes it too – it was always hard in London to find a chance to play.'

'Hard on the chaps if there isn't an opportunity.'

'It was hard in London,' agreed another woman. 'Very nice here, Lady Halifax, to have the space, you know.'

'The garden is really the thing.'

'It is, isn't it? The garden really is something.'

'Awfully special,' another woman agreed, and so they went on, with Laura echoing alongside them.

When the men came up onto the terrace, however, the chorus faltered for a while.

'Ah, so this is Mrs Last,' said Lord Halifax, with that accidental charm that his wife failed to show. 'And you are a born American – how nice for you to be able to come home.'

'I grew up near Boston, not here,' said Laura.

'Yes, it's rather different in America, isn't it? So big – a native of one city feels quite out of place in another . . .' Lady Halifax went on talking, and her female chorus backed her with a twitter of sentences about how different every American city is, but how if you are born in one part of England all of it is your home.

At lunch Laura was seated between two men of about Edward's age. One of them, Archie Platt, turned to her with immediate good manners. He was fairish and tall. It was only really his poor skin, which was reddening and pimpled, which made him unattractive.

'So, the wife of the golden boy joins us at last!' Laura knew she should be pleased to hear Edward described that way, although she wondered whether there wasn't a hint of mockery in Archie's voice. 'Last can do no wrong, you know. Not just with his backhand, either. Tell me, Last, how did you manage to write that report last week when we weren't even allowed notebooks in the meeting? It was so top secret,' he said, turning back to Laura, 'that the Americans said we couldn't write anything in the room, but Last seemed to recall every detail. I must say I was still struggling to tell one American from another.'

Although Archie's praise was lavish, Laura felt a particular kind of English game at work, which she had got to know in London. It was that game in which it was subtly suggested that it was bad form for the person being praised to be trying so hard to succeed, and that the one who was praising was in fact holding the power, even as he seemed to be putting himself down, by showing that he didn't have to make such efforts. She was pleased when Archie's wife Monica joined the conversation and moved it on, asking Laura what she was planning to do in Washington and whether she was going to get involved in charity work. Her horsey face, brightly made up, was smiling, but Laura had to say that she didn't have any plans, and then was afraid that she might have sounded rude. 'Do please find something for me to do,' she said.

'Gosh, you'll be able to take your choice, then – it's all funds for the wounded with me, and all displaced children if you go with Veronica. Stick with me, our supporters are much more fun,' she said.

Laura nodded, but after a while she heard Edward mentioning to Lady Halifax that she had recently suffered a bereavement. 'My condolences, Mrs Last,' her fluting voice came down the table. Laura wondered why Edward, who was usually so private, had put her misery on show. After that she made even less effort to join the conversation, and sat there turning over her food with a fork, feeling like a black crow among the chattering English flocks.

When they got home, late in the afternoon, a silence fell between them. Edward walked towards the drinks cabinet. Laura asked if he really needed another drink, and wondered at the shrewish tone that seemed to have come into her voice. He put down the bottle of whisky.

'How would you like to spend the evening?' The words could have been interpreted as an olive branch, but Laura was in a stubborn mood after what she had sensed was her social failure at lunch, and she failed to take it, shaking her head.

'I don't know – I don't know.'

'This isn't my city either, you know,' he said.

Laura couldn't agree. The people at the embassy were part of the group, and just as in London she was beginning to recognise that she would never be at home in it.

'Shall we go and see a film?' Edward asked.

'You hate American movies, you've told me so.'

'We can go and see one if you want.'

'The night we heard,' she said, 'you told me you had a message for me. You never told me what it was.'

'I thought this wasn't the time. When you're ready, they want you to go and visit the Botanical Gardens on Tuesday morning, any Tuesday at eleven.'

So all the wheels had gone on turning. 'This Tuesday is fine,' she said, and took the glass that Edward held out. 'Let's go see that movie.'

Out on F Street there was a rush of energy: too many people, government secretaries, young soldiers desperate for demobilisation, all drunk with the promise of Saturday night, striding in and out of the bars that were brilliant with neon. Laura had forgotten that a city could be like this; all the unquenched lights, the arrogant voices, the unbroken streets. Cinema after cinema had 'standing room only' signs, until at last they found one that showed second runs. Edward slept during the movie, but Laura could lose herself for a while in the satisfying dance of a thriller which suggested that people's secrets are always knowable and explicable. Still, her mood did not lift and when they made love that night, for the first time ever she lost the rhythm of their desire. Their hands, their mouths, their bodies moved against one another, but the energy seemed mechanical. She found herself startlingly apart from Edward even as he came to the crescendo, and as he withdrew her eyes filled with tears. It seemed so wrong that they had gone through the motions without finding one another.

Who goes to the Botanical Gardens in the rain? When Laura saw the wet streets on Tuesday morning she wondered if she should wait for another week, but she remembered how she had always been Stefan's good girl, clever Pigeon, and that drove her on. She put on a raincoat she had brought from London and found an umbrella. Out of habit she took a circuitous route, studying the map carefully before she left so that she could double back on herself once or twice, but there was nobody looking at her through those sheets of rain. Entering the gardens, she was about to walk around the sodden park and then, realising that such behaviour would be conspicuously odd, she went into the huge conservatory. Here, in her raincoat and scarf, the warmth became oppressive. She was going back towards the entrance when she became aware of someone walking a little more quickly behind her, and she stopped as if admiring the lavish display. Sure enough, the stranger, a short man with an umbrella that he was holding away from his body, came closer. They exchanged the passwords that Laura had been given in London in a half-whisper and went on walking. 'It's too quiet here,' he said, 'follow me,' and they went up to the platform in the next room where the drumming of the rain on the roof provided some cover to their words.

Because they were both standing with heads averted, and he was wearing a hat and trench coat, Laura could hardly see him. She turned to get a good look so that she would recognise him at future meetings, and he shook his head and muttered to her not to show such interest.

'Just in case I—'

'We won't be meeting again. I know you worked in England, but it's too risky here to have you working too. I've been asked to thank you.'

'So this is it?'

'This is it.' He was about to move off.

'Wait – what if there is an emergency? In London I had a code.'

'You must work through your—'

'I mean, if he can't—'

'Then keep silent. This is a hard place to work. If I have to get in touch with you for any reason, the same password, the name Alex, here at this time.'

There were footsteps on the iron staircase below them, and Laura moved away from him. When she looked back, he was gone. Although she thought she had come reluctantly to this meeting, Laura was surprised at the shock of disappointment she felt after his departure, as she walked on through the hot, damp room. It was as though a thread that bound this Laura here to the Laura she had built up in London over the last few years had been cut. What would now give direction to her days?

She put up her umbrella as she left the park, and started walking back through the driving rain. This time she took a direct route back. Her shoes and stockings were already soaking, and as she walked she became more and more disheartened. She felt that she moved too slowly among these huge lines of brick and stone. Even when she got to the smaller streets near to the apartment, she felt lost in the grid of the city where nobody cared where she was or what she did.

The apartment was empty. Of course it was. Edward left early each morning and then there was only ever Laura herself to put on the radio, to turn it off again, to lie on the sofa and then plump the cushions, to scatter crumbs and wipe them up. She cut herself a sandwich and sat in the sterile kitchen, eating it. When the telephone rang, it sounded loud in the emptiness. Laura had to ask the caller's name a couple of times before she remembered who Monica was, and why she was asking her to come to a coffee morning the following week to plan a dinner for the charity she supported.

When Laura went along to the coffee morning, she found that her oddness in being an American among the English wives was cancelled out by the fact that Monica took to her. It was that moment when Monica imitated something that Lady Halifax had said and Laura was the only woman in the room to laugh that brought them together. Monica did not take the vaunted charity work all that seriously, but it was an outlet for her energies and Laura was happy enough to execute little duties for the fundraising evening under her direction. Because she was American, Monica assumed she would know her way around Washington, but of course she knew nobody in the city yet. So when Ellen wrote to tell her that Kit had moved to Washington to pursue his vague dream of working on a newspaper, she telephoned him and invited him to the dinner. She was going to be a good sister-in-law, a good Washington wife; she was determined to play her part. Kit accepted the invitation and said he would bring a friend.

But when it came to the charity event itself, a couple of

months later, Laura was surprised by how reluctant she felt to go. Edward was to meet her at the Mayflower, and Laura struggled against an odd sense of sick apprehension as she got dressed. She could not cancel, she had to go and greet Kit, who would know nobody else there. But as he entered the huge room, she saw he was not alone. Looking around the room with his eyes narrowed, lighting a cigarette, there was Joe Segal at Kit's side. 'Of course,' Laura said, trying to sound at ease as they came up to greet her, 'you said you had met in the Navy – how good of you to bring—'

'Fate!' Joe said, putting his hands out to touch her shoulders and smiling at her with a physical directness that seemed, despite the passage of years, familiar. His sunburnt skin and closely cropped hair were new, but he was the same man who had broken through the first conversation that she had had with Florence in the smoky bar on the *Normandie*. As they exchanged pleasantries, his mind was clearly moving on the same path. 'That girl you were travelling with – what was her name? Do you still see her?'

No, Laura was not going to bring Florence into this crowded room. If you surround someone with silence for long enough, they have a life within you. 'I was travelling alone. That girl Maisie – is that who you mean? She was a dancer, wasn't she?'

'Maisie!' Joe was immediately eager to share a story with her. 'I saw her and her sister in a show in London a couple of years later, when I was coming back from France . . .' As he talked, Laura remembered how he loved to arrange his experiences into tales, and despite herself she was warmed again by his social energy. Soon Monica came up to them, and had to be told the full story of the strange coincidence, of how Joe and Laura had met years ago, although she was not really listening, because really it was of interest to nobody except Laura and Joe.

When the dinner started, Joe and Kit were at a table with Laura and Edward, and beside them were a department store owner and his wife, and a senator and his wife. The men seemed to expect the women to make the social effort for them, but in fact Kit and Joe were the only ones at the table who bothered to move the conversation on. Laura noticed that Kit seemed almost anxious on Joe's behalf, eager to introduce him to people and to explain how he worked at the newspaper, to smooth the way for him. She would not have thought of it if Kit's own social anxiety had not suggested it, but of course, she realised, Joe was out of place here; not only a journalist, but a Jew – not even a rich Jew – and it was only his buoyant social confidence that meant he could be pulled into the evening.

Laura left the table at one point before dessert, and went into the ladies' room. The reappearance of Joe in her life had left her unmoored; not so much, she thought, because of him as because of the memories he brought with him. She would not speak of the girl with dark hair who bestrode the boat journey in her memory, but she was all about her now. What would she say to Laura, if she were here? Laura was standing by the basins, looking blankly at her own face in the mirror but seeing another's, when Monica came in too. 'Goodness, you look awful,' Monica said with characteristic frankness. 'What's up – hungover? Sick? Pregnant?'

'All three, I think,' Laura said, but it was only as she spoke that the unconscious knowledge became conscious, pushing like a plant from her body to her mind and voice. The heaviness in her breasts, the sickness in her stomach, the tiredness in her legs; she had not let herself examine those or her missed cycle, but now, in response to Monica, the knowledge became real. She avoided Monica's eyes, suddenly guilty that she had spoken of it first in this way, and washed her hands as she cut off Monica's cry of congratulations and made her way back to the dinner.

Now Laura began to lose the ability to concentrate on the conversations that eddied around them. She remembered the night when she thought it must have happened, and it seemed

260

a cruel irony that it had been the only time they had made love and she had not felt close to Edward. She could not respond properly when Kit and Joe got up from the table to say they were leaving, thanking her for the invitation, making plans to see her again. She needed to get away from this crush. When the long evening of speeches and music was over, and just she and Edward were in a cab heading home, she could tell him at last. It took few words, to communicate such a momentous change.

Edward turned to her in the back seat of the taxi and crushed her into his arms. Her nose was so pushed against his shoulder that she could hardly breathe. 'A new life,' he whispered into her hair, 'you are wonderful.' Laura wanted to feel wonderful, but as she moved her face her hair caught in his watch. She sat forward to untangle it, feeling clumsy for breaking the moment.

3

'It will be just right for us now.' They were standing in the narrow hallway of a small house in Georgetown. 'Don't you think?'

Watching Edward's unexpected happiness bloom was the best part of her pregnancy for Laura, and taking possession of this little house was only welcome because of the way that he had found it and presented it to her. Washington was an over-crowded city in those days, but somehow Edward had heard at an embassy function that a John Runcie from the university was moving from Washington to New York for a new job, and had jumped in with uncharacteristic eagerness to ask him what he was planning to do with his Washington house. The agreement was just for a year, but as Edward said, they didn't really know where they would be in a year's time anyway.

On this cloudy day, Georgetown looked like a corner of

Chelsea or St John's Wood, he said, and Laura could see how he liked the old-fashioned streets with their flat-fronted houses. He took her through the house room by room, up into the bedroom where she saw he had put a bunch of scentless winter roses, wrapped in cellophane, on the bed. It was the most overtly sentimental gesture that she had ever known from him, and she felt almost embarrassed as she carried them back downstairs to look for a vase in the basement kitchen.

Laura never complained to Edward, but the house was difficult for her from the very beginning. The pregnancy affected her hips, so that walking became painful, especially up and downstairs. While the apartment on Connecticut Avenue had been all on one level, this narrow house had only one or two rooms on each floor: a kitchen in the basement; a living room and dining room as you went into the house; and a bedroom on each floor above. Monica came to visit the next day, and exclaimed how darling the house was, and how lucky they were to get it, but Laura's first unease settled into genuine irritation as the days passed, and she hauled herself up and down those stairs, up and down.

What made it worse was that Professor Runcie had not fully vacated the house, and his taste in furnishings was not hers. Faded, coloured rugs covered every floor, there were old oil paintings on every wall, tapestry cushions on velvet chairs, and despite the high ceilings and big sash windows, there was a general impression of dimness. The kitchen, which no doubt he had rarely used, was small and dark, with a worrying smell of damp. He had left his personality behind in shelves and shelves of books on political science and modern history, many of them, Laura was only half amused to see, about the Soviet Union, and in every drawer there seemed to be little traces of him – the odd handkerchief or old envelope, inkless pen or faded postcard.

Once they had moved into this house, Edward made the

effort to come home earlier, and with the help of Kathy, a daily maid she had found, Laura tried to prepare meals for them in the evenings. She started working her way determinedly through an old cookbook she found in the kitchen, but since Edward never seemed to care what he ate, she soon began to repeat the easiest meals. Steak, meatloaf and roast chicken were repeated on a loop in that kitchen.

One night she had served meatloaf for the third time that week, and could hardly eat any of it. Ever since her pregnancy had started, there had been a metallic taste in her mouth, and although she nibbled at saltines and ginger cookies all day, she found most food unappetising. She sat with an empty plate as Edward ate, sipping a glass of cold white wine. 'I had a letter from Sybil today,' she told him. 'She's pregnant too.'

'Yes, Toby told me.'

Laura commented on what a coincidence it was, but her voice sounded dull. When Edward asked her how she was feeling, she found it hard to express herself.

'It's funny, waiting for someone, and you know that when they arrive, everything is going to change.'

'Why not come out a bit more, though, while you still can,' he said, finishing his meatloaf and reaching for the salad. 'Someone telephoned through an invitation to the newspaper man Whiteley's party tomorrow, that house on S Street. I'll tell you who will be there from home: Amy Parker – Amy Sandall now – she's over here. You remember Amy, I'm sure you met her during the war. We never go to parties – but there are parties all the time here now.'

Laura said that she had never really met Amy – though of course she remembered her, disembarking the *Normandie* with her hat like a little flag, entering Sybil's house in a white coat, sitting in the Dorchester in monochrome. She wondered why she was over in the States, and was surprised when Edward told her that she had married again, for a third time, to an American who wanted to get into politics. 'You can't stay in for the next three months. That's why you're feeling low, with nothing to do.'

All day Laura toyed with the idea of going to the party, and she even went out to a hairdresser in the afternoon. There had been a half-hearted snowfall in the morning, but it was already turning to slush on the sidewalks, falling in dirty streaks off the Dupont Circle fountains. She looked into the shop windows; blush lace underwear in the window of Jean Matou, a crocodile handbag . . . pretty colours, soft textures, but she couldn't summon up the energy to go in and see them more closely. In the hairdresser's mirror, which only showed her from the chest up, she could almost slip into her other self, the girl who used to watch herself with expectation in mirrors and shop windows, wondering what people were thinking about her. The woman next to her, middle-aged with dyed aubergine hair, caught her eye in their reflection and smiled at her. 'That style suits you,' she said in a foreign voice, nodding at the way the hairdresser had cut Laura's hair to just below her ears, 'much better than when you came in.' But when she came home to put on a grey cocktail dress that Ellen had sent her in a box of clothes she had worn in her own pregnancy, Laura felt another wave of nausea, and she telephoned Edward and told him she was too unwell to go out.

A bunch of pinks that she had left too long smelt stagnant on the hall table when she went downstairs to make herself a cup of tea, and she picked up the vase and took it down to the kitchen. The stems dripped on the grey dress as she took out the flowers. As she was walking up the long stairs to bed, pain radiated through her pelvis; she unzipped the dress and left it in a heap on the floor, and lay in her underwear on top of the bedclothes, her hands on her belly. Edward did not come in until the small hours, but although Laura woke when he got into bed, she could not stir herself to speak to him. The next morning, however, when she heard the sound of the shower, she dragged herself out of bed to make him coffee and ask how his evening had been.

'We went on to another party – Amy is wild.' Edward shook his head. Laura was puzzled. He must have seen a side of that collected woman that she could hardly imagine.

'Did she get very drunk?'

'Not just drunk. They were going on again when we left. Monica and Archie gave up when I did, though. Your brother-in-law Kit was there too. Someone said he is aiming to get into journalism. He doesn't seem the type, to me.'

Laura asked Edward what he meant, but he was unforthcoming: drinking his cup of coffee, knotting his tie, looking for his briefcase, he seemed distracted by thoughts of the day to come. After he left, Laura roused herself and cooked some breakfast. She had arranged to see Monica for lunch and shopping, but although the house seemed so empty, the thought of going out into the city was unappetising. She went to telephone Monica to say that she was feeling too unwell to go out.

'Thank the Lord, I'm so ill too,' Monica said in a thin voice, and then offered to come over instead. 'I'll bring you something for lunch – what are you craving? Tell me. When I was preggers, I only craved cold martinis and chips with vinegar, and my doctor told me that was the worst I could possibly do for my baby.'

When Monica arrived, pale under her usual make-up, Laura at first thought she would be a welcome distraction. But she quickly found her chatter disturbing. 'Goodness me, Edward and his friends put it away, don't they?' she said, peering at herself in the hall mirror. 'I look like death. I needed the night out, though – everything at home is unbearable.' She paused and walked into the living room, still talking, almost as if Laura wasn't there. 'At home! I suppose that's the problem. It isn't home. I wish we were at home, I do wonder why I married a Foreign Office type when I only really like England.'

Although Monica had often gossiped to Laura in a complaining tone, this was the most negative she had ever heard her, and as lunch went on she opened up more and more: how Archie thought it was time for their elder daughter, Barbara, to go to school in England, but that Monica couldn't bear to have her so far away; how their younger daughter was talking in an American accent and Monica found it horribly disconcerting; and, embarrassingly, how Monica had lost interest in sex. 'Archie keeps wondering why I don't want it any more; I was like a bitch on heat, my dear, when we met – even when I was pregnant – but the last year or two I just can't be bothered. I look around the men at a party like last night's, and I think I'd rather go to bed with you or you or you than my own husband – sorry, darling, I'm shocking you. I'm shocking myself.' And to Laura's dismay, the corners of Monica's mouth turned down. Not knowing how to comfort her, Laura offered her a drink.

As she went to pour the drink, she wondered to herself why it was that she found Monica's confidences so difficult to respond to. She would like to relax into intimacy with her, but she felt apprehensive that the price of such intimacy might be the expectation of similar confidences from her. And even if the inexorable need for secrecy was not always there for her, in a way she felt that Monica was breaking a delicate code of conduct; that there was something threatening to one's married intimacy in telling such problems to others. But Monica did not seem to notice her unease, and took the martini she brought her eagerly.

'I am awful, going on about my own problems when you are still grieving for your father.'

Laura corrected her, startled, telling her that all that was behind her now, but she could tell that Monica did not believe her. Was her manner, so flat and uncertain, that of a grieving daughter?

After Monica left it was almost dusk, and Laura found

herself half asleep on the sofa. She was still thinking over what Monica had said: how could it be that she was grieving for her father, when she had felt more relief than sadness during the funeral? She had walked away from her childhood home the day she had stepped onto the ship in 1939; she had never wanted to go back there. She had left as quickly as she could after the funeral. And yet it did feel as though there was an absence in her life, at this time when surely she should feel more complete than ever. Was it the absence of war? Was it the absence of any work? Yes, she missed having a role, a purpose in this indifferent city. She could not match Edward's excitement about the forthcoming birth.

As she thought about Edward and the fact that they were to be a family, she found her hands moving to cover her mouth. Other families filled her thoughts. She was thinking about Monica, and about her lack of love – her apparent contempt, it seemed – for Archie. She was thinking about Ellen, and the difference between the relationship she seemed to have now with Tom and the romantic letters she had written during the war. She was thinking about Mother, and how she still tried to keep up the pretence that she had never sat across the table from Father in dread of his anger, never walked quietly through her own house for fear of disturbing him. You are the only woman you know, Laura told herself, who can be sure in her love. Don't be afraid of the change to come.

Edward came in late, the tiredness etched into his face. He walked into the living room where Laura was lying on the sofa and sat down with a glass of gin, picking up a book that was lying on one of the shelves beside him. Laura sat up, stretched a little, and realised she wanted to tell him about the thoughts that had been passing through her mind.

'You know you said I was low – I think I am worried . . .'

Edward put his finger in the book he was holding, and looked up. 'It is frightening for you – but I'm sure it will all be all right. The doctor said you were going along fine, didn't

267

he? I found out today that I'm going to be expected to go with the ambassador on a speaking tour in a couple of weeks, but that's still well before your date.'

Laura tried to explain that it was not fear about the birth that was dragging her down, or at least not the physical reality of the birth. Trying to convey what bothered her, she found herself returning to that moment many years ago when she had first been told about the possibility of a finer way of life. Whenever she travelled back to the memory of the *Normandie* in her mind, she found those few days still bright and clear into her mind. The promise of the future. 'When I first met Florence, when she told me what communism would do for people, it was something she gave me to read. It was really impressive. Even today I remember every word—'

Edward said nothing, but Laura pressed on. She was not sure if what she was saying was welcome. The habit of secrecy had intensified between them, but at that moment she longed for reassurance from him, a moment of recognition of their shared dream. 'It was from the *Worker*. About what family life would be like under communism. The writer said: "There we see no selfish husbands who expect servants rather than companions, and no nagging wives who realise life has passed them by. We see women who proudly go out and put their shoulder to the wheel, and men who are not ashamed to rock the cradle." Or words to that effect. It's odd how one can remember something for so many years, if it's really important.'

Laura wanted to go on and talk to Edward about how they could be that kind of family, that they were not doomed to be like the families she saw around them – the distant fathers and resentful mothers, the growing rifts, the possibility of anger, of violence, the secrets that lay at the heart of families. But Edward stood up to get himself another drink, and Laura lost the thread and finished up on a different, more complaining note. 'I suppose now we're having a family I'll never have anything else to do.'

'But that is such an important thing for you to do,' Edward said, sitting back down and opening his book again.

'It's easy for you to say that.' Laura felt frustrated in her effort to communicate her feelings about the way they seemed to be sleepwalking forwards rather than choosing their path. 'What's the book?' She didn't want to make him argue, but equally she couldn't bear silence to descend just now. To her surprise, Edward closed the book and put it under his chair.

'It's nothing – one of the professor's old books, actually. Tell you what, why don't we have another go at chess?' Laura had tried often enough to play with him, and she didn't really fancy trying again, but she acquiesced.

As the days passed and the birth came closer, Laura's mental anxiety receded and all her consciousness seemed to become concentrated in her body. The movements of the baby inside her woke her at night and startled her during the day. There were still some three weeks to go before her due date, and yet she found herself packing and repacking the bag that she was to take to the hospital, putting in not only things for herself but also the impossibly small clothes for which she had shopped with Monica.

She even became infected by a desire to keep the house cleaner than it usually was, and after Kathy had finished dusting, she would sometimes find herself going through the rooms with a cloth, or rearranging things in closets and shelves – not that she ever seemed to make much difference to the dark, unhomely rooms. One day she was in the living room when she noticed how under each of the armchairs there was a faint shadow of dust on the parquet flooring, and, irritated that Kathy had not moved the chairs before sweeping the room, she went to get a dustpan and brush and came back and pushed the chairs to one side herself. Under one of them she saw the book that Edward had been reading the evening after Whiteley's party. Picking it up, and looking at its title, she realised at once why he had not wanted to discuss it.

Even she knew it was a book banned by the Party, absolutely known to be a pack of lies. He had left it open, face-down, and she couldn't help looking at the page he had been reading. It struck her with horrible force: a father trying to speak to his son through a wire fence in some kind of prison camp. 'For a second he turned to me, his face wet with tears, his hands clutching the grille convulsively.' With a movement that almost shocked her, Laura threw the book back onto the floor and shifted the chair back over it.

When Edward came in, although Laura had not planned to do so, she returned to the discovery she had made that afternoon. 'The book you were reading . . .'

'Which book?'

'The Tchernavin book.'

'I didn't read it,' he said.

Laura was startled. She had seen him with it. She knew the Party would frown on it, but she didn't think that even this would be a secret from one another.

Then Edward backtracked. 'I just looked at it,' he admitted, walking over to the drinks cabinet. 'It's all lies; it's all about fear – and cruelty. How can that be?'

'That can't be.' It wouldn't make sense. Fear, surely, was the characteristic of their incomplete lives, of the fact that they were not yet where they should be. Where they were going, that was what they should talk about. They must remember what their joint belief was – for the future, for their child. 'I think—' Laura was about to say more, but just then she was jolted by a clench of pain.

In later weeks, when Laura thought back to that evening, it was as though a crimson curtain came down over her sight. Through the curtain there was only pain, slamming her over and over again to the floor. She had always hoped she would be good at childbirth; she had seen herself as a stoical figure, and both Ellen and Mother had always been dismissive of too much talk of the awfulness of the experience. But by the time the cab Edward called had brought her to the hospital, she was groaning and lowing like a cow, and by the time the doctor was brought in to examine her, long yells were periodically escaping from her.

'Don't make so much noise, you'll scare your baby,' said one cross-faced nurse to her, at which she turned to Edward and said, 'Make her go away,' with vehement intent, before the next wave of pain picked her up and slammed her down again.

The nurse did not go, but was joined by a number of other medical staff, talking in hurried voices. Laura was trying to ask what was happening, when a mask was put over her face and she was allowed to go under the wave entirely and absent herself from the spectacle of the tragedy that was about to unfold.

Much later, Laura learned words for what she had gone through. She learned about a detached placenta, about haemorrhage, and a resultant lack of oxygen. But at the time there was nothing as precise and transparent as words. When Laura woke to the emptiness of the hospital room, there was only a receding tide of pain. She tried to move, and felt the pull of a wound in her abdomen. She saw Edward, asleep in a chair. 'Edward,' she whispered, and then louder, until he woke. 'I'm so sorry,' he said, and lying there she watched the grief take shape in his eyes, just as she had watched the happiness take shape months earlier.

The return to the little house took place some days later. They got out of the cab, Edward holding that bag of clothes and the teddy bear, and opened the door into the quiet hall. It did not feel like coming home, Laura thought; she had never liked that hall table with the curved legs, and where had that stain on the bottom step of the stairs come from? She walked into the living room and sat down with a grunt of discomfort. Edward brought her a cup of tea. 'Shall I put something stronger in it?' he said. She shook her head and watched him tip gin into his own cup.

271

The silence between them was broken by the telephone ringing. It was Mother, saying she would be there by the evening. Edward had dutifully rung her from the hospital, and had been taken aback by her announcement, which he had duly reported to Laura, that she would come to stay with them for a while. 'I wish you hadn't let her come,' Laura said now in a monotone, and Edward said in a similar voice that he hadn't known how to stop her, but that maybe in fact it was a good thing, since he had to leave for this trip with the new ambassador, Inverchapel, the next day.

Laura had forgotten about the trip. 'My head hurts so much, will you help me upstairs?' was all she said.

She was drifting in and out of sleep when she heard the door slam and Mother's voice intermingling with Edward's downstairs. Later, Laura was aware of her looking in on her, and even in her vague state she registered how odd it was that Mother's usual demanding manner seemed to have been put to one side as she drew the curtains, but left the room without speaking. Later that evening, when she came in with a tray – on which she had put a meal that she and Kathy had clearly put together in a hurry, though it was perfectly edible – again she did so more or less in silence.

The next day Laura stayed in bed all morning after Edward left. Through a fog she was aware of those household noises that remind a sick person that they are still part of the world, that cushion them with the warp and weft of daily life; she heard footsteps, a telephone conversation, a vacuum cleaner going, and at lunchtime another knock at the door with a tray. Mother came in and, as Laura ate, she moved around the room folding clothes. Laura heard her trying to open the drawers of the tallboy. 'They always stick,' she heard herself saying.

'We could get you some new furniture,' Mother said.

'It's not our house,' Laura said, and put her hand up to her head. Headaches from the anaesthetic were still troubling her.

Mother was by her bed, but to her relief didn't talk about what had happened. 'I thought we'd try a sponge bath after you've eaten.'

After the bath her mother sat doing a crossword puzzle while she listened to the radio, and then they talked about a novel that they had both read, and about what they thought of the fashions in the *Vogue* magazine that Mother had bought. That's how they passed the next three days, not talking about the baby or the hospital, but in an odd way Laura felt that Mother's presence and inconsequential conversation formed a net, and although every night she dreamt she was falling, alone, with no one to catch her, her baby son slipping away from her as she fell, during the days she began to feel as though she was being brought to shore.

On the fourth day after her mother's arrival, Laura felt well enough to get up, and they sat for a while in the living room. But as soon as her strength began to return, Laura found her mother's presence less reassuring. She began to feel gritty with irritation over her slow-moving conversation and her anxiety about small things such as what they would eat that evening and why Kathy kept burning the potatoes. And she found her tentative movements, as she padded around the house with self-conscious attention not to make too much noise, undeservedly maddening. Above all, Mother's decision not to mention the expected presence who had failed to arrive no longer felt kind. It seemed excruciating. But Laura said nothing, and remained the dutiful patient, eating her soup and playing cards in the afternoons.

It was ten days after her mother's arrival that Edward returned. He had telephoned each day, but had been as monosyllabic as Laura had been, and it was a shock, when he came in, to see her own exhaustion reflected in his face. Mother was not at ease with him, and as he went to get out the gin bottle before dinner, she asked him needling, polite little questions about his trip. In response, he talked about what he had been doing, accompanying the new ambassador on a public relations trip through unexciting areas of Colorado and Oregon, and Laura was surprised by how bitter he allowed himself to sound. 'Poor Inverchapel had to keep telling them how wonderful it is that the empire is unravelling, and to try to play up to their rabid Red-baiting. He did it all better than Halifax would have done, though, I think.' He shook his head. 'Though neither of them finds it that easy flirting with these homespun Americans. Who would?'

Mother and Kathy had cooked roast chicken with creamed potatoes and string beans, and Laura found herself eating properly as Edward sat there, drinking and mulling over his trip. After a while she realised he was talking, for once, simply to ensure that he did not have to hear too much about how things were going with her, but she did not judge him for that reluctance. She felt relieved that he was back. Soon Mother would go and when they were alone again they would have the chance, she told herself as she scraped up her chicken, to recreate the happiness that could be theirs. She picked up her glass of wine and the cold burst of sourness in her mouth was refreshing. She smiled at Edward as he went on talking in that uncharacteristically inconsequential way.

4

'You've recovered so well,' Monica said when they met at a cocktail party held by a senator a few weeks later. Apart from an overriding sense that she had to be careful not to move too quickly, or talk too fast, that the carapace she had built up for herself had to be carefully handled at all times, Laura inwardly agreed with her; she had recovered well. The scar on her belly was itchy now rather than painful, and that evening she had experimented with a dark eyeliner and bright lipstick of the kind she never usually wore, which seemed to compensate for the expressionlessness of her face. And she felt almost grateful that nothing seemed to have changed around her; this was the kind of party she remembered from before her pregnancy – the tables of smoked turkey and ham, the trays of martinis and manhattans. There was Edward still at the British ambassador's side, even if it was no longer the slender, wry Lord Halifax, but the altogether more talkative Inverchapel.

'I hear your trip to Iowa went very well,' Monica said to the ambassador, simply the expected words at the expected moment, as he paused near to her.

'It wasn't too bad,' Inverchapel conceded, and then launched into a would-be amusing anecdote which, Laura thought, must have been trotted out a dozen times already that evening. 'The slight difficulty was that I had asked to stay in a farm for three days, and I'd brought as a gift a quart of Scotch and a quart of Schnapps – I thought the father looked a little tight-lipped. It was only later I discovered they were all strict teetotals.' Inverchapel acknowledged their smiles, and walked on to more interesting conversations.

And there was Kit at the door, scanning the crowd, so she moved towards him. She had known he was coming tonight, but he looked a little embarrassed, mumbling something about how sorry he was that he hadn't looked in on her recently, how glad he was to see her here this evening, and that he was planning to leave to go back to Boston at the weekend. She knew that his attempt to break into journalism had not gone well, and his graceful stance seemed to slump as he said he was not sure what he was going to do next. 'But Joe's coming tonight too – you know he's doing well now. Have you seen him?'

And there Joe was as if on cue, walking into the party behind them. It seemed a little odd that neither Kit nor Joe had been in touch after the stillbirth, but there, that was the nature of such a miserable experience. Nobody wanted to mention it; nobody wanted to say the wrong thing. She wanted to show them it didn't matter, and she put on a friendly manner as she asked Joe how he was finding Washington, and as he turned to her she felt warmed by the unforced enthusiasm of his response. 'Living in a shoebox, working all the hours that God sends, going to parties every night to gawp at the world's players – how could I not love it? And you?'

Laura tried to match his energetic tone, telling him that they were lucky enough to have found somewhere to live that was not a shoebox. As she told the story of how they had found their Georgetown house, she mentioned the name of the professor who owned it, and Kit laughed.

'You're in his house, the mad old right-wing conspiracist?'

Laura was surprised that both Kit and Joe seemed to know exactly who Professor Runcie was. Joe was talking about one of his books, which he seemed to admire, while grabbing a couple of glasses of champagne from a passing tray and putting one in Laura's hand.

'He sees Reds behind every bush and up every tree, nobody takes him seriously,' Kit said.

'A lot of what he says is pretty sensible,' Joe demurred, but Laura could not tell whether he was genuinely disagreeing with Kit or simply arguing for the sake of conversation. He went on talking, saying that people in Washington were simply too blind to how far the Russians would go, and Kit was saying something about how it was ridiculous to exaggerate the threat, and that even Inverchapel had been happy to have a relationship with Stalin when he was ambassador in Moscow. Laura was casting about in her mind for a way to turn the conversation, but when she asked if they were likely to go to Portstone that summer as Washington was simply too miserable when it got hot, she was ignored.

'If you want a good story about Reds,' Kit was saying to Joe now, 'you should go and see that friend of mine I mentioned, Carswell – not actually a friend, but I knew him at college.

276

He used to be a communist and he says there are communists even in the State Department now, that it's almost like a club – all nonsense, I'm sure.'

Despite another little gambit from Laura about what they thought of the party, Joe was caught by this story and was leaning towards Kit asking more about the man. But thank goodness, here was Edward walking over to them. In this crowd, he was as Laura remembered him from London parties, urbane, sure-footed, surrounded by the group, by people who thought they knew him. And here were Monica and Archie again, Monica in a puffball of a dress, Archie talking as soon as he reached them. 'I'm going to blame you for that editorial about British diplomats,' he was saying to Joe. 'I saw your hand in it. "The good fellowship atmosphere of a very uppity club" indeed, "men who understand the faded diplomacy of Kipling's age better than the aspirations of a modern government".'

Joe came back at Archie, insisting that surely he would be the first to admit that he wasn't on the wavelength of the American way of doing politics. And Kit was quick to back him up, quoting further from the article, as if he felt in some way responsible for Joe and how the others saw his work. Archie was about to respond, when Monica broke in.

'For heaven's sake, do you have to talk work here?' It felt as if she were dragging, as couples so often do, the trail of some previous altercation into this new arena.

'More drinks?' Edward said in a vague voice.

'I think they're finishing up now,' said Monica.

'Tell you what,' Joe said, following Edward's reluctance to end the party, 'someone at the *Washington Post* told me about a great little club just opened up on U Street, with a nigger band that plays the best—'

'Or we could just go to the Shoreham – it's kind of pretty there in the evenings.'

'The club sounds fine,' Laura said, and noted a rather

surprised look on Monica's face. It was not usually Laura who wanted to go on. 'Let's go there.'

'I said I'd meet Suzanne later – but I can telephone from the club.' And as they left the party, Joe was explaining to Laura that Suzanne was his new girlfriend, a fine girl he had met at the newspaper.

The air in the evening streets was already filled with the warmth of the summer ahead which intensified as they walked into the dark, crowded club. Here Laura thought they would be conspicuous, all so formally dressed from the previous party, but nobody seemed to be looking at them as they found a small table at the side of the room. The nigger band, as Joe had put it, played in a way she had never heard before, but she liked it; it seemed to mute rather than exacerbate the jagged edges of her thoughts.

Soon Joe's girlfriend Suzanne arrived, and Laura was immediately impressed; she was still in her work clothes, but whereas some girls would have been self-conscious in that blue skirt and cropped jacket next to the other women in the club in their bright evening wear, she seemed to be bestowing the pleasure of her company on others rather than asking for their approval. In other words, Laura thought, watching her, she was a lot richer than Joe and carried her class with a kind of thoughtless confidence. Joe naturally danced with Suzanne, and Monica was swept off by some stranger, so while Edward and Kit seemed happy simply to sit and drink, Laura got up to dance with Archie. At first he tried to talk to her as they danced, but it was irritating when he put his face close to her ear and his voice buzzed, and she was glad when he gave up and was content to turn and turn to the jittery music, and it was well into the small hours when they finally found taxis to go home.

As they went up the stairs into their house, Laura thought Edward was so drunk that he was oblivious to anything, but then he spoke as they were getting into bed. 'Poor Kit,' he said. Why on earth, Laura wondered, did he pity Kit? 'He's obviously in love with Joe, isn't he – and Joe not a bit interested in men. Poor Kit.'

Laura turned with interest to Edward, asking more; he never gossiped about people and this interpretation of Kit's behaviour fascinated her. But Edward was already falling asleep. Laura lay awake for a while, wondering why she had not seen it herself; she remembered how she had been surprised, too, when Winifred had told her long ago about Giles's love interests. Kit had seemed languid and disconnected from others when she first met him, but she had noticed a kind of anxiety when he was with Joe, an eagerness to ensure that Joe was happy. Was that love? Surely love was the great blooming of joy she had known with Edward . . . Why had her thoughts run like that, back into the past, to the kiss on Hampstead Heath? He was here, now, and they had come through so much. Soon the clouds would lift again. She turned in bed, pressing her breasts against Edward's back and fitting her legs behind his as he slept, trying to find a point of restfulness against him.

That evening of drinking and chatter and dancing was not the only evening like it that month – or even that week. This seemed to be Laura's path now, and as the time passed she realised that there was no point trying to step off it – her world was to be the world of the other embassy wives. So during the days she shopped and lunched and helped Monica with her charity; and she and Edward went out evening after evening, avoiding the quietness of the little house with its empty bedroom on the top floor. She started French lessons, as Edward thought his next posting might be in Paris, and surprised herself with her progress; she had so little else to do. Sometimes she went to visit Ellen and Tom in Boston, but Edward rarely went with her, and now and again she had lunch with Joe near to his newspaper. The world of the newspaper and the world of the embassy touched in enough places to mean that they soon had stories and gossip to share.

But it was something else that drew them to one another. It was perhaps that sense of being out of place in the worlds where they had found themselves; to Joe, Laura could recount some story about Inverchapel's poor attempts at humour or he could tell her about a society hostess who had tried to get him into bed, and they could sit there in a little restaurant with a shabby front and good spaghetti, knowing that they would never really be part of the circles that seemed to embrace them.

One day Laura got out her old Leica camera and took it with her on a walk through Rock Creek Park. She started to photograph trees and their yearning reflections in the water, but she realised that bored her, and a few weeks later she asked Monica if she could photograph her children. Then something began to happen. Barbara and Harriet were intrigued by her and she by them; they were seven and five years old and she was fascinated by their physical confidence – they were always cartwheeling or skipping down the long corridor of the apartment or through the communal gardens. She tried to capture that freedom of movement, so different from the constraints on adult women. Most of the photographs were no good, but she was proud of one where the girls were doing handstands against a wall of the apartment. She didn't show it to anyone, as they looked odd with their upside-down faces and strained arms, but she could not forget it. On a whim, she registered for a course on photography that was being held at the local library, and learned how to develop her pictures herself.

As she settled into these limited grooves of activity, she forgot all about the reactivation protocol, so that she was confused at first when, months and months later, somebody rang to ask about her sister and called himself Alex.

She had not returned to the Botanical Gardens since that

rainy day of the first abortive meeting. Bright and busy now, it was a poor place for secrecy, she thought. She walked around for a while without being approached, and began to think that this was just a test to make sure that she was still in contact, rather than a real meeting. So she stopped holding herself in readiness, and sat down on a bench which was splashed with sunlight and with blossom that had blown from a nearby tree, and opened her magazine. These new clothes, with their boned bodices and stiff skirts – she liked their look of control, and she was already imagining herself in a dress with a particularly exaggerated line when the same short man as before came and sat next to her and shook out his newspaper before addressing her. 'We need you to come in again.'

Laura said nothing, turning the pages of her magazine, hearing the words resonate in her mind. The man went on talking. That was all right, there was nobody near them to overhear.

'He keeps saying he can't leave documents with us to be microfilmed, that it is not safe to have them out for more than a few hours. And – we are worried. This town is small. There is nowhere to hide. He is not looking out – he is . . . is he drunk very often?'

Laura remained silent for a moment, considering. The cherry tree was all in blossom across the lawn, thick and pink now, but the flowers would be brown in a few days. 'Yes, he is drunk most nights.'

'He is missing meetings, he is unreliable.'

How alcohol and grief can transform a man.

'Mrs Rostov says she sees you at the hairdresser. She's the wife of another resident.'

Laura was surprised. She went to the same hairdresser regularly; she liked the way he made her hair look thicker and glossier, even when it had thinned after her pregnancy. A couple of times that striking Russian woman had nodded at her there, but Laura had not known who she was.

'If he brings you the documents, you can retype them in your house, and then take them to the hairdresser. We will bring you a bag like the one Mrs Rostov carries, and then you can swap very easily. You can go there every Tuesday at eleven.'

'I used to photograph them in London.'

'You can do this work?'

'Yes, but you'll need to supply the film for the camera. It's a particular type – for a Minox Riga, manufactured 1938.'

'You don't know how hard it is in this town now – I can't meet you all the time to pass things. We will get it if we can and Mrs Rostov will put it in the bag, but otherwise go ahead with copying them – can you?'

'There's a typewriter in our house.' There was, an old Smith Corona, left by the professor on the desk in the small study next to the living room.

'Contact me only in a true emergency.'

They fell silent for a while, as some people walked too close, but she did not leave, just turned the pages of her *Vogue* without reading them. When it was possible to talk again, he fed her a new emergency contact procedure. She was to telephone only from a public telephone box, a number which was written on the newspaper he was leaving on the bench, and which she was to destroy once she had learned the number, and he would find her at or near to the junction of M and 31st Street an hour later. Laura memorised the instructions expressionlessly, and soon he got up. She could tell he did not trust her. But she knew better than to try to reassure him.

That evening Edward came in late, as ever, and without saying much ate the lamb casserole which Kathy had made. He took some documents out of his briefcase as he finished the meal. Laura reached out for them, and he held onto them. 'I wish it didn't have to be like this,' he said. 'Involving you. It's so . . . I wanted it all to be . . .'

Laura shook her head. This was no time for nostalgia. That was what they were getting wrong, looking back instead of forward. She would find a way to stop that now. She took the documents and went over to the typewriter. She had tried it that afternoon. The ribbon was fine, and the action was satisfying, banging hard with every stroke; you could not be half-hearted about typing on such a heavy machine. As she rattled through the first page, Edward stood up and took another book from the shelves. Laura felt her back stiffen as she typed. She wished that she could clean this house of the brooding, alien presence that lay in the professor's books. But she said nothing.

She typed, letter by letter. You can type without understanding what you are typing, and this was particularly hard to follow, being the details of some alien chemical processes. 'Repeated distillation by sublimation and rapid condensation of vapors,' she typed, 'inversely proportional to the partial vapor pressure sustained by a molecule without condensation.' She noted, but did not type out the headings of each page, the stamps saying Atomic Energy Commission, security level – top. Instead, she went on page by page typing the descriptions and then the long equations. After she pulled each page from the typewriter she had to check it through. It took a long while, and all the time there was no need to speak, just to be busy. When she had finished, late in the evening, she opened the top drawer of the professor's desk, which locked with an old key, and put the copies in there, and handed the originals back to Edward.

'I'll go up to bed.'

He looked up from the book he was reading with eyes that seemed bloodshot. 'I forgot: Nick – you remember Nick – is coming to stay next week, to see some American friends. He's pretty miserable in London at the moment. I think he might be hoping for a transfer out here. I told him to come to dinner on Monday, would that be all right?'

Yes, Laura did remember Nick, although the memory came with no fondness. He had hardly ever even acknowledged her existence. But here was another plan, another thing to do, and she agreed with some energy, suggesting other guests – would Nick enjoy meeting Joe? They owed Archie and Monica so many invitations too; they were always being invited to their big apartment near the river. But as Laura ran through other possibilities, Edward was standing up, putting on his coat. 'Where are you going?'

'I have to get these papers back on the right desk before tomorrow. Don't wait up.'

'At this time?'

'Don't worry, I've got keys.'

His steps went quickly and quietly down the hall. Laura stood there for a second and then went downstairs to get a cookbook. She would make this dinner for Nick a fine evening. Ellen had given her a book of recipes for entertaining that she had never used, but now she was going to make something welcoming. She got into bed with the cookbook and read through pages of recipes that seemed much too complicated for her and Kathy to put together. By the time Edward came back she was half asleep, and he was gone early in the morning, but he reappeared on Saturday evening with more papers for her to type, and again on Sunday. She wondered what kind of excuses he was giving for haunting the office all weekend, but that was not her concern.

That week the tight heat of the Washington summer was already closing in on them. Laura woke early under its weight, lying there in their bed with the covers pushed off, but she was already full of plans for the day, plans she had been laying all weekend. She could see herself, at the head of a table of relaxed guests, white flowers, clattering knives and forks, Edward smiling; and then Suzanne and Monica and Nick too would recognise that she was not just an appendage to Edward, that she could create something – an atmosphere, an evening . . . but there was so much to do.

When Laura went out to the fishmongers and the flower shop, she saw in the window of a drugstore how the humidity in the air was already making her hair curl out of its set; she longed to go into its air-conditioned cool and sip a limeade and read a magazine, but she had to struggle back with the bags. One bag caught on her stocking, and the ladder ran down her leg as she walked. Kathy was at home to receive a delivery; yes, there was the fruit – grapes, dusky purple, but over-ripe, already softening, while the pears on the other hand looked woody. Laura gave Kathy instructions and went into the dining room to put the flowers into vases. Monica had mentioned in passing recently that it was not done to interrupt the gaze across the table with flower arrangements, so over the weekend she had bought three greenish glass bowls, and she cut the flower stalks short and pushed them into the bowls. In her mind the arrangement looked charming, but the heaviness of the roses' heads made them tumble out of the bowls onto the oak dining table, and she pricked her finger on their thorns pushing them back in. In the end she took them into the living room instead, putting them on the mantelpiece where the roses could lean against the wall.

That was how the day went; she went through the list of things to do, ticking things off, making things happen, but with a sense that she was rehearsing for a play where the director was missing. At last, at about six, she went up to change. She had thought she would wear a dark dress with a low back; it had gone down well the first time she had worn it, but now she noticed that there was a mark on the skirt that she had not seen before. She should have sent it to be cleaned. She was sitting on the bed, wetting her finger with her tongue and rubbing at the mark, when she saw that on the table next to Edward's side of the bed was a letter. She picked it up, and even when she realised it was from his mother she went on reading it. '. . . Osborne has taken the land to add to his farm, but nobody seemed to want the house as a house – in the end it's gone to this Bristol man, who intends to turn it into a hotel. Toby is taking some bits and pieces for their London house, and I'll put a few of the paintings into the Lodge . . .'

At first the words meant little, and then they fell with force. Laura remembered the house's austere beauty, the chilly setting for the early days of their love, the meadow where he had kissed her as though she were his dream and saviour. She thought of the rose garden, dug up for cabbages, and the avenue bordered by lime trees that led down to the village and the church. And the little boy who both loved and hated it; she felt him in the room, the man he became, tormented by his feelings for his privileged childhood. 'To me, it's the most beautiful place in the world,' he had said at lunch one day. 'But you can't rely on this kind of beauty,' he had said another time.

Why had he said nothing? Laura thought of how he had been that morning. His face had been set – one might have called it cold – but it had been no different to his face every morning recently. She moved to the telephone and was about to ring him at work, but just as she started dialling the number she thought of how strange her commiserations would sound on the telephone, and how she would have to say she had read a letter from his mother that was not addressed to her.

Instead, she slipped on her uncomfortable high-heeled pumps and went downstairs. Kathy was staying late to help with the meal, and in front of her Laura found herself putting on a show of confidence and chattering high spirits, insisting on whipping the cream and mixing the salad dressing. At half past seven Edward still hadn't come home, and at a quarter to eight the doorbell went. Laura pulled off her apron, ran up the kitchen steps and opened the door to find Archie and Monica on the doorstep. 'How funny!' she said. Her voice was as bright as she could make it. 'You're the first! Even before the man of the house.'

'Not really?' Monica came in, laughing.

'But I saw Edward leave his office an hour ago,' Archie said, shaking his head.

'He probably went to meet Nick,' said Laura. 'Have you met him?'

'Well, I've heard about him – friend of mine worked with him at the Beeb before the war. Bit of a player, isn't he?'

'What on earth do you mean?' Monica asked, but Laura started talking over them.

'I shall have to do the drinks in the absence of Edward – so what would you like?'

To her embarrassment, Laura realised that she didn't have ice put out in the living room, and she had to go down and get Kathy to bring some up. The doorbell rang again, but it was Joe and Suzanne. Again, Laura tried to laugh when she told them that Edward and the guest of honour hadn't arrived yet. She noticed that Suzanne, like Monica, had dressed carefully; both of them were in black evening dresses, and Monica was wearing the big pearl earrings she only wore occasionally. That made her anxiety increase, as she imagined them getting ready, full of expectation, zipping up their best dresses and lipsticking their mouths, setting out with high hopes of a good evening. Thank God that Monica and Joe were so talkative, since they seemed happy to start swapping anecdotes and laughing at one another immediately. But as time wore on, even they seemed strained, without their host. 'They must have completely lost track of the time – or maybe there was some emergency,' Laura said after nine. 'But, you know, the dinner will be ruined unless we eat now. Shall we go and sit down?'

The dinner was pretty much ruined, after having been in a low oven for an hour. Laura could hardly meet Kathy's eyes as she served it. They ate the dry fish and the soft, sodden vegetables, and Laura asked Joe to pour the wine, which he did with a generous hand. As they munched their way through the under-sweetened dessert, a silence fell and finally Laura heard Edward's step heavy in the hall. There he was in the doorway with Nick, but any relief Laura felt on seeing him was cancelled out by the state he was in. If he wasn't actually swaying on his feet, he was only remaining upright by great effort of will, and he quickly slumped into one of the free seats.

'Nick – everyone – this is Nick – this is everyone . . .' he muttered and picked up an empty glass.

'So glad to meet you all,' said Nick, smiling, shrugging off his coat.

Laura stood up. 'Let me take that, Nick. This is Joe – and Suzanne . . .' She introduced everybody, took Nick's coat out of the room and then came back to pile some cold food onto each of their plates.

'We've really finished eating,' she said. 'But don't let us stop you. How was your trip over, Nick?'

He was just as she remembered him: his clothes slightly wrinkled and even dirty, as though he had slept in them, but still with the invulnerable manner of the group, still entirely confident despite the discomfort of everyone else in the room.

'Well, you know, the usual kind of boat experience; our dear Miss Austen had it so well – enough of rears and vices – isn't it wonderful to think how the mind of the virgin of Hampshire would run on sodomy, and now I've come here to make amends. But we got sidetracked, you know – in a most amusing bar not far from here, where I think, I'm not sure but I think, we were the only white faces in the room.'

Laura felt all the listeners grappling with what he was saying. No one would really be shocked, she thought, but no one would be comfortable with Nick's obvious desire to shock them – and nobody would know how to respond. Only

Edward seemed oblivious to everything that Nick was saying, and was ignoring the food in favour of his glass of wine.

'Well, if you don't want to eat, shall we go into the living room for coffee? The rest of us have been sitting here long enough.'

At least as they went through, the pattern of the guests reformed. Now Laura was sitting between Monica and Suzanne on the sofa, and she recognised their obvious wish to help salvage the evening, as Monica started telling Suzanne some pointless but amusing anecdote about her daughters. As conversation filled the room, Laura wondered if some pleasure, some little hope of civilised interaction, might now take over.

'I never thanked you for those lovely pictures you sent over,' Monica said at one point to Laura. 'You know that Laura does such good photographs – do show them to Suzanne.'

'I'm sure she won't be—'

'I'd love to see them,' said Suzanne, as she had to, so that Laura felt it would be gauche of her to refuse. She went to get a big folder that lay on the table under the window, where she had put some of her favourite recent prints – oddly, they were all of mothers and daughters, of Ellen and Janet, and Monica and her girls. Suzanne looked at them with what seemed like more than the appearance of appreciation.

'You are good, aren't you? Look at the light in her hair. Not easy, capturing a child's expression like that. Have you ever thought of doing it professionally?'

'Laura just likes to photograph for fun,' Edward said. 'She likes watching people.'

Laura felt that there was some kind of antagonism in his voice, and yet what did he have to be antagonistic about? The feminine circle had become porous to the men again, and Nick started to tell another smutty anecdote in a voice so loud that the women had to listen too.

'I'm off home,' Monica said as it was finishing, standing up. 'I am sorry but I have to be up early with the girls tomorrow.'

It was rare for Monica to break up a gathering – she was usually one of the last to leave. Laura felt the evening must have curdled beyond repair if she was going.

'Do you just have girls?' Nick asked her, with a look of innocence.

'Yes, two daughters.'

'But little boys must love you so much. You are just the kind of woman that we were all in love with at school, weren't we, Edward?'

'Am I?' Laura could see that Monica was flattered. Maybe she would stay, maybe she would enjoy the charm that Nick could turn on if he wanted to please.

'Yes, look, let me do you a sketch.'

Nick went stumbling over to the desk and picked up a pen and paper. As Suzanne went on talking to Laura about her photographs, he was drawing. Laura saw it just before he handed it to Monica: a caricature of Monica as a school matron, with her breasts hanging out of her dress, and a boy lying in bed holding a huge erection.

Monica and Archie were too English and, perhaps, too sorry for Laura, to be obviously angry when they saw what he had done. They simply went on moving out of the room, thanking her for a nice evening. Laura went into the hall with them, and as Monica went to the bathroom, Archie looked at her. She could not bear the pitying expression on his face. 'You've a lot on your hands there, haven't you?' he said, and as Laura made a dismissive expression, he unexpectedly put his hand up and casually, almost as if he were brushing away a piece of dust, touched her cheek. It seemed an intolerable moment to make, as it seemed to Laura, a pass at her, and she stepped backwards, knocking a vase on the sideboard to the ground.

'Let me help.'

'No, please, do go.' Laura was picking up the pieces, so was he, and she was the first to see the blood on his fingers. 'You've—'

'It's nothing.' He pulled a handkerchief from his pocket and wrapped it around the cut.

'We should wash it.'

'No, it's fine.'

Laura could see how embarrassed he was, and when Monica came out of the bathroom she let them go – one offended, the other injured – and she went back into the living room. She caught Suzanne's eye as she came in and Suzanne responded, getting up and saying, 'Actually, we should be going too.'

'Must we?' Joe said, frowning. 'But Nick, you must have realised that if you brought a negro to your hotel you would—'

To Laura's relief, Suzanne prevailed and they left. Edward and Nick started having a blundering discussion about whether they were going to a nightclub.

'No, we're going to bed, I'm afraid, Nick,' Laura said.

'Must I go drinking alone? My first night in Washington?'

'I'm sure you'll be fine.'

As soon as the door shut behind him, Laura found her anger spilling out of her; it was uncontrollable. 'This was your idea, this dinner, and couldn't you even come back on time? Why were you so rude? Why didn't you tell me about Sutton?'

At the mention of Sutton, she suddenly thought of the devils that might be driving Edward to behave as he had that evening, and she reached a hand towards him, but he shrugged her off so forcefully she staggered backwards.

'I'm sorry,' he said, and pulled her back to him, and began to drag her dress off her shoulders, exposing her breasts. For the first time ever Laura pushed him away, reacting against the clumsy touch of his hands and the smell of alcohol on his breath.

'Good God!' he shouted and picked up the first thing that came to hand from the mantelpiece and threw it at the wall – it was only one of those small bowls of roses, but now it was broken, and the water was a puddle on the carpet, and then he walked out of the room and into the hall.

'Where are you going?'

'To find Nick.'

'At this time?'

'He said he was going to that club on U Street . . .'

'You're too drunk, stay here.'

'You're too drunk, you're too drunk – that's all I ever hear from you. So I spoilt your little party – why does that matter so much?'

'It was for you – the whole evening!' Laura said, but she wasn't even sure if it was true; what had it all been for? But Edward went blundering out of the house and she went back into the living room. Despite all the drinking that everyone else had done, she felt clear-headed and cold. She sat down in an armchair and kicked off her high-heeled shoes. One heel knocked against something. That book, that Tchernavin book was still there, under the chair, she realised. She pulled it out and began to read. The minutes, the hours, passed as she did so.

5

The sky was as luminous as ever, that summer at Portstone. Despite their complaints, Tom and Ellen had rented the same house again for a fourth summer. Already memories were being built around the house and the people who came there every year; memories of the summer broken by Father's death would dominate, but the following summer was the one when Janet cut her leg on a rock, the summer when Kit tried to teach Laura to play tennis, and last summer was the one when it rained for a week solidly.

This summer was as yet unmarked, stretching out ahead of them, the first summer of Ellen's new son, and Laura wanted to feel hopeful that somewhere in the huge cleansing charge of the green water or in the high voices of children on the shore they could recapture a lightness that she wanted to be part of their lives again. A renewal. But on the first day, even though she struggled into the sea, Edward lay on the sand, a hand over his eyes.

'You seem pretty tired.' Kit was sitting next to them. He too seemed weary, strung out and expectant as they all were.

'Washington is quite tough.' Edward sat up and looked at the book Kit was reading. 'Is he any good?' It was a book by an American poet Laura had not heard of, and Kit passed it to him. Edward looked through it for a while.

'I can't make head or tail of it.' There was resignation in his voice as he put it down.

'I can't read poetry myself,' said Tom, 'never saw the point of it.'

'I used to,' Edward said, lying back on the sand again, 'but now it feels so hard – to get its secrets out. Reading all these reports, day in, day out . . .'

'Do you spend your life in meetings?'

'That's it.' Edward picked up a stone and sent it skimming over the waves. 'You need some silence in your head to read poetry.'

'Maybe I have too much silence,' Kit said, in a would-be light way, but Laura caught a complaining note in his voice. She knew that since his failure in Washington he had drifted rather, and was currently just teaching tennis in the locality. As time went on, the differences between the two brothers seemed to become exaggerated: Kit was more and more languid and diffident in his manner, while Tom seemed sturdier and more settled.

Laura felt a headache starting, and wandered back up the shore to the house, where Ellen was sitting in a rocking chair, nursing her baby. She was nervous around Laura, obviously wondering how the sight of her second child would affect her sister. But although Laura had held him a few times, the soft-ness of the first hair on his skull and the curled balls of his fists did not touch her emotionally. The wall that she had built around herself, brick by careful brick, was much too high for that. As they sat and talked, Janet ran in with a ball in her hands.

'Where's Father?' she demanded.

'Say hello to your aunt,' Ellen ordered.

'Hello,' Janet mumbled, looking at her shoes.

'Father is probably busy now, why do you need him? You were going to stay with Ora till lunchtime.'

Janet started throwing the ball in her hands up and down, speaking in a singsong. 'Daddy was going to play with me, he was going to teach me tennis,' and just as she said 'tennis' she lost control of the ball, which bounced out of her hands and onto the baby's head.

'Oh, you stupid—' Ellen's voice was explosive, and her hand whipped out and slapped Janet hard, much harder than anyone would expect, on her cheek. Janet put her hands up to her face, and her eyes filled with tears. 'And that,' Ellen said, slapping her again, on her legs, where Laura saw now that the red mark joined existing bruises. Janet ran from the room, leaving a sick, horrible cloud of the consciousness of pain behind. As soon as she was gone, Ellen started complaining about her behaviour. Laura said nothing – she may even have nodded. But in her mind she was lost in their own childhood, lost in the realisation that patterns of violence she had hidden so deep, that she had never admitted, even to herself, ran like veins of coal through Ellen's family life, and as soon as she could she excused herself and went upstairs. She knew that there was a bottle of bourbon in Edward's closet.

That evening, Kit drove off to the station to pick up Joe. Tom had planned a cookout on the shore, and brought together his usual group of holidaymakers – half a dozen couples and a few of their older children who were excited to be out so late. The day had been hot, and for once the heat seemed to be lasting into the evening, as Tom and his friends built a fire of driftwood on the edge of the pebbles for the barbecue and set up the drinks on a trestle table.

'Suzanne isn't with you?' Laura said, when she saw Joe alone, standing near to Kit.

'She finds this crowd a bit stifling, to be honest. Says they remind her too much of her own family.'

'Really? I thought she was—'

'She's Jewish, yes, her mother is, but her dad comes from a good Washington family. She seems to have got the worst of both worlds: her mother thinks she shouldn't be working at all and her father wishes she had done something more rarefied than journalism. They certainly don't think I'm the right man for their princess.'

Laura made sure to look interested, although her mind was running on other things. Where had Edward got to? And should she have brought down a sweater for later on? But Joe was now completely caught up in their conversation; he had never lost that ability to throw himself wholeheartedly into social interaction. He turned away from those around them so that nobody else could hear what he said, and looked at Laura intently as he spoke. 'I just don't know. I think she's a great girl, obviously she's swell, bright and beautiful and all that, but I'm thinking of going off to Europe again.'

Laura could not see why Europe would be the pull for him, but when she asked why he just shook his head impatiently.

'I don't seem to be making my mark here.' As they talked, they moved away from the others and started walking down to where the waves came up over the pebbles. Laura kicked off her cork-soled sandals and he bent to take his shoes off too, when they reached the edge of the water. 'I feel like I keep missing the boat. Truth be told, I'm angry with myself. Years ago Kit told me to get in touch with a man he knew who knew some stuff about Reds in government. I didn't follow it up – did you see the papers today?'

Laura had not, but she knew with a dull certainty what he was talking about.

'This Carswell just went in front of the committee and blew the roof off it – the names he's named . . . to think I could have been in on that story – hey, Kit!' Joe shouted behind him, to where Kit was standing with a young man who had a house further down the coast. 'Did you see Carswell's testimony today?'

Kit shook his head, and said it was crazy, that nobody could take it seriously. The young man next to him agreed.

'That's right,' he said. 'The man they've named at the Carnegie Endowment, I think I knew him at Harvard. This Red-baiting is getting out of hand now, you've got to wonder where it's going to end. They're going after everyone: they picked up one of the girls in my office the other day for investigation. Sure, she's in the union – since when was it an offence to be in the union?'

'They've probably got it in for the man at the Carnegie because he's cleverer than they will ever be,' Kit said. 'You're not falling for this, are you, Joe?'

Joe turned away. 'Let's get our feet wet,' he said to Laura, and they went down to where their toes were nudged by the waves.

'It's not hard to see why Suzanne finds this crowd stifling,' he said as they stood there, and he started to imitate the way that the young man had spoken, his high voice and dismissive tone. 'I think I knew him at Harvard. My days, he can't be a traitor, I think my mother knows his mother; my word, he's not a spy, I got drunk with him last year, he's quite a pal, you know.' Laura went on smiling into the distance as Joe berated Kit and Tom and their friends for being so blind to the threats that might be growing for their generous, liberal instincts.

As soon as she could, she asked him why he was thinking of going travelling. 'I'm older than you think,' Joe said, though in fact Laura had little idea how old he was, 'and what have

296

I done all my life? I thought I'd get some serious writing done one day, get on to some real stories, and what is there to show for all these years? I haven't even looked at these things that are going on now. It's all going on in Washington now – and where am I? On the outside, that's where – I'm always on the outside.'

Laura asked him in a light voice what he thought any of them on that beach had done.

'But it's different for men, you know – if we're not doing something, it's tough, really tough to feel satisfied.'

It's funny how men assume it's so different for women, Laura thought. 'I didn't think my life would turn out quite like this either,' she said. Perhaps Joe thought she was referring to her lost baby; at any rate he fell silent and Laura tried to move the conversation on. 'It all felt different in the war, didn't it? I can't believe that was three years ago. It feels like another world.'

'There was so much at stake then.' Joe sounded as if he regretted that they were no longer at war. They had walked quite far up the beach, and they turned and looked back at the group of people. Laura saw them from the perspective Joe had just described: self-satisfied liberals, sheltered from the world, unable to see the new threats that were gathering for them. But where was she in this picture? Her real existence did not register in anyone's scheme. It was as though she herself had become a blot, a negative patch in a coloured film. Only when Edward or their handler, Alex, looked at her did her true colours show; and she wanted Edward to look up, to see her even at this distance. There he was, but he was sitting on a rock, his gaze turned out to sea.

Someone had brought a wind-up gramophone, and a few couples had begun to dance on the flat sand. Joe and she walked back to the group in silence and then, without warning, Joe caught her hand and put one arm around her waist, to dance with her. That kind of physical shock is unpredictable.

It had been so long. She felt the warmth of his skin, smelt his cigarette-tainted breath and the grassy tang of his cologne against his sweat. The music changed, became slower, and Joe seemed aware of her physical response; his hand moved on her back and brought her closer to him. The certainty of her enjoyment: it had been there nine years ago, it was here again. There was something dangerous in that, and Laura realised she had to break away. She sat down with the others and tried to join in the conversations that were eddying around her.

For a while she gossiped with Ellen and a couple of the other women. Ellen and Tom had now found a house that they wanted to buy, further up the coast, and she and the other women were discussing it in detail; what renovation it needed, how far it was from the station, whether the garden was too small, whether it would be good to start on a side addition immediately or wait until they had spent some time there. Although Laura wasn't at her best in such conversations, never having had a house of her own, she was willing to play her part. 'You must do the addition,' she said to Ellen, in the ingratiating tone that she felt was expected of her, 'otherwise how can Edward and I come to stay with you in the summers? I won't forgive you if you don't.'

'It is a nice house,' Ellen said in a self-satisfied voice. 'And it's near enough to the club – we can all go there for dinner rather than having these kind of scratch parties.'

'But Ellen, it's such fun when Tom does this.'

'It's such a bother, though, with the children too. They took ages to settle tonight.'

Laura went over to the table to get another drink. As she did so, she tuned in to the conversation the men were having around her, and she realised to her dismay that they were still talking about the revelations at the committee hearings the previous day.

'This Carswell is obviously completely paranoid, off his

head. I hear he made his friend walk behind him into the committee in case some Reds took potshots at him to silence him,' Kit was saying, and Tom was agreeing with him, saying that the people he was naming were just old New Dealers. 'It's pretty disgusting to see journalists throwing dirt all over them, they're patriots too.'

'I'm not saying they are evil,' Joe conceded. 'I bet most of them were just naïve – I know the committee is going too far a lot of the time – but he is talking about people who could have sold serious secrets.'

'That's right,' said another voice, a female voice, one of the women who had been talking up to now only about house additions and children. Then she said something more about how there was bound to be another war soon and they had to protect their way of life. That was not the way that Tom and Kit's friends usually talked, and Laura felt the discomfort in the air, but the woman went on burbling about the prospect of a war to come, and nobody challenged her.

'Where's the whisky?' That was Edward's voice, slurred, in the darkness.

'Here,' said Kit, 'No, wait, over there – mind out!' Edward had stumbled onto his foot.

Edward mumbled his apologies, and Laura heard a young woman behind her whisper to her husband, 'Never get between a drunk and his drink.'

The party went on and on. From the outside, one might have thought that this would have been one of those summer evenings that fulfilled all the expectations of the season: the stars, the dancing, the driftwood fire that flamed with sudden spurts. But Laura was constantly aware, like the dull throb of a headache that will not go away, of Edward sitting there drunk on the dunes, replying to questions in a slipshod, uninterested way. As the night wore on, Joe sat down next to her. Laura asked him for a cigarette and bent to the flame of his lighter. She asked him where he was thinking of going in Europe, wanting to turn the conversation onto lighter subjects, but his answer returned to dark places.

'Berlin would be pretty interesting – or maybe I'll go further afield. We need to know more about what's happening in China.'

Laura asked what Suzanne thought about him going away.

'Well, she'd like to go too. She's trying to get a reporting position, get off the home page.'

Laura was not surprised, but Joe's next remark was unexpected, when he said that they were looking for more photographers on the paper and Suzanne had said that he should mention it to Laura, in case she was interested. Laura brushed it off, saying that she was not looking for work and Joe said that was what he had thought, he knew she was busy with the things that embassy wives did.

'I'm not that busy – is there any more gin?'

Joe called out to Tom, asking where the liquor had gone.

'You know, I think we've drunk the lot.'

'No drink left?' Edward staggered to his feet. 'How are we going to get through to dawn with no more drink? Is it naïve, or evil, to start a party with not enough gin?'

Joe laughed. 'Edward, tomorrow I'm going to challenge you not to drink for a week.'

'Tomorrow I'm going to challenge you to stop flirting with my wife.'

There was a pause in which Laura could feel people shying away from what he had said, and then Joe tried to fill the silence, telling Edward that he mustn't be surprised if people flirted with Laura. Edward mumbled something, and then took a step forward, tripped and lurched over onto his face.

For a moment there was silence, and then all was scurrying, embarrassing motion as Joe and Kit came to his aid, pulling him upright again. 'Come on, Edward,' said Joe. 'Let's get you back to the house.'

Laura got up, offering to help, and she and Joe half dragged, half supported Edward through the dunes and along the stone path in the dusky lawn back up to the house. All the way he was breathing hard, and suddenly he said, 'You're not such a bad man really, Joe, but come the revolution you'll be up against the wall, and I'll be sorry – Laura will be sorry too, you know – sorry,' and then he stopped and vomited, and then they went on again. Joe pulled and pushed him up the stairs to the bedroom and together they laid him on the bed. Laura took his shoes off. He was asleep already. When Laura thanked Joe, her voice sounded shakier than she expected.

'Don't take it too much to heart – everyone can let off steam now and again,' Joe said. 'I'm more than tipsy myself tonight. He'll feel like hell in the morning, though – we all will.'

Not quite knowing what she was doing, Laura touched his arm. There was a shudder of warmth in the touch. Did it come from Edward's assumption, or had it been there all along, had it been there for nine years? No, that was ridiculous. Joe did not react at first, and then he put his hand on Laura's wrist, moving his fingers on the skin of her inside arm. For a moment Laura was lost in the heat of the sensation, and possibility flamed, a path never taken opened before her, and then they both, as if by mutual consent, turned away from one another. When he was gone, Laura pulled off her dress and lay there on the bed, next to her unconscious husband. The breeze from the sea came in through the open window and moved over her naked body.

6

In the warmth of the hairdressers, Gervase's fingers were dry on the nape of Laura's neck as he put in the curlers. 'You are going out tonight?' he asked, looking at her in the mirror.

'No, not tonight – just wanted to look nice for my husband.'

'He's a lucky man,' Gervase said automatically. Laura saw Mrs Rostov come in. She had left the bag, as she always did, on the floor in the waiting area, and she saw Mrs Rostov sit down next to it. 'We're ready for you now, Madam,' said one of the assistants, but Mrs Rostov shook her head. 'Wait one minute, bring me a cup of tea, I'm tired out.' As she waited, she put her bag down next to Laura's, and then stood up holding the other bag. They were so accustomed to the exchange now, but always it was an effort for Laura to keep her eyes on her magazine or her reflection rather than following Mrs Rostov's movements with her gaze.

Gervase set the big bubble dryer, and she looked at her magazine. The words danced up and down in front of her eyes; she was tired. Edward had been out all night, coming home reeking of drink just before dawn. When she heard his step in the room, she had asked him where he had been. 'Getting away from it all,' he had said, and rolled onto the floor and fallen asleep there in his clothes. When the alarm went off a couple of hours later, Laura had to rouse him and push him to take a shower, to wash away the smell of stale spirits. Going into the bathroom after him, she noted that he had missed the lavatory when he had urinated, and balling up a wad of toilet paper she had wiped the floor.

'This can't go on forever, you know,' she had said to him over breakfast, looking into his bloodshot eyes, 'you're killing yourself with drink.'

'It won't go on forever, though, will it? Did you see his sentence?'

Laura knew that Edward was referring to Alger Hiss, whose trial had ended the day before, but she couldn't let him dwell on it. The thought that any of their handlers might also turn out to be a turncoat was too destabilising. It was better not to talk about it.

'He did it for his children, for his God,' said Edward, holding one hand with the other, to stop them trembling.

'Who?'

'The man who betrayed him. He said that even though

communism will win in the end, it's better to die on the losing side than to live under the spiritual night of communism. Do you think Alex ever thinks that?'

'Of course he doesn't, he's Russian himself, isn't he?'

'Is he? He sounds American to me.'

Laura knew it was time to end the conversation. She told him to pull himself together, that he was late for work. He mumbled something about how he was indeed late, for the important discussions about better ways to kill one another. 'I mustn't miss them, they could be useful.'

'You know it is useful; I know it is. Here are the papers from the day before yesterday.' Laura was putting the copies into the black bag and brushing her hair as she spoke.

'Look at you, so clean and sure,' said Edward, and moved towards her to give her a kiss before he went. It was a while since they had embraced, and she put one hand on his cheek and stroked it. How dry the skin felt now, how bitter it smelled, the skin of a sleepless alcoholic. Laura remembered it now, under her fingers as she sat in the hairdresser, and, looking into her face in the mirror, she lifted her hand to touch her own face. In the mirror she caught Mrs Rostov's gaze very briefly, but did not engage.

Gervase was distracted by another customer and slow to come and comb Laura out. When he was finished, her hair looked shiny and set, at odds with the tired, sad look on her face. She remembered when she was younger wondering why older women went to such lengths to dye and dress their hair, since when it was most beautifully done it only threw into sharp relief their faded faces. She stood putting on her camel-hair coat before she left the salon; the air was fresh after the thick heat of the hairdresser. On the sidewalk she saw a familiar face. 'Joe! What are you doing round here?'

As Joe greeted her, Laura felt a sudden rush of self-consciousness when she remembered that night at Portstone, but that was long ago now. Ever since that evening, way back last summer, they had hardly met, only in passing at big parties.

'Oh, I'm sorry,' she muttered. Standing there, she was blocking the doorway, and someone had stumbled against her. It was Mrs Rostov, tying a silk scarf over those aubergine curls. They nodded at one another – just the slightest, the most casual nod – and she walked over to a waiting car.

Joe looked at her getting into the car, in her fur coat and large black bag, and then turned back to Laura, silhouetted in the doorway in her pale coat and large black bag.

'Come and have a coffee?' he said. 'I've got the day off. Everyone was all over the Hiss sentence yesterday, but I missed the boat on that one.'

'Did you?' Laura said, as though she simply didn't remember anything she had ever been told about the case. 'I can't really, I'm meeting someone else – I should go.'

'I'll walk with you then,' Joe said. His sudden persistence was not really surprising, it was like Joe to latch onto one quickly, but Laura was uneasy today in his presence. 'I was thinking about Edward, I'd love to ask him more about how Britain is moving; I was thinking of going over to London for the general election. Extraordinary if Churchill gets back in. What the hell will that mean for foreign policy? I'm wondering about Iran, about Egypt – Churchill wouldn't let anything go lightly.'

Laura was dismissive, telling him Edward was unlikely to want to say anything, particularly before the election.

'I don't want to spill any beans, just get more of a handle on the various players.'

'You know Edward never talks about work.'

'He doesn't, does he? He's not happy here, is he?'

The question came without warning. 'He was happier in England,' Laura agreed and went on walking. They were passing a news-stand. She didn't want to see the headlines, so she averted her eyes as always. 'I'm going into the subway here.'

'It's good to see you.' Joe was unexpectedly close to her, and Laura was afraid to look up into his face. 'Tell you what, it's been so long, could I come round for a drink tonight? Are you and Edward going to be in? I wouldn't be disturbing you?'

Later, Laura thought she should have put him off with some light excuse, but at that moment she interpreted his wish to come over as a desire for her presence. Yes, she was lonely. Standing next to him the space between them seemed small. She felt a physical resonance, the memory of his hand on her back, on her wrist. 'Of course, you are welcome, do come round,' she said, but she did not catch his response as she went down into the subway.

Edward was in on time that evening, walking through the door like any husband, hat onto the stand, briefcase on the hall floor, into a house all cleaned up with a bunch of freesias on the dining-room table. Laura had not cooked a special meal, but she had made sure that there was enough chicken casserole in the oven and fruit salad in the icebox for three of them, if Joe did turn up. She didn't mention the possibility to Edward; she started typing up some documents he had brought while he poured them both drinks. 'Just lemonade tonight,' he said when he brought them in. 'What do you think?'

Laura returned the carriage with a bang. The words she had just typed, 'the plan for atomic war under Trojan lays out 133 atom bombs hitting 70 Soviet cities, giving an expected loss of 2.7 million lives' danced in her mind. 'That's a good idea – do you feel awful after last night?'

'Pretty awful,' he said. 'I've been thinking—'

He was interrupted by the ring of the doorbell. Even then, for some reason, Laura affected surprise, saying as she got up that she had forgotten that Joe had mentioned he might drop round. She pulled the typed document out of the typewriter and stuffed it and the originals into the drawer in the front of the desk. Not waiting to see Edward's expression, she opened the door.

Joe came in full of bonhomie, carrying a bottle of red wine and a bottle of bourbon. 'I couldn't decide which we would prefer tonight, maybe one to start and the other to finish,' he said. Laura didn't take them, saying that they weren't drinking that evening.

'Nonsense, Laura – this is good stuff,' said Edward, taking the bottles from Joe and putting them down on the table in the living room. 'So, what brings you over, Joe?'

Edward seemed to have recovered, however briefly, from the horrors that had haunted him the previous night, and for that Laura was grateful. It was hard to keep up with the swinging of his moods these days, but for the first couple of hours of Joe's company they were in the sweet spot, as they talked generally about the new ambassador, Oliver Franks, about his views on the likely stand that Britain would take in Iran, and how odd it was that the Assistant Secretary of State for the Near East, Franks' sparring partner on Iran, had actually been Franks' own student at Oxford. With this kind of conversation Laura was resigned to being rather at the edge of discussions, but she didn't mind, as the evening seemed to go easily enough as they ate the casserole with the red wine, and Edward put some brandy on the table as they started on the fruit salad. Then Laura went to put coffee on as they went into the living room, and when she came in with the pot and cups on a tray, she saw that Joe had opened the bourbon he had brought.

'That's pretty dangerous brinkmanship, isn't it?' Joe was saying, and as Laura tuned into the conversation she realised that they were discussing Russia's recent testing of nuclear weapons. There was nothing in Edward's reaction to suggest any connection with what was happening thousands of miles away; he was as controlled, as non-committal, as ever. It was only the strain in her own mind that made her realise how weak his control might be.

'On whose side?' Edward said. That was his trick – she remembered first noticing it so long ago – to turn the question into another question, and wait for his interlocutor to elaborate.

As Laura poured the coffee she realised she had left the milk in the kitchen, and she stood up again. When she came back with it, she paused for a moment in the hallway to look at herself in the mirror and check her lipstick. It was a huge, gilt-framed mirror and behind her reflection she could see through the door of the living room, and to Joe sitting there. Something held her there; there is an enticing pull about looking into a scene without the knowledge of those you are watching. He was getting out his cigarettes and offering them to Edward, and Laura heard Edward saying that he couldn't smoke those American ones, and heard his footsteps as he crossed the room to get his own cigarettes from the mantelpiece. As she watched, she saw Joe pour away his glass of bourbon into the glossy-leaved little palm that stood on the coffee table beside him.

She came back, remembering to smile, into the living room. 'Sorry to take so long – coffee?'

'You don't buy that argument, then?' Joe was saying in response to something Edward had said.

'The possession of a weapon implies its use. How can anyone believe that an atomic standoff will make for a safer world?' said Edward, looking into his glass as he spoke. It was not like him to make such a direct and contentious statement.

'I guess people here don't want to see the danger – Truman keeps telling us that it's the only thing to keep us safe, and people are buying that line.' In the embassy circle it was quite normal for British people to express anti-American feeling, but it was surprising to Laura that Joe was falling in with that critical tone, and even more surprising that Edward did not seem to think it strange. Was Joe imitating something he had picked up on in Edward, in the hope of getting him to say more?

As Laura drank her coffee, the surreptitious way Joe had poured away his drink replayed itself again and again in her mind. What was it that had brought Joe here tonight? Why was he trying to get Edward so drunk? Was it so that he could take the temperature of his anti-Americanism once and for all? Had he come to suspect him? Was it the crass reference to the revolution that Edward had made drunkenly in a midnight garden? Was it Edward's desperate struggle with his role as the perfect Cambridge-educated civil servant, now refracted in a different light since Joe had watched the unmasking of Hiss, the perfect Harvard-educated civil servant? Or was it Joe's desperate hope, finally, to have a real story, a meaningful journey for his own life, that led him to sit here pouring bourbon into Edward's glass?

Was it, in some way, her own fault? Was it the sudden presence of Mrs Rostov beside her with her identical bag in the doorway of the uptown hairdresser? Was it the memory of Florence on the boat, something Joe had never mentioned since the first time they had met again, the memory of what her influence might have meant for Laura? Was it none of these? Was she going crazy? As Laura sat there, her stomach tense and her hands gripping her cup and saucer, Joe caught her eye and she thought she saw the smile that she had first seen, easy and sensual, in the tourist bar on the *Normandie* in 1939. Was Joe just wanting to get Edward a little drunk in the hope of spending some of the evening with his wife?

Although Laura was only on the periphery of the conversation, she could not leave the room. They went on for so long, drinking and talking. And although she hinted more than once that it might be time for Joe to leave, it seemed almost as though they were locked into some unbreakable dance, as the hours ticked on. Finally, Laura managed to force an acknowledgement of the late hour, and she made Edward offer to find Joe a taxi on the corner of the street. They went out together, and Laura went thankfully upstairs, and fell asleep as soon as she lay down, exhausted, not even waking when Edward came in. So when she woke to the tinny peal of the little alarm clock in the morning, she was horrified when he turned over and said, in a slurred, drink-tainted voice, 'Sorry, he's just on the sofa – couldn't find a taxi for love or money . . .'

'He's here?' Laura was shocked into the most sudden wakefulness. 'Here, now?'

She went out into the corridor. The floorboards were cold under her bare feet, and the little nail that stood out of one of them caught her heel as it had done before. She crept downstairs and saw Joe lying on the sofa, covered with a blanket. Knowledge fell through her, and she went into the study, where the Smith Corona typewriter sat openly on the desk. In the drawer below were the documents she had been typing the previous night, and the drawer was unlocked. She pulled it open. Had she placed the documents like that? She had been in a hurry, forgetful for the first time, casual as she had never been before. How incriminating were they? She saw the top security stamp on them, the numbers, the revelations, and she shut the drawer again, locking it this time, too late, and putting the key into the pocket of her bathrobe. She turned back to the living room. She was almost sure, from the rigidity and self-consciousness of Joe's body, that he was not asleep, but how could she really be sure?

There was no certainty left; the ground was slipping. She went upstairs, turned the shower full on in the bathroom, and stepped under it. When she came out of it, Edward was standing at the sink shaving, but she could not even meet his eyes in the mirror. She put on a plain skirt and blouse and went downstairs and made coffee and toast for Edward.

'No need to wake Joe,' she said when Edward came into the kitchen. 'I'll get him up in an hour or so. I don't think they start so early at the newspaper.' Then she put the radio on loudly, and ran the tap into the sink, and lowered her voice as she put a coffee in front of him. 'I didn't copy all the papers, but take them with you, don't let them stay here another day – take them back. And don't bring anything today – I had a word from Alex, we need to stop, wait something out, give it forty-eight hours.'

'All right,' Edward said. Had he caught the urgency in her voice? As he left, his step was slow.

When Joe woke, Laura was sitting in an armchair, smoking a cigarette, watching him. He sat up and shook his head. 'I feel lousy.'

'I'll make you some coffee.'

'No need – I'll get some in a drugstore – I should get to work.'

Laura insisted, and then picked up the tray from the previous night, and the ashtrays, and opened the curtains. She came back a few minutes later with breakfast to find the room empty, and waited for him to return from the bathroom. He came in, showered but obviously unshaven, and sat down on the edge of the sofa. If only she could tune in to the key of his thoughts, if only she could read his responses. Here they were alone in her house, nothing to interrupt them and nowhere to go, but he did not allow their hands to touch as he took the coffee, and by that more than anything Laura felt that he must know. He was moving away, he was distancing himself. Was it to ready himself before he struck the blow?

He drank his coffee in silence, and then brushed an imaginary crumb from his leg.

'Well, it was good to see you,' Laura said. 'Bring Suzanne next time, won't you?'

'Sure,' he said, not looking at her, and getting up. He, Laura thought, had not yet learned to act, had not yet been steeled into falseness. She said goodbye as he went into the hall. He turned, and they put out their hands, their fingers touched, but his were rigid under her touch. As he left, she stood at the door and watched him go down the street.

After he had gone, she ran upstairs. She kept the Minox

310

still in an old purse at the bottom of her closet. She took it out, wrapped in a handkerchief, and then she was back downstairs, picking up yesterday's newspaper, putting the Minox inside its sheets, pulling the pages she had typed the previous night out of the drawer of the desk, wrapping them too in the newspaper. Her actions were quick despite the confusion in her mind, and then she put on her coat, tied the belt tightly, and went out to a public telephone box. The newspaper with its weight of guilt was thrown decisively into a trash can at the corner of the street. She would have liked to take it further, but there was no time.

She saw Alex approaching the corner of M and 31st Street before he saw her, and she was careful to scan the approaches and not to walk directly to him. She walked past him, slow and measured, and felt him follow her. They went on for a block or two before she dropped back to his shoulder so that he could hear her. Then Laura told him what had happened. She was brief, necessarily, and as she talked she created certainty out of her cloud of uncertainty. She told him that he had to protect them, that the blow could fall any moment; that Joe was on his way to the newspaper. Alex said nothing; Laura did not know whether the silence meant despair or dissent.

'You can't abandon us,' she insisted, still whispering, but spitting her whisper out. 'Hiss had the statute of limitations, it was all in the past; this is today, and he – you know how hard he's finding it already, to keep it all together. When he's drunk he says things – what if people start remembering that?'

'What kind of things?'

Laura told him about how Edward had talked about the revolution to Joe, how he had openly stated his opposition to the nuclear deterrent. 'I don't think he always knows what he is saying, but there it is. You know – he drinks.'

'And he is still bringing such precious stuff,' said Alex. 'Go on then, go home.'

How Laura would have liked to shout at him, to tell him not to dismiss her like that, but she could control her fear for a few more seconds, a few more steps – so she did, and for the next few steps, and so on, and that, as always, was how she got through the day. She imagined nothing concrete, but images came constantly into her head – an instruction would come, perhaps, to go to the airport, or to the Soviet Embassy, once the defection had been arranged, or maybe Alex could be cleverer than that and plant some information on Joe to suggest that Edward was a double agent who was only passing false documents to confuse the Soviets. Anything would do, surely, just to throw him off the scent.

That afternoon Laura had an appointment at a dressmaker that Monica had recommended. It had taken her a long time to lose the weight she had gained years ago during her pregnancy, but now she had slimmed down, and wanted an old evening dress taken in. She stood there in front of the dressmaker's big mirror, while the waist of the dress was pulled tight to her body. 'You're cold,' noted the dressmaker. 'No, it's warm in here,' said Laura, trying to control the shake in her arms.

When she returned to the house, she asked Kathy, her voice urgent, if anyone at all had telephoned, but there had been nothing, and no post either. All evening Edward didn't come home, and Laura sat watching television in a stupor of tension. He came in long after she was in bed, and although he knew she was awake they said nothing to one another.

The next morning, after breakfast, Laura telephoned Ellen. It was routine for them to talk a couple of times a week. But Ellen seemed distracted, her voice a little croaky with a cold. 'Has Kit got in touch with you?' she said. 'He told Tom he wanted to come to Washington, but it all moves so fast with Jewish funerals.'

Laura's question was immediate, and inarticulate.

'Kit hasn't telephoned you? Such an awful accident, Laura, I hope you won't be too upset. They are still looking for the driver – some kind of hit and run – I can't understand how it could have happened. Suzanne is absolutely distraught.'

Laura finished the conversation with expressions of horror that were, she thought later, sufficient without being excessive. But then she left the house without thinking, without her coat, only coming to and realising how strange she must look walking like that through the cold streets when she found herself at the banks of the river, the wind whipping at her hair, blurring her vision, her hand pressed over her mouth. Believe me, she found herself muttering into her fingers, believe me. Perhaps she meant, believe me that I am not guilty, that I did not think of this, that I did not ask for this. But who would be listening? And who would ever believe her? And hot on the heels of shock came fear, so that her body was dizzy with the sense of menace she felt from every side: the streets were too loud now, that man walking behind her was a threat, that car passing too slowly was a threat; she felt exposed, panic like glue in her throat and juddering through her chest.

When she came back into the house she went to the drinks cupboard. Straight from the bottle, burning down, meeting her panic like a friend and wrapping its warmth around it – was this how Edward felt about the first gulp of brandy before lunch? Her bowels were churning now and she ran to the lavatory. Once she was finished she washed her hands, over and over again, and then went to the telephone. She called the newspaper and got Suzanne's telephone number, but found herself, for all her intentions, unable to dial it. She went out again, this time properly dressed in a coat and hat, and found her way, blundering through the grey city, to Monica's house, and made her telephone Suzanne and give appropriate messages of condolence, and made her telephone Edward and Archie at work to tell them, and got her to get

313

out the brandy bottle and distract Laura with her daughters and her gossip until she had recovered her self-control. Her self-control, which was so much greater than Monica or anyone else would ever have imagined, which she was learning to buckle on again, tightening the armour across her chest and face.

Although Joe had not, as far as Laura knew, been observant, the funeral was held two days later, as soon as the body was released, in a synagogue at the edge of the city. There she sat with the other women, in a gallery of the panelled room, looking down on the men who were weaving some kind of rhythmic process of memory and repetition that would mean something to the others there, but not to her. Laura was distant from it all, but intensely aware, in the way one might be in a dream, of Suzanne at the end of the row, and how her legs seemed restless, she kept tapping her foot or crossing her ankles. For a moment Laura felt as if she were in Suzanne's skin and realised how unbearable her physical life had become to her, how she was only keeping herself in the room by a huge effort of will. The service had already begun when Laura saw Edward come in, unfamiliar in one of the head coverings that he must have been given at the entrance, and sit down tentatively, as if he was unsure of his movements, at the edge of a bench at the side of the men's section.

As they walked out to the cemetery, she found herself looking again and again at Edward. There comes a time in a marriage when you stop seeing the man you are living with, and for many months now Laura had not looked straight at him. But suddenly, in that dark moment, when she would have given anything to have been able to walk away from him, and from herself, and all the horror that their relationship seemed capable of creating, Laura looked at him afresh. Was it pity that stirred in her, as she saw how lonely he looked there among those men who were all bound up in a shared ritual about which he and she knew nothing? Once

314

they had been so sure that they were creating a new heaven on earth. And now, how uncertain he looked as he passed a hand over his mouth and listened to the men around him, but did not join their conversation. As the earth spattered down on the coffin in its newly dug trench, she saw him walk away from the mourners, back to work, alone.

Laura was told that the crowd were to go back to a relative's apartment, not far from the synagogue, and when she got there she found the room held a dozen or so elderly Jewish men and women, and various trays of food. She sat with Suzanne for a while, their knees almost touching on the over-stuffed sofa, listening to reminiscences, and at one point Laura found herself telling an old aunt of his about meeting him on the *Normandie* before the war. 'He loved his work,' Laura said, 'being a journalist. He believed that he could tell the truth.' The aunt nodded. 'He was a good boy,' she said, 'a good, good boy.'

Even now, sitting here on the balcony and looking out over a lake in the long evening, this is the memory that flattens the horizon, that shuts down the light. You can excuse your-self, Laura tells herself, over and over again as the memories rise. Remember, you had no idea, you planned nothing, you asked for nothing except safety. They did it all. You did nothing.

There are always excuses.

Air

1950–1953

1

'Y ou haven't changed,' Sybil said to Laura. 'Except you
look so – American.'

Laura only realised as she stepped into the London house
how incongruous she might look now, over-perfumed, over-
made up and, as she shrugged off her coat, over-dressed in
one of the boldly coloured bouclé dresses that all the
Washington wives had been wearing that season. Edward
hung back as they came in, and Laura began to talk, telling
Sybil that she hadn't changed one bit herself. In a way of
course that was true. You can see the kernel of someone's
face and personality even when they have solidified. There
had always been such a density to Sybil's body and now she
seemed even heavier, not fat, but solid and unsmiling, her
square jaw and prominent nose more dominant with that new
chignon taking her blonde hair up and back.

'Just like the old days,' Laura was saying, as if the thought
gave her pleasure, turning from Sybil to Toby where he was
standing in the doorway of the living room. And he too
was planted, but the solidity seemed borne of uncertainty, as
if he needed a moment to regroup as he took in the change

in his brother. He nodded at Edward. 'Sorry to hear you've been unwell.'

Edward nodded back, saying that he was on the mend, and Laura suggested that they should go upstairs and wash, the flight had been so tiring. They were not in their old room, Sybil was explaining, because that was the nursery now. They were further up. And how were the children? Laura asked, injecting eagerness into her voice. They were having supper with Nanny, Sybil told her, but Laura could see them afterwards. Women's voices, going up the stairs, while the two brothers remained silent, following them. On the landing stood a familiar figure. 'Ann!' said Laura, moving forwards, remembering the intimacy they had known during the war.

'Yes, Ann is still here – housekeeper now,' Sybil said, going on up the stairs, as Ann stepped aside from Laura as if it would be bad form for them to acknowledge one another as friends. 'We thought we'd have a quiet evening tonight, but tomorrow, when you've had a chance to rest, everyone – Winifred, Alistair . . .'

And Giles? Laura was careful to sound happy about the plans. Yes, Giles would be there too, it would be dinner at the Savoy, it would be a celebration.

A celebration. Laura thanked Sybil and closed the door on her and Toby, leaving her with Edward in this unfamiliar room up in the eaves.

'Here we are again,' Edward said. In the early days of their love, how she had revelled in his silences. They had suggested they had little need for words. But now his laconic statements were painful; unsaid thoughts pushed against them. She stood at the window, looking down through the watery new glass onto the square that had been given back to ornamental shrubs, taking off her gloves, finger by finger.

'Do you want to go down for supper?' was all she said.

'Yes, of course, can't keep Toby waiting. I wouldn't mind a bath.'

317

'You go first, I'll wait.' We can at least be polite, Laura was always reminding herself.

The room they were in was rather shabby, as if put together from a go-round of other rooms – a too-big bedstead, a too-small wardrobe, curtains that did not quite meet in the middle of the window. But the ground floor of Sybil's house had recovered its comfortable face, and was carpeted and well lit. The living room was now a surprisingly acid green rather than the previous turquoise, so that the old oil paintings looked out of place on the walls. As the evening dragged on, Laura realised that Sybil and Toby were reconstructing a life precisely modelled on their own parents' and grandparents' lives. The children had already been put to bed by their nanny, their dinner was four courses and served in the dining room where the portrait of Sybil's mother had been restored to its pre-war place, and Sybil took Laura into the living room for a 'little chat' before the men joined them.

The chat, Laura was glad to discover, was not going to be about their husbands. The change in Edward and their ignominious return from Washington would not be discussed, and neither would Toby's evident loss of direction now that he had lost his parliamentary seat. Laura could tell his heart was not in his new life as he crumbled a bread roll, talking of the biography he was working on, how the London Library was so helpful. So the two women sitting in the acid-green living room did not talk about the men as they tried to feel their way into some kind of ease. They talked about Mrs Last, and how unwell she had been ever since she had given up Sutton Court, and about Winifred, and how she had still not married, and Laura asked Sybil for all the details of her children and asked if she could photograph them one day. 'It's my little hobby,' she said in a dismissive tone. 'One has to have something,' Sybil said, bracingly.

When they drove over to the Savoy for dinner the following evening, the city fell dimly on either side of them. Even in this,

London's richest neighbourhood, so many holes still gaped, so many façades were still filthy, paving stones still uneven. But then the lobby of the hotel opened before them, polished and coloured, as though private wealth could overcome public squalor with a single confident gesture.

The four of them were earlier than the others, but there were the first martinis to be drunk in a bar where waiters fluttered and a pianist played an unfamiliar song. Here, in public, Sybil retreated into that formal manner that Laura remembered from the past. Now she read it differently, as self-consciousness rather than as a judgement on her, on Laura, but that didn't make it easier to break through. Winifred's arrival brought a new tension with it; Laura knew how curious she always was, and began at once to forestall her, asking her questions as they went through to the restaurant. She knew that Winifred had moved on from the Ministry of Food, but was unsure what she was doing now; her letters had become sporadic recently. That was because she had been so busy, Winifred apologised, and now she was moving on again. 'It's annoying that I'll be off so soon after you're back . . .' Yes, out of London – out of England, in fact; off to Geneva and the United Nations outfit.

Laura was impressed. Not only by the understated confidence with which Winifred talked about one job and another, but by her whole presence. No longer did she seem to be trying to fit herself into a template of her mother's idea of femininity, bursting out of it uncontrollably from time to time. Now she had taken possession of her own personality. Her hair was cut quite short, in a style Laura would never have recommended to anyone, but which made her head and shoulders look so energetic next to Laura and Sybil with their stiffly waved hair. And her dress – sleeveless, almost straight, unlike the other women's wide skirts – gave her a different, more dynamic profile: her arms were strong against its plain lines.

As soon as Winifred began to ask Laura questions in return,

319

Laura turned the conversation to Aunt Dee and what she thought of Winifred's prospective move to Europe. It was not surprising to hear that she found it quite unbearable, all of a piece with Winifred's inability to find a husband. 'As for Giles . . .' Winifred said, and Laura realised she was curious to see him. 'You know he was chucked out of the Air Ministry. The poor thing is out in some odd medical place in Bristol now.' There seemed to be a note of pity in Winifred's voice. That was new. Hadn't she always rather looked up to her brother, even when she had been angry or irritated by him?

And just then Giles came in with Alistair. Giles with an unexpected little beard, rather messy-looking, but Alistair apparently unchanged, his sharp blue gaze taking everyone in. Their gestures were as expansive, their voices as loud as ever, and as everyone was seated the energy rose; there were greetings and explanations, menus were opened, wine was ordered. But soon the group seemed to splinter. Sybil had become even more unbending, and was looking at Giles with a tight face as he recounted some anecdote about his new workplace – where they were researching brain waves, Laura understood him to say, in frogs and monkeys as well as people. There was a fragile edge to his confidence now, as though he had to exaggerate his words to believe them himself.

Meanwhile Alistair was talking sotto voce to Edward, asking him what he thought of his new novel, a thinly disguised autobiography. Edward had been holding it on the journey back, but Laura guessed from his diffident responses to Alistair that he had not read it, or had not liked it. Toby, on Laura's right, had sunk into silence and Laura felt she had to try to rouse him by asking him more about the children. Nobody seemed comfortable in their conversations, and Winifred was observing Edward, Laura realised. Laura was quick to jump in to talk when the shutter came down over his face and he lost the thread of the conversation, but as the evening wore on Winifred's glances towards him were frequent.

After the plates of the main course were cleared, Winifred stood up. 'Come on,' she said, touching Laura's shoulder. Thinking she was just going to the bathroom, Laura stood up with her and left the room. Once they were out of the restaurant, however, Winifred took Laura's arm in a tight grip and led her through to the bar. 'Two martinis,' she said to the barman and then turned to Laura. 'So, what is up with Edward?'

There was a line that Laura had already used a lot, and she used it now, without a pause. 'He's had a breakdown. It all stemmed from overwork – it's just been the most fearful strain. You know he hasn't stopped working for all these years; we've hardly had a holiday. They put too much responsibility on him in Washington. No wonder he had a crack-up.'

The drinks came, and Laura took refuge in hers, fishing out the olive and putting it unwanted into her mouth, where it sat, salty and inedible.

'What sort of crack-up – mad?'

Laura swallowed down the olive and took a sip of the cocktail. Too weak and not cold enough. What could she say about the weeks after Hiss's sentence and Joe's funeral, Edward's days of torpor and sudden breaks into crazed energy, her desperate attempts to stop him drinking? Better to say nothing. At least other people could still believe in their marriage. So she glossed over it, telling Winifred that she had asked the embassy herself for sick leave for Edward so that he could come home and rest.

'And they agreed?'

'Had to, really – he's been so wonderful over the years. They don't want to lose him. They say he has to get treatment; they've recommended a psychiatrist . . .' Laura could not go on. This was her new fear, blotting out the rest. What would happen if Edward did go to a psychiatrist? What might he say? How would he manage, to talk without talking, to try to be frank without ever letting slip a word? She tried to smile, but her face seemed tight. 'You know, I don't know

321

how a psychiatrist will help – I'm not sure of that kind of thing . . .'

To her surprise, Winifred began to give quick advice. 'Don't let them send him to any old quack, send him to Lvov – you remember him? He'll understand.'

Winifred said that as if there was something she understood, something that she knew and Laura knew. And at that moment Laura felt that there might be, like an oasis ahead of her, the prospect of laying down, just for a while, the dragging burden of secrecy. She looked at Winifred, longing and afraid. 'But is he really trustworthy – it has to be someone who can help him get back to work, not just embark on some, you know, trawl through any troubles . . .'

'He will understand. Look, I'll tell you a secret,' said Winifred. 'You'll have to swear not to tell a soul, though.'

Laura nodded, as another gulp of her martini hit her throat.

'Giles went to him. You see, the reason why Giles doesn't work for the government any more is that they got nervous about his – well, his chequered love life. Oh, let's not pretend. They didn't like him fucking all the boys. There was a young man who was determined to make trouble. We only managed to stop a prosecution by the skin of our teeth. Lvov got him out of a tight corner – told his bosses at the Air Ministry he was tackling his perversions. I don't know if he was or he wasn't, but Lvov backed him up. He had to leave in the end, but at least nothing went public.'

Laura realised, with a slow dawning, that Winifred thought that Edward had overstepped the mark in the way that Giles had. Did Winifred think – did she really think, that Edward also . . . ? Laura's mind closed down on this absurd suggestion and she did as she had always done when she felt she had lost control of the situation, she mimicked Winifred's own thoughts and voice, saying in a high tone, 'It's important that Edward gets back to work. It's important that nothing – nothing that would bother the Foreign Office . . .'

322

And Winifred, apparently sure that they were both talking about the same thing, agreed. 'Exactly. It's pretty awful the way that these boys have to toe the line not just at work, but even, you know, in their private life. Lvov understands that, he won't say anything that will put Edward in bad odour with Whitehall.'

'It's worth thinking about.'

'I'll give you his number. You could go and talk to him first, if you think that would be best. Now drink up, tell me how you have been doing.'

After their drinks they went back to the others, and Sybil looked reproving; they had been absent for too long. But the men had not noticed; there were quite enough anecdotes about old acquaintances to sustain them without the women's conversation. Although to Laura the energy of the evening seemed already to have dispersed, Giles was talking about where they would go after dinner. Apparently the Ace had closed down ages ago, but he knew somewhere just like it, he told them.

'I have to go back,' said Sybil, frowning at Toby so that he motioned for the bill.

'Let's go on,' said Edward, pushing away his glass. Laura picked up her purse. She knew she had to go with him, though she didn't know if she could bear to listen to many more of Alistair's descriptions of a hilarious prank a writer friend of his had played on some pompous critic, or Giles's complaints about how some chap at the Maudsley had got all his ideas on delta waves from Giles's own paper on the subject. But there was no stepping off for her now, so she got up with apparent alacrity and accepted her coat from the waiter, and went along at Edward's elbow to one basement club and then another, and even after Winifred had gone home and the clubs were empty apart from a handful of sodden men, she stayed with him and Alistair and Giles, and at the end of the evening she got him into a taxi, and she and the driver dragged him out of it and up Sybil's steps.

Lvov's room, book-lined and carpeted, was screened from the noise and bustle of Marylebone High Street. For an instant, walking in, Laura felt a familiarity with it, but she could not place why. Perhaps it bore a resemblance to Toby's study in Chester Square. Lvov himself was unchanged, and had a reassuring air of finding everything completely unsurprising. It was as though he had expected her one day to walk into his consulting room and tell him about her husband's crack-up. So she talked just a little more frankly than she had with Winifred, although still all the things that could not be said were loud in her head, so loud that sometimes she lost the thread of what she was saying.

'It was after this friend of yours died that he broke down?'

As Lvov asked her a few questions about Edward's relationship with Joe, she realised that, just like Winifred, he was assuming that sexual secrets were driving Edward's horrors. She wished she could confront that assumption, pull it out and destroy it, but she knew that to do so she would need another narrative to override it, and that narrative had to remain dark. She continued to talk about how important it was that Edward became fit enough to work and that he tackled his drinking. As she spoke, she realised how she must appear: an American girl who put all her faith in clean living and hard work. She stumbled, and tried to make it sound as though the obsession with work came from Edward. 'The Foreign Office is his life. But . . . he needs to be reassured . . . that he doesn't have to do everything perfectly. He overworks terribly, you know, he feels every failure – of diplomacy – on his shoulders.'

'And I have to report back on him to the Foreign Office, do I?'

'Well, yes, that's what I understand. But the thing is . . . if anything damaging . . . tell me, Mr Lvov – about confidentiality.'

'I can report to the Foreign Office if necessary about his suitability to work . . . not about other issues. My job is not to investigate crimes.' And then he went on talking about what he could do, how he could explore the motivation for addiction, for unhappiness, but Laura was not really listening. She was wondering whether he could understand a crime that was not an overload of private longing. Would he find it inexplicable, or merely uninteresting, that a man might be driven by a political rather than a sexual dream?

Then he was asking for more details of Edward's breakdown and Laura explained to him that the drinking had been going on for so long, nothing remarkable in that, everyone drank in Washington, the long evenings were fuelled by drink, but it was as though, after Joe died, Edward had lost the brakes, and sometimes, once or twice, the drunkenness had spiralled into violence. Laura said a little about one night when she had been called by the police and heard that Edward and a young man had been fighting on the steps of a Washington hotel. The young man was a mild, intellectual type from the State Department; how he and Edward could have come to blows she still did not understand. Perhaps, she said to Lvov without conviction, it had merely been lost footing, one falling against another while going drunkenly downstairs.

'And you, what about the effects on you, tell me . . .'

That question came as a shock, and Laura shifted in her chair. 'It was so hard – it's so—' She came to a halt, and Lvov allowed a silence to settle.

Ever since the day when she had alerted Alex to her fears, Laura had felt unanchored, the waters around her too unpredictable. She had never spoken even to Edward about what she had done; and sometimes she was filled with a nebulous hope that if it was never said, it had not happened. Perhaps Joe had never known about their secrets, perhaps his death had been an accident, perhaps she could breathe freely again. And then she would wake again to a morning when all the breath was crushed out of her by guilt. Was it that rocking of guilt and hope that left Edward so unmoored?

As those thoughts ran through her, she felt as though she was about to speak. How seductive were the promises of the psychoanalyst, she saw now – here, all would be confidential; here, nothing would leave the room; here, maybe she could lay down the armour for an instant. 'I've always known he is under strain – but it was . . .' But as she began, a sensation almost like falling came over her and she realised why the room felt familiar to her.

With a rush, an old memory was coming back, taking her in its grip: there had been a room, not this one, but similar, a room made for listening. And filled with a similar presence, a doctor she was supposed to talk to, to tell why she was being so difficult, why she would not eat. She was thirteen, fourteen maybe, in Stairbridge, the sounds through the windows were the sounds of Main Street in summer 1934, and the secret she was about to tell was so great she would not tell it, she would never tell it, it had to remain in the place where the lies were kept, where the violence was hidden. Offered a chance to break it open, she did then as she would do now, rising and shaking her head, saying she must go, that she was fine, but now she was in control, she was an adult, she was promising Lvov that Edward would be in touch shortly, she could shift off the danger and free herself from the terrible temptation of honesty by walking away and into Marylebone High Street, walking away from the possibility of opening the door to where all the secrets lay, and there was that little leather shop she had heard about across the street which sold the softest pumps . . . she went in, tried on a pair, saw herself in the mirror, well dressed, quiet, unremarkable.

She was wearing the same outfit, a grey dress with white collar, that she had worn when she had gone to see Edward's superior at the embassy in Washington. That had been the day after Edward had lost control. The day when she knew something had to be done, when Edward realised she had hidden the drink in the house, when he had started to smash up the kitchen and the living room, looking for it, when she had tried to hold him back and fallen against a coffee table. This grey dress with its high neck and long sleeves had been useful to hide the long bruise on her upper arm; in it she looked respectable and well kempt, despite the hopelessness in her face.

Edward's superior was one Robin Muir. He was a silver-haired, tall man with a withered left arm, who had become embarrassed when Laura had allowed herself to cry in front of him – a few tears, a tremble in her voice, as she said that she thought Edward was pushing himself over the edge. He had agreed with her, it was time to get him home. He had murmured with an attempt at reassurance that it was only because he was such a good worker that he was finding it all such a strain. She nodded, as she remembered how Edward Last had once been Halifax's golden boy, Inverchapel's right-hand man, Oliver Franks' trusted confidant. 'I think three ambassadors have rather relied on your husband. He probably has felt the responsibility too much. I'm sure you have too. It must have been difficult for you both.'

As Laura walked back to Sybil's house, her mind was clouded. But she held onto the main thing: Lvov would see Edward, he had promised secrecy, and even if he did not understand what he was promising to be secret about, it was the best she could do. A quick glass of brandy, she thought, and then I'll feel better, but she stopped the thought. She must stay in control. It frightened her that twice recently she had been tempted to tell someone about things that must never be told. But had she really been tempted? Letting herself into the hall, taking off her hat, she wondered. Maybe she had just been testing herself, building the walls again. Building them higher.

Going into the living room, she found Edward looking through a book. He seemed to be writing notes on it, absorbed. When he heard her, he looked up and for the first time in a while there seemed to be a smile on his face. He had changed, as everyone had noticed; his face had slackened and yellowed, his demeanour had lost that characteristic certainty. But when energy returned to him, as now, the change was not so obvious. 'Take a look,' he said, crossing over to the window. Laura was unsure what she was meant to be looking at. The street was wide and bright, there was nobody there, just a woman with a dog, walking slowly. 'I mean the motor,' Edward said, pointing out a blue Austin parked outside. 'Bought it off Alistair – he didn't want it any more. Come on, we're going out for the day, London's too stifling.'

Sliding into the passenger seat next to Edward, Laura wished she had had time to change her grey dress, which was already sticky under the arms. 'There must have been an accident,' Edward said, drumming his fingers on the steering wheel as they sat in a long traffic jam in Bressenden Place. But as they left the city behind, Laura wound down her window and felt the breeze. English spring, later, more tentative, more promising, than spring in Washington, had got into its stride while she hadn't been looking. All through the edges of south London were ribbons of new housing, but eventually a green patchwork of fields and low hills, drenched in sunlight, asserted itself. The silence between them solidified during the drive, until finally Edward slowed down in a village: a wide green, a pond dappled with light, a few rows of well-kept houses, a pub. 'This is the spot,' he said, parking.

As she got out, Laura asked how he knew the place. It was odd to think that he had come here before the war, before they had met, and yet had remembered it. An old university friend had lived nearby, he explained. 'Will you be warm enough here?' Here was a garden behind the pub, with wooden tables worn grey and grass going to seed around them. That politeness, he relied on it as she did, covering up the hopelessness between them with the careful give and take of civilised conversation. As he went into the pub to get drinks, a rather mangy cat wound itself around Laura's legs. She pushed it away, thinking it looked as if it had fleas, and it sloped through the grass as if it did not care, over to another table. Edward came out with a lemonade for himself and a gin and tonic for her, and a menu. She never knew what to choose at places like this, so she let him decide. Although the pie with a thick brown gravy looked unappetising, it was hot and savoury. They soon exhausted talk of the pie, the pub and the cat, which had returned and was pushing its head against Edward's leg.

After they had eaten, they lit cigarettes and looked out over the almost too picturesque scene, and Laura was wondering whether she should start to talk about Lvov when Edward spoke. 'I know you want to move out of Sybil's.' She had raised this already with him, since the retreat back to being guests in that house made her feel as though she was trying to relive something long gone, but she was unprepared when he said that he was thinking that they should move right out of the city, into a village like this. As soon as he said it, she could see why he suggested it. As far as she knew, their handlers had not been in touch. Perhaps they would not be in touch. Perhaps the precious Virgil and Pigeon were both too tainted now. Perhaps this could be the chance for a new start. A quiet life.

She did not know what to say. She stalled, asking if he was serious. 'We don't have to decide now,' he said, getting up, and then suggested that they should go for a walk. They went to the bar to pay, and then Edward took her through the village, onto a footpath he seemed to remember on the other side of the green, which soon ran uphill into a wood. Bluebells lay in electric puddles among the trees, and cow parsley brushed their legs. The richness of the flowers and the birdsong, rising up from all sides, took Laura backwards, to those days she remembered when she had felt drunk with the lavishness of spring, when Edward's body had gathered up the sunshine and brought it into hers. Now, emerging from the wood and seeing the grassy slopes glistening as if they had been washed, it was like looking at everything through the wrong end of binoculars. She could appreciate it. She could say, what a lovely spring day. She could say, how warm it is in the sunshine. But she knew they were not celebrants with the song of the thrushes. She knew they were just onlookers at the spring glory.

They sat for a while on Edward's coat, on the side of the path. London was a distant smudge to the north, and in front of them the downs rolled airily. 'Breathless, we flung us on the windy hill,' Edward quoted.

'You know so much poetry.' Laura realised that her tone sounded dismissive, and she looked at him, trying to smile. So he had thoughts for the future, a future that still included her. She did not even know herself whether that was what she wanted, but if he was serious he must know that he would also have to start the therapy that the Foreign Office had insisted upon. She started to tell him about Lvov, about how Giles had gone to him, how he was discreet, a friend of Winifred's . . . Edward seemed nonplussed at the thought of her going to talk to a therapist for him, but then he changed and there was something like gratitude in his tone. Talking directly about the situation was like plunging their hands into something dirty, and they withdrew as quickly as they could. But not before Edward had said, in a stilted voice, how sorry he was, he was determined to stop drinking.

'I know what you've had to put up with,' he said. Laura was not sure that he did know. But now she wanted to change the conversation, so she smiled at him, saying that he didn't have to give up alcohol and move to the country and go into therapy all at once. That sounded a little overwhelming, she said in a light voice. He matched her lighter tone, but still insisted that it was time for a new start.

'As long as we can still have a martini before supper,' Laura said, smiling.

'A few glasses of wine during . . .'

'And a whisky after.'

'No, seriously, Laura. I do mean it.'

'But how would we manage living here if they give you back a job?'

'It's easy enough from Whitehall. You get the train from Victoria to Oxted. Doesn't take long at all. You'll be able to go up and down to town whenever you like.'

Laura could not bear to throw his tentative plan back in his face, so she lifted her hand and rested it on his arm, turning him towards her, and kissed him. During the kiss she felt the movement of his mouth, and the taste of the meat from lunch still on his lips. She drew back, and pulled at a windflower on the grass beside her, crushing it between her fingers. He stood up, and they started to walk back down the hill; the sun was already beginning to feel less warm.

3

That first evening when they were alone in the new house Laura found her uncertainty dissipated in the rush of organising the move. All day she had been busy supervising deliveries, making up beds, shaking out cushions. The house's demeanour was coy; it sat back from the road to the village down its own little unmade drive, a dark approach lined with rhodo-dendrons and laurels. But upstairs you could see the airy hills where they had walked on their first visit, while the living room and the kitchen next to it had big French windows that led into a walled garden. As the day wore on, she was going

331

in and out of those rooms with the doors open, so that the scent of the garden blew into the house.

After dinner Laura got out her notepaper and a pen, and scribbled letters to Mother and Ellen, to Monica and to Suzanne. She told all of them that they could come and stay if they wanted; she told them about the garden; how close they were to London; how it had been quite easy to find somewhere because other people, the estate agent said, preferred the new developments closer to town; how they had bought much of the furniture with the house, but some of it was rather awful . . .

As she wrote, Edward sat reading. He had had his first session with Lvov that day, and he seemed amused rather than threatened by it. As she wrote, he came out from time to time with little aperçus about psychotherapy and the unconscious. Once she had finished her letters, she made them tea and they drank it sitting opposite one another on the old sofas. They must look so settled, Laura thought.

She had left the window open in the big bedroom, and as she went in she saw there were moths caught in the lampshade. She turned off the light and stood there in the dark, waiting for them to fly out. Edward came in and began to undress. They did not embrace, but the large, high iron bedstead made up with the new linen that Sybil had given her as a housewarming present was comforting in the darkness.

Almost immediately, the house itself insisted on a new rhythm to their lives. Edward's was still mainly based in London: Monday and Thursday he attended sessions with Lvov, and afterwards he would have lunch with Toby and go to the London Library, while every Tuesday, Wednesday and Friday he played tennis at a club in Hyde Park before getting the train back to Surrey. It was Laura whom the house held close: she had to find clothes in the heathery hues that women wore here; to learn to drive so that she could go up and down to the station, to the shops; to choose new cushion covers and curtains; to find a gardener and get a book about borders so that she could learn the names of the flowers she saw in other gardens and wanted to see blooming in her own; to find someone to come in daily and help with the cleaning.

One day Edward was called up to the Foreign Office for a meeting, and she was to join him afterwards at Sybil's for tea before they went back to Surrey together. When Laura had telephoned Sybil to arrange this, she had asked if she could come early and take some photographs of her and her children. She told Edward she thought she could give Sybil some prints as a thank you for taking them in on their return from Washington. But really it was a selfish request; she was missing the shock of satisfaction she had found in the past when the contact sheets were returned from the developer, and there among all the ordinary or muddied images were, suddenly, the sharp contrast and the memorable expression, the recreation of the chaotic world in an ordered arrangement, and the pleasure that gave her.

Laura photographed the twins, George and Alice, on their own and flanking Sybil on one of her wide sofas in the living room, which was filled with oblique light. But she couldn't get into her stride. Sybil's self-consciousness was so off-putting, and George had a way of bouncing up just as the shutter was about to click, so that she was sure he would be blurred and that Alice would be looking towards him.

'Why don't you all come down to Patsfield for lunch soon?' she said, as she was packing the camera away. 'I could try again then, if these don't turn out too well.'

At that moment Ann came in with the tea. As before, her manner suggested that she hardly knew Laura, that she'd forgotten the long nights they'd shared in the stifling kitchen during the war. 'Mr Edward is coming in,' she told her as she set the table. As Sybil went out to find Toby in his study, Edward came in and Laura looked at him with a question in her expression.

'Back to work next week,' he said. And as Sybil and Toby came back into the room together, he spoke about it as if with satisfaction; something really senior again, Head of the American Department in London. Laura dropped the lens cap she was holding. Alice was asking for a scone, and she moved to the tea table to butter one, and to pour milk for the children.

'Jam?' Laura asked Alice, and Sybil told her that the children didn't have jam on their scones, while at the same time Laura could hear Toby was suggesting dinner to celebrate, and Laura was relieved when Edward said they would get back to Patsfield.

The train was crowded at this time, London spilling its workers back into the suburbs before gathering them in again the next day, and it felt impossible to talk with those men and women listening to every word as they read their newspapers and sweated into their dark suits and dresses. But Edward always left the car at the station, and as they drove home through the midge-laden dusk, he could tell her more about the job. She heard the energy return to his voice; it would mean going back to the centre of things, she realised, he would have knowledge again, he would be precious again. Apprehension gathered in her as he spoke.

Back in the kitchen, Laura took some chops out of the icebox. She could not be bothered to peel potatoes, but the bread she had bought the day before was still soft, and there were ripe tomatoes for a salad, the remains of a cauliflower cheese that she had cooked the day before that could warm through in the oven. He stood looking out of the window as she moved around the kitchen, looking into the garden where the shadows were lengthening under the trees.

'So you start next week—'

'You remember Stefan—'

Their voices tangled, and then Edward's statement that Stefan wanted to see her fell into the silence she left.

'I won't,' she said.

As if he was reassuring her, Edward told her that he hadn't been followed, and neither was Stefan, that they had met for a few seconds on the way to Lvov's rooms this morning. Laura could not understand why he was talking in such detail – it was not allowed, and she said again, 'I won't.'

Edward rubbed his hands over his eyes. 'We couldn't have known.' His statement was ambiguous, and Laura chose not to straighten it out. Left as it was, it might suggest that he knew Laura had told Alex about Joe, but that she could not have foreseen the outcome; that he believed she was not to blame. How she longed for that to be the case.

She went to the icebox and got out a bottle of wine. 'Just one?'

They drank together, as the chops sizzled in the pan.

'I'll tell you something else – Archie's coming to London too. Monica will be pleased, won't she?' Edward was clearly responding to Laura's desire to change the subject, and she tried to join in, discussing with him how much Monica disliked Washington, how good it would be to see them again. They went on talking inconsequentially as she dished up the supper, and then as they ate Laura finally said what was on her mind, what had been on her mind for so long.

'If you wanted to, would there be another way – I mean, could you—?'

'There isn't a way out, for me. But I'll tell Stefan you won't meet him again.'

'Is that really true? Is there no other way for you?'

'How could there be? I'm sorry, though. For you.'

It was hard to hear him say that, and to realise how alone he must feel now, in his pursuit of his goal. Laura could not tell if he had also lost faith that the goal could be there, ahead, on the infinitely receding horizon. 'Don't be sorry for me,' she said.

'But you regret it all, don't you? You wish you'd never started. Never met me.'

This honesty was a place they had never been before, a place beyond all the fury and drunkenness in Washington, beyond their recent politeness and their attempts to create a show of a new life. Laura pushed her chair back and its wooden feet caught on the slate floor with a horrible squeal. She took his plate. His hand went out to the wine bottle. She put the plate down and covered his hand with hers.

'No. I don't.' As soon as she said it, she realised it was true. Up to now in Patsfield, although she had been playing the part of the dutiful wife, she had not been doing so with any conviction; really she had felt that she was only playing a temporary role, biding time until Edward was back on his feet. But tonight, as she saw how he was trying to make something good and decent for them, even within the trap they had made for themselves, she was filled with pity and protectiveness. Any mistakes he had made, after all, she had also made – and worse. The disintegration was mutual. It was not something he had brought upon her. And then she wondered, hot on the heels of the softening she felt, was she the drag on his happiness now? Would he feel freer without her? 'Do you regret me?' she made herself say, matching his honesty with hers. He took his hand from hers.

'I've made many mistakes in my life,' he said, as his hand grasped the wine bottle and poured both of them the last of the wine. 'Loving you was not one of them.'

Laura bent and kissed him, and he stood up and took her properly in his arms. In that moment, she was ready to find him again, and they went upstairs. It had been a long time since they had made love, and it was a different journey from the ones they had made in the past. She undressed him, undoing the buttons of his shirt, the cold buckle of his belt, as he undressed her, both of them finding the warmth of flesh and shuddering with the intimacy of the touch. They did not fumble and rush, half dressed, tumbling towards their orgasm, she allowed him to be fully naked and herself to be naked with him. Now that he was no longer drinking heavily, his skin smelled as it had done when they had first met, she realised, as she moved her mouth down his throat and chest; it had that fresh scent she remembered, something like apple peel. From time to time she was afraid of losing the shape of her desire, in this newly gentle exploration, but in the end she found the lines of her own pleasure, flowing through his responses. There was a moment, as she straddled him and he entered her from below, when she realised that they did not have to spin stars out of one another to find one another. It was different, but it was the same. It was no longer being overtaken by desire for her golden hero. They came together as equals, bringing one another through the waves of pleasure, and just at the moment of her orgasm, she lost the bitter consciousness of her divided self, she was no longer separated from herself or from him.

4

A few weeks later, in the height of summer, Sybil and Winifred came down to Patsfield one Saturday with Sybil's children. Edward was in Rome for a conference and Laura had spent the week working on the house. They did not seem to have much money left in the bank even though Edward's salary had now been restarted, but she had spent some of it on new curtains – olive green and dark blue – and a tea table that could go on the terrace. A climbing rose on the west wall had burst into great red splurges, and she had picked some of the bigger flowers and put them in a bowl in the hall. Inside and outside the summer scents wove together. There was no point, she thought, in trying to pretend that the house was like Sybil's, a great accretion of intently hoarded possessions, but she tried to make it into a pretty frame for that summer day.

Sybil was happy for the children to sit for more photographs, and this time Laura knew it was going well. They sat among the geraniums in the wild borders, and she took close-ups of George squatting down looking seriously at a beetle he had found on a leaf, with Alice kneeling beside him. There was the evanescent sweetness that everyone wants to associate with children – there, in Alice's wide eyes and George's pointing finger.

After the pictures were done, Sybil let the children hide with their tea in the spaces behind the dark laurels at the back of the garden, while the women sat on the terrace. Laura had bought a fruitcake at a recent village fete, and they ate it while drinking the Earl Grey tea she had ordered from the village grocer. Sybil seemed unconscious of the effort she had made, which Laura took as a kind of tribute, but Winifred looked at her in an appraising way.

'You are the good housewife, aren't you? I suppose you're not thinking of working?'

What work could I possibly do, Laura thought, imagining herself in an office now, inexperienced and ignorant. 'It's not like during the war, is it? In Washington, none of the wives worked.'

'But aren't you bored to death out here? I wouldn't have thought village life was quite your thing. Does Edward think that you are his mother?'

Laura found Winifred's directness invigorating. It was the idea that she had been thinking about her at all, had been wondering whether Laura was doing the right thing, which touched her.

'It's so much better for Edward coming down here in the evenings and weekends rather than staying in London – you know how he went under before.'

'But you do have a life too. Wouldn't it be more fun to be living in town? I saw Monica and Archie the other day, they said they knew you in Washington, that you were out every night there.'

Of course Winifred would know Monica and Archie, Laura

thought. That was the way of the group; everyone knew everyone else. Laura said that she might look for something to do the following year, if everything was going well. She started to tell anecdotes about her efforts to fit in with village life. 'I've promised to do some baking for a coffee morning next week, but as for me and cakes . . .'

'I can come and teach you,' said Sybil, surprising her. 'It's the only thing I can do in the whole world. Daddy didn't think anything of education for girls, but he packed me off to a cordon bleu cooking course when I was eighteen. I still do some of it, I'm not bad – I'll teach you how to amaze the wives of Patsfield with some fancy confections if you like. Also, Nina asked if you would come and photograph her son one day? She saw those pictures you did of us before and liked them – so much better, she said, than some she paid a fortune for in a Mayfair studio.'

This was unexpected. Laura did not know that Nina was married. Sybil explained that it was some much older divorced man whom Sybil had known all her life, and Laura could tell that she disapproved. Laura could not bear to think of going to Nina's house, putting her and her son at ease, setting up her camera. In a stalling aside, she said she was thinking of charging for taking photographs.

'Do you need to?' Sybil asked.

'I was thinking of making a little darkroom out here in that outbuilding. It would make it more of a project, you know, if I could charge a little bit – not much, obviously.'

'I wouldn't worry about how much,' Sybil said. Just at that moment the children's shouts from the back of the garden disturbed her, and she got up to check on them. The garden was physically richer when children were playing in it, Laura was thinking: you noticed the sticks on the ground they were sorting; you noticed the dandelion clocks they picked, the daisies they made into chains, the ladybugs they tried to catch – small things that were normally passed over. She was wondering how she could show that in photographs, the lines of sight that children brought with them, but Winifred was talking to her now, asking her how Edward's sessions with Lvov were going.

Laura didn't really know any more than that Lvov had written a report that had cleared Edward for work, but had asked if he would continue to come and see him. 'He can't wait to stop, says it's all so self-indulgent.'

'Giles loves it, he's always trying to encourage me to go, but I don't think I'd have a whole lot to say. I'm not like these men with their wicked secrets.' Winifred must still believe that Edward's problems were sexual, Laura realised. She needed to confront that now, to tell Winifred how mistaken she was. There must be a way to put her right without divulging other secrets. But just as she began to speak, Winifred was talking about how she was off to Geneva the following week and why didn't Edward and Laura come and stay with her in the late summer. They could swim and walk in the mountains; they would enjoy the scenery. Laura liked the idea. Her mother and Aunt Dee had gone to school near Geneva when they were young women; she remembered seeing an old photograph of them against a picture postcard background of exquisite peaks. There was something so clean and charming about mountains in the sun. Winifred must be looking forward to moving there, Laura said.

Winifred agreed, clearly excited about it. She started to talk about the need for countries to come together in the face of the threat of atomic war, the importance of the United Nations – 'as an idea,' she said intently, 'whatever we manage in practice'. Laura would have liked to know more about what Winifred thought of the American domination of the United Nations, but as Sybil came back the conversation moved towards the personal. It was Winifred's new boyfriend Peter, apparently, who worked for the British mission in Geneva, who had found her this opening there. She would like Sybil and Laura to meet Peter some time. He was the son of old Bennett, Sybil must know who she meant, who used to be in the diplomatic service before the war.

That Bennett, Sybil remembered, whose house was near theirs in Derbyshire? Hadn't he had to resign in disgrace, though? That was all nonsense, Winifred said; Peter said he had taken the rap for someone else. So the conversation drifted into the social meanderings where Sybil was happiest; anecdotes were told that framed people in the group, judgements were handed down, until Winifred said she had to go, she was meeting a friend later. She got into the little car she drove, blowing a kiss to Laura out of the window, making her promise she would see her soon in Geneva.

Laura expected her departure to trigger Sybil and the children to leave too, but Sybil showed no sign of wanting to go. As the children scrambled back under the rhododendrons and out of sight at the back of the garden, she went on sitting on the terrace, crumbling a last slice of fruitcake. The sun was weaker now and Laura was cold, but she was also pleased that Sybil wanted to stay. She had never got over that sense that Sybil looked down on her; that Sybil felt that however long Laura was married to Edward, however well she served tea in her English garden, she would never belong inside the group. But now, by showing no sign of wanting to go, it was as though Sybil had decided to move for a moment into Laura's world.

'Don't let Winifred make you feel unsatisfied with your life,' she said, clearly thinking about Winifred's critical observations. 'Obviously you have to look after Edward right now.'

Laura was glad that Sybil wanted to support her, but she had to admit that she thought Winifred had a point. After all, it was not as though she had children. She had only this house, this garden, empty while Edward was at work. She said something about how it was different for Sybil, who had a family to look after.

'Well, I don't do that much – Nanny does most of that side, you know. Which is a blessing, given that they run rings around me. I can't understand how she keeps them under control.'

Laura had never heard Sybil say anything against herself, anything that suggested that she was not entirely the arbiter of all that was good. She quickly moved into the role that Sybil was presumably asking her to occupy, that of reassurance, telling her how beautifully the children were behaving. But Sybil's voice in response was raw.

'Because you're here. That's why I can't face going home till bedtime, when Nanny will be back from her day off. They'll just rampage if it's only me and them. I don't know why – it's as though they sense some weakness in me. They know I can't say no to anything.'

Laura reassured her again, saying that wasn't weakness, it was love, a mother's love.

'I don't know.' Laura knew that Sybil's own mother had died when Sybil was very young, but she would not have dared to mention that herself. It was Sybil who gestured towards that knowledge. 'I just don't know whether I can be that. I didn't have it. And Toby, he's like my father, he hardly sees them. Not that they seem to care. They only like one another.'

Laura was disoriented by this new Sybil, angry and vulnerable, sitting there on the terrace because she was reluctant to go home with her children. She knew that she should feel sorry for her, but in some way Laura felt energised; Sybil had always been so confident, so removed from Laura's own awkwardness and mistakes, but now the power balance in their relationship seemed to be shifting. Sybil was still talking, and for some reason she was talking about Edward and Toby and their mother. Laura and Edward had been up to see Mrs Last in her new home the previous week, and Laura had found the visit excruciating. 'Of course she can't bear us,

342

taking her sons away,' Sybil said grimly. Laura asked whether that was it, and said that Mrs Last didn't seem to care much about whether Edward was happy or not; she didn't seem to care for him at all.

Sybil was silent for a moment, and then her words were puzzling to Laura. 'The first time I met her, there was something so strange in the atmosphere – it was as though . . . Laura, can I say something? When I got to know Edward, I'm not sure, I felt . . .' Laura was held, riveted by the sense of a confession coming. 'It's been on my mind so long,' Sybil went on, and then she stood up without warning. 'Alice! Stop that!'

The children's play had degenerated; there was shouting, tears, stamped feet and folded arms. Sybil rushed forward and tried to find out what had gone wrong, and tried to make Alice say sorry to George, but Laura could see how the children screened out her words, that her repeated reprimands were melting before their intransigence. In the end Sybil had to drag George towards the car, as he yelled in crescendos. Laura heard her muttered threats, felt her embarrassment, and tried to look as though it was all nothing, that she had hardly noticed the children's bad behaviour.

When the children were both pushed into the car, Sybil got into the front seat and Laura saw her shoulders sag as she got out the key. But she rolled down the window. 'Thank you for a lovely afternoon,' she said, reverting to her usual formal manner. 'Sorry it had to end so abruptly.'

'You were going to say something – about Edward?'

But the moment had passed. Sybil shook her head and put the key in the ignition.

Learning to bake, learning to develop her photographs, learning to prune the roses – as the weeks went on Laura began to appreciate these little physical triumphs over the shapelessness of the world. Deep within her was a sense that she and Edward did not deserve happiness now. But gradually she realised she was still determined to find some kind of contentment anyway, and maybe this was the way one built it, day by day, out of small pleasures and gentleness. It was on a fall day she had spent digging holes in the cold earth to plant what seemed absurd numbers of snowdrop, scilla and white narcissus bulbs alongside a taciturn gardener from the village, that she found herself counting days in her head, noting the changes, the sickness, the heaviness in her body, and realised she was pregnant again. When Edward came in she was in the kitchen, washing the earth from her hands in the sink, wearing a green sweater of his over an old grey dress.

On the kitchen table were some prints of the photographs that she had taken of Sybil's children, and as Edward stood there drinking lemonade he started to look at them. 'Funny to think that you started taking pictures of documents, and now this.'

He was looking at a photograph of Sybil's son. It was one of the best pictures she had ever taken, Laura thought, with a very shallow depth of field so that all one's attention was drawn to the boy's wide eyes and slightly parted mouth. He was glancing off to one side, as if he had seen somebody he was delighted to look at. There was an inviting charm in that glance that she knew any mother would love. Under it was another that Laura had printed off to look at, although she knew she would not give it to Sybil. This time there was anger in George's pursed mouth, and his curly hair made him look impish. Beside him was a dandelion clock, and the perspective made the dandelion as big as his head.

Edward held it up. 'You are good, aren't you?'

Laura said something about how mothers liked her photographs, because they captured time that passed too fast. And then she told Edward her news. The expression in his eyes was so hopeful, it hurt her.

She put the radio on, as they often did over dinner so that

they did not have to think of new stories to fill all the silences, and some piano music that Laura thought she recognised fell into the room. 'Didn't you play that once?' she asked, and then, struck by that thought, she suggested that they should get a piano, so that their child could learn as Edward once had. He agreed, and asked her about her plans for the dark-room in the garden. She realised, as they talked and she heated the soup and the pie she had bought from the village shop, that the news of the pregnancy had made this quiet life feel like the beginning of something rather than the end. When they were in bed that night, Laura felt a new current of exploration driving her pleasure, as if she had found a kind of confidence in her body, a confidence that she had not known before, and when Edward tried to enter her from behind she pulled herself up and turned over, embracing him again as she wanted to be embraced, and insisting through her move-ments that he follow her.

Those bulbs that Laura had planted with such effort did not do very well on their first spring outing. The scillas all began to raise their heads through the soil, but the snowdrops hardly made any appearance to speak of. When she asked the gardener what had gone wrong, he was clear. 'They are hard to raise from bulbs, you should have ordered them in the green,' he said. 'Order them now and you can plant them later in the spring, and then next year you'll have a pretty display.'

Laura felt irritated that he hadn't given her this advice before, and annoyed that the display she was hoping for hadn't arrived. But then, as she went back into the house, leaving the gardener to tie in the rambling roses, she turned and looked back into the green space and imagined how it would look next year with the snowdrops in bloom, and the year after, when the pear tree she had planted would be lifting its head above the walls. This rhythm is sustaining, she thought. Although she did not feel the mad rush she used to feel at the onset of spring, the sense of the inexorable march of the seasons and the turn of the year was in some way allied to the new life in her belly.

And out in the garden was now her own little room, her darkroom. To her, it had become the heart of the house. Whenever she went up to town for lunch with Sybil or Monica, or to the theatre or a concert with Edward, coming back to Patsfield it was always the darkroom that seemed to be pulling her home. She had no illusions about her talent for photography; it was not great, but she had the enthusiast's ability to stick with it, to take advice, to practise, to do something that was just good enough to make it worthwhile.

She went on photographing mainly children, and the narrowness of her subject matter bore fruit, since that was the one area where other women were prepared to pay her to do a good job. In April she had completed a session with Monica's daughters, who were now twelve and ten. It had been hard to stop Monica disrupting the afternoon with her importunate need to talk, so instead Laura had told her she would have lunch with her the following week in town. When the day came, she found herself reluctant to leave the house and the garden, there was so much to do in it and she found herself moving through her chores slowly these days.

They met in the Royal Academy; the stated intention was to look at the exhibition, but after they had eaten their chicken salad and lemon cake they walked instead into the Ritz bar and ordered a couple of martinis, while Monica smoked and cried and went on talking interminably. She had decided to leave Archie. She was taking the children. In Washington, she could pretend she didn't like the place, but now she was home she realised that it was all about Archie. He smothered her. He bored her. She was getting old – she was still young. He hadn't even cared when she had had an affair. 'I think he is missing a vital part; he doesn't seem to be able to talk about it.'

346

Laura listened, and tried to say the right things, reflecting Monica's desires back to herself and helping her to muffle her fears. But what she was thinking about were Monica's daughters; how uneasy they had seemed on the day that she had photographed them. The onlookers to unhappy lives, as she had been, as Ellen had been, as they all were. Could one ever break away from that mould? When she mentioned them, however, she could see that Monica thought she was being critical, so she just told her how beautiful they were, how the photographs had come out so well.

On the train back to Patsfield, Laura found a newspaper on the seat next to her. Death sentences for the Rosenbergs; the news fell like a dark bar across the day. Yes, the court had agreed that Ethel Rosenberg had typed up the information her husband had brought her about nuclear weapons, and yes, their judge had said their crime was worse than murder. 'By your betrayal, you undoubtedly have altered the course of history to the disadvantage of our country.' Laura let the newspaper drop to the floor. She would not think about that.

Instead, she found her mind turning to the contact sheets she had printed out the previous day. As soon as she was through the door she went to the darkroom, and started to make a bigger print of one of the most successful images, which showed Barbara, twelve years old, in a pose that hinted at the woman she would become. Laura was intrigued by the picture; it wasn't beautiful, but it worked. Barbara looked self-sufficient, her eyes levelling with the viewer, a grown-up glance that was at odds with her childish cheeks and mouth. It was the face of a haughty survivor rather than a child, and Laura felt pleased as she pegged it out to dry and walked back up to the house. As she went into the kitchen she became aware of the dragging heaviness in her hips. At nearly eight months pregnant, such a long day was a strain. She was glad to sit down now, in the quiet.

So it did not bother her that Edward was late for dinner, although it was odd that he did not telephone. He had had to work late a lot recently, as the brutish standoff in Korea continued. She ate by herself, and then sat on the sofa, manicuring her nails, which were weak and splitting – was that the pregnancy, or the chemicals she was using in the darkroom? – and listening to the radio. As dusk fell, it seemed odder to her that Edward had not telephoned, and she began to doze, listening to a radio programme about Chopin. She snapped out of the doze as soon she heard Edward's key in the door, but was confused, sitting up on the sofa – for a moment she thought she was in the old house in Georgetown – and then she came to properly and got up, going into the hall.

It fell on her like a blow – the staggering gait, the sour breath, the clumsy movements – everything she thought was behind him. She went up to him and pushed him, her hands on his shoulders, not knowing what she was doing.

'Why? Why can't you stop?' she was saying, pointlessly, angrily, but instead of coming in, he put his arms around her there in the hall and drew her out with him, back out into the front garden. It was freezing cold for April, with a damp fog in the air. Laura resisted. It was too cold, she was tired. He was maddening. Was it the Rosenbergs' death sentence that had tripped him over the edge? Was it the threat of atomic destruction in Korea? She could not bear it. He had to learn to survive in the world as it was. He gripped her arm fiercely and pulled her to the gate, she went draggingly along, and then he put his mouth close to her ear. She still could not understand what was behind the violence of his movements – and then she realised: he was afraid to speak in the house.

'They know.'

He was drunk, he was whispering, but nothing could hide the force of what he was saying. That they had known since the new year. No, they did not know for sure, but they suspected. She shuddered with the cold, and clung to him as he went on speaking. 'It was when Archie said something in a meeting that made no sense to me that I realised – I've been pushed out of the loop. I'm not getting the blue folders any more. They've downgraded my security clearance. I thought I'd get to the bottom of that, brazen it out somehow if they knew about some leak. But this lunchtime, there was a tail on me. Every time I left the office he was there; I zigzagged around Green Park a few times, thought I'd lost him when I went into the Reform after work, but he was still there when I came out. They trailed me to the station. No one at this end – they'd stick out a mile in the village – but maybe they're listening . . .' They turned to look at the house, which loomed up over them in the darkness.

So it comes back, the fear that dazzles your mind, that grips your stomach. Laura was back again in the medium she had lived in for so long in Washington. Terror makes your breath shallow, it makes your jaw clench, the sweat break under your arms. Stupid, she thought to herself, stupid to think you could live a different life, stupid to think you could nurture shoots of revived love all the way to their fruit. Stupid. She leant against Edward.

'Stefan says we might have to run,' he said. Laura's hands were on her belly, and Edward's hands went round them. It was only just over a month to go. 'I know we can't.'

'You must go, if it comes to it.'

'I can't go without you.'

'Don't be stupid.' They went back into the house, and she wondered, as they re-entered and Edward began to take off his coat, whether she had put him in danger by withdrawing from the work. If he had been meeting Stefan day in, day out, passing documents, picking them up again, how much more obvious had he become? He was not as drunk as he had seemed at first, and they went through to the kitchen where Laura made cocoa and they drank it like children, with a box of cookies between them, munching and sipping.

349

There was nothing on the radio so late. Laura told Edward about Monica. He already knew from Archie. It was sad, he said. Laura said she was thinking of the children, and Edward nodded. At last they went to bed, and lay the way they did now, with Edward's front against her back, so that her belly was not in their way.

Laura turned her head, and whispered into his cheek. 'Tell Stefan that if he needs to see me, I will.'

The next time Laura went into town, just after she gave up her ticket at Victoria station, she heard someone say, with quiet clarity, at her shoulder, 'Pigeon.'

She went on walking, but her steps found pace with him. 'You know why I had to stop.' Stefan said nothing, and for a moment she thought he was about to go. 'Don't use him again – use me.'

'If someone rings you, just rings, three rings and then stops, take the next train to Victoria. That's where we'll find you.'

They went on walking for a few paces, and then he spoke again from just behind her. 'If we have to take Virgil over, we'll take you too. We won't forget.'

'What are our chances?'

There was no reply. Laura went on walking for a bit, and when she turned he was nowhere to be seen.

As the days went on, everything seemed to slow down. Day after day, Edward came in late, drunk. Laura didn't have the heart to remonstrate with him, although some nights, when he didn't come home at all, she lay awake into the grey dawn, wondering if they had finally caught up with him. But as the days moved into weeks, she thought that maybe the danger had passed, and that maybe this low-level sense of uncertainty, this reliance on alcohol to get through each night, was simply their inescapable normality.

One Thursday evening in May Edward was home at a reasonable time, but as he walked heavily into the kitchen,

Laura realised he must have been drinking all day. He pulled open the French windows and, without needing to be asked, Laura followed him into the garden, down to the tangle of shrubs at the back, where the rhododendron flowers were browning and dying. As she came up to him, he was snapping the flowers off their stems and throwing them down onto the dark earth.

'Stefan's heard from Washington – from another contact – they've broken some old codes. Old telegrams. They've found something that seems to point to me. They're still not quite definite. But soon, they'll get there for sure. They've got dozens of cryptographers working around the clock.'

Laura asked him, as if she was asking for the time of a train, how long he thought they had.

'I don't know, let's hold on as long as we can.'

'Not too long,' she said, putting her hand on his arm and stilling his fierce plucking at the flowers. Dinner was almost ready, she said, and she made him come back in, eat and listen to the Schubert sonata on the radio.

The next morning they were both awake before the alarm. Laura went downstairs and made coffee, and Edward came down in his dressing gown. They sat drinking it, and talked a little at first about whether they would go to the piano store in Marylebone that weekend. It was only when the letterbox snapped that Laura realised that a silence had fallen, the noise of the post tumbling onto the mat seemed so loud. She had not really forgotten that it was Edward's birthday today, and there were cards there from his mother, Sybil and Toby, and others. She brought them into the kitchen and he began opening them while she made toast. 'We'll celebrate tonight, remember,' she told him. 'A special meal, and your present – unless you'd rather have it now?'

'No, no, tonight is good.'

'I'm sorry I can't come up to town to celebrate – I'm just such a lump now.' It was only two weeks to go before the birth. Edward rose from the table and went upstairs to dress. Another day to get through. A birthday.

Once he had gone out, Laura gathered herself. She went into the study and wrapped his present, which she had been keeping concealed behind the desk: a new tennis racket. He had been complaining about his old one. There was a ring on the doorbell. It was just the girl Laura had found in the village, the niece of the postmistress, whom she had engaged to come in daily to clean. Really, Laura wanted to be alone, but she forced herself to be bright and easy in front of Helen. Laura had taken to her at first because she did not seem to fit easily into the role of servant; she was obviously clever and observant, and when she had first started to work in the house Laura had enjoyed talking to her. But now Laura had to watch herself to keep Helen at a distance; she did not want any intimacy at this time.

After Helen had started making the bed and dusting the rooms upstairs, Laura laid out a recipe book on the table, and started to make a Victoria sponge. She saw it in her head, golden and perfectly risen, with icing spelling out 'Happy Birthday'. She beat the butter and sugar until her arm ached, but when she added the eggs she saw the mixture separate, flatten and curdle. She remembered when Sybil had shown her how to do it, and the smoothness of the mixture she had created. She stirred the flour disconsolately, not knowing whether to start again or use the mixture as it was. The telephone rang in the hall and she put down the spoon. As she walked towards it, it stopped, after just three rings. It was already after eleven o'clock.

'Helen!' Laura called, and when she came out of the living room where she had been dusting, Laura asked her to take the cakes out of the oven when they were done. 'I'm just going to put them in now. I have to go up to town; I forgot something for tonight.'

'But Mrs Last, are you well enough to—?'

'I'm fine, really,' Laura said, cutting her short, although the last thing she wanted was to get on the London train. She rang for a taxi to the station, and before it came she poured the cake mixture into two buttered tins and put them in the oven. She had just taken off her apron and brushed her hair when the taxi arrived; as it drove up to Oxted she saw one of her neighbours walking along, a tall, untidy-looking woman who had often spoken to Laura when she was out and about in the village. She was about to stop the taxi and ask her if she wanted a lift to the station, but held herself back; now was not the time.

As soon as she got to the station, she saw Stefan on a bench on the platform. She walked straight past him, knowing it would be too dangerous to speak in the open where any waiting passenger might see them. As they got into the train, they both hesitated in the corridor. 'Do you have a light?' she said, getting out a cigarette, and he fumbled in his pocket.

'It's over,' he muttered as flame met cigarette. 'He must go tonight. They're planning to interrogate him on Monday. Valance, the man who broke Fuchs, will do it.'

Laura drew on the cigarette, and then as other passengers got on she went to look for a seat, holding back her thoughts. None of the compartments was empty. They could not talk any more. Soon, outside the window, the suburban muddle of London began. Buddleia and cow parsley along the railway tracks. A magpie flying too close to the window. She got up and back into the corridor. Stefan was still standing there, smoking, and she went up to him. She had to risk it. Under the rattle of the train he spoke to her.

'They broke an old telegram that pointed to him. One of our men heard about it in Washington; he broke out two days ago, arrived here last night.'

'How can he get away, if they know?'

'They aren't setting a tail in Patsfield. They don't know he knows, they don't want to alert him, they are only watching him in town. He can go tonight, from the house, by car.'

Laura flicked ash out of the window, and asked what she should do.

'Make him go tonight. Hang on until Monday before you tell anyone. We won't be able to talk to you for a long time after he goes, probably, but we'll hold on for you. Give him something – give him something for a signal that another agent can show to you. I might have to go over with him.' The train was pulling into a station, and Laura went back into a compartment. Being seen here, talking to a stranger, it was too dangerous.

At Victoria, they walked in opposite directions. For her cover, Laura made her way to a little shop she knew in Jermyn Street and bought Edward's favourite shaving cream and a new badger shaving brush. She thought of lunching in Fortnum's, but she had no appetite; London was a great roar of indifferent noise and too many people, any one of whom might be dangerous to her. She was glad to get back, but when she got out of the taxi at Patsfield and put the key back into the door, she felt her hips aching. She was exhausted. Helen had finished cleaning, and the house smelt of the baked cakes and jasmine; Laura had put a few sprigs of the flowers into a small blue vase on the hall table. As she walked past the telephone, it rang again; she let it ring three times, but thankfully it went on ringing, and she picked it up.

'Darling – just to let you know, Nick's in town. I'm going to bring him up to dinner tonight.'

'Tonight! Edward, you can't. And – Nick . . .'

The line went dead. Laura longed to ring him back to explain, but she couldn't think how to speak on the telephone without alerting possible listeners. Above all, it was essential that nobody realised that he knew anything at all. She would have to delay telling him what was going on until after Nick left. But what would those few hours mean for the plan?

Helen had left the cakes on a cooling rack in the kitchen. Once Laura had turned them onto plates, she saw how uneven they were, and when she put them together with cream and jam, the sloping tops meant that the whole thing listed to one side, and the cream, which she had not whipped stiffly enough, began to spill out of the middle. It was surprising how annoying it was, this failure. You can't do anything right, Laura thought, and again she noticed how her pelvis was aching. A warm bath might relax her.

Lying there in the cooling water, she saw the shape of her belly change as the baby shifted and pushed, as if it too were unable to settle. She hauled herself out and wrapped herself in a towel, and out of the window she saw a car sitting on the road outside the house. Just sitting there. It had to be one of Stefan's men, keeping an eye on the house. It must be.

Once she had dressed she took the bowl of peas that she was to shell for supper out into the garden. Sitting on the terrace, she podded them, trying to make her mind slow down with the repetitive movements. That was where she was when the light began to fade, and Edward came home. He walked onto the terrace in his dark suit, his homburg in one hand, pulling off his tie. Sir Edward Last in the making, or the NKVD's precious Virgil, she thought as he came. In the fading light he was still the tall young man she had met at Sybil's party, the man who had listened to her. He knelt down beside her and took her hands and put his face to her belly. 'Be good to your mother,' his muffled voice said.

'I saw Stefan today,' Laura said, pulling away from him.

'I know what you're going to say. There's someone out in the road, in a car.'

'Stefan said there would be somebody, keeping an eye out.'

Edward stood up. He seemed to be considering. 'Do you want me to go?'

The evening around them was alive with the soft alertness of squirrels rustling in the bushes and a blackbird flickering in and out of the trees. The scream of the doorbell broke the peace.

'God, is that Nick?' Laura said. 'How are we going to get rid of him?'

'He's coming out with me – not all the way – but to make it look like a jaunt to start with.'

'Nick? Nick is—?'

'He's one of us.'

Shock flooded through Laura. 'Why did you never tell me before?'

'He got me into the whole thing.'

Laura could not take in this new information, and as Edward went to answer the door, she went into the kitchen and put the bowl of peas and the bag of empty pods down on the table, next to the absurd cake which had now slid completely over to one side. Nick came in and Laura saw in an instant how the exodus was exciting to him, how he was buoyant with nerves and expectation.

'I can't believe this is where you've made your nest,' he was saying with sarcastic relish. 'A return to my childhood neighbourhood – how sweet.' So he was the university friend with whom Edward must have walked in the woods, many years ago.

'You should eat before you go,' Laura said, going to get out bread, ham and a half-open bottle of wine, ignoring the celebratory champagne in the icebox. Nick immediately helped himself, but Edward went out and upstairs, and Laura followed him. When they reached the bedroom, he put his arms around her; it was impossible for her to know whether there was true communion in that kiss – it was so laden with fear and memory, it hardly existed as a present moment. Edward turned and packed a few things into a small case. He put the radio on, as loudly as he could, and she picked up a small framed photograph that sat on the bedside table. It was a picture of the house that she had taken last summer, when the roses were out on the walls. She opened the back of the frame to take it out, tore it in half and handed one half to him. 'Give that to Stefan or whoever it is when you know you're through, to get in touch with me.' He took it, but he hardly seemed to register it.

'Stefan suggested it,' Laura said.

He put it in his pocket. 'Try not to be alone,' he said.

'Mother's coming next week anyway, remember, to help with the birth.' At the word 'birth', they were unable to bear the conversation and they went downstairs, to find Nick standing in the hall.

'Look at you and your stiff upper lips,' he said. In front of him, Laura found it necessary not to cry. They were looking for coats, they were going to the lavatory, they were downing a last half-glass of wine. She went with them to the doorstep, heard Nick swear as he tripped over a stone, and saw the lights of the car disappear down the road, into the damp night.

5

Even now, Laura could not allow herself to feel alone. She had to act precisely in character, in every way, for as long as possible. She had put up with Edward's absences often enough. Indeed, she knew that the fact that she had always put up with them with such apparent insouciance would be an important building block in the story that she would now create, a story that might be the key to their survival.

Although she still felt the physical exhaustion that had troubled her since the morning, she was too restless to lie down. Instead, she sat on the sofa for a while, listening to the radio and sipping automatically at a small glass of whisky. Then she began to go through Edward's large walnut desk which they had put in a back bedroom. She did so with a methodical bitterness, knowing that if there was anything there that was incriminating in any way, it was essential that she found it before MI5 did. And so she went through every paper, every notebook, and then through every garment in the wardrobe and every coat hanging in the hall, checking pockets, feeling linings. She found letters from Giles and Alistair, which they had sent to him in Washington, and through them she read for the first time the sad story of Giles's downfall. She found a card from Nick, wishing him luck on his work at the American Department – 'though I feel the charms of the Newfoundland have palled on you in more ways than one!' – and she took the card and burned it in the grate, pounding the ashes with the poker until they were a tiny heap of nothing. She found lines of poetry that Edward had scribbled in the back of a notebook over the last few months, featuring trains and gardens, hills and birdsong, and heard his voice in them. At dawn she ate a piece of the pathetic birthday cake, and fell asleep on the sofa, only waking at about noon.

It would have been quite in character for her to have telephoned Sybil or Winifred during the day, but she held herself away from the telephone, in case they asked about Edward, in case someone had heard that Nick had disappeared – in case the chase began. It was raining, a dreary drizzle, but she made herself walk down to the village and pick up some provisions she did not need in the local store. She stood in the shop for a while, talking to the tall untidy woman she knew a little, who said she was thinking of setting up an amateur dramatic society in Patsfield. Would Laura be interested? After the baby, obviously. Laura was not interested, but she was glad to talk, to hear about the plans, to walk slowly by the woman's side back down the high street. Letting herself into the house, its silence oppressed her. She could not bear to make herself a meal, but stood by the kitchen table, eating handfuls of raw peas, and then two more slices of the cake, the crumbs falling onto her belly. Even though she knew it was a dangerous thing to do, she couldn't help herself, she needed to speak to someone, and she went to telephone her mother.

'No, nothing is wrong yet, but I wondered – you know, I just have a feeling that it's going to happen soon. I know we planned for you to come next week, when the Caesarean is booked, but how would you feel—?'

'I'll see if I can change the flight,' Mother said. Her immediate response threw Laura back in her mind to that time four years ago when her mother had risen to the crisis after the stillbirth. As she replaced the telephone receiver, she found herself kneeling on the floor in the hall, gripping her own wrists painfully in an effort to keep hold of her calm.

The next morning, she went to church. She had been in once or twice before, for Easter and carol services. She liked the whitewashed simplicity of its interior, the airy setting up on the hill. But the regular congregants were standoffish with her, since neither she nor Edward were regulars. There was no presence there for her in the coloured glass and the scent of lilac, but it was good to be with other people and she stayed this time for the coffee and cookies, seeing again the woman who had talked to her about the amateur theatrics. When she got back to the house, she went straight to the darkroom. She had found some old negatives among Edward's papers, old photographs from school. As she printed the pictures, she saw his young face looking up at her, unshadowed.

It was another sleepless night, characterised by fear and heartburn. But finally she could act: at nine in the morning she telephoned the Foreign Office and asked for Edward, and when she was told he was not there, she asked if she could speak to Archie Platt. Her mouth seemed dry as she said that she had not seen Edward since Friday evening and had thought he must have stayed the weekend in town. 'I hope he's not ill or . . .'

'God, what a time for him to behave like this,' Archie said. 'I'll pass the word along and we'll have him ring as soon as he gets in.'

The prints in the darkroom were dry. She brought one to the house and propped it on the mantelpiece. She did not think Edward had taken a photograph of her with him. But maybe that was a sign that he didn't think they would be long parted. She threw the stale cake in the bin before Helen came and changed her dress which, she suddenly realised, catching sight of herself in the hall mirror, she had worn all weekend; it had a stain on the front. She must look normal; she must look as though she had slept, as though she was the usual Laura.

It was after lunch when Archie finally rang back, a new tension in his usually lazy voice. 'Look, everyone's a bit concerned that he hasn't turned up here either. Could I put Spall on the telephone? He's one of our chaps – looks after this kind of thing.' The receiver was slippery in Laura's hand as she waited for Bill Spall to come on the telephone and introduce himself. He asked her when she had last seen Edward and where he had said he was going.

The next day, in the consulting room, the doctor measured and listened. His hands were cold on her skin. Turning away from her, looking at papers on his desk as she pulled down her dress, Dr Turner said that they would go ahead with the Caesarean as planned, a week on Thursday. Laura felt dismissed; she had liked that momentary sensation of being looked after. Outside the consulting room the world returned, too sharp, too loud, as she walked down the steps into Harley Street.

She drove the short distance through London to Sybil's house. When Bill Spall had asked her to meet him the following day she had immediately suggested that they could go to Chester Square. Would Toby and Sybil not be a kind of protection for her? They both sat with her as Spall talked, and often interrupted him in their confident tones. Spall asked Laura to describe what had happened on Friday evening, and Laura told it the way she knew she would be telling it from now on: Nick, an old friend, nothing to that, the two of them coming back for a drink after work, then back to town in Nick's car for dinner – and why not, it was Edward's birthday; she could not do much in her condition. Yes, Edward often went to the club after work with his friends; yes, he was rather unreliable; certainly, if he had wanted to stay up in town for the weekend it was unusual of him not to telephone her, but she had assumed nothing was wrong. She had been rather tired out recently, it was nice for her to be able to rest. She had only really begun to worry on Sunday, and then . . .

It was Toby who tried to turn the interview around. Irritable and impatient, he began to question Spall, wanting to know exactly what the Foreign Office was doing to find Edward and Nick. So Spall told them that Nick's car had been traced to St Malo, and two men answering the description of Edward and Nick had been seen on the ferry that connected with the train to Paris. There, he said, the trail had gone cold – but the French police were involved now. The French police, Toby said with a groan, as if they were talking about comedy characters. Paris! Sybil said, folding her lips together and straightening her back. Laura could see the judgement forming in her expression. Had Edward gone off on an unforgivable alcoholic binge with a well-known pervert and drunk? Was he right now sleeping it off in some French gutter? If Edward had not been one of them, her own brother-in-law, the verdict might have escaped her lips. As it was, there was enough bad feeling in the room to bring the conversation to a halt quite quickly.

After Spall had gone, Laura found herself longing to go too. She had to stay for a while, though, to allow Toby and Sybil to circle around what had happened and try to situate it in everyday life. Toby remembered how he had once gone with a friend to a house party in Cumberland, and Sybil had mistaken the date, and hadn't known where he was all Saturday. 'It came out all right in the end,' he said, and Laura felt a deep coldness within her as she thought that, for the very first time in their lives, something was not going to come out all right. She had to escape their expectation that she would stay with them, now that the house in Patsfield was empty. 'My mother is arriving tomorrow, you know,' she had to say more than once. 'I'd rather be there, really – in case Edward telephones, or comes back tonight.'

'Surely he'll guess where you are,' Sybil said, but her insistence on this point seemed to be tempered, Laura thought, by her own growing anger with what she thought Edward had done, and after tea Laura was able to escape.

During that night, as she moved in and out of sleep, dogged by heartburn and cramp in her legs, unable to find a comfortable way to lie, Laura found the conversation with Spall playing again and again in her head. Stefan had said that the man who broke Fuchs was to break Edward this week. He had mentioned his name; it wasn't Spall, but Valiant, something like that. Stefan had been quite sure that the code-breaking in Washington had pointed straight to the truth, and yet Spall seemed so unsure about what he was handling – it was almost as if he had no evidence at all. Perhaps he had not been given all the material. Perhaps he was bluffing to catch Laura out. Or perhaps he knew the truth, but saw Laura as irrelevant to it and believed there had been no need to tell her or ask her anything. She saw herself as she had been that afternoon, sitting on the sofa in Sybil's room with her hands clasped over her huge belly: the epitome of femininity, alien, outside whatever masculine narrative, whether of espionage or alcoholism, the Foreign Office was constructing from Edward's disappearance. A pregnant woman is even more invisible than other women, Laura thought as she fell asleep, or rather, only her pregnancy is visible.

362

She felt that truth even more forcefully when Mother stepped into the house the next day. Mother was with Aunt Dee, who had met her at the airport and driven them both down to Patsfield. As soon as the two sisters looked at her, Laura was aware that this was the one thing that united the three women: the life inside her, the experience of motherhood. They stood in the hall as Laura explained the extraordinary news of Edward's disappearance, but as if that was immaterial they began to ask her how she was feeling, and made her go and sit down in the living room while Dee helped Polly to unpack.

It was a relief to hear them going upstairs; to have voices in the house again. Laura had asked Helen to prepare a cold lunch, and how good it was that the sisters' reminiscences and anecdotes rather than Laura's strange situation dominated conversation over that lunch. Laura had never seen her mother and aunt together before, and despite her own self-involvement, she was intrigued. She saw how they were trying to orient themselves against one another. Mother, she saw, might have stood once in the same relationship to Dee that she had to Ellen, as the plaintive younger sister; but now they were older, both widowed, both long past their shared childhoods, they were looking at one another with new eyes. And the fact that Mother already had two grandchildren, and was now expecting a third, undeniably gave her a kind of seniority. They talked about pregnancy, about birth, about the pleasures of young children, as they ate ham and salad and asked Laura about the house. This ignorant calm could not last long, Laura knew.

It lasted only until the following morning, when the doorbell rang, peal after peal, over breakfast. 'I'll get it,' called Helen, opening the door, and then Laura heard voices raised in anger. The door slammed, and Helen came back in confusion, saying that someone had asked for Mrs Last, but when she had asked him to wait, he had put his foot in the door, and it was only his fault if he had got hurt as she shut it. As Laura moved to the door, the telephone began to ring, and when she picked it up she heard a stranger asking for Mrs Last. She said Mrs Last was not available, and heard the stranger on the other end saying the name of a newspaper, promising money for her side of the story. The person outside the front door was rapping hard, with his knuckles, and calling out the name of another newspaper. Laura put the chain on the door and locked it, aware as she did so how thin it was, how her body and the man's body on the doorstep were divided only by a few inches.

People agreed later that the leak came from France, from a French policeman who told a reporter that he was looking for two missing British diplomats and understood that they had gone east. Laura never knew if that was true, but she knew that the story of a drunken jaunt to Paris had been broken with shocking suddenness. Going back into the kitchen to make coffee, she saw before Mother did a figure appear over the wall, jumping down into the laurels, a young man with longish hair and an eager expression. She pulled the blinds over the French windows and checked that they too were locked. When she got Spall on the telephone he was unhelpful, clearly bothered himself by what was happening.

'Just refer any reporters to the Foreign Office,' he said. 'We'll prepare an official statement shortly. Have you heard anything else?'

Laura insisted that she needed protection now in Patsfield, somebody to keep the reporters away, and when he said he wasn't sure if he could do that, she put the telephone down and called Toby instead. Now, surely, his intimate knowledge of the corridors of power would be helpful. But his tone, as he promised to see what he could do, was uncertain and full of pauses, as though he was listening to something else other than her words.

All day the doorbell went on pealing. At lunchtime Aunt Dee came in a taxi and had to push through the knot of reporters, who all started to offer her money for her story, assuming she was Edward's mother. The plan had been for the three of them to go out for lunch, but obviously that was no longer possible; instead, they were penned into the house, which was warm in the May sunshine. They opened the windows upstairs, but kept the curtains drawn and the doors locked downstairs, and sat in the living room, Laura dozing on the sofa, listening to Mother and Aunt Dee talking.

Laura had taken the telephone off the hook during the day, but when she replaced it in the evening it began to ring again: Monica, who must have heard the story from Archie; Giles, who must have heard from Toby; Winifred, who must have heard from Giles. 'Are you all right?' they were all asking. 'You're not alone, are you?' All Laura could hear in their voices was the taint of curiosity, and she told each of them she couldn't talk, she had to keep the line free.

'Do tell Helen she can go now,' Laura said to Mother. 'And could you ask her to bring in the newspapers in the morning? I wonder what nonsense they will print.'

If only it had been nonsense, Laura thought the next day, looking at the newspapers that Helen had put on the kitchen table. 'British diplomats missing', 'believed to be on their way to Moscow' . . . Set down like that it was so histrionic, like the opening scene in a film that you knew would be all chases and shoot-outs and would never tell you anything about the complexities of life. Mother and Aunt Dee, reading them after Laura, seemed to be waiting for her to speak, and so she said what they wanted to hear, that it was all crazy, how anyone could believe such a thing of Edward she had no idea; the Foreign Office should put a stop to all this. They both approved the idea that the Foreign Office was in some way in the wrong, and liked to hear her expostulate about how stupid that man Spall clearly was.

But had there been enough time? That was all Laura was thinking, as she left the kitchen and crossed the hall to telephone Toby. Was Edward safely across now? Or would the massive pursuit that must now be underway catch up with them? There would be no hiding for him now if so; the attempt to go east would be too obvious, the treason too clear. Her baby pushed further into the well of her pelvis, sending a dense pressure through her vulva, just as the doorbell began to peal again. 'Don't answer it, Helen,' she said. But the bell gave way to a furious knocking, and then a voice called through the letterbox, 'Telegram for Mrs Last,' and she let Helen go to the door to take in the message.

Misspelt, laconic, it was obviously a telegram written for public consumption more than for her eyes, and yet there was still meaning in it for her. 'Had to leav unexpectedly. Am quite well now. Don't worry. I love you. Please don't stop loving me.' 'Am quite well now.' Laura read those four words with hope, almost chanting them to herself. 'I promised to tell Spall if I heard from Edward at all,' she told Mother. 'I can't make this out, really, but – I must go and telephone.'

This time, Spall's voice was distant. He would come up to Patsfield that afternoon to talk further, he said. But as he spoke, Laura felt a different sensation in her belly, not just the pressure, not just the tightening, but a clench of pain, more definite, more insistent. It was not the sudden agony she had felt five years ago, but it intruded with absolute certainty, clearing a place in her mind. She waited, listening for its return, as Spall went on talking.

'I'm so sorry,' she said. 'I don't think I'll be able to do that. I think I'll be going to the hospital.' She put down the receiver and waited for the pain to go and to return and to go, and then she picked up the telephone again to order a taxi.

6

As Laura woke, she heard another's breath, coming and going, coming and going: a sound that was feather-light, but which bound her with a grip like steel wire into the new life. She was too tired to do anything, the anaesthetic was still swirling in her head. Where she was lying, she could not even see the baby in her crib by the wall, but the new presence filled the room. In that state of suspended animation, feeling the pain from the wound in her belly grow as the anaesthetic wore away, it was strange to hear voices at the door, breaking out in anger, 'No, I'm sorry, Mrs Last is not yet able to have visitors.'

'I'm her cousin, she's expecting me.' But it was an unfamiliar Englishman's voice, a loose Cockney intonation, not one of Edward's family. A bouquet of roses, bursting with freshness, came into the room, but behind them was that eager face Laura had last seen in the garden at Patsfield. Laura tried to sit up, wincing from the pull of pain in her abdomen, and as she did so the flash of the camera came with shocking brightness, and the nurse's shriek for someone to come and help turn him away cut through the room.

'I'm so sorry, Mrs Last, please accept our apologies.' Another nurse and a doctor were in the room, concerned, crowding out the peace.

'Make sure it doesn't happen again,' Laura said, but her voice was weighted with tiredness rather than anger, and she soon fell asleep, waking only when the nurse came to help her feed Rosa. Rosa, too, seemed sleepy, but when she found the nipple and sucked a rhythm fell into place between them. Whorls of hair failed to cover that too-naked skull, her feet were too soft, her vulnerability too extreme. When the visitors Laura was expecting, Mother and Aunt Dee, came later, she found it difficult to speak to them. They bore with them fears about the rumours building outside, but Laura was slow to respond. She needed to learn the contours of a new face and the rhythms of a new life, and all her energies were being taken up by those imperatives.

This is the unanswered question of motherhood, Laura came to realise over the following few days. Had her life got bigger, enlarging itself around this new being? Or had it got smaller, fixing itself to the well-being of this tiny person, cutting out any dream of freedom? The actual physical space of her life was so constrained now as to be claustrophobic. This was not entirely Rosa's fault. The reporters would not give up, and even once they had driven back to Patsfield after Laura had spent a week at the hospital, they were unavoidable. The women kept the curtains closed on the ground floor; they never answered the door unless they knew who it was; they did not use the garden because reporters would hide in the shrubs to listen to them; they could not walk into the village without their footsteps being dogged. Outside, the summer was flowering and lengthening, but Rosa and Laura could see nothing of it. So it remained a close, warm, female world, in which the smallest person became the largest, and all Laura's energy was concentrated on the feeding, the sleeping, the crying – a slow circling in which days moved on without changing shape. All the time, the telephone rang, but even when the voices of friends and acquaintances were heard, Laura put them off visiting.

The only person Laura wanted to see now was Sybil, and she was the only one who had not been in touch since the birth. Toby had telephoned, telling Laura he was off to see his mother, who was obviously quite distracted with worry. Laura asked if Sybil would come and visit, and Toby replied, absolutely, very soon. His voice was always so clipped. But Sybil's silence continued. Laura needed to break through it, she thought, she needed Toby and Sybil; she needed the protection of the group.

So one morning, when she had slept reasonably well, Laura telephoned Sybil and asked if she could come and see her. Sybil's voice was always flat on the telephone, but she agreed. It was odd, Laura thought, that she did not offer to come to her, but presumably she had heard about the ring of reporters around the door – who would expose themselves to that? She held onto the fact that Mother and Aunt Dee had long been insisting that they could look after Rosa for a few hours now that she was taking a bottle, and Helen had said that she could drive Laura about, since the Caesarean wound still made it impossible for her to drive herself.

Even though Helen drove Laura's car right up to the door, and Laura rushed out with a scarf over her head, the reporters saw what was happening immediately. There were cars right behind them all the way through the village, disconcerting Helen, who began to drive erratically. Laura wanted to ask her to try some tricks on them: to drive south for a while, perhaps, and then double back, or jump a light to put distance between them. But just as she opened her mouth to speak, she stopped herself. She found Helen more trying than ever these days; there was something too watchful about her manner. So she sank back into the seat, wanting to pretend she was unaware of their followers. It was not hard just now to seem passive. This was the first time since the birth that Laura had been apart from Rosa, and her milky, aching body felt the absence.

Eventually Helen parked in Chester Square, and the reporters' cars found places next to them. Laura realised there was no avoiding them. She agreed that Helen should remain with the car rather than come in with her, and put on her sunglasses. As she stepped out, the door of Sybil's house swung open immediately. She must have been watching for her from the window, and there was Ann on the doorstep. Laura tried to ignore the shouts of the reporters. One of them – that long-haired young man – was offering money, absurd sums, just for a few comments. He was trying to get in front of her as she walked, to take a photograph. Laura was sweating by the time she gained the steps, but then she was standing in the hall, pulling off her sunglasses, and Sybil was at the top of the stairs.

'Every time I come here I remember the night I first met you – and Edward . . .' Laura said, walking up to meet Sybil.

It was surely a statement that laid claim to a particular intimacy with her, an intimacy that had grown between them over the years, the long years that they had come to know one another little by little, up to that strange moment in the Surrey garden not so long ago when Sybil had been about to tell Laura some confidence.

But as Laura walked up to her, Sybil moved backwards, and Laura followed her heavy body in its starched dress into the living room. Sybil sat on the corner of a sofa, and nodded at Ann, who had followed them up. 'Do bring tea now,' she said.

Laura said how much she had wanted to talk to Sybil, feeling that surely Sybil would appreciate this appeal to her judgement. But Sybil said nothing. Laura said that Giles and Alistair had been in touch, hoping that this mention of other members of the group might move them onto common ground. 'Alistair's article was quite unforgivable,' Sybil said. Laura knew that he had covered pages of a Sunday newspaper with his views on Edward's disappearance and anecdotes about their friendship, but she had not had the stomach to read it. 'If you haven't read it, don't,' Sybil said.

'Why did he do it, do you think?'

'Fame. Edward's made him famous. He's everywhere now – the spy I knew, my friend the traitor.' There was such bitterness in her tone.

'But he isn't a traitor – you know that, don't you?'

'Of course,' Sybil said. But her voice was strange. It was as though she was deliberately echoing the willed blandness of Laura's voice. Surely that was not possible. Tea came and Laura drank a little. She asked how Toby had found Mrs Last, and how the children were, and Sybil asked about Rosa and the birth. There were pauses between sentences, and gradually Laura had to accept that this went beyond Sybil's usual stiffness. 'Toby's having rather a hard time of it,' Sybil said at last. 'He had been hoping to move into the House of Lords soon, you know.'

Laura should have felt resentful, perhaps, that Sybil seemed to be putting her husband's career above Laura's husband's very existence. But she did not feel resentful. She felt ashamed, realising that the horrible mystery that surrounded Edward had made her a blot on Sybil's world, that her presence now was an embarrassment or worse. She muttered something sympathetic, and was not surprised when Sybil did not respond. Instead, Sybil asked her a question. 'Did you know Robin Muir?'

'I remember the name, someone from the embassy. Yes, I met him to ask for Edward's leave—'

'That's right – rather senior chap. His wife's an old friend of the family. He died two weeks ago.' Laura tried to voice condolences, but Sybil went on talking. 'His wife says he had a heart attack when he saw the news about Edward. He died of it. And Lord Inverchapel is very ill. He's been ill for years, of course, but this has pushed him over. They say he won't be long for this world.'

Not long for this world. It was a phrase that seemed very unlike Sybil, as though she was moving into a kind of tragic cliché. Again, Laura tried to say how awful such news was.

'Isn't it?'

Now Laura recognised that the intimacy she thought they had found that day in Patsfield amounted to nothing; Laura was beyond the gates, she was the outsider. She could never be forgiven for the path Edward had taken away from the group, away from Sybil's certainties and traditions. There was no bond, no loyalty now between the two women, and Laura felt the break of it as she walked to the front door and went alone and vulnerable down the broad white steps to the waiting car and the dazzle of the flashbulbs.

It was nearly three months after the birth that Laura and her mother went to Dr Turner together with Rosa, for a check-up. Dr Turner was pleased with Rosa: 'Bright as a button,' he

371

said as she made pursed faces at him. But he was not pleased with Laura. Laura was startled into self-consciousness as he took her pulse and asked her questions about her diet and sleep and commented on her thinning hair and dull skin. She had spent the last few months focused on Rosa rather than on herself, and it was only now under Dr Turner's frowning scrutiny that she realised she was failing at her own work of femininity, that she had forgotten about the face she turned to the world.

She had healed slowly from the Caesarean, so that there was often a current of physical pain running through those days, which made them all the more exhausting. Rosa was a fussy baby, always wanting to nurse or be carried, so that even with Mother and Aunt Dee and Helen to help there was never respite for Laura. Nothing, she thought, prepares one for the overwhelming physicality, not so much of childbirth – the anaesthetic and the surgery had, after all, shielded her from that – but from the experience of looking after a new baby. Whenever she was not with Rosa, her skin craved her touch, and yet whenever Laura had her in her arms she felt restless, weighed down by her needs. This push and pull of desire and frustration was too extreme for her to understand; it was an intensity of sensation from which, it seemed, there was no release.

Dr Turner told her she needed to engage a nanny and get more sleep, to take a nap every afternoon, to eat more red meat and drink more milk, to go for a walk in the fresh air every day, and he enlisted her mother in the argument. Laura could not be bothered to explain to him that finding a nanny was not very easy when you had become the notorious wife of a traitor and every prospective employee who answered your advertisement for help turned out to be in the pay of some newspaper. The interest in the Last story had not died down. She still could not step outside the door without being photographed. Every time the reporters left for a day, they seemed to find a new lead or a new angle, and swarmed back again. One week, Herbert Morrison made a statement about the missing diplomats in Parliament; another week, there was a supposed sighting in Warsaw; another week, a statement by an old colleague of Edward's that he had once boasted of being the English Hiss; another, a page of vile gossip in a Sunday newspaper that the two had fled because they were being blackmailed over allegations too depraved to repeat in a family newspaper.

And with the press camped by her door Laura could not imagine how Stefan was ever going to reach her. How would she receive any message that was more informative than Edward's anodyne telegram? There could be no straightforward escape for her now, no flight over the borders under cover of night. No wonder she looked strung out, but of course she could say nothing of that to Dr Turner. She smiled and said yes, she would try to rest more, she would think about where they could go for a holiday.

On the way back to Patsfield, Rosa whining on her grandmother's lap as Laura drove, Mother picked up the subject. 'He's right,' she said. 'Never being able to have a normal day – not able to go for a walk or go shopping or anything – you can't go on like this. He said your nerves are all to pieces, that you're not recovering properly from the birth.' Out of the window Laura saw that reporter with the longish hair, whose face she might have found quite attractive had he not posed such a threat to her, walking down the village high street, talking to the woman who had been keen on amateur dramatics. Laura realised that she never stopped watching out in this way now, she was never unaware of being watched, of watching the watchers. Her mother was right, it could not go on.

When they got into the house, it was nearly lunchtime. Rosa began to get restless, and while Mother and Aunt Dee ate, Laura was pacing the floor, trying to calm her. 'Let Helen take her for a while,' her mother said, but Laura believed that

Helen would unsettle her, and it was easier to hold her herself, carrying her through the maze of her tiredness until she reached sleep and Laura could go upstairs and put her into her cot. Then she went down and ate some cold, tasteless chicken pie while Mother and Aunt Dee talked.

She had noticed how the relationship between Mother and Aunt Dee had grown over the last few months here. They liked to drift back into the past, and Laura could catch echoes of the young girls of the Edwardian age they had once been, the dreams and ideas that had fuelled their youth. But then Laura would hear them talk about the excruciating present, and they were unable to sidestep the dead ends of their lives: the unfulfilling marriages and bereavements, the children lost to a strange confusion of modernity and abandonment. Giles and Winifred and herself all became rolled up into the same narrative of anxiety, while only Ellen, with her apparently perfect family life, was outside their complicated tales of worry and woe.

But at all times they tried to avoid the mystery around Edward. That taint of espionage, those suspicions of homosexuality were too filthy and complicated for them to want to discuss. Laura could see how hard her mother tried to focus on the needs of the moment, rather than thinking of what might lie behind the disappearance. She knew that strategy very well; it was the one she had used for years. You must keep your gaze on the immediate scene: the plates that needed clearing, the dresses that needed ironing, the vases that needed fresh water, while the clouds above you gathered and dispersed and gathered again.

Now, they were focused on the idea that Laura must get away from Patsfield. Aunt Dee had the solution, one that she had been putting forward for some weeks already: they should go and stay with Winifred.

'She says she knows lots of quiet towns around Geneva – you know the sort of thing, mountains, hotels – she can take time off work and settle us in. I haven't forgotten my French, so there won't be any problem finding our way around,' Dee was saying.

'It's not a bad idea – the Alps, do you remember our first skiing lesson when we were at school there?'

'I could hardly stay upright. What do you think, Laura, shall I tell Winifred we'll come soon?'

Before they made any certain plans, Laura said, she would need to talk to Bill Spall. She had promised to stay in touch with the Foreign Office, after all. Mother and Aunt Dee shied away from that statement, and Laura waited until they were settled in the living room with their cups of tea before she went to the telephone. She did not really want them to overhear her conversation with Spall, but in the event it was truncated. 'I just need to get away for a bit,' Laura tried to explain. 'My doctor said—'

'I'll call you back,' he said. But when the telephone rang later, the voice was not his. 'I'm calling from Mr Valance's office,' a woman said. 'He'd like to come and see you this week. He'll come to your house tomorrow.'

Valance. That was the name. Laura had had no sense, up to now, that anyone in the security services was interested in what she might or might not know. She had not been questioned. The house had not been searched. The statements made by Herbert Morrison and Anthony Eden and others in Parliament about Edward had been made without any reference to Laura Last. You are just the wife, Laura thought to herself, you are nothing to them. But Valance was the man whom Edward and Stefan had feared, and neither of them was here to advise her. As she walked the corridors that night, holding a fussy Rosa, inhaling her scent, longing for her to rest, she wondered whether now it was the beginning of the end.

As the black Austin parked in the drive outside the house the next day, Laura was rather glad to see from an upstairs window that the photographer who staked the house night and day was trying to snatch a picture of the man who got out, and that his driver was having to go out and remonstrate with him, explaining no doubt that while Edward's family was fair game, you could not photograph members of His Majesty's secret services. Laura was waiting for him in the living room, holding Rosa. She had tried, in a way that felt unfamiliar to her now, to dress well and to put on make-up, but the face that looked back at her from the mirror seemed changed – not just tired, but flattened, worn down by the overwhelming events of the last few months, and there were silver hairs showing along her parting.

As soon as Valance came in, Laura disliked him. He was a large man who might once have been good-looking, with a shock of strikingly white hair, but whose jowly face now looked doglike and whose belly strained at his jacket. There was something about him, indeed, that seemed familiar, but Laura was not sure what it was. She went out and gave Rosa to Mother, and returned to the room.

'Would you like some tea?'

'Let's just get down to business, shall we?' he said. He had a voice which wanted to be as certain in its vowel sounds as Toby's or Edward's, but there was a memory in it of a regional accent which Laura could not place. He shut the door. 'Let's not start with Mr Last. Let's start with you. Tell me about your involvement with communism.'

The shock was physical, in the pumping of her heart and the dryness of her mouth. Given Spall's obvious assumption that she was superfluous and ignorant, she had not expected this opening. But the long weeks of waiting had helped her. There was no question she had not run over in her mind at some point during these weeks, no scenario that had not already unspooled in her restless imagination as she paced the floors with Rosa.

'Well, I never was involved. I read a little of the *Worker* when I first came to England – a girl I met gave me one – but I'm not really political.'

'Who was this girl?'

Laura screwed up her mouth in what she hoped looked like willing concentration. 'I think she was called Florence. I talked to her on the train from Southampton to London, you know, years ago.' His face didn't flicker. Laura had decided to admit to a couple of slight encounters with people she knew were communists, in order to make her other denials sound more convincing.

'Did you go to meetings organised by the Communist Party?'

'No, not at all. I once heard Florence speak. It was at a Co-operative Guild meeting, I think.'

'Were you ever approached to become a member?'

'I suppose Florence may have mentioned it, but I wasn't as involved as that.'

'Did you know that Edward was a member of the Communist Party?'

'You know, that's impossible. He is absolutely loyal. He loves his country. No, that's impossible.'

It was not anger, but something like boredom, as if she had simply said what he had expected, that she saw on Valance's face. If Stefan had been right about the evidence that had fallen into the hands of the Foreign Office, Valance must either know that Laura was lying, or think that Edward had kept her totally in the dark. Was he going to bring her in now, was the game over?

But Laura knew she had one thing on her side. Over these quiet weeks she had realised that there was no appetite on the part of the British government, unlike in the States, for any open accusations, any courtroom arguments or public statements, any airing of evidence and counter-evidence. Whenever she thought about why that was, she put it down to embarrassment – the embarrassment of admitting that they had kept a traitor in the American embassy all those years, sending him to those sensitive meetings, allowing him to hear every word of the nuclear policy, every nuance of the negotiations for the North Atlantic Treaty Organization, and feed it all drip by drip, day by day, year by year to Stalin. But now, confronted by Valance and the regional accent that he was so eager to cover up, Laura recognised that it was also all about class, the intense fidelity to all that Edward's family represented, everything that Laura had come to know as the group, whose every characteristic – the accents, the humour, the education, the clothes, the pastimes – compelled deference from everyone else, even from this man who was not quite part of it and yet wanted to be part of it. Even if he had the evidence, did he have the will to drive it home and destroy her?

So as Laura heard and responded to Valance's questions, in a dance of half-revelation and retreats into secrecy, it was as though she was making him a silent promise – if they wanted to build some kind of wall around what they would see as this cesspit of treachery, she would help them build it. If they wanted to keep Edward's secret close to their chests, she would do nothing that would mean they had to show their cards. Over and over again, as he questioned and she responded, she thought that he saw through her, but nothing was explicit and nothing became dangerous, until the end.

'Tell me about why Mr Last chose that day to go away.'

'I have no idea. I've told you, I don't know why he went or where.'

'We need to know how he knew things had become dangerous for him. Unless you give me the information, you – and your family – will not be left alone. Your daughter is young. We would not want to separate you so early.'

The air in the room seemed thick and lacking in oxygen. Laura was silent.

'And tell me about Mr Last's relationship with Nicholas Fergus.'

'He rarely saw him. I think I met him once or twice, that's all – only at parties.'

'When Last was seeing a psychiatrist . . .'

'A psychoanalyst.'

'He reported that . . .' and Valance made a great show of referring to his notes. Had Lvov given anything away? Would he be the weak link? 'Ah, yes, that Last was suffering from homosexual tendencies.'

'I beg your pardon?'

'Were you aware that your husband's connection to Fergus was of that kind?'

'That is a vile insinuation.' But strangely, Laura found that it was no easier to speak the truth than it was to lie, and her voice sounded too reedy to be persuasive.

'We have it here from this psychiatrist that Last was seeing on his return from Washington. Of course, Mr Fergus was notorious in that regard, it was why he was sent home from Washington. And we understand that Mr Fergus had often boasted about his . . . relationship with Mr Last. One colleague of Mr Last's has told us that he saw them in a . . . compromising situation, on that Thursday at their club.' He was looking straight into Laura's face. It doesn't take much to make a new mother break, but just at that moment Laura heard Rosa cry out in the next room and she stood up, saying she would be back in a moment.

When she returned, she was more composed, freshly powdered and lipsticked, and Valance moved on to the question of her travels. He told her that they had the powers to prevent her travelling, but that they would prefer not to do so, so long as she stayed near. Geneva was acceptable. But there was one condition. She was not to speak to the press under any circumstances at all. 'It could seriously disrupt our investigations if you did.'

Laura understood, and she was quick to agree. She told him that he could rely on her silence at all times. At all times.

'And will you let us know if your husband or anyone acting for him tries to contact you?'

'That goes without saying.' The interview was at an end. It was a relief, but as Valance left, how weak Laura felt. Mother came into the room some time later to find her sitting on the sofa, her head in her hands.

'Can we go away?'

'We can,' she said, standing up and taking Rosa from her. Her weight was both reassuring and exhausting. 'We can go.' This place that once felt almost like home had become unbearable. It was time to leave.

7

Nothing could prepare one for the breadth and depth of the Alpine panorama, its cleanliness, its washed, bright lines. Edward would have quoted poetry, Laura thought, but Winifred was more down to earth. 'Rather cheering, isn't it, the mountain air – and hopefully the reporters will leave you alone here. Giles told me they've been ferocious in England. There was debate in Parliament about your treatment, wasn't there?'

There had been. In the end, the long-haired reporter had got tired of waiting and had published a lengthy, entirely fictitious interview with Laura in a Sunday newspaper, detailing her anguish and her belief that her husband would soon be in touch with her. When she had seen it, Laura had felt sickened not just by its content, but by the fact that she had to grovel to Valance, explaining over and over again that she had not been culpable. For once Toby had stepped in to help, and a letter of complaint was published in *The Times* by a friend of his, imitating his own pompous voice. 'The repeated invasion of the privacy of the family,' it had said, 'an invasion amounting at times to persecution, is surely indefensible.' Toby had also been behind questions in Parliament about the press. He had sent Laura a copy of the entry in Hansard, in which some politician she had never met had talked about the 'public misgiving' that the fictitious interview had caused, and how this showed the need for a Press Council. All Laura knew was that none of this kerfuffle had prompted the newspaper or the reporter to apologise or admit wrongdoing. She found the complaints as tiring, in some ways, as the original publication, but she could not explain that to Winifred.

They were eating heavy Alpine food on the terrace of a restaurant in the picturesque little town and, seeing the great valley falling away below them and spiralling up into the cloudless evening sky, Laura felt as though she were coming out into the open after weeks locked in a dark room. It was only the next morning, however, as they were breakfasting in the hotel, that she realised how elusive her freedom still was.

An English family was having a good look at them from another table, and passing a newspaper from hand to hand. Before Mother and Winifred could notice what they were doing, Laura quickly asked a waiter for a newspaper herself. There it was on the second page: a picture of her holding Rosa on the tarmac of Geneva airport and a story about how the bungling secret services had let her leave England, and how speculation was rife about whether she was likely to make contact with her traitor husband while out of reach of their surveillance.

Laura found herself looking at the photograph of herself as if she were looking at a picture of a stranger. She had not noticed the photographer in the crowd at the airport, and all she remembered from the moment of disembarkation was the weight of Rosa in her arms, how difficult it was to go down the aeroplane stairs with a baby and how the heels of her shoes kept sticking in the corrugations of the steps. But in the photograph she looked as though she was deliberately posing, her head high and her expression knowing. The picture did not show Mother; Laura seemed to be alone, striding into the future with her daughter. If she had seen such a photograph of a stranger, Laura would have said that the woman in the picture was relishing her notoriety.

She did not show the photograph to the others, but went on turning the pages as if she was interested in international news. A few pages further in was a picture of Amy Sandall, in Monte Carlo for the weekend, walking on the esplanade and wearing a rather outré get-up which bared her midriff. Although she was with her husband, you would not have noticed him in the picture, and there was something similar about this and the photograph of Laura. Looking at it, Laura remembered the first time that she had seen Amy tackled by the photographers on the platform of the boat train at Southampton. Laura had thought then that Amy relished her fame, that she felt energised by it as she forged forward. Or did she?

As they crossed the lobby back to their rooms, Laura could see through the big doors that there were photographers waiting outside the hotel, and when they went out to drive over to Megève for lunch, they were followed all the way by two reporters, one on a motorcycle and one in a car. Discouraged, Laura and the others soon returned to the hotel, where they spent the afternoon in the hotel grounds. Mother and Aunt Dee went early to bed, and Winifred and Laura sat on the restaurant balcony, drinking cognac and smoking.

'I can see it's absolutely impossible for you,' said Winifred. 'But they will get bored soon, don't you think?'

Laura said she was sure they would, and then she said she hoped they would. It had already been so long.

'It's absurd that they think they are going to land some scoop, following you about. What do they think will happen, that some Soviet agent is going to jump out of the bushes and carry you off to Moscow?' Laura smiled at the very absurdity of the notion. 'I suppose you'll just have to sit this out.'

'I don't know how much longer I can, though.'

'You've coped up to now.' The two women sat in silence for a while, and then Winifred asked what she must surely have been dying to say for some time. 'Don't you have any idea what has happened to Edward?'

But it was easy now for Laura to respond. She had answered so often, the words came without hesitation. 'None at all. I know that he isn't a traitor, though, whatever they say.' And then she spoke about what was also pressingly on her mind. 'The problem is, I don't know how to go on practically. I don't have a cent, you know – I'm living off Mother.'

'Doesn't the Foreign Office look after you?'

Laura had to explain that the very week after Edward drove off into the night, the Foreign Office suspended him. No pay, nothing. They had not responded to any questions from Laura about what she was meant to do. The mortgage payments for the house in Patsfield, doctor's bills, Helen's pay, diapers, food, taxis . . . 'I don't know what Rosa and I will do if—'

'But surely Toby and Sybil – and Mrs Last—?'

Laura had to confess that she had become unwelcome there, and Winifred shifted in her chair as though the thought made her uncomfortable. 'God, they would prefer to be living in the last century, wouldn't they?'

'You remember telling me I should think of getting a job?' Laura said.

'Not the ideal circumstances now in which to look.'

Winifred's directness was refreshing. But it was true; as the wife of the missing diplomat, and with a small child, how would she work? And if she couldn't, who would support her? She would have to sit down with Mother and Aunt Dee, she realised, and talk them through the situation and find out exactly what Toby would contribute. It would take a lot of direct, aggressive honesty about money. The thought was exhausting. Instead she asked Winifred about her work, and about Peter, who had got her this job and whom Laura still had not met.

'You'll be surprised when you meet him, everyone is. He's much too young for me, is the truth. People keep saying, he's not what we expected, he isn't your usual type, but what they mean is, how did anyone as old and cynical as you snare someone so young and fresh? Not that I have snared him. In fact – he's been talking about marriage, but I'm not so sure.'

Laura asked why. At first Winifred was vague, and then she talked more about her work, about how she enjoyed the sense of building something for the future at the United Nations. 'I'm someone there – not someone powerful, but someone . . . reliable. I'm not quite sure – I know it's an odd thing to say – that I want to stop that. If I married Peter, you know, he could be posted somewhere else tomorrow.'

Up until just recently Laura would have found Winifred's view strange, but now she saw how she had built a life that rose directly from her own personality. At work, with Peter, with her family – people took her for what she was. Laura wondered what that would feel like. She could only hold herself together by a great effort of will; she was always aware of the mask she had to wear, but there was Winifred unafraid of the judgement of others. Admiration stirred in her.

And it was Winifred who made the move to Geneva possible. By the time the month in St-Gervais came to an end, Laura and her mother had had the conversation about money, looked through the bank statements and bills, and recognised that the mortgage on Patsfield was unsustainable. Once that had been understood, Mother wanted Laura to come back to the States at once – to live in Boston, near to Ellen. Mother had given up the old house in Stairbridge and now lived in Ellen's neighbourhood, in a little apartment.

Why shouldn't Laura find something nearby? She could stay with Ellen until she found the right place. Laura knew that would be impossible for her. She had to be in Europe. She had to be where Stefan could reach her. Even if he had been put off so far by the circling reporters, or the fear that MI5 had set a tail – though she had not been aware of one – it would not be much longer. The contact might be made at any time. So she told Mother that the move to the States would have to wait for a while. She said that the Foreign Office would not allow it yet. That was true, after all; that was what Valance had said.

It was Winifred who suggested that at least the press were better in Switzerland than in England, and it would be nice to have Laura near to her. She found an apartment that was being vacated by someone who was leaving the United Nations. The view from the front was endless, filled with circling swifts and the changing clouds, out over the rooftops, the lake and the mountains, even if the back rooms were dark. What's more, the family who was leaving had a nanny, Aurore (awfully competent, said Winifred), who would be looking for a job. Laura talked by telephone a few times with Valance and his assistant. They agreed that she could stay in Geneva for the time being, but that any further travel would have to be agreed with the British consulate.

She went back to Patsfield just to pack up the house, leaving Mother and Rosa in Geneva. She had asked Helen to meet her there, but as soon as she saw her she felt it was a mistake. Helen asked her questions about Rosa, about Geneva, the new apartment, but Laura could hardly speak to her. Everything here is corroded now, she thought, I can trust nobody. All day they packed personal belongings into boxes, wrote on them the address of the new apartment, with that sense of unease between them. Edward had books about Russian art, Russian music, a couple of volumes of Marx, all of Tolstoy's novels in a beautiful set. Laura felt Helen's gaze on them as she put them in a box of things to be given away. At the end of the day Helen rose. 'Good luck, Mrs Last,' she said, brushing down her skirt. Laura could not meet her eyes.

But when Helen was gone, the past crowded in instead. All the things that she had planned to do and never done; the piano she had not bought, the sofas she had not re-covered. All the things she *had* done: the pretty curtains, the tea table that would now belong to the buyer, a local doctor. How neglected the garden looked with summer at an end, the grass yellowing and overgrown, peonies toppling into it. She opened the door to her beloved darkroom. Soon it would be a garden shed again. She gathered up the photographic paper stacked in a corner and carried it through to the bins. It was silly to dwell on what might have been, she said to herself as she pushed it down on the other rubbish.

8

Winter bites hard in Geneva. In the frozen days Laura felt that she was waking up to the new reality of her life. One January morning a man in a grey trilby started following her around the fruit market near to their apartment, and Laura allowed herself to catch his eye, willing him to speak one of the usual passwords or mention Edward or Stefan. When he suggested to her that she should join him for a drink, she realised that her eager manner had made him assume she was an easy pick-up. Irritation pulsed through her as she climbed the long flights of stairs back to the apartment.

She rattled the keys in the door. One of the locks turned one way, one turned the other, and she still muddled them most of the time. The flat itself seemed to resist her, refusing to fit itself to her shape. Yet Aurore had Rosa sitting in a pile of cushions on the floor in the living room, and as Laura came in she heard a gurgling laugh. That was the only thing to hold onto now: since Aurore had started to help her to look after Rosa, Laura had felt some of the overwhelming pressure of motherhood lessen.

Now someone else was doing the work, feeding her baby and bathing her, alongside Laura, she could see how it was possible to survive becoming a mother with one's personality intact, even to enjoy it. She could also see that Aurore's physical presence, her scent and voice and face, were becoming imprinted on her daughter; that this slow growth of trust was love, and this was a gain for all of them. She still found motherhood often overwhelming, especially during the long nights and weekends without Aurore, but she could stand away from it enough to say, no, this is too much; yes, this is fine. Before, she had not even been able to become conscious of how she felt, in the deluge of experience.

But while her relationship with Rosa had become easier, that did not make life in the apartment straightforward. As the urgency of Laura's need for her mother lessened, their relationship became gritty, constantly irritable. Out of duty and the fear of solitude, Laura tried to be a good daughter, tried to bring her little nuggets of news, tried to encourage her relationship with Rosa, tried to find people – middle-aged Americans, mainly – with whom Mother might find common ground. Tonight, Laura wanted her mother to accompany her to a cocktail party in one of the big hotels; she had been invited by an Italian man to whom Winifred had introduced her a few months earlier. But Mother felt unwell. She was lying on the sofa. She motioned to the telephone. 'There are messages,' she said. Laura looked at the notepad; someone had called whose name she did not recognise. 'A reporter,' her mother said brusquely.

The repose they had hoped they would find in this quiet city seemed to be eluding them. There was no longer a pack of reporters camped outside the door, but still Laura never knew when the camera flashes would suddenly go off again, sparked by some new piece of gossip or simply a quiet news day; she never knew when the telephone or doorbell would ring and some enterprising writer would be there with a reason why it was time for her to tell her story at last, and why he or she was just the person for her to confide in. No doubt this latest message was one of those, and Laura threw it in the bin without looking at it. 'If you won't come out, Mother, you don't mind if I do?' she said. 'Aurore can put Rosa to bed before she goes.'

Her mother acquiesced, getting up heavily and saying she might go to bed early. Laura made herself go and get changed. It's funny, she thought as she put on an old velvet dress and lipsticked her mouth, that even though she no longer had the crippling shyness of youth, there was always that reluctance just before she left the apartment to go out. She had partly wanted Mother to come with her to protect her from the possible expectations of Roberto Peri. He was a smooth-voiced man, an aficionado of Wagner and Mahler, and she had enjoyed going to a couple of concerts with him, where she could lose any self-consciousness in the waves of sound, but she did not want the friendship to go any further. Her strange status – neither widow, divorcée nor single woman – made her an object of interest to too many men.

But tonight, as Roberto steered her around the room, she felt that his interest in her was not really sexual. It was as though she was a little curiosity he had collected as he might have picked up a picture or an ornament; the wife of the missing diplomat, how fascinating. She saw the usual knowledge jump into people's eyes as he said her name and saw that he was pleased to have brought such an intriguing object to a dull party. So many people seemed to pass through Geneva in those days; she was not really surprised when she saw a familiar face nearby her.

'Why, Archie!'

'Winifred said you might be here,' he said. 'It's been so long.'

What was he doing in Geneva? Had the Foreign Office sent him over for some posting?

'Just this,' he motioned at the cocktail he was holding, and Laura was puzzled. 'I don't mean drinking, but just having fun. I came into a huge inheritance a few months ago – quite a shock – my cousin Rupert died without children and left the whole thing to me – massive estate, house, pictures, the lot, but all up in the Scottish Highlands. I can't be doing with it, so I've sold everything, to the horror of the family. I've chucked in the Foreign Office and I've been travelling for the last six months – had a whale of a time. Egypt, Italy, and now back here. I think I'll stay in Europe for a bit. You know I'm no longer with Monica?'

Laura did know, obviously. She exchanged letters with Monica from time to time, although they had not seen one another since before Edward's disappearance.

'I knew you'd left England and come over here. Can't blame you, the papers were beyond belief – I'm sorry I didn't get in touch. What with the divorce and then Rupe's death – I've been a bit all at sea. I didn't want to impose on you. You've had so much on your plate. But it's great to see you.'

Laura understood what he was saying; he had had enough to deal with, he could not have confronted her trouble too. But it was good to see him. There was a sort of humour about the way he talked, as though he refused to see things tragically, which she found refreshing after the hushed tones so many adopted when they met her. When he told her that he was meeting Winifred and Peter later for dinner, they decided to leave together. Roberto was not really irritated when she told him she was dining with a friend and she saw that she had fulfilled her role for him for the evening.

As they walked through the lobby of the hotel, Archie excused himself to go to the lavatory. There was an English newspaper lying on the reception desk, and Laura saw Edward's face in the photograph before she read the headline.

What a dreadful picture they kept using: Alistair must have given it to the press. Over-exposed and taken from an unflattering angle, it made him look chinless and smug. But the story was worse. New allegations, new sources, new gossip: in this version, the British secret services had followed Nick and Edward from Patsfield on the momentous night, and then murdered them and dumped their bodies in the English Channel in order to keep them forever silent and minimise the international scandal that would ensue if the extent of their spying activities was revealed to the Americans.

Laura had Edward's telegram that had been sent a week after he left, and had not lost faith that it was his voice in those misspelt words. But when Archie found her again, the newspaper abandoned on the floor, he could not help noticing that her expression was closed. 'Don't ask,' Laura said, and she was glad when he didn't.

In the taxi ride to the old town, she found herself trying to ignore all the questions in her mind. It had been nine months already: why no word, why had Stefan not made contact, why had no message been brought to her, not even a line about Rosa's birth? This silence was corrosive, destructive, she thought, taking a cigarette from her bag. Archie lit it for her. The smoke filled her mouth with a moment of comfort.

'All right now?' he said, smiling, and Laura smiled back.

'It gets to me sometimes,' she said.

'Things do,' he responded, and again she was glad of his wry, accepting expression.

When they got to the restaurant, Peter was there but Winifred had been delayed, he said. Laura had not warmed to Peter. He worked for the British mission to the United Nations, and was one of those men who is always keen to show off his faultless French, his perfect German and his elegant Italian. He came from a diplomatic family himself, and seemed to revel in the rootlessness that a travelling childhood had given him, as though he was more at home in huge marble rooms

390

and at impersonal ambassadorial functions than anywhere else. But in that moment, with the fear nagging away at her again, she was glad of the way that he and Archie could fall so easily into the patter of the group, talking about Archie's travels, about whether he had visited Freya in Ventimiglia, Edith in Florence, Cecil in Alexandria.

Winifred finally joined them, obviously straight from work. She was working early and late hours that year, as a convention neared its final stages. At first she seemed irritable, clearly bringing with her a frustration from the meeting she had just left, but then she relaxed, telling Peter something Laura could not catch about how in the end the Australian ambassador would come round, it was only a matter of time.

Halfway through dinner, she turned and started speaking to Laura in an undertone. 'Giles is coming to ski in March. None of my business, I know, but he is awfully hurt that you wouldn't see him when Edward left. He said he rang and rang but you kept giving him the brush-off.'

'I just couldn't bear all the intrusion.'

'He isn't like Alistair, you know, he won't blab all over the place. He's been . . . rather changed by Edward's disappearance. Also, I should warn you, Alistair's turned those bloody articles into a book, to come out in a few months – the anniversary, you know.'

Laura did know. 'What sort of book?'

'I'll get you an early copy, if you want."

'It does sound a bit rich, him making a book out of it,' Peter said, the sort of bland remark that was typical of him.

'More than a bit rich – absolutely beyond the pale,' said Winifred, 'but it's made him a star. He's got a new novel coming out too, about espionage and sex. He sees himself as something of an expert.'

'Aren't we all experts now?' Archie said, but his voice had a joking, rather brotherly tone that made it protective rather than needling, Laura thought. His relaxed presence took the edge off her anguish that evening, so it was a pity he was moving on the following week – to Italy, he explained, to the south, right down to Puglia.

A few weeks later Laura acquiesced to Winifred's request, and brought the whole household – Mother and Aurore and Rosa – to St-Gervais for a couple of weeks, so that they could ski with Winifred and Peter and see Giles again. They stayed at the same hotel that they had gone to in the summer, one of those Alpine hotels with vast rooms and bad plumbing and postcard views at every window. Laura had a couple of skiing lessons and then gave up, finding the loss of control in that immensity of space too disorienting, but strangely her mother rather took to it, weaving her way slowly down the slopes with Winifred after a few lessons. One day, when Rosa was happy in the hotel crèche with Aurore, Laura agreed to go for a walk through the town with Giles. They were muffled up, and looked pale and tired and out of place, Laura thought, seeing themselves reflected in a bakery window, in this town where most people seemed to be rosy and laughing with the mountain air and exercise.

Laura knew what Giles wanted to talk to her about, and although for a while she kept the conversation on other subjects, asking him about work and telling him about Rosa, in the end she succumbed, and as they walked, she lived through his sense of loss and envied him the fact that he could be so open.

'For me, he was a kind of hero,' Giles said, kicking at the snow as he walked. Kick, kick, kick, leaving dirty marks on the white sidewalks. 'When I think of him now . . . I remember him leaning on the bridge at Trinity, quoting some bloody Horace. I thought he had everything – brains, so charming too – I never really thought I was good enough for him. He was the only man who made me feel like that. He invited me to his house in the holidays. I remember him reading Edward Thomas to me. He thought there was so much in it, the poetry of everyday life, but I couldn't see it.' That brought Edward suddenly very near, and Laura tuned out of Giles's train of thought for a while, but when she tuned back in he was still on the same theme. 'He told me about Tolstoy, about the need to get away from possessions. I thought, how extraordinary he was, right at the centre of that class, you know, but with this social conscience – and sensitive: he knew all the names of the wild flowers when we went walking. He made me feel at home there, at Sutton – the other boys like him at Cambridge made me feel a bit – you know, I was a scientist, I wasn't rich.' Laura remembered Giles in the garden at Sutton, and realised how she had misread him, seeing his pleasure at being there as confidence, when in fact it was just eagerness to belong. 'I was jealous of you, because he married you. I thought, you'll never understand him as I do. But of course neither of us understood him at all – nobody did; except, I suppose, we must assume Nick did.'

Perhaps fresh snow was about to fall, the sky was greying and there was a wind coming up. 'Let's go and get a hot drink,' Laura said. They were passing a café, and they went in and ordered hot chocolate and brandies. In the glass-fronted counters were gleaming confections of pastry, cream and bilberries, and Laura ordered a couple of cakes that were left untouched between them. Nothing could stop Giles talking as he was swept down such a river of reminiscence.

'He was a pacifist at heart; he hated the whole war machine. The last conversation we had, he was talking about Korea. He could see the evil on both sides. How could he have ever put his trust in Stalin? He must have been so utterly duped.'

Laura said nothing except that she didn't know. As the drinks arrived, she realised that she wished that she could ask Giles more about his assessment of Edward's politics. When the world was embarking on the showdown between fascism and communism, she wanted to ask, where did you want to be? But she remembered Edward reading Tchernavin on the

Soviet prison camps, and being unable to speak about what he read. When you saw the pictures from Hiroshima, she wanted to ask Giles, did you believe American power should have no counterweight at all? But she remembered Edward expressing his fears to Joe about the Soviet atomic tests. She could not begin that conversation with Giles about the rights and wrongs of the great political standoff of their age, because, even now, a year on, every step of the way, her mask must never slip. She had to be an empty-headed wife who knew nothing about politics. And even if she had been able to start that conversation, would she have done so? For so long, after those first conversations in 1940, she and Edward had avoided talking directly about what it was they were working for, and now when she looked back she felt unmoored by the uncertainty she felt about what he had really been thinking, all that time. She just said, 'But Giles, he was never a traitor.'

'Do you think it was just a mistake, then – that Nick was going and Nick dragged him along, that Edward didn't know what he was getting into until it was too late?'

'I just don't know,' Laura said, her voice a rush of cold on the heat that had been building from Giles's words. She stirred her hot chocolate, which was gritty at the bottom. 'Nothing about it makes sense to me. Have you talked to the security people?'

'You mean MI5? God, I tried to talk to them at the beginning. I told them I knew him – come and talk to me – but they weren't interested. Some junior chap popped over one day, but hardly listened to me. Alistair tried to talk to them for his book – his vicious book – but they wouldn't spill any beans. Nothing said, nothing done, if you ask me.'

'Is his book really so nasty?'

'I brought you an advance copy – Winifred told me to. It's in my room, back at the hotel.' Giles lapsed into silence, brooding and looking into his glass. He was unshaven and rather crumpled, but not, Laura thought, unattractive; he had the kind of energy that clever, emotionally thwarted people often have, as though some passion was only being held in check by an intellectual effort. Laura wished that she could have spoken, could have talked about the things they were both struggling to understand, and brought down the barriers between them. But she could not. So as they went on talking, she kept on parrying, going sideways, and at the end, as they walked to the hotel, through the snow that had begun to fall around them, she sensed anger brewing in him. He might not have realised it, but he was furiously disappointed that his confidences had not been received with the interest he thought they deserved.

So, as he went on talking, it was not so much about how important a figure Edward had been in his life, but how significant he had been in Edward's. 'Of course, I know that he was lonely. I wish I could have spent more time with him – but being posted to Malvern, and then working in Bristol, made it difficult. I wish I could have been with him more; maybe I could have persuaded him out of whatever it was that made him put his trust in Nick.' Laura still said nothing except that there was no point in regrets. When he handed her Alistair's book at the door of his room, she felt that he did so with pleasurable expectation, as if he knew and approved of the pain it would cause her.

After dinner, once Mother and Rosa were asleep in their rooms, Laura began Alistair's book and went on reading it all night. While reading she remembered how Winifred had told her seven years ago that Alistair was not quite able to see another's full humanity, and the force of this observation struck her as she saw Edward become, in his hands, a mere caricature of a traitor. But it was not an unlifelike portrait. With Alistair's description of Edward on his return from America, Laura was plunged back into that dinner at the Savoy when they had all tried so hard to play their roles: 'His appearance on that evening was unexpected. He had lost his serenity, his hands would tremble, his eyes were hooded and he looked as if he had spent the night sitting up in a train . . . Though he remained as detached and amiable as ever, I felt it was clear that he was in a very bad way. From time to time, even in mid-conversation, a kind of shutter would fall as if he had returned to some inner and incommunicable anxiety.'

But there were other, less expected cruelties in the way that he wrote about her. 'It is clear that Laura Last is as confused as all her friends about the circumstances of his disappearance. Any latent political beliefs he had were obviously not confided in a wife whose inability to interest herself in any aspect of politics is at times painfully obvious. She is a woman dedicated to dancing and flirtation, and her eagerness for admiration could often be an embarrassment for Last, who would detach himself from her social life.' And Laura was forced down the hidden lanes of memory again, those nights when she had insisted that Alistair took her dancing at the Dorchester, when he had been the witness to her naïve attempts to flirt with Blanchard. Shame coursed through her, as it had done all those years ago.

The next morning Laura waited until Winifred and Peter and Mother had gone off skiing again and Aurore had taken Rosa into the hotel crèche, before turning to Giles over the breakfast table and restarting the conversation. 'He is cruel.'

'And the editors got him to take out Edward's relationship with Nick . . .'

'Whatever do you mean?' Laura's temper sparked at last; how could it be that even Giles, who claimed such knowledge of Edward, would believe such a thing?

'We don't have to beat around the bush any more, do we? They went off together, didn't they – how much more obvious did they have to make it? Alistair told me that you'd known and you'd turned a blind eye, for years.'

'That's nonsense.'

'I'm sorry if I offended you,' he said, in a stiff, satisfied voice that showed he was not sorry at all. 'Alistair said you knew. I loved him at Cambridge. Well, I fancied him, but it was Nick he cared for. We can see that now.'

There was no more for them to say. Social niceties were at an end. 'I must go and get ready for skiing – it's absurd to come all this way and not even bother to go on the slopes.' She stood up, throwing down her napkin, and went out of the restaurant. She did not go out to the mountains, however; she could not face the great whiteness of the outdoors. She went into the crèche to find Rosa and to roll coloured balls with her, while her mind travelled back over the years.

The interest aroused by the book's publication was intense. Laura could gauge it by the increased numbers of telephone calls she got from journalists, and when it was published in America there was another surge. Mother had tried to push Laura to go to America that summer, and every week, it seemed, she received letters from Ellen, telling her she should think of coming home. But she was very aware of Valance's warning that she could not travel too far, and once or twice Ellen enclosed cuttings about Edward from American newspapers with her letters and Laura quailed at the anger they revealed. She wrote impersonal little notes back to Ellen, suggesting that she should come to Geneva herself.

It was not until the following spring that Ellen finally took up the invitation, without Tom and her son, but with her daughter Janet, who was now ten. As Laura saw them walking towards her, she felt she was looking at the future of motherhood – the child who grows apart from you and looks with bored eyes as you fuss with suitcases and passports. Of course one knows that it will happen, Laura thought, but it was the first time she had felt the future with that kind of physical shock: what it would be like for her and Rosa when they were no longer locked into the double step of infancy.

Although it was their mother who had been asking Ellen to come over, the first evening the chatter was mainly between the two sisters. Laura put on the bright persona that she had honed for visitors, telling them what a lovely city Geneva was, how she was so happy to be in this part of it – the shops! The restaurants! The cosmopolitan crowd! And they could go for drives along the lake, and up in the mountains. But after a day or so her mood corroded. She felt, as she always had – but worse now than ever – Ellen's critical gaze on her life. And she could not warm to Janet, who seemed to have inherited Ellen's negative view of the world; Laura found herself irritated by the ten-year-old's passive attitude, her lack of enthusiasm for the holiday. Gradually the apartment, crowded with the two sisters, their mother and two little girls, began to feel impossibly claustrophobic.

The night before her second birthday, Rosa was unable to settle; it seemed that she was sickening for something, though she had no rash or fever. Whatever the reason, the broken night made the morning feel too bright and noisy, with Ellen and Mother making plans for the day and Janet trying to play with Rosa, but only succeeding in upsetting her. They went out for the day, in the little train up into the hills, with Rosa in a stroller, and at the lunch in a hilltop café Laura felt that she should drink only one glass of wine. But as soon as they returned to the apartment, she poured gin into a glass of orange juice while the others were setting the table. They had invited Winifred to come around for a birthday tea after work, and Laura could see that Ellen and Winifred took to one another immediately. That made her feel resentful rather than pleased; she realised it was childish of her, but she saw them as belonging to such different parts of her life, and she did not want Winifred to value Ellen – dull Ellen – with her terrible American sandals and her bright red nail polish. But here they were, talking in a down-to-earth way about where Ellen should go shopping the next day and about Winifred's work. Laura cut the over-iced chocolate cake and stepped back onto a balloon whose explosive burst caused Rosa to collapse into tears.

Immediately Mother and Ellen began trying to calm her down, but Laura could see that their well-meaning distractions were only upsetting her more, so she pulled her out of her high chair and took her out onto the balcony, alone. Rosa strained away from her, her bottom lip trembling, and as Laura tried to distract her she could hear the women talking in the room, thinking she was out of earshot.

'Why won't she come back to America?'

'False hopes,' said Winifred.

'I thought there was a problem with her passport?'

'I thought it was hoping that Edward might turn up in Europe.'

'She's got to move on.'

After a while Rosa relaxed and let Laura tickle her into hiccupping giggles. Laura went back into the room, feeling a pool of silence spread around her as she did so, and put the child into her high chair. She had planned to take a photograph of Rosa for her birthday; these were the only photographs she took nowadays – studies of her daughter. But when she took the camera out, she found that nothing was going well: the light was too dim and Rosa began to complain again.

After Janet and Rosa were finally in bed, the four women sat in the living room, eating more birthday cake. At least Winifred's presence gave Laura an excuse to open a bottle of wine. It was not long before Ellen moved into the open. Clearly, she had been emboldened by the agreement of Winifred and Mother that it was time for Laura to move on.

'I've found out, Laura, that if you come back to the States you could get a divorce from Edward quite easily – don't, don't, please listen,' Ellen said, irritated that as soon as she started talking, Laura stood up.

'I am listening,' Laura said, although she had such a headache that it was hard to concentrate on her words. 'I'm just getting another drink.'

'It doesn't mean that you couldn't be with him again if he comes back, but at least it will regularise your position. It's impossible like this. If you come to Boston, I could help with Rosa, and she'd have her cousins to grow up with.'

Laura tried to sound reasonable. 'It's kind of you, but I can't decide just like that. The Foreign Office agreed to Geneva, but it took some persuading. They would never let me go to the States. And I can't bear the thought – you can't imagine what the press was like in England. They'd all be out again in full force in America. He was secretary of the Combined Policy Committee, you know. It meant he knew everything about the bomb. I'd never hear the end of it there.'

'Nonsense, Laura. I'm not saying it wouldn't be bad for a bit – but you faced it down in England—'

'I didn't. I ran away. It was impossible.'

'It was impossible,' their mother agreed.

'Mother,' cried Ellen. 'I thought you were on my side!'

'I am,' their mother said. 'But, Ellen, you've no idea. We couldn't leave the house.'

'That was two years ago, it's not a new story any more. Come on, Laura, you can't stay here forever. It's not fair on Mother, or Rosa.'

'Who says it's going to be forever?'

In the face of Laura's continued faith in her absent husband, Ellen and Mother fell silent. Winifred spoke next.

'They do have a point, darling. Maybe you should look for a job? It's not good just brooding all the time.'

Again, Laura tried to sound reasonable, and talked to Winifred about what might be possible during the time that Rosa could spend with Aurore, and given Laura's minimal experience. The women were glad that Laura seemed open, at least, to letting them discuss her impossible, rudderless life, and so they went on talking in circles for a while longer, and then Laura said she had to go to bed.

Once in her room, she lay fully dressed on her bed, looking up at the ceiling, which was painted a pale, shiny grey. There were cobwebs in the corners, she noticed, and on the ceiling light. She should get a broom and knock them down. She should tell the cleaning lady tomorrow. Her headache was growing at the back of her eyes. She felt isolated by the way that Mother and Ellen and Winifred had attacked her, all wanting to change her life. She could see herself through their eyes: drinking too much, a nervous and irritable mother, wandering through life with a vain, stupid hope, not thinking about how her choices affected those around her, selfishly making her mother stay with her when she wanted to be back in America.

If only she could just give in, go to Boston, let Rosa grow up with her cousins. A normal, suburban life; wasn't that what she wanted, really? Maybe it was all she had ever wanted, maybe her other dreams had been only adolescent illusions. But as soon as she thought of it, she knew how distant that was from her now. She had seen something of the temper of the times in Washington; she could not return to the fire that had destroyed Hiss. The silences of the British secret services chilled her, but their cold inertia gave her a way of surviving.

And then there was the pure physical distance such a move would put between her and Edward. If he was now in Russia, silenced for some reason but still alive, he was not so very far. There was always the possibility that Stefan would walk into her life again, passing her in a narrow Swiss street, handing a card to her in a crowded train. In Boston, miles and oceans would divide her from them.

But as Laura thought of this, and the possibility of Edward's presence just across the borders, or Stefan in this very city, the silence, unbroken for two years, screamed in her ears. What had Stefan's promise actually meant? When he had said that they would bring her over, was he just reassuring her with empty words so that she would let the precious Virgil go without her? She thought of the network of contacts that had been knitted around Edward. Thinking back, unpicking conversations, she recognised that Nick was not the only one. There must have been one other source in Washington, with a link to the cryptographers' discoveries, and another one in London, who knew when Edward would be brought in and who would interrogate him. Laura had never been given the keys to that kingdom of secrets. She had not realised it all these years, but she had always been an appendage, locked outside the masculine relationships that they said might endanger her, but which, she also saw, could have been the route to her survival. Outside one group, she had also been outside another. She really was alone, as Edward had never been alone.

As she thought that, other fears began to crowd in. She could no longer push away the insinuations that Valance had made, that the press had been running with, that Giles had stated baldly and that Alistair had wanted to include in his book – that Edward and Nick had gone off together, not just as spies, but as lovers. And as that thought entered her mind, other pictures from the past that she had been trying to forget, that she had always refused to look at directly, were sharp, scissoring through her memory: an evening at the end of the war and Nick's hand touching Edward's neck, laying claim to a long intimacy with him; a dark night in Washington, and Edward blundering out of the house to go drinking with Nick; the secret that Edward had blurted out on that final night, that Nick had recruited him at Cambridge. What form had that recruitment taken? What memories had Patsfield held for him that had drawn him back when he needed to make a new life? She remembered Nick's excitement the night that they set off, the exuberance in his face as Edward came down the stairs to him, ready to leave his pregnant wife, to set off into the darkness for their final adventure.

And now, was it as Giles imagined it? That even now he was with Nick, safe in their dream country, happy, free, making love, more content without Laura than he had been with her? Maybe he had only stayed with her all these years because she knew his secret. She had been a useful dupe, a good mask for him. Was that all she had been? Laura heard Rosa crying out upstairs and as she went to hold her and comfort her, finally bringing her down to nestle against her in Laura's own bed, she found herself confronting the possibility that she had refused to consider ever since she had heard the car drive away that damp May evening – that Rosa might never know her father. More, that Laura had never, really, known him.

9

'I'll telephone the consulate,' Laura found herself saying to her mother the day after Ellen's departure. 'I'll go and talk to them about us going back to the States.' One says things, Laura realised, without necessarily meaning them, because the moment seems to make them essential. It wasn't possible any more for Laura to find excuses that would make Mother happy. She had to talk as if a return was on the cards. She picked up the telephone later that afternoon, with Mother listening in from the living room, and dialled the number of the consulate.

Although Laura found it hard at first to explain why she was calling, still, the first person she spoke to knew who she was; her fame had not faded. But she was passed on from secretary to secretary, and then was told that someone would call her back. Nobody did, for some days, and when she was finally telephoned, she was asked to come in for a meeting.

Still, she was not nervous. Entering the building that cloudy spring morning she assumed that they would simply refuse her permission to travel to America, and she could use that as an excuse to Mother and Ellen.

So she was off-guard when she was taken into a room where Valance was sitting alone, behind a desk, his jowly face as ugly and inexpressive as when they had met two years earlier. But this time she was not lost in the hazy fog of new motherhood, and it dawned on her with an immediate jolt where she had seen that face before – in 1944, in the swaying ballroom of the Dorchester, between Blanchard and Victor. What had he been doing with them, with the Soviet spy who had gone over to the Fascists, and the arms dealer whom Edward could not countenance speaking to? The miasma of corruption that had hung around those nights was there again in the dull room of the British consulate in Geneva.

A secretary was just bringing him coffee. 'This might pass for coffee in London – but we can do better than this dishwater here.'

Laura sat down on the high-backed chair that she was motioned to. Outside long windows, she could hear children playing in the Parc Beaulieu.

The secretary went out, and came back in with something that she obviously thought would be more to Valance's taste. Laura saw how nervous she was around him; saw his pleasure in bullying even this clumsy woman. When they were alone, he spoke.

'You've kept your side of the bargain.'

Surely it was wrong of him to start by talking of bargains, she thought; surely that was too open a move.

'But now you are asking about moving to America. We have evidence . . . you know what I'm talking about. We didn't want to take you in when your baby was so small – but now . . . You seem to assume you are free, that we have lost interest.'

Laura had not prepared herself for this kind of blatant attack, this talk of evidence and arrest, and she simply spoke as she had so often: with a statement of ignorance. Edward was not a traitor; she had no idea where he was going that May evening. Valance did not react to her statement, but asked whether, if she did know, she would tell him. This time she had to do better in her acting, but her voice seemed forced even to herself as she told him that of course she would.

'I need you to do a job for me, which will bring us both closer to the truth.'

Now she did not trust herself to speak. She kept very still, pulling her eyebrows together as though puzzled, and he began to speak about her network. He wanted more of it. He wanted more of what she knew.

'I don't even know what you mean,' Laura said. Her voice came out childish, almost petulant, rather than innocent.

'Tell me about your cousin Giles.'

The box. The key. The diagrams. Sweaty hands slipping on the camera; the anti-aircraft guns booming around her. That was not poor Giles's fault. Laura said something about how she was sure that Giles had been such a tireless worker in air defence, and then she backtracked and said she knew nothing about what he did in the war. It was all so confusing now; what should she say?

'All that depravity,' Valance was saying, 'but maybe you don't mind that sort of thing. Your husband's friend Alistair says you were free to go your own way; you knew Mr Blanchard in the war, didn't you?'

Now Laura felt as though her body, with its banging heart and short breaths, was not under control. She was no good in a crisis. How could she ever have done the work she did when she was like this; it was pointless, impossible, she might as well give up now and tell them everything. Valance was getting up and for a moment she thought that he was going to touch her, to force her; when he stood up, she realised how tall he was, and she was weak with panic. But he was getting a file from another desk. 'Whatever you knew yourself, you will have to help us find something now. What about Peter Gillett? Was he the one who discovered your husband had to leave?'

What was this? Peter? That was nonsense. 'He was in Geneva then,' Laura said. 'I met him here for the first time last year.'

'I'm getting tired of all these lies. He would drink with Mr Last at the Reform whenever he was in London. You must have met him on occasion. You know his political sympathies.'

'Peter? But he – he's my cousin's boyfriend . . .' This was wrong. Peter had never even talked about Edward. He had never mentioned politics. His job with the Permanent Representative to the United Nations was dull, bureaucratic. What would he be doing there if Valance was right?

Valance was still talking, saying that Laura knew well enough what he was talking about – 'his father, Cuba, all that' – and then asking about the messages he used to run. 'We know he was involved, but we just need a little thing to clinch it and bring him in. He's not much in himself. Why don't you find out who else he was working with? That will be enough to keep you safe for now. One name. Who tipped off the network about Mr Last's impending interrogation. Just the name.'

Laura looked out of the window, past Valance's face. She made a gesture of submission and denial, a big breath and a sigh, and told him that she had no idea how he could say such things about Peter, he was such a nice man, she hadn't even met him until she came to Geneva.

'Do you want us to put real pressure on you? I've said we don't want a trial, especially while your daughter is so young.' He then said something about the Rosenbergs, who were clinging on, still on death row, but Laura had found some breath at last, and was speaking over him, speaking for all the world as though she was on trial, saying clearly that most of what he had just said to her was a mystery to

406

her, that neither she nor her husband had ever done anything wrong, but that she did understand he wanted her to talk to Peter Gillett. She would do that, and would tell him what he said, although she didn't think she would find out anything useful because she thought they were all barking up the wrong tree. And one day, when her husband was found, everything would be clear.

'Failure isn't really your best option,' he said. It seemed that the interview was at an end.

The weather was so changeable in Geneva; clouds were coming over and Laura was shivering in the wind as she walked down the streets where the cars were too loud, the people stepped too close to her. She went into a café on the corner, almost empty but for a couple of middle-aged men reading newspapers, but she ordered coffee rather than brandy. The story that Valance had just peddled seemed full of holes. She could not believe Peter had been any kind of messenger in the drama. He was too much out of the loop, here in Geneva: how would he have heard what the cryptographers in Washington were doing or who had been given the task of breaking Edward that week in May? Valance was sending her up a cul de sac by talking about him, but she was aware that even if it was all nonsense, and even if Valance knew it was all nonsense, the demand for some information in return for her safety might indeed be real. The request to go to America had not even been considered; she was expected to stay here and help MI5 – that was clear. Maybe her failure on this first task was a given, so that she would feel she had to do better the next time.

And who would blame her for giving in? Just as Laura had done anything once upon a time to save herself and Edward, so now she would undoubtedly do anything to save herself and Rosa. She could hardly bear to recall the horror of the end of their time in Washington. You knew nothing, she reminded herself. You planned nothing. You only asked for safety. They did everything. But there is irreducible guilt that never goes away, however much one goes on weaving the excuses that enable one to carry on and take the next step and the next through a banal life, one foot in front of the other, slow, unremarkable, through the streets of London or Washington or Geneva. The weight of fear settled on Laura again as she walked: she was just a tiny thing, a fly in a web whose corners she could not see.

As she came into the apartment, Rosa came and clung to her legs. Above her burble Laura heard the telephone ringing, and she picked it up as Aurore came to distract Rosa. Archie's voice came on the line; it was the first time he had telephoned. Yes, Yugoslavia was so interesting . . . yes, winter in Morocco . . . but back here now it was spring . . . and what was Laura planning to do in the summer . . . ?

'Well, we aren't quite sure yet.' Laura tried to make her voice light; it was not so bad, she wanted to convey, quite fun, living the drifting life that she did now. 'Mother might go over to Boston. But I'm not sure that I want to go there . . .' She was not ready to tell Archie that she was not yet allowed to go so far.

'I'm taking a house in Italy for the summer,' Archie said on the crackly line. 'Cyril's house, as he's going off to India on some mad expedition. Why not join me? Down on the Adriatic Coast.'

'I do come with others, you know . . .'

'There's masses of room – that's the thing, really: too much room. I'll see if Winifred and Peter can come too, for some of the time. Do come, with your daughter as well.'

The invitation could hardly have come at a better time, Laura thought. When she told her mother that evening that the consulate would not give immediate permission to travel to America, she was able to move on to the invitation to Pesaro and tell her that she thought she could probably get them to agree to that.

'I'll go to Boston for the summer, then, and see Ellen,' Mother said, clearly relieved. 'Tell me more about this Archie.'

In front of her, and for Aurore and Rosa, Laura had to be confident about this arrangement for the summer. Valance sent the message through a secretary. A trip to Pesaro was acceptable; a month away from Geneva was no problem if it was just to Italy. They would meet again later in the summer. So, with a manner of airy confidence, Laura made plans, bought new swimming costumes for herself and Rosa, and told Mother that it wouldn't be long before the consulate saw sense and gave permission for her to travel to America.

But only once she'd got onto the train in the summer did she realise how uncertain she was about this trip. Aurore did not look as if she had dressed for a holiday, in a grey skirt and blouse, and there was always that tension between mother and nanny when they were alone with Rosa: which one of them would respond when Rosa cried, who was really responsible for the mistake of putting orange juice in her bottle, which was upended on her new white dress?

That sense of uncertainty deepened on their arrival at the house. It was a tall villa overlooking the ocean, bleached out in the bright afternoon light. But when one stepped out of the taxi and into the hall, the house seemed different from what one anticipated from the exterior, rather dark and faded, as though the sunlight had not permeated its huge rooms with their painted ceilings and their stone vases in tall alcoves. In the living room Laura noticed the rings that glasses had left on the coffee tables and the unemptied ashtrays. Archie was obviously casual about this borrowed house; he was talking about the friends that had been staying up until the previous day, how he was keeping the house full all summer. Rosa was whining, bored and hot from the journey, and Laura felt apologetic. Archie was no doubt expecting her to be the smiling, sociable woman he had known in Washington, and here she was, a distracted mother in a crumpled cotton skirt.

She tried to cover her uncertainty with enthusiasm. 'What a lovely house,' she said in a bright voice. A garden opened out from the living room, laid out in a geometric pattern, with box hedges lining beds of lemon trees and herbs and geraniums.

'Gah-den,' Rosa shouted, stomping along the paths. Laura scooped her up and showed her the lemons on the trees, and pulled a sprig of rosemary, crushing it in her fingers for her to sniff.

'You are lucky to have this,' Laura said, but Archie sounded bored as he agreed. Laura had not even planted a window box in Geneva, and breathing in the scented air she was overwhelmed by a memory of the mulchy odour that used to linger under the laurels in Surrey. The wet earth of that garden in Patsfield, with its straggling scillas and damp leaves, came into her mind like a vision of a glass of water to someone desperate with thirst.

'Do you miss England?' she asked Archie, in a casual way.

'Not at all – the rain, you mean? The cold? The food?'

'Well, and the countryside – the—'

Rosa had a new habit, when she thought Laura was talking too much, of putting her little hand hard across her mother's mouth to stop her speaking. Laura tried to pull it off, but the child began to whine again and Laura stepped quickly towards the house, looking for Aurore.

Laura felt that the price of her holiday was to be amusing, so once she had given Rosa to Aurore and made sure that the nanny knew where everything was and was happy with the arrangements for her room and her supper, she touched up her make-up and ran down to talk to Archie before their dinner.

As she sat down and her cotton skirt flew up a little, she noticed his gaze falling on her legs. She brushed it down over her knees and felt self-conscious. For some reason she had not thought up to now that his invitation might include a

410

sexual expectation; now, as he poured her a gin and tonic, she felt that had been naïve. So she kept a quick artificial conversation going, asking him for details of all his travels, telling him dull stories about Winifred and other acquaintances. But the conversation did not seem to become easier between them. They were sitting on the terrace, eating figs and goats' cheese as the sky darkened, and Laura was thinking that she might soon escape upstairs, pleading tiredness, as Archie talked about the plans for the following weeks. Winifred would come in a couple of days, with Peter, and then he was also expecting Amy to stay for a while, and there were some very amusing neighbours the other side of Pesaro. 'You know Amy, don't you?' he said.

'I don't; Edward knows her. I saw her now and again – I didn't know you knew her?' Laura said. Why did her voice sound nervous? Amy Sandall, divorced again, she knew that, was still someone whose face Laura saw in magazines. She had no idea that Archie would know her, and it seemed an incongruous friendship. Archie was not nearly grand enough, surely, for that charismatic woman. He seemed to realise what Laura was thinking, and told her that they had only really met in Monte Carlo the previous summer, when Archie had just come into his inheritance and run away from London. 'Her crowd is a bit too full of themselves really; I don't know why I asked her. But I bumped into her last month in Bordighera and asked her to come down for a while, and she telegraphed yesterday to say she would.'

When Winifred and Peter arrived a couple of days later, Laura did not find the holiday any easier. She had not seen Peter since that conversation with Valance; he had been on a trip to Sweden in May, Winifred had told her, and then to London for a while. And although she had been so sure that Valance had been talking nonsense when he said that Peter had been part of the network, as soon as she saw him, sitting on the terrace after he arrived, sunglasses blocking out his gaze, a rustle of fear began. He was asking about the swimming at the beach; he was talking about taking a speedboat out one day; he was accepting a glass of limoncello before lunch – it was all so civilised. Archie hardly knew him, had only met him a couple of times before, but of course they were easy with one another, they had the urbane understanding of the group, a shared sense of humour, shared acquaintances. Laura felt the ripple of unease deepen. How easy it would be for him, as it had been for Nick, for Edward, to hide a secret for years: nobody ever suspected men like them.

She could see that Winifred was assuming that something was going on between her and Archie, and she had to accept that, it would be gauche to tell her that she was wrong. There would be no shame for Laura, after all, in finding a lover now – on the contrary, perhaps it had been rather extreme for her to have remained so obviously faithful to her absent husband for so long. Laura noted in turn that Winifred seemed irritable with Peter, leaning back in her chair, criticising something he had said. As she looked at Winifred, she thought how young she looked: her childless body was the same, slender and energetic, as it had been when she had first met her, and her cropped hair was short and thick as a boy's.

They talked of going down to the beach that afternoon, but then Archie said that Amy might be arriving soon, and everyone was held, uncertainly, in the garden, awaiting the new arrival. When Amy did walk out through the French windows onto the terrace, Laura was surprised. How she had changed. She remembered how Amy had looked on the boat, at the Dorchester, in Sybil's house, so relaxed even in those striking monochrome and scarlet outfits, as if she had just thrown them on, but now her clothes did look thrown on. She was wearing grey trousers that looked too big for her and a white straw hat whose wide brim was bent. Beside her was a young man, too eager to please, shaking everyone's hands too energetically. 'Gianni . . .' was all Amy said by way of introduction as he did so.

If there was one word Laura would have associated with Amy in the past, it was repose. She had always seemed to be the still centre of any room, an exquisitely calm presence among the chatterers. And yet now she was irritable, sitting on the edge of her chair, smoking quickly and nervously. When she took off that straw hat, Laura noticed that there was a tide mark in her make-up at the edge of her jaw, and in the corners of her eyes the black flakes of her mascara showed. Archie had planned for dinner in the house, but before they ate Amy insisted that everyone pile into cars, Peter's and Archie's, to drive to Pesaro for a drink. She gripped Gianni's arm and whispered to him in the hall as they were getting ready to go.

Nobody else but Laura noticed the motorbike starting up behind them as soon as they left the house, but she saw it, too close behind them, swerving in and out as if to get a good look at the passengers, and as they parked the cars, another Vespa screeched to a halt beside them. Laura expected, they all expected, that it would be Amy he wanted to photograph, but the bulb went off in Laura's eyes. In shock, she turned away, holding her hand over her face. 'What comment do you have on Ethel Rosenberg's death?' shouted the man on the back of the motorbike. 'What do you have to say about the traitors?' Fear was there on the esplanade.

Archie hurried Laura inside the bar, pulling her along by her arm. She sat down, but then realised the photographers were waiting outside, and she turned so that her back was to the window. Archie and Peter were calling over a waiter, trying to pretend that nothing had happened, offering Laura a cigarette. But Amy was chilly, her eyes narrowed.

'Still no news of Edward?' she asked in her rather rasping voice, tapping a cigarette on the table and lighting it.

'Nothing – I mean, the press has all sorts of sightings all

413

the time – but they never come to anything.' Laura went back to her usual line, like a worry bead that she had to click into place. 'I just know that he couldn't have been a traitor.' She felt the others shy away from the statement, and only Amy went on looking at her in that appraising way.

'Where do you think he is, then?'

But Winifred, as if to drown out the rudeness of her question, was asking where Amy had been staying last week. Amy ignored her and started saying something about the Rosenbergs, about their children. Laura turned away from her, glad that drinks were arriving and a cold vermouth was put in front of her. It was as though Amy was angry with her, she thought, and she tried to push Amy's attention away from her.

'Where's Gianni?' She had only just become aware that he was missing. Was he still in the car?

'He'll be back.'

He didn't come back for a long time, and when he did, Amy didn't let him have a drink but insisted they went back to the house. The photographers were still waiting, but Laura was braced now, and Archie drove fast, zooming dangerously along the coastal road. As soon as they went in, Amy and Gianni ran upstairs. Laura looked almost laughingly at Winifred, assuming it was sex. But they were only gone briefly, and when they returned Amy seemed languorous, coming out with a slow step onto the terrace, smiling more easily at everyone.

It was the kind of meal that any onlooker would think was straightforwardly bright with chatter and laughter. The citronella candles did not really keep the mosquitoes away, and the first bottle of wine was corked, but the sound of the ocean could be heard on the warm night air. The neighbours Archie had mentioned came over at the end of dinner, two young couples who were eager to meet new people, and Laura could see that they found Archie and his group glamorous in a rather seedy way. Here were the notorious Amy Sandall and the infamous Laura Last, drinking with younger men in this Italian garden; she felt embarrassed by how they must seem to these young English couples. But Amy's low laugh filtered out over the group, making Laura feel, as she had in the past, that they were all satellites to her self-sufficient charm. She remembered how Amy had studded her life with these distant appearances and, suddenly, caught up with the wine and the evening, she wanted Amy to know what she had meant to her.

'I've always admired you so much,' she said. 'You won't remember, but I saw you on the boat on my way over to England when I was just nineteen. And the first party I went to at Sybil's house, you were wearing a white satin coat. And then I remember seeing you at the Dorchester during the war.' As she spoke, Laura realised how limp her words sounded: she could not express what Amy's image had meant to her; how she had seemed to Laura to be a unique woman who did not need the world's approval, who was able to follow her own star. But as she spoke it dawned on her how empty her admiration of Amy had been, like the callow admiration of a teenage schoolgirl for a film star. 'I think I aspired to the way you looked.'

Amy leant forward for another drink. 'That's sweet of you,' she said, but her words were cold, and she turned back to Winifred, to the conversation they were having about why monogamy is unnatural. Amy had obviously taken to Winifred, and the two of them seemed to be taking delight in talking frankly about sex in front of the younger couples.

Laura was soon glad to go upstairs. In her room she opened the shutters and leaned out, eager for the sea breeze to penetrate the room. Amy and Winifred and Gianni were still sitting on the terrace; the others had gone down to the end of the garden for a look at the moon on the sea. Amy's words were borne upwards on the night air. 'That tedious woman. Still thinks she's an ingénue. If there's anything I hate, it's an ageing ingénue. Did you read what Alistair wrote about her? You should hear what he said that couldn't be printed – she looks such a prig, but underneath she's a tart who was always running after other women's boyfriends. Nina told me the same – apparently she was almost sucking Blanchard off in front of her. So Edward drank and drank, desperate to get away from her, and really had fun with his boys from university. I doubt he was ever really a spy – probably wanted to escape that ghastly marriage, at least Nick would spice things up for him.'

Gianni's laughter was heard, and Winifred's voice was too low for Laura to catch what she said in response. After that, the conversation became general. But Laura lay awake a long time that night. She relived the horrible time when she was trying to seduce Blanchard, following Stefan's instructions, and thought again about how her behaviour must have struck observers. And again she travelled back through the years, remembering Edward's unhappiness, his drinking, and wondering whether they had ever been side by side on their long journey.

The next day Laura woke early with Rosa. She liked these mornings, when the freshness of the night seemed to linger in the air. But as she walked down the corridor, holding Rosa's hand, she passed the open door of Winifred's bedroom. There, in a tangle of covers, lay Winifred naked and Amy with her. The two women were tanned and blonde, Amy's legs were apart and Laura could see below the thick pubic hair the dark, almost purple, labia. She was shocked by the swell of desire she felt at what she saw, but she went on walking, trying to pull Rosa's attention towards herself, and the two of them went down into the living room. There she found Gianni, the neighbours and Archie talking in a roundabout, drunken way; it was obvious they had stayed up all night – the gramophone was playing some needling jazz music and the room stank of cigarette smoke.

As Laura backed out of the room with Rosa, she felt the floor was slightly tacky under her feet and there was a smell of grappa; someone must have spilt a bottle. She went out through into the kitchen, but the maid was not yet there, so she clattered around making herself coffee. The milk had turned. She squeezed a couple of oranges for Rosa to drink. She felt as though she was out of step with the holiday, trying to create this peaceful morning for her daughter.

After their scratch breakfast she took Rosa down to the beach, where other families, Italians and Germans, were settling under big umbrellas. The air was close and humid and Laura longed to get into the ocean. Last summer, Laura remembered, Rosa had been terrified by the sudden slap of the sea, even the warm Mediterranean, and had clung to her and cried when she tried to hold her in the waves. But this year she was delighted by it, and Laura was able to hold her chubby arms and pull her along at the top of the warm, thick water. 'Look, you're swimming!' Laura said. 'You're my little fish . . .'

'Swim me, swim me,' she called back. Nothing is as untainted as a child's smile in the sunlight. When she tired and they came slowly out of the waves, she laid her head heavily on Laura's shoulder and pushed her face into her neck, and Laura thought, at least I have this. Back on the sand, she rummaged in her bag for the Leica and photographed Rosa standing there, her hair all spiky from the water, but soon Rosa got tired of the game. She began to complain, and Laura saw that the salt water seemed to have irritated a rash she had on the back of her legs. Aurore had come down to see if they wanted anything, said that she shouldn't have gone in the sea with that rash, and took her back, crossly, to the house. Laura began to gather up her things to go back too.

'You've been in the water already?' It was Archie, his eyes tired behind his sunglasses.

417

'Yes, but not really swimming – just with Rosa.'

'She's such a sweet child.' Archie seemed to speak with conviction. 'She reminds me of Barbara at that age. I hardly see her now, you know – I think Monica has poisoned her against me.'

'That's awful, I had no idea – I'm so sorry.'

'Swim again?'

'How do you have the energy? You haven't been to bed,' Laura said. 'Don't feel you have to amuse me.'

'It's all right – Gianni had cocaine with him. Have you tried it? You can go on all night. Goodness, I felt bright. I'll probably crash soon.'

Laura sensed again how out of step she was with the others on this holiday. Keeping up good behaviour was a constant necessity for herself and her daughter. The others had the luxury of putting all that aside for the vacation, while she was never able to relax. She and Archie swam together, but soon they heard the dark rumble of thunder, and as they came out of the sea the first drops of the gathering thunderstorm fell on them, and they ran back to the house. The villa was not made for rain; it seemed damp, dark and inhospitable in the living room as the storm rattled the shutters. The others were all asleep now, and when they got up around lunchtime they all sat in the living room, drinking coffee and taking aspirins, looking haggard. Peter and Winifred were clearly not talking to one another, and Laura was vividly aware of the energy that now existed between Winifred and Amy. She herself was locked out, she knew, she with her careful feminine ways and her tedious adherence to convention.

Winifred suggested they played cards, and they all sat in a ring. Amy was in her nervous mood again, and as she sat there one leg kept jiggling on top of the other and one eyelid seemed to be twitching. It was as though she was two people, Laura thought, but she was unable to keep the one hidden inside the other, so instead they existed side by side. At least the others were trying to keep the holiday mood going, laughing and gossiping as they slapped down the cards. When the rain eased off, Winifred insisted, they would drive over to Ravenna to see the mosaics.

'Winifred, you're so energetic. We could just laze on the beach.'

'We've been lazing already, Archie. Don't you miss work, all this lazing?'

'Not at all. This is what life is about, isn't it, trying to get a few good hours, a few good days?' he said. 'Monica used to say I was too frivolous for words. She liked Edward,' he said, turning to Laura, 'because he was so ambitious. Why don't you work as hard as Edward? she used to say . . . I'm sorry . . .' It was the wrong thing to say, but it was Peter who steered the conversation into easier waters, saying something about the good life and leisure, and how it was only in modern times that people associated work with the good life.

Laura saw how his statement irritated Winifred, who interrupted him, arguing that without proper jobs they were just drifters, exploiting the work done by others. Laura wanted to tell Winifred that even with her job she was still reliant on the work of others; it wasn't as though she produced anything – but of course she said nothing. She didn't have a leg to stand on. They were all, in that room, exploiting others, relying on the wealth of their class, of the group, eating, drinking, taking drugs, playing cards, while others cleaned up after them and cooked for them and made and washed and ironed the crisp cotton clothes for their ageing, sweating bodies. It all seemed so ugly to her.

But she must not forget the game they were playing. Laura played her lowest diamond to follow Archie's king, and looked over to Peter as he sat contemplating his cards, with his deadpan face, and suddenly asked, out of the blue, 'I can't remember if you met Edward, Peter – did you?'

His expression did not change, as he threw down his six

and said, 'A few times, at the club.' Winifred put down a queen, with a heavy sigh. Peter looked up from his cards and caught Laura's gaze. Caught it, held it and looked down again. That rhythm was too slow. Like the wrong chord on a piano, held too long. Did it mean something? For a moment Laura wanted to believe it did. Could Valance be right? As she let that possibility grow in her, she thought that, if so, if Peter really was part of the network, then maybe she had finally found a route to Edward. Maybe she could discover something from him – how to pass a letter, how to find out what was going on, what was being planned. She felt an answering note of expectation sound inside her.

But as soon as she heard it, it died. This was too unlikely; she could not be such a fool. Would she trust a suggestion – almost an introduction – from MI5? More likely it was a trap. It would be absurd for her to trust anyone ever again. The looming shadows – the Rosenbergs, the executions, their orphaned children – they were the darkness of the summer still.

The next trick started with hearts, and Laura tried to follow the game, but was aware that she had lost track of the conversations around her. She had moved back into the world where nobody was what they seemed. Her whole body seemed to rebel against the thought of being trapped in that net again. She felt a pain in her stomach and her hands slipped with sweat.

'Is it time for a cocktail, do you think?' she asked, as the cards were slapped down.

'Good idea – I'll go and get the things,' said Archie. As he mixed martinis, Amy and Gianni left the room again.

'Pretty sad seeing Amy in this state,' Peter said, gathering up the cards. 'I'd heard she was a complete addict now, but hadn't realised how bad it had got.'

Laura took the cold glass from Archie's hand and crossed over to the window, looking out, saying that it looked as if the rain was easing off and maybe they could go to Ravenna after lunch.

On Sunday night, all the others left. She saw how Amy looked at Winifred as she wished her goodbye: it was a complicit, amused look that made hot jealousy rise in Laura's throat, a look that was followed up by a quick, almost aggressive kiss on Winifred's mouth. What a relief that they were all driving off to other parties and travels; the house was easier and fresher when it was just Archie with her and Rosa and Aurore. There were a few days to go before Laura had booked the train back to Geneva, and even Archie seemed relieved that the relentless partying of the others was over, and the days asserted a more gentle rhythm.

One night they were eating dinner alone together, after Rosa had been put to bed and Aurore had gone to her room, and Laura found herself watching Archie as he ate and talked. He must be ten years older than her, but he seemed younger; his skin was still bad and his eyes were rather bloodshot, but his body was rather like Edward's in outline, with broad shoulders and long limbs.

There was eagerness in his expression as he noticed her watching him. When they walked down to the end of the garden to smoke and look at the ocean, she allowed him to kiss her. She felt distant from him at first, too conscious of each aspect of his touch, the fingers in her hair, the tongue pushing at her teeth, and then suddenly she broke, almost madly straining towards him, desperate to lose control, to feel again, not to be always on guard, grappling at his shoulders, opening her mouth wide and opening her thighs as she stood there. He stumbled back, and she realised she had been too ravenous in her response, and she laughed, brushing down her skirt, saying she had drunk too much. He laughed too, and lit a cigarette, and she smoked one as they walked back to the table.

As they came near to the house, she heard the sharp cry of Rosa, rising out of sleep. She went upstairs and settled her to sleep again, feeling the damp curls of her hair, kissing the soft curve of her cheek. This, she realised, was the only touch she had known in these two years, a touch that was as careful and controlled as holding a glass vase. She went back into the living room where Archie was sitting with a glass of grappa, and went towards him. She wanted to go into the lost world of sensuality, and that night she experienced sex in a way she had never done before. It had little to do with Archie and his personality; his body was pleasing and warm against hers, but her body was the centre of her experience, and by the end she felt that she was riding Archie's body to a destination that was hers alone, the torrent of her orgasm was all that she was seeking.

Transition

August 1953

When they re-enter the apartment in the late afternoon in August, it feels close and musty. Laura pulls back the shutters with a bang. She asked the cleaning lady to leave milk and bread and fruit for them, but obviously she has forgotten. There is that puddle of water under the icebox again. Laura is tired, she wants to rest, but she has to let Aurore go home. She knows that Aurore is not pleased about the holiday; she found the group too decadent and too drunk, the weather too hot. Laura feels guilty as she pays her what she owes her, plus a little extra, and tells her to go and have a rest.

Laura takes Rosa with her and goes to the local shop, and then down to the public garden along the street with a ball, and encourages Rosa to kick it, trying to make her use up her energy so she will not resist going to bed tonight. It all seems to be working well and Laura feels that the two of them, mother and daughter, are a happy addition to the other families in the park, and then disaster strikes: Rosa screams – a bee has stung her hand. Laura gathers her up and takes her, weeping, up the street and up all the flights of stairs to the apartment. It is hard carrying her and the shopping up all that way. Cold water, kisses, cream – nothing seems to help, and when Mother comes in tired from her journey, Laura feels almost embarrassed to be here in her dark flat with her crying daughter.

Maybe that is why Laura is more dismissive than she should be when her mother says something that evening about how Ellen and Tom were talking about why Laura should move back to America to get her divorce. 'So I can come and be pitied by them forever?'

'You've always been so hard on her,' Mother said. 'And on me. Ellen said once, it's almost as if you hate us.'

Those words are too shockingly honest, and Laura feels the blood beat up in her face as she insists that she is sorry, she did not mean to sound nasty. She is grateful to them both for all they have done for her, all they are doing for her. Mother seems to accept the apology, and to move on, but afterwards, when Laura is lying awake in her bed, she hears her mother's words in her head and she realises what fidelity it has taken for Mother to stay with her, Laura, through these years, even though she knows Laura does not really want her. She does not like to give this fidelity its name, but she knows now it is love. It shames her. For the first time in her life, she thinks of the journey her mother has made, the moment when she left her family to go off with the man she adored, the slow disintegration of her dreams, how that relationship curdled into misery, and her dogged, thankless loyalty to her indifferent daughters. To her dismay, Laura sees in it an echo of her own life, but the light it casts on her own journey is not a kind one, and she turns in bed, banging at her pillow.

The next morning, she tries to cover up the awkwardness of the previous day. She tells her mother about the holiday in Pesaro, about Archie, and lets her understand how that relationship might have developed. When Laura left Pesaro, Archie had asked her if she and Rosa and Mother might join him for another holiday at the very end of the season, near

Lake Annecy. 'Talloires is meant to be so pretty,' Laura says now. 'We could just go for a few days.'

Her mother seems happy to fall in with this plan, but Laura feels that something is coming to a head between them. This life in limbo cannot last forever, she knows. Maybe Archie will be her way out. Maybe she will go to Ellen in Boston with Mother, and face down the fear of exposure. Maybe she will have to make her own independent way, and learn from Winifred to find work. Each path is fraught with uncertainty, with the need for endless lies. The coffee is bubbling in the coffee-maker. She picks it up. The top has not been twisted on properly. Some of it slops out as she moves it and she burns her hand. 'Mummy sad,' Rosa says, watching her as she screws up her face and holds her hand under the cold faucet. 'Poor Mummy.' When your child shows empathy, it heartens you, you realise she can care and not just be cared for. But also, there is a hard question in it. Rosa is watching her, learning from her day by day. What is she learning?

After she has put ice on her hand, Laura realises how late it is. She has the appointment to keep with Valance that he made with her before she went to Pesaro. She asks her mother to look after Rosa, as she has given Aurore a few days off, and starts to dress with great reluctance. Walking through the city up to the consulate, her legs feel heavy. Geneva itself seems in a dull mood today, the clouds are dense, the air hardly stirring, even under the trees in the Parc Beaulieu. Valance is sitting at a desk in that purple-papered room. He looks ill or hungover and he is in a bad temper. She puts on her air of injured innocence, and tells him that she tried her best with Peter, but got nowhere.

But after a while, obeying a new script that has just occurred to her, she begins to behave differently from the way she has acted the last two times they have met. She begins a false performance of openness, as if she has succumbed to his persuasiveness. She acts as if she is fishing from her mind any possible story that might interest Valance.

First of all, she confesses a couple of things she thinks he must already know – about how Edward seemed to receive some message that he was in danger a few months before he left, and about his belief that he was being followed in town. She makes much of saying these things, as if she is confiding in him. And then she takes a new turn. She talks about Robin Muir and about how close he and her husband were. As she speaks, she remembers that mild, silver-haired man in the British embassy, and in her mind she apologises to him for using his memory in this way, as she begins to weave innuendo around his readiness to send Edward home suddenly from a suspicious Washington.

At first, Laura can tell that Valance is not convinced, but gradually she can see that the idea of the involvement of Robin Muir intrigues him. Could he, the dead diplomat, another apparently impeccable member of the group, be the missing link? To her relief, she feels that his attention is moving away from her; perhaps her continued play of ignorance is beginning to convince him. After all, at the end of the day, Laura is just a woman. She forgets names and places; she has no head for politics. Valance has no doubt read Alistair's book, has no doubt heard other people's opinions of her. A woman. A wife. A mother. Why would her husband have confided in her? After a few hours, Valance smiles without warmth and dismisses Laura. He tells her that they will meet again in a few months, and that he will have work for her. She feels that they may have moved into a different place. For sure, it is a safer place for now. But not a comfortable place, and as she walks out, she feels hot nausea in her stomach.

She goes to pick up some photographs, ones she took before Pesaro, from the developer, and takes them home to the apartment. She realises as she opens them, sitting on the sofa in the living room, that she already knows which ones are going to be good. Before, the developing process itself had seemed a revelation of the unknown; now, the camera seems to do what she wants, the contrasts and compositions that she planned for are almost exactly what she sees. Looking through them, she is caught by a desire to see how she has improved, and she gets out a box of old photographs. Rosa is sitting beside her on the floor, playing with a toy train, but she clambers onto her lap when she sees the pictures. 'Rosa,' she says, putting her thumb down on the prints. 'Don't touch the picture, darling,' Laura says automatically, leafing through the others. 'Mama,' she says, pointing at the picture that Winifred took of Laura's wedding day. 'And that's Father,' Laura says. Rosa does not respond, looking at the stranger in the picture, and Laura suddenly stands up, dislodging her from her lap so quickly that she cries out.

When Rosa is in bed that night, Laura puts the prints back in their box, looking back over them. The photographs she has taken of Rosa are such a detailed record of a child's change and growth, her gradual strengthening and consciousness. She is surprised by some of them, even though they only document two years, but the older face of the child becomes laid over the younger one in one's memory, so that one quickly forgets what at the time seems unforgettable, and the photographs gain this power to surprise. Love for a child is so different from love for a spouse: it rests on this transience. Could she also have learned to love change in Edward? Could they have aged and moved forwards, together? Could they have forgiven one another for all the mistakes, and built something honest out of the imperfections and littleness of everyday life?

She wonders. When she was younger, she had idealised people who seemed to possess, in their self-sufficiency and separateness, a secret path to joy, a superior knowledge of the right way to live – people like Florence, Amy and Edward. But they have fallen away from her now. None of them could teach her how to live. Maybe it is only a quiet, day-to-day loyalty that is worth having; maybe the grand love or the great gesture is always doomed. Maybe that year in Surrey was the only time that she and Edward began to fumble towards something worth having, when they started to try to be honest with one another, and gentle. She thinks about Rosa, and what she will teach her about how to live. She wonders how she can ever teach her about honesty, when she lives a series of lies, laid one on top of the other. She wonders how she can teach her about love, when she is still trying to understand herself what is illusion and what reality. She does not even have a garden, she thinks, she does not even have a proper home for her child. How can she teach her about security?

That evening, when the others are in bed, Laura sits as usual on the balcony, looking over the lake, watching the light change, talking to her ghosts. As she fills her glass, she realises she is drinking the way Edward drank – to drown out the insistent sense of an irreconcilable life, a script that she cannot make her own.

And then, a few days later, at the end of August, through the trees, up above the lake, the car is roaring, the road is ribboning into the distance, when it turns. At last. She is driving up to meet Winifred for lunch in St-Cergue, thinking of her new coat, when the car in front of her screams to a halt, and the other half of the postcard that she tore with Edward is put into her hand. She is Pigeon again, and Edward is alive.

All through lunch with Winifred she is distracted; she is used to covering up her thoughts, but now she wants to stop, she wants to be silent and to consider what has happened. Everything has changed. Everything. He has not abandoned her. But she does not yet know what this means. All she knows is that in this moment the world is sharper, the colours stand out more, the operatic Alpine landscape that she has been coldly appreciating for several years seems to be charged with energy; even the olives they eat with their first glass of wine are saltier, juicier, tastier than anything she has eaten recently, and she herself feels more awake. But she is not listening to Winifred. She must tune back into the conversation.

Winifred is at that very moment telling Laura that she thinks she could find her a job – at a rather lowly level, to be sure – in an English library that has recently opened to serve the British in Geneva. Winifred knows the woman who is setting it up, whose husband works in the United Nations. Laura expresses enthusiasm, although she is not really listening, and Winifred promises to call them for her that afternoon.

Then they start to talk about Peter. Winifred says they have broken up. Laura does not tell Winifred what she saw in Pesaro, but as they sit there the image of Amy, the attitude of sexual abandonment, the sleeping woman in flower, is there in Laura's head. She cannot imagine how to mention that to Winifred, however, and she says nothing, although she feels the pulse between her own legs as she remembers it. Then, without being asked, Winifred says something about Amy, about how she was planning to come to Geneva in the autumn, but that she, Winifred, has told her she will find the city too dull. There is a dismissiveness in Winifred's voice and Laura realises she has packed that experience away with the summer. Looking at Winifred there, so confident and contained in the sunlight, she thinks that perhaps this is the secret to Winifred's happiness; that she can pack each thing into its proper place, she can retain boundaries at each point of contact, can go on learning and growing, without losing herself in pursuit of a grander dream.

When Winifred wants to know about Laura's relationship with Archie, Laura finds it easy enough to talk about that. She remembers when Winifred first asked her about Edward, and how it all seemed too sacred for words, but this is so different. Winifred teases her a little, and says she can see that

Archie is her type, by which she means that he reminds her of Edward. Yes, he is tall, and fair . . . Laura cannot see other similarities, but she is happy for Winifred to tease her. There are other, much more pressing things to think about now.

Although she is longing to be alone with her thoughts, when she leaves Winifred and drives back down to the city, Laura does not think directly about what has happened. She cannot. Everything has shifted, and yet she cannot see what the new direction is to be.

As she and her mother pack that evening, Laura can hardly hear what she is saying. She is moving in a dream now, and the next day, as they drive to the train station, she finds herself nearly colliding with a stationary car. Archie is there to meet them at Annecy station, and drive them to an old-fashioned family hotel in Talloires. Yes, it is a pretty place, as Archie said it would be; yes, it is perfect for families at the end of the season. Archie is polite to Mother, friendly, more talkative with her than Edward ever was; they all seem to get on so well, like a little family. Laura wonders how he can shift so easily from the hedonist she saw in Pesaro to this civilised chatter. It does not seem fake, he is just easily influenced by those around him, she thinks. She watches his pleasure in Rosa; it is not false, he does remember his own daughters, and enjoys having her there. Before supper they swim in Lake Annecy, and Rosa enjoys his physical strength, sitting on his shoulders as he swims, fast, across the cold fresh water.

But dinner flags. Again, Laura is distracted, wanting to be alone, and finds her control slipping, her attention wandering. To excuse her manner, she says she is listening out for a cry from Rosa from the room above them, that she is not sure that she would be able to hear her. She goes and checks the room a couple of times, which annoys Mother, who thinks she is being too fussy. When they go up to bed, Laura sees Archie's hopeful smile, but she ignores it. She does not go to him. She wants to be with her memories tonight. She wants to pleasure herself, and that night she does. Just at the moment of orgasm, a face she has not seen for so long, a young woman's face, is in her mind, and the body she glimpsed only once, in the cabin of a dark ship, in all its innocent nakedness, springs into her thoughts. For a moment, she feels a pang of longing, not just for the girl's body, but for what she might say if she could see her now, words that could touch and tangle, as well as hands and legs. But the thought fades, and she sleeps.

The next day her mood changes. After breakfast, she asks her mother to take Rosa down to the swings at the lakeside and says she must go into the town to buy something. The way she says 'something', she can see that Mother thinks it is sanitary protection or contraception; something that nobody wants to talk about. This is why you can tell big lies, she thinks to herself, because people are so eager to keep all the small lies hidden. She is walking along, smoking, thinking these pointless thoughts, when suddenly she ducks into a café and asks for a brandy. She is beginning to see what is at stake. Silence has been her friend for two long years; there is absolutely nobody in the whole world that she can talk to about what has happened. But now she begins to see the magnitude of what she is facing.

She does not know what the next step should be. For so long she held onto the fact that Stefan said he would bring her over. But gradually the promise faded. She has built a life now, a life without Edward. Is the old dream strong enough to bring her back? How can she know? The brandy should be comforting, but the doubts about Edward that have been growing are unfolding in her mind again. Why was he silent for so long? It could not have been impossible for him to communicate. There are always channels, she knows that as well as anyone – letters, whispers, codes, telegrams. Why was there that monumental silence? What did it mean? What would she be going to if she went over? What sort of life would she be giving Rosa?

She remembers how they used to imagine the Soviet Union: the visions that Florence and Edward held out to her. For Florence, although she may have talked about it intellectually, it was something emotional, the possibility of an authentic, fully lived life. For Edward, it was also something almost spiritual; it was the way, he believed, that the great guilt of the upper class could be absolved, so that he would no longer have to drag around the burden of being the one who had benefited from the toil of the working class, from the colonial oppressed, their broken, miserable lives; that he could be their servant rather than them his servants. Servants. It was funny – not funny, but ironic – that all those years she had been the one who had had to deal with the servants – Mrs Venn, Edna, Ann, Kathy, Helen, now Aurore – all the women who had cooked for her and cleaned for her and looked after her child. She would like to be in a society where she no longer had to look back into their questioning and judgemental eyes. Or would she? Laura flicks, out of her thoughts, back into the café and her situation. Why is she thinking about Ann and Helen and Aurore rather than about herself and Edward and Rosa, and what she will do now?

As she finishes her drink, she is thrown back to the past. Thrown back to the dark times in Washington. It is nonsense, surely, to think that she was in any way responsible for Joe's death. It came hot on the heels of her meeting with Alex, yes, but it is the stuff of a cheap thriller, a fast movie, to think that the two were connected. It makes no sense. Why did Alex not bring them out then? Why did she not talk to Edward about what it all meant? She and Edward were so schooled into secrecy by those instructions, she thinks sadly, and then she begins to wonder. Was it really the orders of their handlers that made them so silent even with one another, or was it simply his character, his desire to live without revelation, keeping himself to himself, even when he was naked with her? Whatever the reason, she can see clearly now that they never had the conversations they should have had.

Even if she is not guilty of that horror, what was she really doing all those years? She thought she was on the straight path to justice, but it all faded and snarled. Is that why Edward found it all unbearable, she wonders? Was it just the threat of exposure that unhinged him – or was it the nature of their work? They were passing the secrets of death, the ways to kill, from one empire to another. No, she stops herself. There is still the hope, everything Florence and Edward believed, the authentic life, equality, freedom – the hope is not dead. But how tinny those slogans sound now, after all she has read, all she has heard, over these years. She thought she was on a path to truth, but it led her to a world where every step, every word, is false.

If she goes, maybe she will be safe at last. She will be able to relax, finally, for once. And Rosa will no longer be the daughter of the traitor; she will be the daughter of a hero. She at least might be able to live a life free of secrecy. Surely Laura owes her that. Laura remembers the trial of Hiss, the imprisonment of Fuchs, the death of the Rosenbergs. She does not have to think of them directly; they are always with her. In Geneva, in London, in Boston, she and Rosa will never be safe. But she has been cleverer than all of them, she thinks to herself. No one suspects her. Valance even thinks that she will work for him, if he needs her. Even Mother, even Ellen, even Winifred; nobody thinks that she was anything but an innocent wife. Her mask has been a good one. Has her face stayed intact behind it?

In her mind a huge battle has begun, an enormous fight of two opposing forces. Consciously, she flutters away from it again, she stands up and walks away from the café and goes back to the others. They swim again before lunch; she wants to fold into the water and be lost in it. They have a delicious lunch of perch, on the lakeside terrace; ice cream with real plums in it. Rosa is in such a good mood, she is happy to play on the swings in the little park in the afternoon and Mother agrees to watch her in the evening when Archie asks Laura if she will come dancing at a neighbouring hotel.

All the physical pleasures are a welcome distraction; she throws herself into them, and even, yes, after the dancing, she goes up to Archie's room and tries to lose herself in sexual pleasure again. But it is elusive to her. What is she doing, rubbing herself against this man? He knows nothing of her; her mind is a blank to him. He is holding a naked woman in his arms, he does not care who she is, and this makes her self-conscious – if he does not care for her, for her personality, for all she has given and all she has lost, then is it just her small breasts, the slope of her stomach, he wants? Again she is thrown back through the years, to the time when she believed erotic joy meant perfect communion. She remembers how she felt entirely taken over by Edward and his ability to rouse passion in her. And now . . . now she sees sex the way others have always seen it. They could be any woman, any man lying there. There is nothing unique, nothing irreplaceable, in this. She cannot find her pleasure tonight, but she lets him have his. He says how wonderful it was, how lovely she is. She realises that he does not know that she was not there for him. She rolls away from him, burying her head in the pillow, and he puts out a hand and strokes her back.

And so the holiday goes on. It is all as it should be, Laura realises; everyone is so well mannered, everything is so pleasurable. Even when an electric storm comes over on their last day, they go into Annecy to shop and lunch in the driving rain and manage to enjoy the afternoon. When they part, and Mother and Rosa and Laura get back on the train to Geneva, they are all agreed: it was such a good break. They must do it again soon.

The next day she wakes early. It is Monday. Over breakfast, she tells her mother that she can't go to the doctor with her that day, even though Mother would like her to help her talk to him about the pains she has been having in her legs. She makes up a pointless excuse instead about the new job and needing to go and talk to Winifred. She feels selfish as she says it, but she has to do this now. She drives back up the road to St-Cergue. It is a good choice of theirs, she thinks as she drives. You can see forever, and be sure there is nobody following. She parks the car a little below where they had stopped before, and finds the footpath into the woods. She goes some way down it, holding the camera, and after a while she lifts it up to her eyes. You cannot see the lake clearly here, but there is a glimpse through the trees, a sliver of blue, misty in the distance. She frames the view until she hears footsteps behind her, and turns around.

'Stefan.'

After all this time. Older, more tired, than ever – he seems to be walking with a limp. If she has been through a lot, what must he have been through? He nods at her, and they walk together. Then he puts his coat on the ground and they sit down. There are wild strawberries there in the grass, below the trees. Laura picks one; it is just a few seeds, a little sweetness, in her mouth.

'Will you come?'

'It's my choice?'

'You will do it,' Stefan says. 'You believe in the revolution.' Laura does not know whether that is a question or a statement, but she knows those are not the words she would use.

'Tell me all about Edward – what does he say, how is he?'

'I haven't seen him. But I know he wants us to bring you over. He wants to see his daughter.'

There are so many questions that Laura could ask: about what Edward has said about Rosa, what his life is like, is he working, where is he living, does he feel at home there?

Is he drinking? Is he with Nick? But it is hard to get your tongue around questions when you are so used to silence, so Laura just asks why it has been so long. Stefan talks about an agent intercepted at the borders, about difficulty in getting clearance in Moscow for certain activities, about a letter that was destroyed when another agent lost his courage. Laura cannot sift truth from lies. She gets up and tells Stefan that she doesn't know yet, that she wants him to come back tomorrow, same time, same place. It is the first time that she has ever given instructions to him, but he accepts them.

The next day, they meet again and walk a little way in the shady woods. Stefan tells her that he understands why she feels adrift now. For once she feels him trying to be frank with her. He tells her that the stories he told her the previous day were true, but – and here he stops for a while and Laura sees that he is gathering his strength to be more open than ever before – it was only when Stalin died that the authorities became flexible enough to respond to Edward's request to make contact with her. Laura takes this in, and recognises that her status as the appendage, the wife, quite outside the grand narrative, will never change.

Stefan tries to bring her back to him. He tells her that Edward has been impatient for news of her; he repeats that he wants to see his daughter, and he reassures her that he is not drinking much. Again, Laura cannot tell what is truth, what is a story concocted to persuade her. In the end she falls silent, and lets him talk through the instructions he has been sent to give. She takes notes in her mind, just as in the old days.

In three days, he says. They will keep a tail on her all the time; two men who will alert her if there is any danger. She will drive to Lausanne and from there take the train to Zurich; from there she must take the Arlberg Express, but she must leave it at the Austrian town of Schwarzbach St Veit, where she will be met by a driver. He has her ticket ready. Here it is. Rosa will need no ticket. Just like Edward, Laura must leave on a Friday, and she must give an excuse to Mother and her friends about where she is going so that nobody is alerted until Monday. Just like Edward, she will be taken quickly across the border. Just like Edward, she will be able to prepare one telegram, to be sent once she is across.

'What if I can't do it?'

'If you think someone has broken the secret, you must try to alert our men. Thread a scarf through the handles of your shutter on your bedroom window. We'll wait a fortnight, and then try again here at the same time.'

As she drives back along the lake to Geneva, Laura is thrown forward into what it will be like for everyone if she goes. To her surprise she realises that she feels excited by the prospect. It is childish, she thinks, like the adolescent who says how sorry you'll be when I'm dead, but she cannot help thinking of how Alistair, Sybil, Giles, Amy – all the people who made their own judgements, who dismissed her and patronised her – how they will finally know. She thinks of Valance, and is filled with elation when she thinks of winning at his game, of pulling out from under his nose. She thinks of a woman she has not seen for many years, who might read the headline in the newspaper, and might remember an eager girl on a transatlantic crossing, and might recognise the twisted journey she has taken, and why she lied to her and left her so many years ago. She knows she should feel sad about Mother and Archie, and even Ellen, and Winifred, who have stood by her all this time, but at the moment she is unable to think of them. As she thinks of the future, they seem to blur and recede.

Now, she clatters up to the apartment with a little more energy. She hears the telephone ringing as she puts her key in the door. 'I'll get it!' she calls to Aurore. It is Archie. 'Thank you for a lovely weekend,' she says. 'Yes, I'd love to meet next week.' When she comes off the telephone, Aurore is

437

telling her about the new playground they have found in the Parc Beaulieu, the other nannies she knows go there, Rosa had so much fun playing with little Marcel. Laura scoops Rosa up, nuzzling her neck as Aurore speaks. She has kept her safe all this time. She is not such a bad mother. She smiles widely at Aurore, thanking her, and tells Rosa she must show Mama the new park soon.

It's the usual salad and cold meat for supper, once Rosa is in bed, but Laura finds herself humming along to the radio as she is preparing it. She is aware that she must say something to cover her change of mood, her elation and alertness. 'Mother,' she says, 'I've been thinking – you are right, it's time for us to go back home. We can't stay here forever. I've got to start thinking about getting that divorce – it's been more than two years.' Her mother is so pleased. They sit a long while over dinner, talking about how they will go back to America and how Tom will help with the divorce, and Laura enjoys helping Mother imagine this new future.

The next day Laura goes to the hairdresser. She has her hair washed and set. She picks up some clothes from the dry cleaners, and goes to a lingerie shop to buy some new underwear. She goes back home, and still the decision is not quite made, the time is running out. The next day, when her mother goes to meet a friend for lunch, Laura packs most of her and Rosa's clothes into two big cases and puts them into the trunk of the car. She watches herself doing it. So, she says to herself, you have decided.

When Mother comes back, Laura tells her that she has met Charles and Tamara Hamilton in the market. 'You remember Tamara, don't you?' she says. Her mother is puzzled, as well she might be, because Tamara is nobody, but Laura reminds her impatiently about their children and how Winifred introduced them last winter in St-Gervais. 'They've asked me to come and stay with them in Montreux tomorrow, just to catch some last sunshine. They've got a nice pool for the children.

I said I would go with Rosa, I hope you won't be lonely here by yourself.' Mother insists she will be fine, and the next day in the late afternoon Laura packs a small case, just right for three days, in front of her, and puts on a grey skirt and white blouse, and the blue Schiaparelli coat.

'You've dressed up,' says her mother, noticing that she is wearing her pearl necklace too.

'Tamara is quite elegant, isn't she, though?' Laura says. Mother comes down with her, holding Rosa's hand on the stairs as Laura has the case to carry. They walk over to the square where Laura has parked the car. Mother kisses Rosa and settles her into the back seat. It would be odd for Laura to embrace her mother now, here, in this crowded city square, as they never do, or to encourage Rosa to do more than pucker her lips at her. Laura is suddenly shocked by the thought of the parting of grandmother and grand-daughter, much more than by her own parting, and unexpected tears prick her eyes as she starts the car.

All the way to Lausanne, the tears will not go. That heart-less mood that had infected her the day before has gone. What will this do to Mother, and how . . . but the road is unfurling.

Laura begins to drive more and more slowly, as she feels the pull of the daily round of life, dragging her backwards to her mother, to Archie, to Geneva. She realises that nobody will understand what she has done, and why she has done it. Nobody will believe that she was in full control of her actions. She is too fixed in everyone's minds now as the dupe in a manipulative relationship. They will think that she was threat-ened by Soviet agents; they will think that she was fooled. Nobody's opinion will really be changed, nobody will let themselves be surprised. They will continue down their fixed paths, only one or two of them saddened by her long betrayal and her sudden departure.

But as the road to Lausanne unspools, she realises that she fell in love too early and too late to go back on her wager now. It is no longer the golden ideal that sustains her, but the dogged hope. We all realise sooner or later that love does not last, Laura thinks as she drives, just as we realise that utopia does not exist, but it still seems right to her to live as if they do. She can no longer put all her faith in Edward, or in the Soviet Union: she knows too much, she has worked out too much. But there across the border is the one place where she may be able to live honestly, and build a truthful life for her daughter, and she cannot now turn away from that imperfect and desirable future.

And so she parks the car at Lausanne station. She drags the bags out of the trunk and shouts for a porter. She sees another car drawing up beside her, and the usual fear beats in her, but she knows that Stefan said they would have watchers every step of the way, and sure enough the driver is a passive spectator of her departure. She holds Rosa's hand, and they go slowly under the station's great arch of an entrance, but then the porter calls to her to hurry, the train to Zurich is already waiting.

She looks for an empty compartment, but they have to share, and they have to sit with their backs to the engine. Laura gets in, settles Rosa beside her and takes out the bottle of milk for her. As the child begins to drink, the train starts up. The exquisite, unseeing Swiss landscape fans out past the window. Laura pulls Rosa onto her lap, and tells her about what they are passing. 'Moun-ten,' Rosa says, naming her world, as she always does, object by new object.

Laura has not slept properly for days, and as Rosa begins to doze on her lap, she too falls asleep with her forehead jolting against the window. She is flung awake as the ticket inspector comes around, and light flashes into her eyes as she opens them. For a moment she thinks it is the dawn, and then she sees the streaks of the setting sun across a dull sky, and realises it is the same day, moving towards night.

Acknowledgements

This is a work of fiction.

However, it was inspired by some aspects of the life of Melinda Marling, the wife of Donald Maclean. As such it stands on the shoulders of a number of books about the Cambridge spies and occasionally borrows directly from the historical record, particularly around Donald's defection in 1951, when he left the family house at Tatsfield with his friend and fellow spy Guy Burgess, leaving behind his pregnant wife, Melinda.

A few times the real words of historical characters are very closely echoed by the characters in this book; for instance, what Alistair writes about Edward in this novel is very close to what Cyril Connolly wrote about Donald Maclean in *The Missing Diplomats*; the telegram Edward sends to Laura is almost the same as the telegram that Melinda received from Donald, and the letter that appears in the press about Laura's treatment is almost identical to the letter written by Violet Bonham-Carter to *The Times* about Melinda.

Laura also comes into contact with some real writers' work which I have quoted verbatim; she reads Harry Pollitt's *Will It Be War?* before going to a party, she reads George Orwell's 'Inside the Whale' in a café in London when trying to find a convincing reason to leave the Communist Party, and she and Edward both read Tchernavin's *I Speak for the Silent*. The article she reads on the Normandie appeared in the British *Daily Worker* in August 1939, while a joke made by

441

Edward about Native Americans was made by Beverley Nichols and is found in his book *Uncle Samson*.

Aside from these direct quotations, I am grateful to all those who have written about the Cambridge spies, particularly Phillip Knightley, Ben Macintyre, Geoffrey Hoare and Yuri Modin, whose work has helped me to imagine those strange times. I am also grateful to a number of books about communism in the first half of the twentieth century, particularly *About Turn: the British Communist Party and the Second World War*, edited by Francis King and George Matthews; to those writers such as Philip Ziegler, Matthew Sweet and Juliet Gardiner who helped me to imagine London in the Blitz; as well as those historians and memoirists from Alger Hiss to Whittaker Chambers whose work gives insight into McCarthyite America.

I am grateful to Katharine Viner, who as editor of Weekend magazine at the *Guardian* published my feature article on the women in the Cambridge spy ring, which first encouraged me to track down all I could about Melinda Marling, the communist in the Schiaparelli coat.

But this is not a history book, and I apologise in advance to readers who may be irritated by my inaccuracies and inventions. It is fiction above all in one central respect: there is not a shred of evidence that Melinda Marling ever participated in espionage. It has now transpired that she knew about Donald's double life before she married him, and supported him up to and beyond his defection, but everything in this book to do with Laura's own secret life is complete invention.

This book has been a while in the making, and I would like to thank all those who kept me smiling during the trickier moments. Thank you particularly to Harriet Gugenheim, who helped me stay on track, and to Maggie Baxter, who as chair of Women for Refugee Women enabled me to take the sabbatical that allowed me to complete the first draft. Thank you to Rebecca Gowers, Linda Grant, Don Guttenplan and Robert Winder who read and commented on drafts, and to my mother Ruth Walter and my sister Susannah Brunert. Thank you too to my agents Derek Johns and Anna Webber at United Agents who took me through this journey on relays. Thank you to Katie Espiner who brought me to HarperCollins, and to Kate Elton, Suzie Dooré, Charlotte Cray, Ann Bissell and Cassie Browne.

And to Mark Lattimer, Clara and Arthur, for all the love and loyalty and laughter, thank you.